Forsaking All Others

FORSAKING
All
OTHERS

✳✳✳✳✳✳✳✳✳✳✳✳✳✳✳✳✳✳✳✳✳✳✳✳✳✳✳✳✳✳✳✳✳

THE SISTER WIFE SERIES

✳✳✳✳✳✳✳✳✳✳✳✳✳✳✳✳✳✳✳✳✳✳✳✳✳✳✳✳✳✳✳✳✳

ALLISON
PITTMAN

Tyndale House Publishers, Inc.
Carol Stream, Illinois

Visit Tyndale online at www.tyndale.com.

Visit Allison Pittman's website at www.allisonpittman.com.

TYNDALE and Tyndale's quill logo are registered trademarks of Tyndale House Publishers, Inc.

Forsaking All Others

Designed by Jacqueline L. Nuñez

Edited by Kathryn S. Olson

Published in association with William K. Jensen Literary Agency, 119 Bampton Court, Eugene, Oregon 97404.

Scripture quotations are taken from the *Holy Bible*, King James Version.

The Scripture quotation on the dedication page is taken from the *Holy Bible*, New Living Translation, copyright © 1996, 2004, 2007 by Tyndale House Foundation. Used by permission of Tyndale House Publishers, Inc., Carol Stream, Illinois 60188. All rights reserved.

Library of Congress Cataloging-in-Publication Data

Pittman, Allison
   Forsaking all others / Allison Pittman.
     p. cm. — (Sister wife series)
   Sequel to: For time and eternity
   ISBN 978-1-4143-3597-1 (sc)
   1. Married women—Fiction. 2. Mormons—Fiction. 3. Marital conflict—Fiction.
4. Utah—History—19th century—Fiction. I. Title.
   PS3616.I885F68 2011
   813'.6—dc22
                                          2011023617

Printed in the United States of America

17 16 15 14 13 12 11
 7 6 5 4 3 2 1

TO MY LORD AND SAVIOR, JESUS CHRIST,
IN WHOM I CONTINUE TO LIVE . . .
OVERFLOWING WITH THANKFULNESS.

"Don't let anyone capture you with empty philosophies and
high-sounding nonsense that come from human thinking and from
the spiritual powers of this world, rather than from Christ.
For in Christ lives all the fullness of God in a human body.
So you also are complete through your union with Christ,
who is the head over every ruler and authority."

COLOSSIANS 2:8-10

ACKNOWLEDGMENTS

I am so grateful to my parents, Dee and Darla Hapgood, who made quiet, noble sacrifices in order to raise my brother and sisters and me in a healthy, Christ-centered home. I love our family story: how Jesus Christ became Lord of our family the minute he became Lord of your lives. Thank you for that example.

For Mikey and my boys—Jack, Ryan, and Charlie—you are the blessings of my life. Thank you all for your patience and understanding during deadline week (or weeks). How lucky I am to be surrounded by men of God.

Thank you, Bill Jensen, agent extraordinaire, who continues to be my champion. And the wonderful people at Tyndale—the dynamic duo of Jan and Karen, who let me run with this story, and the fabulous Kathy Olson, who can truly bring magic out of a mess.

Always, I am so grateful for my Monday night group—all of you! Your prayers give me strength, and your words give me joy.

Finally, to all of those readers of *For Time and Eternity*. Thank you for your warm reception of this story and for your enthusiastic longing for its continuation. Every e-mail fed me, and each word of this story was composed with you in mind. Your support allows me to continue to do what I dearly love to do—write stories that reflect the awesome power and grace of our God. I sincerely hope you find it worth the wait.

Escape from Zion: The Spiritual Journey of Camilla Fox (née Deardon) as Written by Herself

Of all the questions I am asked—and there are many—none arise as frequently as this: How could any loving mother abandon her children? Each time I face such a query, I am reminded once again that we, God's very children, are nowhere near capable of extending the same grace to one another as he has given us. It assumes a selfishness in my action, portraying me as a woman so determined to master her own fate that she cared little for the consequences. But there are so many other questions that beg to be answered before one could begin to understand the circumstances that led to that fateful decision.

How, I wonder, can a young woman be raised in a Christian home, yet know so little of Christ? Yet that perfectly describes my spiritual condition at the time these events began to unfold. I lived my entire childhood never missing a single Sunday service, and I faithfully read one chapter of the Bible each night as soon as my education allowed me to do so. Perhaps I can blame the stern nature of my father or the weakness of my mother in his wake, but I knew nothing of Jesus Christ as my Savior beyond the nature of vocabulary.

My fellow Christians wonder: How could I have been so deceived by the Mormon doctrine? To that, I must reference my earlier point. If the light of Scripture is given no opportunity to pierce the most superficial layer of the heart, false teachings are bound to find purchase. The Latter-day Saints speak with a Christian vocabulary. The teachings of Joseph Smith are so intertwined with biblical truth that the latter, like cream, may rise to the top but never break free of the mire beneath it.

And so it was that when I met Nathan Fox, I did so harboring a heart untouched by love of any kind. My parents were sparing with their affection, my faith was a matter of rote exercise, and being just fifteen years old, I was a more-than-willing victim to any semblance of passion. I've often wondered, had Nathan been a nice Christian boy from my village church, would I have been so drawn to his charm? Conversely, would the Mormon doctrine have been as enticing if spoken by some dull, homely boy? But they—Nathan and the Mormons—came to me like two twisted cords, and I allowed myself to be braided within them. Such a cord is not easily broken, which is why it is best suited to anchor a boat to a shore.

Or to create a noose.

And so, bound as I was to both Nathan and his faith, I left my home. My parents had nothing to offer me; the teaching of my church fit neatly in the back of my mind. For a while, my heart blazed with new truth—or what I accepted as truth. I can hope that, had I been left to my own study, I would not have been so easily taken in. But I warmed in the glow of my husband's fire, content enough with my fellow Saints to risk such light.

Together we built a little home in a valley near the canyon

where men like my husband quarried the stone for the Temple. And it was there that I truly felt myself cast from light into shadow. I watched my husband slave, wrenching stone as was his Saintly duty to the Prophet and presenting his carpentry in a vain attempt to win the Prophet's favor. Even so, I might have been content to remain in that shadow to this very day were it not for two developments that I could not countenance: raising our two daughters in such darkness and being asked to share my husband with a second wife.

It is this—the matter of a sister wife—that brings the collective gasp of shock when I am afforded the opportunity to speak to women about the plight of polygamy. And behind the gloved hands that hide their titters, women ask, "How could you ever submit to such indignity?" To that, I have no answer, for as a woman inclined to obey what I knew of Scripture, I felt I had no recourse but to submit. Those who live outside the Mormon faith—Gentiles, as they are called—like to envision a great, lascivious nature that drives the Latter-day Saint to engage in such practice. And perhaps there is such, for some. But my Nathan was driven solely by a desire to please the only god he knew and the Prophet he worshiped.

Despite my own faithlessness, God was very gracious to me, giving me a home, two beautiful daughters, and a dear, if unlikely, friend in Kimana—an Indian woman who lived on our property. Both my daughters and I loved her as one would a mother. In his sovereignty, though, God also took away, claiming the life of my first son mere hours after his birth. This brought to me a sadness that only a Savior could comfort, and I claimed Jesus Christ as such.

By the time Sister Amanda came to be my sister wife, my eyes had long been open to the falseness of the doctrine that would allow such a thing, and my heart abandoned the Mormon church. By the grace of God, I truly believe that my own soul was safe from its clutches at that point. But every day, I saw my daughters growing more and more indoctrinated by its teaching, which forced the question I could not ignore.

How could I let my children grow up in a house where they would never be allowed to hear the truth about Jesus Christ?

And so I set out on a journey to create a better life for them. When men do the same, they are hailed as heroes, while I, in the literature of Mormons, Christians, and secularists alike, have been maligned as the woman who abandoned her children.

So to revisit the question with which I opened this missive, while I am often bombarded with questions, I do not take the luxury of a retrospective examination. I never stop to ask myself if I should have done anything different. After all, how can you look at the assembled pages of your life and decide which should be ripped out and which should remain to press the treasures of your memories? Seems to me the greatest joy comes out of the pain that nurtures it, and you cannot keep one without the other. So I am forced, here at the end of it all, to fold every leaf together and say, as God did of his early people, that I did the best I knew how. I lived according to my conscience. He alone can forget the depth and breadth of my sin, and I claim the blood of his Son, Jesus, to all others who would judge me. I have lived now nearly forty years with my choices, and sometime hence I will die in his grace. That is the hope no man can steal from me.

Not again.

Ladies' Home Journal
July 1896

CHAPTER 1

Near Salt Lake City
January 1858

Smoke. And darkness. And warmth.

"I think she's wakin'. Go fetch the colonel." A man's voice, one I didn't know. A momentary blast of cold air, and I remembered the storm, the roaring wind and swirling snow that carried me here.

"Ma'am?" Closer now. I felt a warm hand against my cheek. "You're going to be just fine."

I wanted to smile, but my lips felt dry, tight. When I tried to speak, they peeled apart, grating against each other like thin, dry bark.

"Don't you try to speak none. Just show me, can you open your eyes?"

I wanted to, if only to see where it was the Lord had brought me, but already the voice was falling away, like words being dropped down a well. Sight seemed too heavy a burden, so I contented myself with what senses I could muster—the soft sound of a crackling fire, the sweet smell of the wood burning within it, and the warmth, blessed warmth, covering my body from my toes to my chin. The weight of it pinned me down.

Time passed. How much, I couldn't know, but enough for me to develop an unutterably powerful thirst. I pried my lips apart, worked my tongue between them. Just that little movement brought the presence to my side again. A new touch to my temple, a new voice in my ear. Deeper, stronger.

"Ma'am?"

Of their own accord, my eyes opened. I saw nothing at first, but then he moved into my sight. Long hair brushed behind his ears, a full moustache covering his top lip. His eyes were closed at first, and the moustache bobbed as he said, "Thank you, Lord." Then they opened, and in the fire's light they shone warm and brown.

"Where—?"

"Shh." He held a finger to his lips. "Time enough for that later. I'm Colonel Charles Brandon of the United States Army. Outside of Jesus himself, you couldn't be in better hands. Now, how about some water?"

I gave no response, but I didn't need to. I tracked him with my eyes as he reached behind himself and produced a blue tin cup. He took a sip.

"Just testing. Don't want it too hot."

Then my head was cradled in his hand and he placed the cup against my mouth. The first sip burned, then soothed as I swallowed.

"Little more?"

I opened my lips wider in response, and I heard him whisper, "That's a girl," as he gauged just when to take the cup away. He must be a father, too.

"Now," he said, laying my head back, "if you'll consent." He reached into his coat pocket and took out a thin, silver flask. "I'm in no way a drinking man myself, and I don't want to lead you down the path of evil, but if you'll permit me to mix just a few drops of whiskey in that water, it'll toast your blood right up."

My first instinct should have been to say no, but speaking was still beyond my strength, and truthfully, my thoughts were still cloudy enough that his words had no impact. He took my silence as permission and twisted the lid off the flask. With caution and precision, he drizzled a bit of the amber liquid into the water remaining in the blue cup and swirled it.

"For this, you'll need to sit up a little straighter."

He moved behind me and, this time, put his arm beneath my shoulders. I could feel the brass of his cuff buttons against my skin, hitting me with the realization that I was fully naked beneath a pile of wool blankets and bearskin. I twisted my head, panicked, and he instantly interpreted my terror.

"I know and I'm sorry. But we couldn't have you wearing twenty pounds of wet clothes. Now I wish we'd had some old Indian woman to help us out, but we're just a bunch of soldiers. If it helps, I held a gun on 'em and kept 'em blindfolded."

I didn't believe him, but I cared a little less.

"When you're ready, drink this down."

Just the smell of the whiskey in the water brought new life to my senses. Sharpened them, somehow, opened me up to the thought of drinking it down.

"All one drink," he said behind me. "If you sip it by half, you won't drink the rest."

I nodded, braced myself, and closed my eyes. I don't know what I was expecting, but I felt only warmth. Heat was followed by clarity, and when Colonel Brandon lowered me once again to what I now recognized as a buffalo skin–covered cot, I was fully ready to speak.

"Thank you." My voice was hoarse, and then I remembered screaming into the storm.

He cocked his head. "Doesn't sound to me like you're quite up for telling your story."

He was right. I couldn't. But it had nothing to do with my throat.

"If it's all right, though, I'd like to ask you just a couple of questions." He set the cup down on the ground next to him and took a small piece of yellow paper out of the same pocket where he kept the flask. "Can you tell me who Missy is?"

The name shot through my heart. "My daughter. Her name's Melissa. And Lottie."

He checked his paper, and the pleasant expression he'd worn since my eyes opened to him disappeared, replaced with a furrowed, worried brow. "Are they—were they traveling with you?"

I shook my head as tears gathered in my eyes.

"They're safe at home?"

"Yes."

"Well, thank God for that."

And I did as my head filled with visions of them, cozily

tucked into their bed or sitting on the braided rug in front of the stove, happily playing with their dolls at the feet of—

"Nathan? Is he your husband?"

"Yes." I tried to sit up. "Is he here? Did he come for me?"

"Shh . . ." Again his warm hand soothed my brow, and exhausted, I lay back. "No, ma'am. Nobody's come for you."

"Then how do you know?"

He showed me the paper. Three words—*Missy*, *Lottie*, *Nathan*—and one letter: *K*.

"Kimana."

He smiled. "Private Lambert wasn't sure of the spelling."

"She's taking care of my daughters."

"I see." I could tell he wanted to know more, but I hadn't the strength. It wasn't the time. "You've been sleeping on and off for close to twenty hours, and that's just since we found you. Now, for me you've been nice and quiet, but I guess when Private Lambert pulled his shift, you decided to talk a little bit. He picked out a few names."

"Oh."

"And he said you seemed to do a lot of praying."

"Yes."

"The way I figure, those prayers brought my scouts out to find you. Nothing but unbroken snow, they said; then there you were, hanging on to that horse. Why, that animal herself is a miracle."

"You have to send her back. To my husband."

"Time enough for that. We'll get you feeling better, and then we'll get both of you safely home."

More tears, and now they fell, sliding straight down into my ears. "I don't have a home."

He leaned forward, elbows on his knees. "Now, don't be silly. Everybody's got a home."

"Not me. I had one, and I left it. I had to."

His voice dropped to a whisper, even though as far as I could tell, the two of us were quite alone. "Are you one of them, then? A Mormon?"

"Yes." Then quickly, "No. I mean I was, for a time. But not really, not in my heart. And now—God, forgive me . . ." Whatever else I meant to say disappeared in the drought of my throat. I mustered what strength I could and turned on my side, my back to Colonel Brandon, and curled up with my regret.

Taking a liberty I could have never imagined, he put his hand on my shoulder, tugging me to face him. As I complied, he smoothed my hair from my brow and brought his face so close to mine I could feel his breath.

"Now you listen to me. I don't want you to be frightened for one more minute. Not for yourself and not for your girls. I'm here for you. The United States Army is here for you. And as I've sworn my life as a sacrifice for freedom, I will make it my promise that you'll have a home."

"How?" I'd brought the blanket up to my face, and it muffled my question. Still, he heard.

"You leave that up to me. Another drink?"

As an answer, I sat myself up on my elbows, holding the covers nearly to my chin.

Silently, he filled the cup with water from a pot sitting on a grate by the fire and added a little from a clay pitcher. Then he lifted the flask, holding it like a question. Remembering the pleasant warmth, I nodded, and as before, he measured in a tiny stream and swirled the cup. I continued to hold the covers as he tipped the cup against my mouth, and this time I took the drink in several satisfying gulps.

"That's the last of that for you."

"That's fine," I said, lying back down.

"Now sleep. And don't worry. When you wake up, I'll be here."

"And then?"

"And then, it sounds like we might have a bit of a battle on our hands."

CHAPTER 2

On what I judged to be the second day after waking, a soldier backed in through the tent's door. He barely twisted his torso to turn and drop a bundle of folded cloth on my feet, but it was enough for me to get a glimpse of a face where a battle between faint, sparse fuzz and angry blemishes raged along sunken cheeks and a sharp jaw.

"Here y'are, ma'am," he mumbled before stumbling back out again. Still weak, I struggled to sit up and inched the bundle closer to me. I found it to be a man's long shirt made of fine, thin wool and a pair of thick wool socks. With some effort I managed to drop the shirt over my shoulders and pull my arms through the sleeves. The shirt was laced along the front, and while I could pull the laces to pull it closed, I could not tie it, as both my hands were bundled loosely in bandages. This was the unpleasant surprise that had greeted me when I was fully awake. Frostbite, Colonel Brandon told me, which caused unbearable tingling. I'd not yet been permitted to see them, so I had no idea the extent of the burning, but I knew I could no more pull on a pair of wool socks than I could pull a sleigh across the snow. Besides, my feet felt warm enough under the pile of blankets and bearskin; in fact, I appreciated the shirt more for its measure of modesty than warmth.

Exhausted from dressing, I fell back upon my pillows, but I did not sleep. Instead, I listened to the conversations around me. Most of what I heard seemed to meld into one constant, masculine hum, but if I concentrated very hard, I could pick up recurring themes. The blasted cold. Those blasted Mormons. That blasted woman goin' to mean nothing but trouble . . .

Apparently the bedside vigil enacted upon my arrival was suspended once it seemed clear that I would not become "that blasted *dead* woman" anytime soon. I was left largely alone with my thoughts—memories interspersed with dozing dreams—to be interrupted only by the appearance of one young man or another with a cup of hearty broth or tea. I judged time by their greetings: "Morning, ma'am." "Afternoon, ma'am." "Evening, ma'am." If any noticed the unworn socks folded across my lap, no one mentioned them. I learned no names, ascertained no ranks, and after two days of this, I knew little more about where I was than the day I arrived.

On the morning of what must have been my third waking day, I opened my eyes to see—for the first time—a strip of sunlight along the bottom of the tent wall. Before that, there'd been only the steady, low light from the constant burning of the little woodstove. This tiny sliver brought to me the sense of hope that comes with a new day: the snow must be some-what clear, and I could go home. Well, not *home*, exactly. I had little hope that my husband would welcome me. And if he did, I knew he'd never again let me out of his sight. But I did wish to get away from here and find my way safely to the home of Nathan's sister, Rachel, in Salt Lake City. Just for a while, until God directed my next step.

Moments later, when the young man who'd brought me my shirt arrived with a tin plate of scrambled eggs and a cup of tea, I thanked him and asked to see Colonel Brandon immediately.

The young man, too tall to stand comfortably within the tent, maintained what posture he could. "Colonel Brandon is not here, ma'am."

"Not here?" His promise to deliver me rang in my ears, and I tried to keep the fear out of my voice. "Where is he?"

"Not at liberty to say, ma'am."

"Is he coming back?"

"Not at liberty to say, ma'am. Anything else I can get for you?"

I wanted to tell him to take this food away and bring me my clothes and coat, shoes and horse, and let me set out for Salt Lake City, but something about the tightness of his lips told me that such an action was highly unlikely. I sat up—easier now as I'd grown stronger—and held my bandaged hand out for the plate. This was to be my first bite of solid food, and while my stomach growled for it, my bandaged hands were too clumsy to grip the fork.

"I'm going to need help with this."

"Yes, ma'am."

"What is your name?"

"Excuse me, ma'am?"

"Your name. If you are going to feed me, I insist on knowing your name."

"Lambert. Private Casey Lambert, ma'am."

"Good morning, Private Lambert."

"Good morning, ma'am."

He found a small stool and brought it to my side, folding his long body into a piece of bric-a-brac to sit on it. With great precision, he speared a bite of egg and brought it to my mouth, his own opening slightly as my lips closed around the fork—something I remembered doing when I fed my own daughters. The memory of that made it difficult to swallow, but the moment I managed it, he was ready with the next one.

"You have a knack for this," I said, hoping some conversation might loosen his lips a little. "Do you have children?"

Even in the dim light of the tent I could see how deeply he blushed. "No, ma'am. Don't even got a wife. But I helped my ma with my little brothers and sisters."

"Oh? Are you the oldest?"

"Yes, ma'am."

"And where are they? Where are you from?"

"Ohio, ma'am."

"You must miss them terribly."

There was the tiniest crack to his facade, no more than the sunlight running along the tent floor, and then the military mask was back. "It's an honor to serve my country, ma'am." He punctuated his sentiment by nudging the fork ever closer to my mouth.

After just three bites, I could eat no more.

"Are you sure, ma'am? Make you strong."

"It's delicious," I said, though truthfully it needed a little salt, "but I don't have my appetite. I think, though, it's only a matter of days before I'll be strong enough to leave. Perhaps Colonel Brandon will be back by then?"

Nothing, not a flicker of an eyelash nor a twitch of a lip, gave me any answer. Instead, he put the teacup between my bandaged palms and waited for me to drink it down before removing himself and the dirty dishes.

I knew I'd be left alone until noon, if not longer.

Private Lambert was right about one thing, though. Even those few bites of food gave me a new strength, and with the aid of my teeth to loosen the fastenings, I managed to unwrap my right hand to assess the damage. My fingers were red and swollen. I flexed them with very little pain, though it felt like each would come snapping out of its own skin. The tingling seemed more unbearable with the bandage removed, and I had to fight against the urge to rub my hand against the scratchiness of the wool blanket. No doubt such an action might bring a temporary relief, but I knew well the damage of doing so could be permanent.

Then, clumsily, I unwrapped my left hand, not nearly as pleased at what I saw. My thumb and first two fingers seemed well enough. Swollen and red, but otherwise in as fine a shape as my entire right hand. But the skin had swollen up and over the wedding ring I wore on my third finger; both it and my pinkie were black nearly to the second knuckle.

I knew what that meant.

Dear God, please—heal my hand. I knew I was asking for a miracle because the flesh of my fingers was now as dead as any rotting corpse. *But you, O Lord, are a God of miracles. You have raised men from the dead. You brought me from the brink of death to this place.*

"It's just two little fingers." *What are two little fingers in the scope of creation?*

I felt myself wanting to cry, but tears would not come. Even they had dried up and deserted me.

13

There seemed little point in rebandaging my hands, though I did loosely wrap the gauze around my left one, if only to shield me from its ugliness.

How had this happened? I'd been so careful. I remembered the morning I'd left—crisp and cold, but clear. Two pairs of gloves I wore. Three pairs of socks under my boots. And when the storm hit—that great wall of snow—hadn't I been careful? Although much of my memory was as clouded as that gray sky, I remembered tearing my petticoat, wrapping my hands and feet, knowing the danger. And still, this?

I thought back to all those glorious days, with sunlight blinding off the surface of new snow. How my girls loved it. Played for hours. And I'd bring them in, set them by the stove, carefully pulling off gloves and boots and stockings. They'd complain about the cold, and my first instinct was to rub their little hands and feet until they were warm, but Kimana always stopped me. "No, Mrs. Fox," she'd say, the wisdom of her people shining within her bright brown eyes. "Just warm by the fire. Let the blood dance by the fire." And soon enough the girls would be dancing too.

I wiggled my toes, pleased to feel that they, at least, seemed intact. No pain, no tingling, not even numb.

But my hand . . .

I hazarded another look, surprised that the flesh of my fingers seemed even blacker than it had the first time, and a new fear invaded my soul.

Oh, God, don't let it be . . . don't let it be . . .

"Mrs. Fox?"

To my recollection, this was the first time anyone had announced himself before entering my tent, and this small measure of courtesy took me off guard. I said nothing, seeing as I had no idea what right I had to allow or disallow a visitor. The flap opened and with the always-welcome burst of fresh air came one of the smallest men I'd ever seen. He had to have been within an inch of my own height, and he seemed to float within the now-familiar blue hat and coat rather than wear them.

"Ah, yes," he said. The pitch of his voice was high and nasal, almost unpleasantly so. "I heard you were alive and well, sitting up, eating and talking and all that. Very good, very good. I don't want you to think I've abandoned you, but there are a lot of sick men around this camp. Sicker than you, I'm afraid. But now—"

"You're a doctor?"

"Captain Buckley, United States Army physician." He took off his glove and held out his hand as if to shake mine, a gesture that made him seem both insensitive and ignorant of my condition. Still, I lifted mine, and he caught it, gently holding it aloft with his soft palm. With the swelling, my hand was actually larger than his. "Not bad, not bad." He turned it over and over, inspecting the flesh at all angles. "Pain?"

"Not really."

"Tingling?"

"Yes."

"You took it upon yourself to remove your bandages?"

"Yes."

His small, pink lips were surrounded by a neatly trimmed moustache and a beard that just covered his chin. He twitched his lips, moving the whiskers from side to side. "Let's look at your feet."

"They feel fine, not at all—"

But Captain Buckley was already at the foot of the bed, lifting the covers. He took my foot in his hand, and I could not recall any other time a man had done such a thing. I flinched— more than that, I kicked out, surprised at my own strength.

"Whoa, there!" He feigned being thrown against the wall. "You're a feisty little filly."

"I'm sorry." I willed myself to hold still. "I don't feel . . . I mean, my feet feel fine."

"They're good. Now, at the risk of my own life, I'm going to put these socks on you to keep them that way."

I held my breath as I felt my foot descend within the woolen sock, but the immediate sense of warmth proved to be a great comfort, and I relaxed.

"Now, Mrs. Fox, I believe you have one other hand?" He made his way back to my side and settled on the little stool as naturally as I'd seen any man sit in any chair. "May I?"

Carefully, he unwound the soft folds of bandaging to reveal my damaged hand and made a small, repetitive *tsk*-ing sound. "This does not look good."

"It's my fault."

"Don't be so hard on yourself, Mrs. Fox. I was here when they brought you in. It was obvious to me that you took every precaution—"

"That's not what I'm talking about. They warned me. The bishop and the elder. They warned me. It's a curse."

I felt the cool back of his small hand against my forehead. "Mrs. Fox, I'm afraid your fever has returned."

"They warned me." And I could see them, both of them. The leaders of the church. In my home. By the light of my fire. Telling me. Accusing me. "It's the mark of my sin."

"Nonsense."

"I'm an apostate, do you see? I was a good Christian girl. I became one of them."

"Mormon?"

"Yes. But after a while, it all seemed . . . Their teachings felt . . . *wrong*. That's why I left. I was leaving my husband and the church."

"Wise move, if you ask me." He brought my hand closer to his face, sniffing.

"They said, 'You will forever bear the mark of your sin. Your skin will turn as dark as that Indian woman you keep.' And now, look."

"I'm looking. And it's no different than I've seen a hundred times over. Frostbite, pure and simple."

"What if they were right? What if this is God's punishment?"

"For leaving their church?"

"For joining in the first place, maybe."

"Mrs. Fox, I am a man of God only insofar as I see him through the lens of science. This—" he held up my hand— "is the result of poor blood circulation due to extreme cold. Nothing more. I will never purport to be one to claim where or how we are to acknowledge God, but I do know that we were not meant to live unsheltered in extreme temperatures. Our blood requires warmth. And when it is denied that warmth, we die. Sometimes we die all at once; other times we die a little at a time. That is what's happening here."

"It's because I abandoned my daughters. I left them there."

"How many daughters do you have?"

"Two."

"Two daughters. Two fingers. Which would you rather have lost?"

The finality of his words struck my core. "Lost?"

There was an immediate softening to his character. "I think right here—" his finger grazed the first knuckle—"just at the hand."

"No."

"You'd rather wait? Let the death spread?"

"God could heal me. He saved my life, after all."

"Do you know how God heals?" He answered his own question by letting go of my hand and holding up his own—both of them, like spindly branches growing from the trunk of his overlarge sleeves. "For you, healing will come when these are gone." He folded down his fingers that corresponded to my ruined ones. "Does this look like too big a price to pay to live?"

I studied the image, squinting my eyes to imagine my own hands. "My wedding ring . . ."

"Wear it on another finger, if you choose to wear it at all."

"I just don't know if I'll be able to stand—"

"The pain?"

I nodded.

He chuckled. "I've seen men snap off their own toes with their bare hands to keep this from eating them alive. But seeing that you're a lady . . ." He opened the black leather satchel he'd carried in with him and produced a glass bottle of clear liquid. "Chloroform. A few drops of this, and you'll be sound asleep. Won't feel or remember a thing. I promise."

"Shouldn't we consult with Colonel Brandon? He—he said he would take care of me."

Captain Buckley puffed up a full inch. "And just how efficient would an Army surgeon be if he consulted with his commanding officer for every medical decision? Soldier or not, you are encamped here with this regiment, and therefore under my care. I don't know why I am flattering you with the illusion of choice in this matter. Now—" he produced a clean white cloth—"will it be with anesthesia or without?"

"What if I don't wake up?"

"You have made your peace with the afterlife, I assume?"

I know he meant his retort to be lighthearted, but it chilled me. Of course I had, hadn't I? I knew my life to belong to Jesus Christ, both here and eternally, but that did not give me the courage to face this unflinchingly.

"May I pray first?"

"Of course."

"Would you pray with me?"

"Mrs. Fox, I do not know how much of a comfort that would be."

I found myself longing for Colonel Brandon's strong Christian comfort. "There's no one else here."

He sighed—"Very well"—and took off his hat.

"Most gracious Lord," I prayed, "I ask now your favor. I offer you my hand as I've given you my life, and I ask that only one be spared completely. Bring me again to life after this deep sleep, that I may return and bring my daughters to the truth. And my husband, should he seek to know you. If you choose to take me in my sleep, I'll welcome an eternity spent with you, for I'll know you have another plan to save the souls of my children. Please guide the hands of Captain Buckley, and may he see your miracles in his work. In the name of Jesus, I bring my petitions. Amen."

Captain Buckley grunted something akin to an amen, then poked his head out the tent door and ushered in Private Lambert, who might have been standing outside the whole time. "To assist," he said.

The three of us seemed very crowded indeed, and the cold winter air lingered as Captain Buckley gave the order for Private Lambert to keep the tent flap open.

"We need to let the fresh air circulate," he explained, rummaging through his bag, "lest we all succumb to the chloroform. That wouldn't do."

"No, indeed," I said, trying to make light of the moment. Private Lambert remained stoic as ever.

From the bag came a one-foot square wooden block, which the captain covered with a clean piece of linen. This he set on the bed somewhat near my waist.

"Now, are you ready, Mrs. Fox?"

"Yes."

He folded the cloth, held it over my mouth and nose, scowled, refolded, and repeated the process until he had the size and thickness he sought. Then, careful to hold the bottle away from him, he eased the cork out and silently counted each drop as it fell.

"Now," he said, perfectly positioning the cloth, "just breathe normally. And count, if you like."

I did not count. Instead, I repeated, *Lottie, Missy, Nathan, Kimana . . . Lottie, Missy, Nathan, Kimana.*

Over Captain Buckley's shoulder I could see Private Lambert holding a knife above the flames of the fire in the little stove. They danced orange and red upon the blade.

Lottie, Missy . . .

Let the blood dance by the fire.

CHAPTER 3

I don't know that I would call it pain, exactly. More like a constant awareness that what once used to exist is no more. Like a half-remembered thought, a name on the tip of the tongue, or the lost verse of a song. I'd hold my hand up, stare at the packed and bandaged wound, and think, *My goodness, shouldn't this hurt more than it does?*

Then again, no part of my body felt as it ought. My head was heavy beyond the point of lifting, my legs all but disappeared, and my intact hand a throbbing ball of numbness at the end of my arm. The silence screamed louder than any noise, making words spoken within inches of my ear seem swallowed up in the constant haze within the tent walls. I tried to explain all of this to Captain Buckley, but the words were too thick on my tongue. I could only manage a cumbersome "I can't feel . . . I can't feel . . ." before he told me that I should count myself blessed, then administered a few drops of black liquid to the back of my tongue.

"Five more days, and no more of this," he'd said. At least that's what I thought he said. But I could not trust my judgment anymore. Sometimes the shadows on the tent wall took on frightful shapes—giant bears reared up with their massive claws outstretched. Low, sleek foxes running circles around the walls. I'd hear the sound of men chopping wood and imagine my limbs being hacked off one by one. The touch of a hand to my face would usher in searing pain, and I didn't know if it was the burning of the hand or my fevered brow beneath it. The shirt I wore would soak through with sweat, and I'd think myself back in the snowstorm, desperately clinging to Honey's bridle. Once, when that happened, I actually stumbled from my cot and wandered out into the camp, only to be brought back by two soldiers. Later I learned that I'd put up quite a fight. After that, somebody was always beside me.

I begged to go home. To see my daughters. To talk to that man, the Christian. Colonel Brandon. I prayed to Jesus, pleaded for healing. For grace. For forgiveness and release.

"No more." I'd turn my head whenever Captain Buckley came at me with the dropper full of morphine.

"You couldn't bear the pain without this."

"I can. God will give me strength."

To my surprise, he shrugged and said, "As you wish," before returning the precious drops to the small black vial and proceeding to change the dressing.

This time, I didn't look away. I fixed my eyes on the white bandage, growing dizzy as I watched him unwind it from my hand. He let it fall like so much ribbon on my chest and lifted the gauze that covered the spot where my fingers once were.

"You don't want to see this."

"Yes, I have to."

He set his face grimly and began to pull a thinner ribbon of gauze from within what was left of my finger itself. "I didn't have enough healthy tissue to sew a flap," he said, "and the flesh is too delicate to risk cauterizing, so you're healing from the inside out. A little each day until the skin grows over."

"You don't look happy at what you see."

"I'm worried that I didn't cut far enough down the bone."

"What does that mean?"

He reached down into his ever-present bag and came up with a small silver tool, something like a pair of pliers.

"What is that?"

He squeezed the handles. "It's called a bone nipper. Now, would you—?"

The tent flap opened, and Private Lambert nearly fell inside. "Captain Buckley? Sir? We have a problem."

Captain Buckley didn't turn around. "What is it?"

"The w—" His eyes met mine and he stopped. "I'm sorry, sir. I didn't know she'd be—"

"What is it?" I struggled to sit up, but Buckley tightened his grip on my hand, and the resulting pain stole the very breath from me. I was working up the strength to scream when I heard his voice.

Even in my fevered, drugged state, I knew it. I'd heard this voice every day of my life for the past seven years, save for the one summer we spent apart. The summer that ruined everything. I was fifteen years old the first time he ever said my name, and I could hear him say it now.

"Camilla."

Only it wasn't the soft, breathless, love-struck sound it had been all those years ago. No, this was angry. Accusing.

"Camillaaaaaaaa!" Calling for me.

And then, an answer to him. "She isn't here, sir." I knew that voice, too, though I hadn't heard it but once in my life, and that days and days ago.

"You cannot keep my wife from me."

Nathan.

"Na—"

A cool, small hand clamped itself over my mouth before I could make another sound.

"I will search every one of these tents if I have to." My husband, the man I'd pledged my life to. He was here. Home was here. I strained to turn my head beneath the surprisingly strong grip of such a minuscule man.

"Private Lambert," Buckley said calmly, much too calmly given the scene, "it appears I need to perform a second surgery on Mrs. Fox. Will you prepare the anesthesia?"

"Yes, sir." Private Lambert could no longer look me in the eye.

"You would do well to remember, sir," Colonel Brandon was saying on the other side of the canvas, "that you are on military property. We are in a hostile situation, and I don't want to treat you like an enemy combatant."

"Nathan!" But my plea went no farther than the soft, white palm against my lips.

"Listen, Captain—"

"Colonel."

"—Colonel Brandon, is it? There's no need to create hostility where none exists." That was my Nathan, his voice as slick with honeyed peace as I'd ever heard. "I'm simply a man looking for his wife."

"Who isn't here."

"Seven drops," Buckley said.

No! My silent scream.

"If that's the case," my ever-charming husband was saying, "then you have no reason not to let me look around."

"Given what your people did at Fort Bridger, you're lucky you haven't been taken prisoner on the spot. Now, I suggest you leave, Mr. Fox."

For a split second, the hand was ripped away, but I had only time to squeak out, "Na—" before the familiar square of white cloth was clapped over my mouth and nose.

"I'll be back." I pictured his eyes, narrowed the way they did when he had that crescent-moon grin—the one that started at the middle of his mouth and curled up to one ear. The one he gave when he wanted you to think you'd won.

"Come ready to defend yourself."

I locked eyes with Captain Buckley, holding my breath until the pain in my head threatened to split my skull and I exhaled against the cloth.

Then inhaled.

Then, black.

⁓⁓⁓⁓⁓

My stomach roiled; bile filled my mouth. In an instinctive panic I rolled to hang my head over the side of the cot, but that put weight on my left arm, and the crippling pain of the action sent me flat on my back, gagging.

"Here, now." Captain Buckley's voice came through the darkness and I felt myself being raised to sit up. A cool, smooth surface grazed my chin.

My heaves produced little, as I'd had nothing more than

water and broth for days, but my stomach fought valiantly to expel even this meager content.

"It happens sometimes with chloroform," Captain Buckley said.

My throat raw from effort, my body came to a shuddering rest, and I relaxed against him. He slowly lowered me to be propped up by a bedroll and blankets, and I willed myself to die. But I had a final request.

"I want to see my husband."

"I can't help you there."

"He was here. I heard him. Right before—" My stomach cramped again, and my entire body responded.

"You see? You're in no shape to see anyone."

There was one man to whom we all answered, though, and as I found myself once again at rest, I risked saying only two words.

"Colonel Brandon?"

"Hm." Buckley seemed to be waiting for me to settle; then, without a word, he left. My hope that he would return with the colonel was short-lived because in an instant he returned carrying a tin cup filled past its rim with snow.

"This is fresh. Clean. Sent down from the heavens just a few hours ago." He produced a spoon, scooped it full, and held it against my lips. "Don't need to swallow. Just let it melt against your lips."

I took a measure of comfort at the coolness of the snow. It was, after all, the first contact I'd had with the world outside this tent in so many days. I savored it, fresh against my lips, and felt my entire body succumb to its nourishment.

"Better?"

I nodded.

"I know you are probably in a great deal of pain right now.

But we need to wait until it's safe to give you anything more. Do you understand?"

I nodded again and looked at the cup in a silent request for more snow. He complied.

"As for Colonel Brandon—" his narrow eyes remained focused on my mouth—"you'll be happy to know that he is just as anxious to see you. He's waiting only on my word that you are up to the meeting. You need to be strong. We don't want him to think you're not up to travel, now, do we?"

I shook my head, fighting to keep my breath steady, my stomach still. Captain Buckley wiped away the melted snow that dribbled down my chin.

"Very well, then." He set the cup squarely by my side and went to the tent flap, opening it but an inch to say, "Fetch the colonel." A long, lanky shadow moved to obey. Private Lambert, no doubt.

"I know you are in pain," he repeated upon his return. And I was, so much so that the throbbing of it rang in my ears, making his voice seem very far away. "You mustn't let on to Colonel Brandon just how much. Do you understand? He needs to think you are much stronger than you are, for all our sakes. Otherwise, he won't move the camp, and we'll all be stuck here like open targets in the snow. Can you manage?"

I nodded, saving my strength to speak my mind later.

"Good girl. You just let me speak for you."

At that moment, Colonel Brandon stooped to Captain Buckley's stature and came through a bright gash of sunlight. He removed his hat and held it to his chest, saying, "Mrs. Fox," in a greeting fit for the queen's parlor. I attempted to return his salutation, but Buckley's steadying hand on my shoulder gave me permission to remain quiet.

"How is she?" Colonel Brandon asked as if I'd suddenly disappeared.

"Weak," Buckley said. "Extremely so, I'm afraid."

"And the, uh . . ." I couldn't be certain whether he himself was aware of wiggling his fingers.

"You're no stranger to such surgery. You know it'll be a week at least before we'll know the extent of her recovery."

Brandon lowered his voice. "We don't have a week. Can she be moved?"

"With great care, I believe so, sir. In fact, the fresh air might do her a world of good. I assume more suitable quarters have been arranged?"

I followed their conversation, my eyes darting from one to the other, full of unanswered questions, but something told me the less I spoke, the more I'd learn.

"Two buildings left intact," Colonel Brandon said, frustrated. "Well, one in good shape and half of another." For the first time since saying my name, Colonel Brandon focused his attention on me and went to his knees at my bedside. "How are you feeling, Mrs. Fox? Be truthful with me."

"I—" I swallowed and tried again. "Is my husband here?"

"Your husband? No."

"He was. I heard him."

"I've tried to tell her," Captain Buckley piped up from behind. "The medicine and the cold, it can all play tricks on the mind."

I scowled over Colonel Brandon's shoulder. He'd said no such thing, but there was a particular purse to the doctor's lips that warned me to keep silent.

"The situation is very complicated right now," the colonel said, calling my attention back to him. "And very dangerous.

I have to do what I think is best for you and, equally important, what is best for my men."

"What could it matter—?"

"I'm not in the habit of planning military strategy with women."

"I want to go home, to my husband. Before there's any real trouble."

"That isn't possible."

No softening of his eyes. No sympathy. No promise.

My heart began to race, and with its fury, the pounding in my head increased, bringing with each beat the intense, throbbing pain. "Am I a prisoner, then?"

"Of sorts."

"More like property," Captain Buckley interjected, to the colonel's disdain.

I closed my eyes while the remnants of fresh snow turned bitter to my taste. "I don't understand."

"If it's any consolation, Mrs. Fox, I don't know that I fully understand either."

He stood then, clapped a gentle hand on Buckley's shoulder, and ushered the doctor outside for a moment, leaving me alone with my fear.

Father God, this is my deliverance? To be maimed and imprisoned? I will trust you, as I have no choice. But please, Lord, be not far from me.

Moments later Captain Buckley reappeared and went immediately to his bag and retrieved the small vial of black liquid.

I turned away. "No." While the pain might have been close to unbearable, I did appreciate the clear head. I needed to think. To understand. To pray and listen for the Holy Spirit's comfort. Guidance. "You said I had to wait. That it wasn't safe."

"Those were my orders, yes, but unfortunately your physician is outranked." He caught my chin in his hand and forced me toward him. "Now open."

I gritted my teeth.

"Please, Mrs. Fox." He wedged his finger between my lips, and seizing the opportunity, I bit down. Hard. Hard enough to feel his delicate bone between my teeth. He yelped and I released my grip, only to feel the sting of his slap against my face. As shocking as that was, it came as a welcome distraction from my ever-throbbing hand.

"Give me a wounded soldier any day," Buckley muttered, shaking his hand. "They understand the perils of war."

With that, he grasped the bundle wrapped to my wrist, and while at first his grip meant nothing, given the padding of gauze and bandages, soon the pressure eked its way through, and what had been a constant, familiar pulsation now became a silent, tangible scream as he pressed and pressed upon the wound. I fought not to cry out. Clenched my jaw, bit the inside of my cheek until I tasted blood. I arched my back in protest, thrashed my head, but soon it all rose within me, and the tiniest pressure of his thumb made its way to the place where I'd once worn my wedding band.

I screamed, calling out, "Nathan!" And when I opened my mouth to call his name again, the bitter, familiar black drops landed on my tongue, to be chased away with pure white snow.

CHAPTER 4

I recognized the sound of heavy sleds scraping over the snow and the muffled clomp of hooves. The gentle jostling woke me—the opposite effect of being rocked to sleep. The sweet, clean, cold smell of snow pierced my lungs, such a refreshing change from that of the ever-burning fire. I opened my eyes and saw peach-colored canvas stretched above me. On the other side of it was the sun.

From what I could tell, I was lying atop a pile of skins— most likely buffalo—with my arms folded across my chest. My left hand throbbed mercilessly, but there was nothing I could do to alleviate my discomfort. I was wrapped—swaddled, really— in several wool blankets, cocooned like an Indian baby on its mother's back. However, I was alone. I craned my neck, twisting it in hopes of getting a glimpse through the front opening to see who was driving. Remembering the conversation between Colonel Brandon and Nathan, I almost hoped it was my husband taking me home, even if I felt like some trussed-up prey. At least I would see my girls.

My mouth and my throat felt like they'd been lined with tree bark. Still, I fought the pain to swallow before attempting to capture the attention of whoever might be at the reins.

"H-hello there!"

My best effort at shouting was nothing more than a croak no louder than the sound of the sled's runners, and even that had robbed me of what little strength I had. This, then, was what Jonah must have felt all those days in the belly of that great fish. I tried to take some comfort in knowing that I was surely in God's hands, as my own will had been handed over to him the moment I left my home so many days ago. Unwilling to succumb one more time to the depths of unconsciousness, I forced my mind to dwell on what I knew to be true: I had broken away from the bonds of the Mormons' false teaching.

And quite possibly been thrust into the hands of a greater danger.

No! I pushed the doubt from my mind. Colonel Brandon was a fine Christian man.

Who lied to your husband. Then lied to you.

My eyes ached to produce tears, but none would come. I forced down the bile threatening to rumble up from my empty stomach. Now was the time for strength. Bracing against the pain, I rolled my shoulders once, twice, until I could move within the confines of the blankets. That helped, just to breathe a little. I lifted and contorted myself until my legs were equally free, which is when I discovered I was still dressed in the long shirt and woolen socks. No clothes, no shoes, and no way to find such items in the surrounding darkness. Not that I had any plans to jump to my escape, but the state of my undress restricted me as much as the blankets. I sat up—straight up—for the first time since awakening in the Army tent. Whether from the chloroform, the motion, or my lack of food, I immediately felt dizzy and reached out for the side of the wagon to keep me steady. Still, even that bit of initiative strengthened me, and I gingerly turned my body around until I was on my knees.

I clutched at the canvas opening to hold me steady and, taking a deep, strengthening breath, tugged it open. The onslaught of sunlight sent me reeling backward, and I buried my face in my sleeve until I felt I could look up again. When I did, the shocked expression on Private Lambert's face made me wonder if, in fact, I hadn't died sometime prior and come back to haunt him this snowcapped morning.

"You need to lie back down, ma'am." Private Lambert's voice cracked in surprise.

"Where are you taking me?"

"Please, lie back down, ma'am." He sounded desperate, and I almost felt sorry for the boy. The cold had brought the blemishes on his face to a raging red, and he seemed about to snap his neck as he divided his attention between the horses and me.

"Tell me where we're going, Private Lambert, or I promise you I'll throw myself from this wagon and let you crush me under the runners. Would you like to explain that to Colonel Brandon?"

"No, ma'am, but honest, we're almost there. You'll be able to talk to the colonel yourself."

The strength that was allowing me to sit upright and hold my balance was beginning to wane, so without another word I retreated to my pallet. Slowly, carefully, I took the top blanket and draped it across my shoulders, clumsily wrapping it around me not only for warmth, but as some sort of decent covering for my next confrontation with Colonel Brandon. I kept my head clear, rehearsing my questions: *Where am I? Why am I here? Why did you send my husband away?*

In my mind I was strong and forthright. I imagined myself six inches taller and infinitely stronger. I was no delicate hothouse flower after all. He didn't know me. He didn't know what happened the night before his men found me lost in the snow. What it took to stand up to my husband. To stand up to his church. The Lord had infused me with the power I needed to get away, and it was only by his strength that I'd survived since then. Surely he wouldn't fail me now.

I was rehearsing my litany for a third time, including an imaginary contrite spirit on the part of Colonel Brandon, when I heard Private Lambert click, "Whoa," to the team and the wagon-sled came to a smooth stop.

"We're here, ma'am," he said without bothering to poke his head through the canvas opening. Then the squeak of a wagon seat, and he spoke in a much more formal tone. "Subject ready for transport, sir."

"Relax, Private." Colonel Brandon's voice rang clear.

"Yes, sir." The crack in his voice reinforced his enthusiastic pride.

The two exchanged a few more words that I couldn't hear. Moments later, I heard Colonel Brandon on the other side of the canvas. "Mrs. Fox?"

"Yes." I hoped I sounded as indignant as I felt.

"If you'll wait just a minute, I'll send for someone to help you down."

"I'm fine." I'd been inching my way toward the back

of the wagon, unable to truly crawl, given the injury to my hand. Indeed, the smallest movement sent blue sparks of pain throughout every inch of me, but weakness had long ago worn out its welcome.

"Nonsense." The wagon rumbled as he opened the tailgate. "At least let me—"

But I was already at the back of the wagon, ready, with what dignity I could muster, to swing my legs over the open gate. He looked at me and smiled, lifting one gloved hand to the brim of his hat.

"At least let me help you down."

Before I could stop him, his hands were at my waist—lost as it was within the layers of blankets. As he readied to set me down, though, he held me suspended. "You don't have shoes."

"My socks are thick enough." There, one strong sentence.

"Warm, dry socks are a luxury around here. No need to soak 'em through."

In a move that made me fear I would snap in two, he wrestled me around until I was cradled in his arms, held close against him.

"Where are we?" Somehow, being thus carried, my inquiry lost its fervor.

But he did not answer. His steps were amazingly steady, given that each foot sank into the snow as he carried me around the corner of the wagon, and then a simple turn of my head answered my question. Almost.

I was looking at an enormous stone wall—ten feet tall, or so it seemed—stretched across the vast, snow-covered plain. The wall, at least, resembled a place I'd never been to but had heard of many times.

"Are we . . . Is this Fort Bridger?"

"Yep." He hitched me closer, an angry gesture that accompanied the grim set of his mouth.

Besides the massive wall, nothing else resembled the great structure that was a part of so many conversations around our own hearth and especially when we visited with family in Salt Lake City. In my mind, it had always been a massive, fortified structure, designed to protect newly arrived Saints from the onslaught of Indians while they replenished their stores for the final leg of the journey. But this? The stone wall bore signs of scorching, and as Colonel Brandon carried me through what used to be a gated entry, I saw nothing but the charred remains of burned buildings poking up through the drifted snow.

"What happened?"

He said nothing, and my grand plan to remain resolute began to crumble just as much as these buildings had, and my own smoldering anger was doused under a cold blanket of fear.

"Why have you brought me here?"

"We'll talk when I get you inside. There's just one building left, and a room's been set aside for you."

Sure enough, a long, low building ran along the back side of the stone wall. Ducking his head, he carried me through the doorway, and a young man sitting behind a rough-hewn table jumped to his feet in salute. Colonel Brandon nodded in acknowledgment and took me through a passage of two other rooms, before coming to what I estimated to be the end of the building.

"Home sweet home," he said, depositing me on the bed.

When he stepped away, I had the chance to take in the small space. Behind me, morning light poured through the single, small window high on the wall. Fire burned within a single-burner stove, and two spindly chairs were tucked up to a little round table. A wooden trunk sat at the foot of the narrow bed.

"What do you mean *home?*"

"This is where you'll be staying for a while."

"Colonel Brandon, I have a home."

"That's something we need to talk about." His response gave no credence to my protest.

"Well, that would be nice, actually, seeing as nobody has said more than two words to me since—"

"Since we saved your life?"

"If that's how you want to see it. I might classify it as more of a capture."

"Then you are naive, Mrs. Fox. Now, I've asked Private Lambert to bring you something to eat, and then you can get some rest—"

"I've had quite enough rest. I want to know why you've brought me here and what you intend to do with me."

"How is your hand?"

"My hand?"

"I can send for Captain Buckley to give you something for the pain."

"No. I'm fine."

"You're not a soldier, Mrs. Fox. No need for you to suffer like one."

I steeled myself. "Exactly what am I, then?"

He smiled. "A guest."

"Who is free to leave?"

"Who isn't strong enough to leave."

"And when I am?"

"We live in a world that changes every day. A few weeks ago you would have been nothing more than a woman in the snow. And now . . ."

"A few weeks ago I would have been at home. My *own* home."

"And so it seems we both have stories to tell."

Just then a series of quick knocks sounded at the door, and at Colonel Brandon's command, Private Lambert entered balancing a tray which, at yet another, silent, command, he placed on the table.

"Anything else, sir?"

"No thank you, Private. Assume your post, please."

Private Lambert glanced in my direction before giving a well-practiced salute and backing out of the room.

"Now, Mrs. Fox, while you may not feel in need of any rest, I did not have the luxury of sleeping through the drive here." With that, he touched his fingers to his brow and followed in Private Lambert's path, but this time when the door closed, I heard the distinct sound of a sliding lock.

"Oh, Lord," I spoke aloud into the sparse, empty room, "give me strength."

It occurred to me then that I'd never know the extent of my weakness without testing my limits, so I stood—rather, I attempted to stand. My legs lacked the strength to bring me to my feet, and while the small bed had iron bedposts that I could grasp to help me up, I knew the bundle of bandages that encompassed my left hand would never be able to grip one. Besides, just the thought of the pain such a gesture would bring about made me dismiss the idea entirely.

I knew Private Lambert was just on the other side of the door, no doubt ordered to listen for my slightest cry for help, but I would not give my captors that satisfaction. The table was, at most, three steps away. If I could stand, I could walk; and if I could walk, I could sit again. By now my stomach rumbled in anticipation of whatever might be steaming in that bowl; perhaps that was the final impetus needed to propel me to my feet. Once standing, I wavered just a little, then one, two, three steps, and I lowered myself into the narrow seat of the wooden chair.

My reward was a rich potato soup, crackers, and a small pot of black coffee. My right hand had almost healed completely, though my fingers were still swollen to the extent that I could fit only one through the cup's handle. No milk, no sugar—just onyx-black and pungent, and as I took my first sip, my eyes closed in gratitude. Immediately I felt the blood within me bring itself to the coffee's warmth. Years—years it had been since I'd had even a sip, and I set the cup back down to cool so I could reward myself with more satisfying gulps later on.

I soon learned the thickness of the soup came not from any kind of cream, but from yet more potatoes, but I devoured it and even used the wrist of my bandaged hand to lift the bowl to drain it. After an initial salty crunch, I dipped the crackers in my coffee and savored how they dissolved in my mouth.

Strengthened as I was from the meal, the bed beckoned, but I did not want to have yet another bedside conversation. Instead, I rose to my feet—much more steady this time—and walked to the trunk at the foot of the bed. It was plain, but well made, with leather hinges and the words *Property of the United States Army* branded on the lid.

Not knowing what to expect, I bent to open it, hoping for nothing more than some form of colorful quilt to take the place of the monotonous wool Army blankets. Instead, I found something quite more rewarding. A Bible. My Bible, actually—the one given to me on my wedding day. It was small and fashioned to look like a tiny, velvet trunk with a brass clasp. It sat atop my dress, my skirt, my petticoats, and my stockings. Rummaging around with my good hand, I found the contents to be everything I'd had with me when I was lost in the storm, with the exception of my shoes and coat.

"In case the lock doesn't hold me, I suppose." Still, the sight of my Bible infused me with a sense of power tenfold what the coffee had given me, and I scooped it up, bending my lips to touch its cover. With a renewed thirst I carried it back to the table, letting the pages fall open in front of me. No surprise they fell open to the Psalms, as those were the passages that spoke clearest to me. In fact, the page I saw had its corner folded and a thin penciled line drawn beneath the words:

I will walk within my house with a perfect heart. I will set no wicked thing before mine eyes: I hate the work of them that turn aside; it shall not cleave to me.

With these verses, I lost my fear of what I would confess to Colonel Brandon. I, after all, had done nothing wrong. What had I to fear?

Though I had not returned to the bed, I had let my head rest on the pages of my open Bible, and it was in that state that Colonel Brandon found me. I don't know if it was his gentle "Mrs. Fox?" that woke me or the sound of wood being added to the stove, but I opened my eyes to the blurred vision of words on a page. A tiny stream of spittle gathered in the corner of my mouth, and I quickly swiped it away as I sat up, grateful to have found my favorite shawl among my belongings. With it wrapped around my shoulders, a still-full stomach, and an almost-clear head, I felt a little more like myself. In fact, I had a few seconds of feeling whole before the pain in my hand manifested itself, but I simply squeezed it as best I could and braced myself for conversation.

"I see you found your things," Colonel Brandon said, closing the stove.

"Yes. Thank you."

"And I trust your time with the Scriptures served as a great comfort to you."

"As always," I said.

He took the chair across from me—the dirty dishes had been whisked away in my sleep—and braced his elbows on the table, leaning forward. "Now, tell me. How is it that a good Mormon wife and mother finds herself alone in a snowstorm?"

"Perhaps I'm not a good wife." I swallowed tears, thinking of my daughters, and wondered if I could even be called a good mother.

"Were you leaving your husband?"

"I was going to Salt Lake City. To visit my husband's sister."

"Her name?"

"Rachel."

He raised his eyebrows, clearly wanting more information, but I met his gaze, offering nothing.

"Why would your husband allow you to take such a journey alone? In winter, no less?"

The shame of my departure burned so, it surely registered on my face.

"Mrs. Fox—" he took a deep breath—"how many wives does your husband have?"

Had he reached across the table and slapped me, he could not have shocked me more. "I—I beg your pardon?"

"We are fully aware of the Mormon practice and the toll it takes on its women. Did we find you as you were trying to escape?"

Escape. Such a desperate word, and I did not want to paint the picture of my past life in that light.

"My husband, Nathan, took a second wife recently, but that isn't why I left."

"Then why did you?"

"Perhaps, Colonel Brandon, to be fair, we should take turns answering questions. Such as, why didn't you tell my husband that I was in your custody?"

"*Custody?* Interesting. I kept your presence confidential for your own protection. Now, why did you leave?"

"Protection from what?" But apparently Colonel Brandon was intent on taking turns, and when he refused to answer, I resigned. "I left because I found I no longer accepted the teachings of the Mormon church. And I refused to be rebaptized, so I knew I wouldn't be able to stay any longer."

"So you left to protect yourself?"

"To some extent, I suppose."

"And so you must now understand why we are protecting you. It's not a secret—at least not to us—how your church treats the less, shall we say, faithful members."

"Rumors," I said, oddly defensive of the people I'd so recently renounced. "Besides, my husband would never let anybody harm me."

"But he would put you on his horse and send you off into a blizzard."

"The storm came up so suddenly. There's no way anyone could have known—"

"There's no way any man would let a woman take that horse." He leaned closer. "In fact, he seemed not to have known you'd left home at all. Odd, considering you were planning to visit his sister. Rachel."

I felt, somehow, that I'd been caught, though when I

retraced my words, I couldn't come up with a single lie. "He—he knew. I was to be escorted from our village by two of our ministers."

Colonel Brandon seemed to fight for a second to keep his composure. "And why weren't you?"

"Because I couldn't wait."

"And why not?"

I thought back to that late night. My husband. Elder Justus, his dour face stretched even longer behind the candle's flame. Bishop Childress, with the voice that sounded like it had been scraped from the bottom of a kettle. My daughters asleep in the next room; my sister wife no doubt with her ear to the door. The accusations. The dire predictions that my skin would turn black with the blasphemy of an apostate. The request, over and over, that I confess to a sin of disbelief. The command that I be rebaptized into the church. Every word a snare, and the thought of climbing into their big black coach an even bigger trap. Thinking about it now, my heart raced, pounding like a rabbit's, carrying through until my entire body quivered.

"You're safe now."

I looked up. "Am I?"

"More than that, the safety of a lot of people might depend on your staying here."

"Why would that be?"

"Look, Mrs. Fox, we're at war."

"War?" I went cold despite the adequate heat from the stove. "Is that why you burned down the fort? To take it over?"

"*We* didn't burn the fort. One of *you* did."

"That's ridiculous. Why would that happen? This belongs to us—to them. Rachel's husband is a lawyer, and I know for a fact he advised Brigham Young on the purchase."

It was all Tillman could talk about during a particular

family dinner. After years of conflict, Fort Bridger was to finally become a post to supply the Saints heading farther west. Tillman had nearly burst his vest buttons with pride.

Colonel Brandon opened his hands in a warm gesture of surrender. "Apparently the church still owes on the note, and therein lies the dispute. Young knew we were planning to hold winter quarters here. Bridger himself guided us, and when we showed up, nothing. Scorched earth, if you will."

"But why would he burn his own—?"

"I don't know if Governor Young himself ordered it or if some zealot took it into his own hands. All I know is my men are facing a winter in tents because this is one of the few rooms remaining."

"And you've given it to me."

"For now, yes."

"Why?"

"As I said, to keep you—and all of us—safe. We don't want any of your people to misunderstand and think we captured you. We don't want anybody storming our camp to rescue you, firing upon our men and getting fired upon in return. We don't want them to think you're a prisoner."

"Yet you lock the door."

"Only for now, until I had a chance to explain."

"And you'll leave it open?"

"If you wish. I could even give an order that the lock be put on your side."

I smiled, though it cracked my lip to do so. "And you'll give me my shoes? And my coat?"

He raised his eyebrows in surprise. "Are those not in your trunk? Must have been an oversight. I'll have Private Lambert reprimanded in the morning."

"Don't be too hard on him," I said, playing along. "But you

don't really believe you fooled my husband, do you? He'll come back." At least, that's what I wanted to believe.

"I sincerely hope that doesn't happen. Because if it does, we'll respond as the president has given us orders to do."

"But what if I *want* to go home? What if I've realized I made a mistake leaving in the first place?"

"You can, once this is all blown over. Trust me, if we can win this war without firing a shot, that's what I'd prefer."

"You keep saying *war*. And we don't know—I don't know what you mean."

"How far outside of Salt Lake City is your village?"

"Not far. Fifteen miles."

"And your husband? What does he do?"

I thought back to Nathan's workshop in the barn, packed full of his frustrated attempts to have his work worthy of the temple. "He's a carpenter."

"We know Governor Young's arming a militia, so the war's no secret. You didn't know a regiment was encamped here?"

"No. We knew—that is, Bishop Childress told us we needed to dig in. With our faith and allegiance to the church. That's why I became a problem. I guess I still am."

"Not a problem. Not a prisoner. A guest. Stay here, get your strength back, and we'll decide where to go from there."

All of a sudden, I felt a peace wash over me and an inexplicable feeling of safety. The room was small but warm. The food simple but filling. And for the first time since I was a very young girl, my fate was in the hands of a man who shared my dedication to Jesus Christ. But like the touch of a tiny hand, one doubt beckoned me.

"What about my daughters?"

"What about them?"

"They'll want to know what happened to their mother."

"What did you tell them?"

"The truth. That I was going to spend time visiting their aunt Rachel."

"And what was your plan after your visit? When were you planning to return home?"

I didn't need to answer his question. We both knew the answer to that. Never.

"Your children are safe?"

"Yes," I said, knowing Nathan would die for our daughters. Along with that, the shadowy thought that his life would be easier if I died instead. They would have their father, and a mother in his second wife. "We have an Indian woman who helps me care for them. She is a Christian, too." For some reason, it was important to me that Colonel Brandon realize that I'd done all I could to protect my girls.

"Then you can sleep easy."

"But I want somebody to know the truth. To know where I am."

"I know. My men know. And God knows. For now, that's enough. Give us some time, and I'll see what else we can do."

CHAPTER 5

I wonder if we don't mistake the comfort of routine for the comfort of home. Within a week my small room had come to feel almost cozy. The western exposure of the window allowed me to sleep late into the morning, and I was never disturbed until I knocked on my own side of the door, at which time whatever soldier happened to be on duty would escort me to the facilities outside. For these brief forays I was granted a pair of men's boots, which fit perfectly given the layers of wool socks I wore, and I felt my strength growing little by little each day. Once back inside, I'd find a bowl of porridge, sometimes accompanied by a slice of bacon, waiting for me at my little table. And always, coffee. At noon the ritual was repeated, only the meal was replaced with potato soup and crackers, and in the evening, with johnnycakes and molasses.

Twice a day, once after breakfast and again after supper, Colonel Brandon came to my room to visit. Our conversation was always the same.

"Have you heard from my husband?"

"No."

"Then can I leave?"

"Not yet."

"When?"

"When it's safe."

Sometimes I found myself wanting to talk about other things, like whether or not he had a wife and children, or to tell him more about my own daughters, but the night I tried to do this, he held up his hand.

"It's not a good thing for me to know how wonderful and loving my enemy is."

"We aren't your enemy, Colonel Brandon. My family—we're just honest people."

"Living in a traitorous theocracy."

The words slammed against each other in my head, making no sense at all. "What does that mean?"

"Brigham Young, as governor, is the political leader in the territory, right?"

"Yes," I said, though I'd never really thought of him in that context.

"And he's also your religious leader."

"Yes." Now that was a much more familiar picture.

"Well, for a territory looking for statehood, that's not a good combination."

"I can't see that it would matter. Aren't other political leaders religious men?"

"Yes, but they don't exercise their power in a religious manner. Their citizens are still free to make their own choices."

"And you don't think the citizens of Utah Territory are given that same right?"

Colonel Brandon sat back in his chair. "You lived there for how many years? Seven? You tell me."

"He would tell you that he brought his people here to find religious freedom. That's what my . . . what Nathan used to say. That the Mormons were driven out of the United States for the very same reason that our forefathers settled there. And now you bring this conflict to us? It isn't right."

"Governor Young had ample opportunity to step down, let the president appoint another leader, and he refused. He brought this upon himself. He brought this upon his people."

"You don't know . . ." I stopped and questioned my own thoughts. How was it my heart could be so full for these people from whom I was so desperate to flee? "So many have already lost so much. Lost as they are, they have homes. And lives."

"Which they would die for if their leader asked. You know that's true."

"Is that a bad thing?"

"Is he worth dying for?"

The question didn't warrant an answer, but it did prompt another question. "Have you met him?"

"Not yet. Have you?"

"Once. He came to the wedding."

He furrowed his brow. "Your wedding?"

"No." I instantly wished I hadn't said anything, but his gaze compelled me to continue. "Not my wedding. My husband's, to Amanda."

"Oh." He had the grace to look embarrassed before turning his moustache up in a smile in a valiant attempt to lighten the mood. "So tell me. Suppose, through some great feat of military strategy, I manage to get this guy cornered. What's Brigham Young's weakness?"

Smiling despite myself, I said, "Pastry. And women."

We laughed together, and I think both of us saw our enemy diminished in our amusement. To have said such a thing in my own home would have incurred the wrath of my husband, and I'd never dare say such a thing in public. But this room was safe. Small and warm with a lock on the door, even if the lock was meant to keep me in.

<hr />

Two weeks after Captain Buckley had come after me with the bone nipper, he unrolled the bandages to reveal the final result of his work. He cocked his head and clicked his teeth, examining my hand from one angle, then another, beaming as if he held a new creation.

"Outside of actual fingers, I don't think anything could be more perfect."

I suffered his gloating, finding it only slightly less painful than the wound he declared healed. On all of his previous visits, I'd averted my head, not wanting to face my hand's mangled fate, but I knew I couldn't ignore it forever, especially knowing it would no longer be hiding in a mass of bandages.

"Let me see."

Captain Buckley released his cold, thin grip. I held my breath, and there it was. Two soft, pink mounds where my fingers used to be.

"See that?" He fairly bounced on the bed with glee. "Healed from the inside out. No stitches, no infection, just brand-new skin and scar. Second best to the real thing."

I attempted to move them and was rewarded with a stubby budge. After so many days of bandaging, I'd grown used to doing everything with my right hand—eating, drinking, dressing. I maneuvered my fingers—even the phantom ones—imagining what it would take to move on to more complex activities. How would I lace my boots, were they ever returned? Or tie a corset, should I ever decide to wear one again? I thought of the day when I would return to my daughters, how one of them would be forced to wrap her fingers over this place of amputation. Would they recoil in fear? Or fight for the privilege? And then, a thought—to my shame, an afterthought that hadn't occurred to me until this very moment.

"My ring."

"What's that?" Captain Buckley barely looked up from his task of rolling up my bandage.

"My wedding ring. Where is it?"

"Ah, yes." He tapped his finger to his temple, making himself look all the more like a marionette as he pondered. "I believe I gave it over to Colonel Brandon with the rest of your property."

"He hasn't mentioned it."

"Hasn't he?"

"Where is my ring, Captain Buckley?"

"Let me check." He stomped his little feet on the ground before jumping up, moving in a miniature, jerking fashion that always made me think of a fish on a line. His black leather bag sat on my table, and I heard the odd clattering of metal objects as he rifled through it. "Is it . . . is it . . . ? Here!"

Once again proud and self-congratulatory, this simple feat on par with a successful surgery. He handed the ring—a thin, simple band of plain gold—and as I took it, I marveled at the fact that his fingers were the same size as my own.

"Are you married, Captain Buckley?"

"Not yet. Oh, there've been some ladies willing to step out, but my heart belongs to medicine. She's a jealous mistress. You know a man can't go and give himself to two . . . Oh, beg your pardon, Mrs. Fox."

If I thought for a moment that Captain Buckley had misspoken, I might have been inclined to grant him grace, but the smug look when he caught his gaffe made me wonder just how long he'd been waiting for such an opportunity. Instead, I ignored him.

"I suppose I'll have to wear this on my right hand," I said. "The, um, stub is too wide."

"Oh, that's some swelling. Might go down in a couple of days. Might not."

I slid the band over the third finger of my right hand, surprised to see it stop at the knuckle.

"Still some swelling there too, eh?" He crooked his pinkie at me. "Looks like a last resort. But I wouldn't worry. There's more to being married than wearing a ring, isn't there? You're just as married whether it's on the right hand or left hand, or even a ribbon around your neck, aren't you?"

"I suppose."

He picked up his rolled bandages and took a few shuffling steps back to the table and dropped them in the bag. "You know," he addressed the ceiling, "I've always wondered if . . . No, no. Never mind."

Tiresome as his company was, I knew he'd prolong his exit unless I indulged his question.

"Go on," I said. "Wondered what?"

"Well, if you Mormon women shouldn't get a new ring with every new wife. Sort of like a prize. Three, uh, *sister wives*, is it? Well, then, three more rings. One on each finger."

He held up a spindly hand looking like a bare branch growing from the cavernous pot of his sleeve and wiggled his fingers, something dark dancing in his eyes. I narrowed my own.

"Don't be ignorant, Captain Buckley."

"But it's not a bad idea, is it? Think about it. Then everybody would know—"

"Just stop." For the first time I felt threatened in my safe little room, and I balled my hand into its first real fist, feeling my nails—long after so many days' growth—digging into my palm. "Thank you for saving as much of my hand as you did; now I suppose you won't need to visit me as frequently. Or ever."

He looked genuinely shocked but not at all hurt. Any insult I intended deflected off him like a bullet hitting brass. He snapped his bag shut and hauled it off the table, trying very hard not to stagger at its weight.

"Oh, absolutely, Mrs. Fox. And I daresay I'll be glad to get back to tending the men, which is what I'm out here to do anyway, isn't it? I didn't exactly sign up to spend my time with a . . . Nope, no. Not going to say it."

This time I allowed his words to go unspoken, and after a fairly civil good-bye, he left. Of all my visitors—including Colonel Brandon and the myriad of shifting guards—he was the only one who continued to latch the door on the other side. I found myself waiting for the sound of that metal bar before allowing my tears to fall. Seeing my hand, the finality of amputation, settled an overwhelming sense of loss. This, then, was all the healing I could expect. What kind of healing could I hope to see for my family? Twice I had done this—run off in pursuit of freedom, only to find myself enslaved. The first time when I was just fifteen years old, lured by the promises of love and adventure in the arms of a handsome boy. And now I was here, trying to escape those promises. For the first time in my life I was utterly alone. Not because of a locked door, but because of a lost life.

"Father God . . ." I buried my face in my hands, cognizant of the new absence. I didn't know what to speak to him. I simply repeated my cry and waited for an answer. And then I heard a long, wailing sound coming from the yard outside my window.

". . . *aaaaaalllll.*"

It was an unfamiliar summoning, and I cocked my ear to hear more clearly. Still unsatisfied, I hopped out of bed and slid a chair next to the wall under the window and climbed upon it. Raised to my tiptoes, I could get my eyes just over the sill. Outside, the men—some bundled in buffalo robes, others braving the cold in just their woolen uniforms—were running from all directions toward a man who stood on a tall wooden box. He held a canvas bag over his shoulder, and once again, cupping his hand to his mouth, he issued the call that was echoed by the crowd that had gathered.

"Mail call!"

I jumped off the chair and ran to my closed, locked door. For the first time in my stay I pounded upon it, demanding that it be opened, and to my surprise and relief it was, immediately, revealing the shocked and somewhat-frightened face of Private Lambert.

"Is anything wrong?"

"I need to speak with Colonel Brandon."

"He's probably out at mail call."

"Go and find him. Send him in to me." Private Lambert's eyes fluttered, and I softened. "Please, if it wouldn't be too much trouble."

"Not at all, ma'am."

We stood for a few minutes as he rocked back and forth

on his heels. Finally I backed into my room. There was an odd sense of respect as Private Lambert closed the door between us.

I paced the room during those moments I waited for Colonel Brandon to arrive, and when he did, I nearly pounced upon him.

"You have mail."

He looked confused and moved a hand to his breast pocket. "How did you—?"

"I heard the call outside. How is it you have mail delivered in the middle of winter?"

"Oh," he said, his voice a mixture of understanding and relief. "Yes, of course. We have our own delivery system."

"So you'll be sending a post out?"

"This isn't something I need to discuss with you."

"I need to send a letter."

"Mrs. Fox, I don't think—"

"I need to send a letter home. Back home, to my parents. I need them to know the truth. Where I am and why I'm here."

I'd worked myself into quite a state by then, and Colonel Brandon gripped my shoulders. "Of course you can write your letter, and I'll send it back with our carrier. I'll give it my personal seal, so there'll be no delay."

"Thank you." I felt calmer now. "In fact, would you be so good as to write the letter on my behalf?"

"I could." He stepped away, his gaze dropping to my mutilated hand. At some unspoken request, I lifted it for him to see, and he encircled his fingers around my wrist, turning my hand at all angles for his inspection. "I'm so sorry. But I'm sure in time you'll learn to write with the other."

Embarrassed, I snatched my hand away. "Oh no, that's not the reason. You see, I've been writing to my parents for years—twice a year, actually, since leaving home. And they return my letters. Unopened."

"I see. Wait here."

He was gone for just a moment before returning with several sheets of paper and a small black box. In a gesture I'd just recently begun to recognize, he held one of the chairs out for me, and I took what had at some point become *my* place while he sat opposite. The little black box contained a bottle of ink and a pen, and the paper turned out to be good, thick stationery with his own name emblazoned across the top in fine calligraphy flanked by two waving flags.

"Look official enough?"

"Indeed."

I scooted my chair closer and propped my elbows on the table as he dipped the pen's nib in the ink, touched it to a piece of blotting paper attached to the underside of the box lid and then to the paper, where he wrote the date in an elegant hand: *January 30, 1858.*

"Your parents' names?"

"Deardon. Arlen and Ruth." I couldn't remember the last time I said their names aloud, and I repeated them again, just to double the familiarity.

Colonel Brandon narrated as he wrote, telling my parents that he was writing on behalf of their daughter, Camilla, who was in excellent health and currently under the protection of the United States Army.

"Wait," I interrupted. "If you say that, they'll think I'm in some kind of danger."

"It's my belief that you are." He lifted the paper and blew across the ink before continuing.

"Please tell them that I have two daughters—Melissa and Lottie."

"They don't know?"

I shook my head. "They've never opened my letters. Once,

I even sent a lock of Lottie's hair so they could see how very much it is like mine. 'Straight as a plank' is what my mother used to say. And almost the same color."

He didn't share my smile. Instead, he looked right past me, and I imagined his mind was miles away from this little room.

"Do you have children, Colonel Brandon?"

"Yes," he said, shifting his gaze back to me. "A son. Robert. He'll be twelve years old this spring."

"It must be hard to be separated from him. I know I miss my little girls terribly. But at least you know . . . I mean, I assume your wife is a good Christian woman."

"She was, yes."

That word, *was*, lingered between us, leaving nothing more to be said except "I'm so sorry."

"Well—" he pushed the ink bottle and paper across the table and held out the pen—"I think it best you continue from here. They might be more reassured seeing the rest of the letter in your hand. I'll leave an addressed envelope with Private Lambert."

Having made this decision, he stood, and if I had any objection, I was given no opportunity to voice it. But I didn't. Instead, I faced this empty page like I had so many others, from the first letter I wrote telling them I had become Mrs. Nathan Fox, to the last one with its words blurred with tears as I wrote about the death of my tiny son. What was I going to tell them now? It seemed somehow pointless to tell them every detail of the life I'd lived since I last saw them. There wasn't enough room on the page, not enough ink in the bottle, not enough strength in my hand or heart to wrap it all in words.

I stared at Colonel Brandon's writing, decisive and strong. He'd written *your daughter, Camilla,* in such a way that all the letters of my name were tucked inside the C. Protective even in penmanship. I wished I could bring my girls here. To this place.

Surely the three of us could live in this tiny room for a while. Until spring. But I knew Nathan would never stand for such a thing, and though I missed them, I had to remind myself that the girls were safe and warm and loved. But what of their faith? What of their hearts?

Much as I tried to recall my father's voice speaking to me in any kind of warmth or love, only one sound followed me from the home he provided for me to the home I made with Nathan: his shouting about the Mormons. *"Those blaspheming, whoring heathens."* I know now that he was afraid of them, of what they would do to me. What they would mean to me. He was terrified that I'd join my life to them, the charm of their teachers blinding me to the falseness of their teaching. And now, here I was, scared of the same thing for my children.

I hadn't added a single word to Colonel Brandon's. The pain of all my returned letters stilled my hand, and I knew my words alone wouldn't break through the wall built between my parents and me. What would I say? That my father was right? I couldn't justify the bile behind my father's words. Would I simply say that I had left my husband? Certainly I wasn't the first woman to feel cheated and disillusioned, and I couldn't bear to tell them about Nathan's taking a second wife. I didn't want to be tainted by his sin. I needed them not only to welcome me home, but to forgive me, and how could I ever pour my repentance through a pen?

Words flitted through my head, each emptier than the last, and almost without thinking, I reached across the table and found my Bible. What question could I possibly have that wouldn't be answered here? Since I couldn't rely on my own voice, I turned to the voice of my Savior, because he'd told my story in the parable of the lost son. I read the story over and over, seeing myself in the young son who abandoned his father and home. That final sight of my father on the riverbank, gun and torch in hand, gave me little hope that he would be waiting for me with open arms at our farm's gate. I looked around my cozy little room, hardly seeing it as the vile pigsty the vain young man encountered, and not long ago my life with Nathan had been full of love and children and joy.

But then, there had come the night—that first night when he brought Amanda to the house. I don't think I ever really believed he would take a second wife. It didn't seem real until the day he brought her into our home. More so the night he took her into our bed. That's when I found myself perishing.

Unwilling to face the memories, I faced the words on the page.

"And when he came to himself, he said, How many hired servants of my father's have bread enough and to spare, and I perish with hunger! I will arise and go to my father."

That was it. Finally I had come to myself. Free from the tide of Nathan's affections, free from the never-ending needs of my daughters, free from the relentless pressures of the Saints to join myself more ardently to their faith. I was in the same place I'd been before leaving home almost eight years ago. Alone in a room, Nathan out there somewhere, an undecided part of my future. But while he had pulled me into his life all those years ago on the riverbank, he could not touch me now.

Gripping the pen, I wrote:

Mama, Papa—I write now in my own hand.
I have come to myself. I have sinned against
you, my parents, and I have sinned against God.
I pray that you will welcome me home. Look for
me at the gate come spring.

Truly, I had no idea how that reunion would come to be, but I would not think past that moment of reconciliation. After signing the letter, *Your repentant daughter, Camilla*, I blew gently across the page and, satisfied the words were solidly attached, folded the paper and took it out to Private Lambert, who stood and fumbled with an envelope.

"I'm instructed to take this directly to Colonel Brandon, ma'am?"

"Yes, please."

He handled my letter as if it were glass. "Not sure when the next post'll be out."

"Don't tell me when it does."

"Ma'am?" The catch in his voice gave the word three syllables.

"If it's tomorrow or three weeks from now, I don't want to know. I'm going to assume, Private, that by placing it in your hands, it's as good as sent."

"Yes, ma'am." But he didn't seem any less confused.

I didn't have the heart to tell him that the few lines in that letter brought to light the depth of my sin and my urgent need for grace. He didn't seem to be strong enough to carry such a burden, and I didn't want to spend the ensuing months with my ear turned toward the window, listening for mail call. Anticipating an answer, waiting for grace. For I would stay here as long as Colonel Brandon and his troops would extend their hospitality. Come spring I would make the journey home alone, and I would need this time to gather my courage and my strength, because one look, one touch from Nathan Fox, and both would melt like snow.

CHAPTER 6

I did not see Colonel Brandon for two days after watching him pen the opening of the letter to my parents. I passed the time reading my Bible and, having kept the ink and pen, pestered the soldier posted outside my door for more paper time and time again. Finally Private Lambert knocked softly at the door and, with a covert glance over his shoulder, presented me with a ledger book bound with red cardboard. Several sheets had been ripped from the front of it, leaving me with pages upon pages of empty lines. True, they were divided into columns, but I soon learned to ignore them as I wrote.

At first I returned to my childhood habit of noting a meaningful Bible verse each day, but that was the practice of a girl who struggled to read even one chapter per evening. Now, as I spent hours poring over the Scriptures, it seemed unfathomable to choose one verse, one sentence to carry more meaning than the next. Every word seemed precious, and the more I studied, the more I wondered how anyone could choose the ramblings of a false prophet over these sacred writings.

And so, rather than pick and choose to expound on God's truths, I set out to write my own story. How I came to meet and love and follow Nathan Fox. How I let the lies of Joseph Smith grow like yeast in my heart and mind, how the death of my child and life with a sister wife brought me back to truth. Exactly who I was writing this for, I didn't know. Much as I wanted to believe otherwise, I knew there was some chance that my parents would refuse to welcome me back into their home. This, then, would tell my story. Sometimes I feared I might never see my daughters again, and this would tell the story of why and how I left. But I flicked this thought away, quickly and often, like a pesky summer fly. If anything, we would read these pages together. All of us, my daughters on my lap, my father at the table, my mother stirring supper on the stove.

I relived it all as I wrote, remembering those days when my future was as uncertain as it seemed now. Someday I would be somewhere, looking back on this time. I tried to borrow on that future assurance that God was with me, just as I could look to my past and see him guarding my steps, no matter how wayward my path.

Although I couldn't imagine why anyone would risk reprimand to give me such a treasure, I nonetheless treated it as well-meaning contraband and took pains to have it tucked away under my mattress long before I could expect any of my regular interruptions—mealtime, a stroll to the outhouse, and the like. Therefore, after such a long absence, when Colonel

Brandon interrupted my afternoon composition with a harsh pounding at my door, I chose to forgo the usual hiding place and simply stood, slipped the book onto my chair, and sat back down upon it, trying to sound calm and natural as I beckoned him to come in.

His face gave away nothing to enlighten me to his current mood. Instead, expressionless, he strode in and, with no prelude, set a black bottle of ink on the table. "I figured you must be running low by now."

"Thank you," I said, offering no explanation of my own.

"You've been writing."

It was impossible for me to tell whether his statement was intended as a question or a reprimand, so I treated it as neither and said nothing. Instead, I sat with my hands folded in my lap in a new fashion I'd adopted meant to conceal the amputation of my fingers.

After a few moments' pacing he asked, "May I sit?" which he went on to do without awaiting my permission. "I see you presume to return to Iowa."

"You read my letter."

"It's customary for a prisoner's correspondence to come under a certain scrutiny."

"You sound as if you disapprove."

"I've been thinking." He drummed his fingers on the table, and I waited. I'd grown so comfortable with silence. "You said you intend to travel back east in the spring."

"I hope to, yes. If you'll allow."

"And how do you intend to get there?"

"If I remember correctly, I arrived on a horse. I assume she is corralled somewhere, or will I have to charge the United States Army with horse thievery?"

He raised a brow, along with a corner of his moustache. "And what of your daughters?"

I felt myself bristle in defense of my decision. "I can't stay here—in Deseret, I mean. I need a home to bring my girls to. I need to know that I can have that with my parents, or at least with their help. It seems to me a logical conclusion, Colonel. Hardly worth days of stewing."

"In fact, Mrs. Fox, I've been thinking about my own boy. How he lives day to day unsure of his father's well-being. He's cared for and loved, of course, but the uncertainty of his father—well, I know it's hard. I write as often as I can, but still, he may go years without seeing me and even months without hearing any news. It hardly seems fair to saddle him with so much worry."

Something flickered within me—a twisting of hope and dread. "So you're going to tell me to go back to my husband?"

"The idea has crossed my mind. Since you won't be able to travel until spring. But naturally, it's up to you."

"I have a choice?"

"Of course."

"*Of course?* Two minutes ago I was a prisoner and you were reading my personal letters. Now I'm just, just . . . nothing?"

After initial, unchecked amusement, he settled into a quizzical look. "You have always been here at my discretion, Mrs. Fox. And like any reasonable man, my discretion is rarely absolute."

"So I'm no longer in danger of being the spark that would ignite a war?" I was being sarcastic now, pouting a little. I must admit to having been somewhat hurt by my diminished importance.

He looked clearly uncomfortable. "It could be that my decision to keep you here was not entirely motivated by military protocol. Call it old-fashioned chivalry, a natural, protective nature. But I realize now my decision is keeping you away from your children. I don't know if I have the right to do that."

"I chose to leave them, Colonel Brandon. So I can bring them to a better life."

"Which you can still do. And I'll do all I can to help you. But for now—what was your original intent?"

"To stay with family. In Great Salt Lake City, until the spring."

"Perhaps, then, that would be best after all."

I thought of Rachel's home. I'd never felt unwelcome there, and surely if I came to her—wounded and cold—she would willingly give me refuge. Surely her home would be a greater source of creature comfort than this primitive encampment, and Nathan might consider my residence there less of a betrayal than my remaining a willing prisoner of Brigham Young's enemy. It seemed I had no recourse to argue. Colonel Brandon looked every bit a man settled in his thoughts, and beyond the fact that I'd grown comfortable, I could come up with no compelling reason to stay.

"Well then," I said, attempting to inject some light into the graying room, "I'll have to insist that you give me my shoes."

I did, in fact, get my shoes back, but days of inactivity had swollen my feet so that tying the laces proved more cumbersome than I could have imagined. I was red-faced with the effort when Private Lambert came to my door.

"Can't leave today, ma'am. Storm's on the horizon."

For two solid days it snowed. Grateful for the reprieve, I tried to gather my thoughts, deciding just what I would say to Rachel and Tillman upon my arrival on their doorstep.

Rachel was more than Nathan's sister. Though a year younger, she was his fierce protector, and in some ways the bond between them rivaled that between Nathan and me. Both were fiercely protective of each other. It was Nathan who'd joined Joseph Smith's church first, bringing his beloved sister to join him soon after. He'd arranged a marriage with a strong, prominent man—the imposing Tillman Crane—who'd promptly filled his spacious home with wife after wife. Four, in fact. The rooms teemed with women and children, and here I was set to add myself to the mix.

If they'd have me.

The hospitality of Rachel and Tillman was nothing new for our family. In fact, Nathan had encouraged such visits before, hoping I would see the domestic beauty of plural marriage. The sisterhood. The camaraderie. The preview of heaven on earth. But there was a canyon of difference between being a guest and a refugee. As gracious as he might be to his first wife's family, Tillman's loyalty belonged to the church. After all, we had done nothing to line his pockets.

I knew the morning I woke up to sunshine flooding through my tiny window would be my last in this room. Without waiting for confirmation, I broke the thin layer of ice in my washbasin and splashed my face with the frigid water beneath. Nathan had always said this was his favorite part of any day. He never heated his wash water, claiming the chill of it wakened the blood within. I felt my blood awakened that morning, though my hand ached terribly at the base of my missing fingers.

The soldiers had never been able to procure a proper brush, so I did what I could with the small comb that had appeared after days of appeal. Luckily, my hair was thin, straight, and soft—its condition an advantage for the first time in memory.

The comb's small teeth slid through easily from my roots to the ends just past my shoulders. Amanda, my sister wife, had a shining blue-black mane, thick like velvet clear past her waist. In the evenings, my daughters would squabble over the right to brush it. She slept with it plaited in three braids, which she twisted together like a rope, and each morning, nearly half an hour was devoted to its styling.

I wondered what she would choose that morning, though the sun was hardly high enough for her to be out of my husband's bed.

My own hands could barely manage the simplest twist, secured at the nape of my neck with a few pins. I was thus engaged when Private Lambert's familiar knock sounded. When I summoned him to come in, he poked his head through and immediately blushed bright pink, as if catching me in some much more intimate act.

"I see you're ready to go, ma'am." He kept his eyes trained on my feet, perfectly respectable in their laced-up boots.

"Then we are leaving today?"

"Within the hour, Colonel says, providin' you're set."

My stomach twisted. I was anything but *set*, but God had directed my path this far. I had no reason to believe I shouldn't follow.

Not long after, I was presented with my coat, hat, scarf, and mittens. Then a new step outside into the unforgiving glare of a clear day, I was presented with another longed-for sight.

Honey. I hadn't seen her since the day I left home, and if she were any measure as happy to see me as I was to see her, she gave no sign. Her breath steamed in tufts from her nostrils as she stood, ever patient, in the snow. Her coat had grown thicker and her mane had been denied the careful attention that Nathan bestowed, but her eyes were brown and bright.

She'd been well fed, I could tell, and seemed quite at ease with the man holding her rein.

"She's a fine horse." Colonel Brandon had come up to stand behind me. For the first time in our acquaintance, he was not wearing his familiar blue uniform. In its place were sturdy, plain, brown wool pants tucked into the legs of thick leather boots, with a thick sheepskin coat over all. A black knit cap sat just above his brow.

"Why, Colonel Brandon," I said, taking in the sight of him, "I would hardly have recognized you."

"This is not official business," he said. "More of a civilian errand. And I figure I'll attract less attention if I'm not parading you through town in all my decorated glory."

The gathering of men around us laughed, something I couldn't imagine them doing had he been in full uniform. He held the reins of a prancing white stallion that snorted impatiently, pawing at the patchy snow. Both he and Honey were ready to ride, and while Private Lambert deposited my small bundle of worldly goods into the bags hanging from my saddle, my eyes were drawn to the rifle holstered at Honey's side.

"I don't expect you'll have to use that." Colonel Brandon read both my mind and my fear. "Most anything that could be dangerous is deep in hibernation right now."

"You telling me them Mormons hibernate?" The comment, coming from the back of the crowd, spurred on a chorus of resounding laughter that might have given way to a dozen more comic threats if not for the silencing glare of Colonel Brandon. Civilian attire or not, his authority commanded almost immediate silence. He said nothing, though. Nothing in my defense nor in that of the Saints. But he didn't have to. I knew. Were the need to arise, he would protect me, defend me with his words or his gun. I could only pray for a peaceful passage.

And in his great mercy, God granted it. The sky maintained a gauzy haze, enough to soften the glare of the sun but without the darkness that threatened storm. We were a party of four: myself, Colonel Brandon, and Private Lambert, who had been instructed to change into civilian attire. Apparently his overcoat was either borrowed or came from a time before his final uniform fitting, because the sleeves stopped just shy of his bony wrists, making him look even more the vulnerable youth. Riding ahead was a man they called Coyote Tom—a small, dark Paiute Indian whom Colonel Brandon described as the finest scout he'd ever met. A master at reading the land, Coyote Tom had vision that bored through hills and trees and snow. We followed the tracks left by his sturdy, spotted horse. Keeping a steady pace, barring deep drifts or new snow, our party was due to arrive in Salt Lake City late tomorrow night.

"Would be more comfortable in a sleigh or wagon, I know," Colonel Brandon spoke over his shoulder, "but harder on the horses. We've got a lot of miles to cover. We'll be pushing our mounts to their limit just to make it in two days."

"I'm fine." The scarf, wrapped twice around the lower half of my face, muffled my words, and we continued in purposeful, comfortable silence.

It was one of those winter days when, after days of being cooped up inside, I would have shooed the girls outside to play. Cold, yes, but windless and still. Before long I'd unwrapped my scarf and taken off my hat. The temperature must have climbed up to something close to forty degrees, and we shed our overcoats. Every hour or so, we rested the horses, allowing them to nibble at what exposed grass they could find and lap from puddles of melted snow. For our rest, we walked in slow, stretching circles, chewing strips of salty dried venison. Colonel Brandon had his familiar flask, this time filled with brandy, and he insisted I take one or two sips, just to "keep the blood warm." From what I could tell, Coyote Tom had nothing to eat or drink all day, and he remained respectfully distant when we stopped to do so.

"It's their way," Colonel Brandon said when I mentioned we should share what we had. "He has his own. He'll eat when he's ready. Probably not until the end of the journey. These are proud people."

"And private."

"That's right. You keep an Indian woman, don't you?"

"*Keep* is an ugly word. Makes it sound like slavery. We had . . . There was some trouble a while back with the natives. Kimana's family—her husband and child—were killed. She was wounded. Nathan and I cared for her, and then she just . . . stayed."

"That was good of your husband."

"He's a good man, Colonel Brandon. In all of this, we must remember that."

CHAPTER 7

After two endless, exhausting days of riding, we arrived at the northernmost ward of Salt Lake City under a cloudy veil of muted moonlight.

"You lead us from here," Colonel Brandon said, his horse pawing impatiently in the muddy street.

Coyote Tom declared he would go no further into town, and I couldn't blame him. It was a strange relationship the Saints had struck with the native Indians. Joseph Smith's revelations taught that Jesus walked among these people, but they themselves garnered little reverence. Few were ever seen within the city, and being in the streets at night would bring Coyote Tom—and all of us—unwanted attention.

"This way, toward the temple." I sounded more confident than I felt, as I'd never come into town from this direction before. However, Brigham Young's meticulous planning—straight, ordered streets—soon displayed the logic he'd intended, and we moved through the grid with measured, quiet steps. Even the horses seemed to sense our clandestine intent, as each hoof was raised and lowered almost silently upon the packed mud and snow. I held Honey's reins loose in my hand, guiding her right, then left, then right again as the streets became more familiar. After a time, the houses on either side of the street ceased to be simple, wood dwellings with darkened windows and became grand, multistory brick structures with soft lights glowing from within.

I whispered over my shoulder, "This is the street," and Colonel Brandon responded with a low, appreciative whistle.

"If I'd known you came from this kind of money, I'd have considered holding you for ransom."

"None of this is mine. I have a sister-in-law who married well to a man who married often."

"You mean there's profit to be made in polygamy?" Private Lambert asked.

"No," I said, lowering my voice and indicating he should do the same. "There's profit to be made in obeying Brigham Young."

Rachel and Tillman lived in an enormous, three-story home built of bricks the color of overripe cherries. A wide porch ran the length of the house; I'd spent many a summer evening sitting on the bench swing watching our children chase fireflies in the front yard. A short picket fence surrounded the lot, and I called our party to stop at its corner. Although lamplight shone through the front window and several upstairs, the hour was late and we were hardly expected. I could only imagine the ruckus that could follow if Tillman came to the door to greet this wayward Saint accompanied by two soldiers. Besides, I hardly knew how I was going to explain myself, let alone my escort. To my surprise, Colonel Brandon agreed.

I said a quick prayer, asking God to guide my words as surely as he had guided our steps here, and dismounted Honey, handing her reins to Private Lambert. The street was otherwise deserted, making my steps sound louder than had any of the horses'. I ran my gloved hand along the tops of the pickets, remembering the rattling sounds the girls and their cousins made by racing along them with sticks. Those were the memories that made me think I could make a home for us here. For a while, anyway. Until the spring.

I was still at the gate when I saw Rachel through the window. Her blonde hair with its long, loose curls tied back by a single, thin ribbon glowed golden in the firelight. She was laughing at something, her head thrown back, and for just a moment I panicked. More than anybody, Nathan could make her laugh like that, and the thought of his being just outside my line of vision stopped my heart. But then, one of her sons—Bill, I think—ran into her arms and she embraced him in a hug I could feel all the way out in the cold. Whatever he'd done or said to inspire such joy in his mother I could only imagine, but then I'd shared such moments with my own daughters, and I knew that the smallest gesture, the tiniest trinket could lead to such a treasured embrace. The cold night air turned to fine crystal within me, and I ached to hold my children.

Just then, Rachel picked the boy up and gave him a spin, turning his back to the window while bringing herself to face it head-on. And that's when she saw me. I know she did because all trace of mirth left her face. Her hand came up to cup the back of her son's head, pressing him more closely to her, and she looked straight at me over his fine blond hair. I don't know how long we stayed there, staring at each other—she in the light, I in the dark—but it felt like a small eternity. Her gaze held me frozen at the gate and I sensed Colonel Brandon approaching to my rescue. Wordlessly, I held up a hand to stop him—just the slightest flicker of my wrist, never taking my eyes off the warm tableau on the other side of the glass.

Inside, Rachel put little Bill down and stepped away, saying something that sent him out of the room. Moments later she came through the door, and then it was I in her embrace, the small iron gate between us.

"Camilla Fox—you had us all scared half to death."

Her words, though whispered, were urgent, and she held me so tightly, I could not respond until she stepped away, and then I could manage only "I'm sorry."

"Where have you been?"

"I can't tell you that right now."

"What happened? Why did you leave?"

"Nathan didn't tell you?"

Before she could answer, the front door opened and Tillman's body filled the doorway.

"Rachel? Sweetheart, what on earth are you doing out there?"

In one fluid motion, Rachel grabbed my arm and turned me so that my face was hidden. "Just chatting with Sister Delia, darling. Learning how she makes that walnut cake you liked so much at the last Sunday supper."

"It's late," he grumbled.

"Well, it's not often we get a chance to chat, dear. I'll be right in."

Rachel's was a voice that could soothe any beast, and without a word her obedient husband turned and walked inside. She looked over my shoulder, waiting for the sound of the latch before turning her attention back to me.

"I've been hoping that what Nathan told me wasn't true," she said, picking up our conversation.

"So he told you I left?"

"He told me that you were leaving the church. That when the bishop came to question you, you renounced our faith and refused to be rebaptized. He told me you left him without a word, that you abandoned him and your children." All of this she spoke through perfect, gritted teeth as if she herself had been wronged by my actions. "So, please, Camilla, tell me he was wrong."

"It's true. All of it."

She frowned with an expression more like pity than anger. "You stupid, stupid girl. What were you thinking?"

"I—"

"I told you, give yourself time to accept the new wife. The first few months are hard, but you'll adjust. It's the way things are."

"I didn't leave because of Amanda. Not entirely."

"Oh yes, you did. You were jealous. Not about a new woman coming into your home, but the fact that my brother chose to obey Heavenly Father and Brigham Young over your selfish wishes."

"I cannot be part of a church with the false teachings that would encourage a man to make such a choice."

"Stupid girl," she said again, and this time she grabbed my arm and hauled me through the gate. Such a bold action would surely bring Colonel Brandon to my side, so I once again held up a hand to stay him. Once we were safely tucked around the side of the house, true darkness settled all around us. She spoke close—close enough that I could feel her breath on my face. "Do you know what kind of danger you may have put yourself in?"

"There was no sign of a storm when I left," I said, recalling that morning when, fully assured I was within God's will, I'd walked out of my home. "I was going to come here to see if you could take me in. Just for a while, just until—"

"I'm not talking about a *storm*. I'm talking about when Nathan couldn't find you. You'd disappeared after speaking such ugliness against the church. These are difficult times, Camilla." She gripped my arm, and I could tell she was shaking. She'd left the house wearing only a heavy shawl, but her tremors were not from the cold. "You know the persecution we're facing. The troubles Brigham's having. We have to stand together."

"I assure you, I'm no threat to Brigham's church."

"You're tearing your family apart. You're choosing to be disobedient to your husband, to the prophet, and to the church. They won't stand for it, Camilla. You have to go back home. Throw yourself on Nathan's mercy. He still loves you—he loves you so much. You're the first wife. Go reclaim your place."

"I can't," I said, but a gentle tugging on my spirit amended my words. "Not yet, anyway. I want to go home—to my parents. I'm planning to leave come spring. All I'm asking is for you to let me stay here with you until then."

"Here?"

"Yes."

"Absolutely not. I'm sorry, Camilla."

"I wouldn't be a burden. I'd do my share—"

"I have three sister wives. Do you really think I'd risk my marriage to have a little extra help with the dishes? Tillman wouldn't stand for it."

"If I am in danger as you say, how can I risk bringing that to my children? I—I can't go back home."

Rachel took a step back, studying me as she wrapped her shawl more tightly across her shoulders. "You never answered my question. Where have you been since you left?"

I felt a guard built up around my tongue, and I knew with absolute certainty that this was not the time for total truth. "Somebody found me after the storm died down. They took me in."

"Somebody who?"

I chose my words carefully, picking my way across cobblestones of facts. "A man named Charles and his . . . family."

Rachel furrowed her brow. "Do I know them?"

"They've just arrived. I was sick—from the cold, you know. They were quite kind. But I could never impose on them further."

"Then you'll need to find someplace else."

"There is no place else."

"Of course there is." She spoke as if willing me to see a giant, invisible secret. "I'm not going to have a hand in this misguided adventure of yours, but surely there's someone who'd welcome a little bit of company to while away the long, dark winter. A friend in need of a friend?"

As I listened, Rachel's intent became clear, but with that clarity came a shadow of reluctance. "Oh, Rachel, I could never—"

"Rachel!" Tillman's voice boomed into the night, no doubt alerting every neighbor.

Rachel stepped away to poke her head around the corner. "Just finishing up, darling. I'm on my way." Then, back to me, every ounce of sweetness drained. "I'm through talking. And for both our sakes, this conversation never happened."

I remained in the shadows of the side of the house until I heard the opening and closing of the front door. Drawing my hood down to hide my face, I moved quickly through the front yard and out the little iron gate, making my way back to the corner where Colonel Brandon and Private Lambert waited with the horses.

"Private Lambert will carry your things," Colonel Brandon said. Indeed, the young man already bore my small bundle of belongings over his shoulder.

"Not here," I said before giving a brief rendition of my conversation with Rachel. "But there's one other place I can go."

"More family?"

"Not quite. It's a little way from here, but the horses will attract too much attention. I'll be fine on my own."

"Nonsense," Colonel Brandon said. He turned to Private Lambert. "Coyote Tom is setting up camp just outside the city. Take the horses, and I'll meet you there." He took the bundle from Private Lambert and slung it over his shoulder before bowing to me in a gesture that clearly said, "Lead on."

The wide streets that comprised Rachel's neighborhood and those just past it, hosting every kind of shop and boutique, were lined with lights that would blaze until midnight—at least one more hour, according to Colonel Brandon's timepiece. Heads down, we walked swiftly and spoke very little, our silence complementing the muffled sounds around us. When we came to Temple Square, however, I brought us to a stop.

"Normally," I said, "this place would be a beehive. Just the way Brother Brigham likes it. Men hauling stone, climbing scaffolds. Constant, constant noise. Hammers and wagons and—"

"Shh." His gloved fingers came to my lips. "Listen."

I saw. Low-lit lanterns hanging from the scaffolds. Oxen and wagons positioned in the street. And men. Absent were the rich baritone voices raised in songs glorifying the sacrifice of their labor. Instead, nothing but muffled footsteps and the occasional whispered command.

Colonel Brandon drew me close to his side and brought us under the eave and against the window of a print shop on the corner opposite the temple. As we watched, it soon became clear that while this late-night workforce might lack joyous tribute, they exhibited no shortage of fervent dedication. It was constant motion—dark, shadowy figures milling all around the temple's foundation. Shovels and buckets and spades in an ever-marching brigade. One wagon being led away, and another falling in line behind. All in a perpetual silent agreement of purpose.

"They're burying it," Colonel Brandon said, his voice no louder than that of a shovel stabbing soil.

"But why? They've worked so hard . . ."

"They're hiding it so it won't be destroyed."

"But who would—?"

"We would. Or so Brigham Young seems to think."

Somehow, the sight of those men burying that temple struck a chord of fear in me that no enemy's blaze ever could. Every stone in that foundation came from the quarry not far from the home I shared with Nathan. I'd seen the men toiling under the weight of them—each giving one day in ten as free labor to the church. I'd seen the great slabs lashed to the wagons, pulled by teams of eight oxen one brutal step at a time, making a journey of three days out of one that would normally take an afternoon. It was all we talked about, that temple. Its blueprints were almost as sacred as *The Book of Mormon*. Men and women alike devoted as much to it as to God himself. The workforce of the pharaohs of Egypt was no more enslaved than Brigham's Saints. And to think, now, at his word, to tear down what they'd built? To create one massive, domelike grave?

"They'll do whatever he says." I spoke my fear aloud.

"Just between you and me?" Colonel Brandon tipped his head low. "He scares me, too."

The activity in Temple Square gave us license to be less furtive in our own movement, even if I was the only woman in sight. We moved quickly, though not so much so as to attract attention, and I continued to give directions.

"Left at this corner. Now straight across."

After a time, the streets grew more narrow, and the sturdy brick structures gave way to those made of whitewashed planks. Sidewalks disappeared, and each step required a little tug out of the mud before taking the next one.

"Definitely a change in fortune," Colonel Brandon said. I allowed him to take my arm.

"But no less devoted."

We came to one of the last streets in the ward, one lined with identical, narrow, two-story houses. Most of the windows were black, although a few boasted a low, gray light. My eyes scanned each door, but there was no way to find the correct door in this darkness. The doorposts were marked with crudely painted numbers, and I whispered the one we sought.

"Here it is." Colonel Brandon stood in front of the dilapidated porch, and I wondered how I could ever have missed it. Three sad little steps—the bottom one half-buried in mud—and a railing that had been detached for as long as I could remember. Winter had taken its toll on the few plants and shrubs in the front yard. In daylight, I knew the color of the clapboard exterior to be gray; it was no less so in moonlight. These windows seemed darker than the others on the street, and I knew that they were covered in thick drapery on the other side of the cold glass.

I took hold of the railing, thought better of it, and put my foot on the bottom step. "You need to go now," I said, reaching for my things.

He held them back. "I'm not leaving you alone out here."

"And I don't want to have to explain who you are. Go down the street a little, if it makes you feel better."

"Just who is it that lives here?"

"A friend."

"And this *friend* . . ."

"She'll take me in. I know it."

"And if she doesn't?"

"This is the door God has led me to. If he chooses to close it, well, I'll pray about the next one."

"Here." He took the bundle off his back and handed it to me before reaching into his pocket. From it, he withdrew three candle stubs. "I have night patrols in the city on a regular basis. From now on they'll sweep down to this street. Promise me, if you ever have any problem—"

"I'll be fine."

Colonel Brandon opened the sack, dropped the candle stubs in, retied it, and continued as if I hadn't said a word. "If there's ever a time when you don't feel safe, put these candles in the window, and I'll send someone to fetch you back."

"Back to where?"

"Back to me."

The moment hung between us like so many stars. Standing on the porch step, I was eye level with him for the first time. Stripped of his uniform and stature, he became just a man. A kind one at that, with his plain woolen cap and soft brown eyes. A man who wanted to protect me, shield me from harm, take me away. And in this I felt the fresh pangs of a new danger. A threat delivered not by his hand but from within my own heart.

"You mean, back to Fort Bridger?" My voice held no malice, but still he recoiled.

"Yes, yes. Of course. Or to your home. Whatever you choose."

I reached out my right hand and took a firm grip of his shoulder. "Thank you, Colonel Brandon. I shall never forget your kindness."

The moment I released him, he took on a soldier's stance and touched his cap. "Farewell, Mrs. Fox."

We turned our backs to each other and went our separate ways—he down the street and I up the two remaining steps to the wooden door. I knocked twice, and when there was no answer, I took off my glove and knocked again. As I waited, I allowed myself a glimpse up and down the street, but there was no sign of Colonel Brandon, though simply knowing he was within earshot gave me some comfort.

I had turned and raised my fist to knock again when the rough metal doorknob turned, and with painstaking caution, the door eased open, revealing a small wedge of a pale face and one narrowed green eye.

"Camilla?" My name was spoken in that familiar voice—as if the letters were being dragged across burlap.

"Yes, it's me," I said, and the door opened wider. "Hello, Evangeline."

CHAPTER 8

She wore a yellowed nightgown underneath an enormous gray shawl. Standing in her dark doorway, she seemed little more than a shadow herself. Her skin was pale beneath its carpet of freckles, and her hair—the color of sunset—sprang from beneath a flannel cap in a mass of thick, coarse curls. Eventually, her thin, pinched face broke into a smile, revealing small, crowded teeth, and she flung the door open wide.

"Come in! Come in!"

I did, and we were immediately in each other's arms, embracing as we always did, as if ages had passed since we last saw each other. This time, however, such sentiment was warranted, as we hadn't seen each other since before my husband's second marriage. We were almost the same age, Evangeline Moss and I, but as I held her in my arms that night, she felt infinitely older. There was a frail, brittle quality to her body, like she could snap beneath my touch, but when I attempted to pull away, she clutched me tighter.

"Oh, when I said my prayers tonight to Heavenly Father, I felt something in my spirit that you would come to see me."

"Really?" I disengaged myself carefully and stepped back. Her entire upper arm—sleeve and shawl and all—fit comfortably within my encircling fingers. "Well, then, maybe we could go inside. You must be freezing out here."

"Of course. And you too, I suppose, although you're wearing a cloak and hood and everything, but still . . ."

She chatted nervously, giving me time to turn and send a final wave to where I assumed Colonel Brandon was watching. And then we were inside.

Truthfully, air on this side of Evangeline's door was not much warmer than that in the street. The only light came from a single candle sitting on a small table just inside.

"Let's go into the kitchen," she said over her shoulder. "I'm afraid the parlor's not very tidy."

"Anywhere I can sit down." The day's ride and recent walk were beginning to take their toll.

"Parlor, then, but you must excuse the mess." She picked up the candle, and only the long shadows on the wall indicated that we were not merely two friends visiting. We talked about the weather—the welcome break from snow and the pleasure of a mild winter afternoon. "So I'm surprised you didn't bring the girls with you to visit."

And that's when I realized—Evangeline had no idea that I'd left my husband, that I'd been in hiding for nearly a month, that this was no ordinary call. But the lateness of the hour, the fatigue I felt clear to my very bones kept my conversation from plunging to anything deeper than polite replies to Evangeline's chitchat. I balanced on the side of truth, saying I knew the girls were safe and sound at home, and I simply wanted to get away for a while.

"It's getting a little crowded at our house," I said, forcing a lighthearted tone.

"I can imagine."

But I wondered if she could. I'd known Evangeline almost as long as I'd known Nathan. We'd traveled together in the same emigrant party and become as close as sisters during the journey. Her mother died of fever on the trail, and it was I who'd brushed and braided the woman's hair to prepare her for the grave. Days after we arrived in the valley, Mr. Moss suffered a terrible stroke and Evangeline devoted herself to his care for the six long years it took him to die. Her younger brothers lit out for England the minute they were old enough to serve as missionaries for the church, leaving Evangeline utterly alone.

As the candle's flame slowly filled the room with light, I began to see why she would be so reluctant to entertain a guest in her parlor. There never had been anything posh about her furnishings, and from what I could tell, she had the same threadbare sofa she'd always had, though there did seem to be a new addition of two upholstered chairs. I couldn't be sure, however, because on this night the furniture wasn't even visible. In fact, very little about the room would identify it as a front parlor. The floor was littered with blankets spilling down from what I knew to be a lovely floral-print sofa hidden underneath. Dresses and stockings draped over the matching chairs, and the short-legged oak table in the center was littered with assorted dishes. Even in this dim light I could see they were dirty.

"I mostly stay down here during the winter months," she

said, moving piles aside. "It saves on fuel if I only light one stove."

"Very frugal of you." I dropped my bundle on the floor next to the newly exposed chair before dropping myself down into it. From what I could see behind the cold grate, this room had known very little warmth.

"I'd offer you something to eat, but the fire's already out."

"That's fine." It took all my grace to ignore the rumbling in my stomach.

"Maybe a slice of bread? And I have a jar of pumpkin butter—" she drummed her fingertips together and glanced side to side—"but it's late and one really shouldn't go to sleep on a full stomach. Bad for the digestion. Unless you're going to be leaving right away? Are you?"

It was the first question she'd asked of me since my arrival, and her utter lack of curiosity tore at my heart. Was she so lonely that the midnight visit of a friend prompted nothing more than an apology for a messy parlor? Her credulity swathed me in guilt. Short of those in ministry and my own husband, Evangeline was the most fervently dedicated Saint I knew, and had she any clue about the state of my faith, she never would have deigned to offer me bread and pumpkin butter. Still, though the darkness and cold outside were only marginally less inviting than those within her walls, I chose to hold my tongue. There'd be time enough for truth in the morning.

***

It certainly wasn't the worst place I'd ever slept. Wagon beds, barn floors, even hard ground under a star-filled sky—all at one time had served as substitutes for a feather-filled mattress. But in terms of ironlike discomfort, nothing compared to stretching out on a threadbare quilt spread over the solid plank floors of Evangeline's parlor. I couldn't give my make-shift bed full credit for my sleeplessness. My left hand throbbed with cold, like a thin steel blade thrust clear to my elbow, and Evangeline's distinctive snore—an endless succession of three short whistles—robbed me of any sense of peace. Sometime just before dawn, the cold and the noise and the pain surrendered to my exhaustion, and my eyes dropped down to the back of my head, smothered in sleep.

I dreamed of my daughters during those short hours. Our little home sat in the middle of a shallow basin, and when-ever we came back from a church meeting or the trading post, they would run ahead, drop at the top of the swelling hill, and roll to the bottom—over and over again—while Nathan and I strolled, hand in hand, wrapped in their laughter. My dream captured such a scene, so real that I could feel Nathan's fin-gers intertwined in mine. I awoke to find my own fingers laced across my heart and my daughters' names caught in my throat. Oh, how I didn't want to open my eyes, not while my mind echoed with Lottie's sweet laughter, but soon enough another voice invaded, and I felt a twiglike grip on my shoulder.

"Good morning, sunshine!" Her voice was as close to sing-ing as it could ever be. "I see you're a late sleeper, too. I usually don't get up until I absolutely have to. Sometimes it's nine or ten o'clock."

"Ten o'clock?" I struggled to my elbows and sat up.

"Relax. It's just past nine. But you must have needed your sleep. Here, I'll help you up."

Evangeline stood above me, her hands extended down. Without giving it a thought, I reached up to grasp them.

"Camilla! Your hand—what happened?"

"Oh, that." Even then I knew I was in for a lifetime of

explanation, but I was not compelled to give my friend the entire story that morning. "Frostbite."

"Oh, how terrible. I hope Nathan wasn't affected the same way."

"Nathan's fine." I was steadily on my feet by now and, short as I was, nearly a head taller.

"He wasn't out with you?"

"No."

"You were out alone?"

"Yes." Already I longed for the girl from last night who seemed never to ask a single question.

"And so what did he use? I mean, was it Nathan? Or a doctor? Was it a knife? Or I've heard sometimes toes can be snapped off with your bare hands. But not fingers. Although yours are small—"

"Evangeline, please. This was not the most pleasant experience of my life, and I'd rather not talk about it if you don't mind."

"Oh." She sulked then, just as my daughter Melissa did whenever she couldn't have her own way.

"I'm sorry," I said, squeezing one of her hands with my whole one. "It's just that we haven't seen each other for ages. Surely there are more pleasant things to talk about."

Immediately she was beaming again. "Of course. You must be half-starved by now. Come into the kitchen."

I followed her into the small, gray room just past the stairway. Here, finally, a small fire in the stove waged battle against the icy room, and I took to it like a moth, alternately blowing on my hands and holding them out toward it.

"You know," Evangeline said with pride, "Brother Brigham himself set my fuel allowance for the winter. I went straight to him and said, 'Just because I live alone doesn't mean I need to freeze in my own bed.' He's really the kindest man I've ever met. So generous. He says I'm to stay in this house until my situation changes."

Had there been some way to capture the tone of her voice, the room would have transformed to a desert at high noon in July.

"That is quite generous of him." The coolness behind my own words did not daunt her in the least.

"And I happen to know that he personally sees to it that his wives send their mending and washing to me so I can earn a little."

"Enough to pay a tithe, no doubt."

"As we all should," she said, suddenly quite serious. "These are dark times we're facing. But you might not realize, living as far away as you do. And now that we have this bright new day, you can tell me what brings you into Salt Lake City."

"I don't wish to be rude," I said, inching away from the stove, "but perhaps we could have a little breakfast first?"

Evangeline slapped her palm against her forehead. "There, see how I am? I'll get to talking and then I'm likely to forget my own head. You, you're the guest. Sit."

I obeyed, though it was difficult to relax in the wake of her nervous preparations. First on the table was a pitcher of milk brought over by a generous neighbor. It was, I could feel, still warm, and I longed to drink great gulps of it, knowing full well I'd not have the cup of coffee I'd grown so used to having in the morning.

Evangeline reached inside a larder and sliced two thin strips of bacon, which she set to sizzling in a large pan. She apologized for not having any eggs—they would have to wait until her next Ladies' Aid basket arrived. She did, however, produce a loaf of bread from which she cut two lacy-thin slices.

These she threaded onto a long metal fork and placed inside the oven to toast.

"Helps to melt the butter," she said, giving the yellow ball in the middle of the table a convincing pat.

"No pumpkin butter?" My eyes went to the jar full of the orange stuff sitting on the shelf above the sink.

"Oh, I thought we'd save that for a treat with supper. If you're going to be here for supper. You will, won't you?"

"I will now," I said, and she laughed, clapping her hands with girlish glee. Once again, her joy ripped at my heart, and I wondered just how long two people could live with an unspoken falsehood between them. Soon enough, though, I had a slice of bacon on the plate in front of me and a thin slice of toast so crispy the sound of my chewing drowned out whatever conversation came from the other side of the table. In between bites, I drank my fill of warm, fresh milk, and tears pricked the corners of my eyes as I thought of my girls sharing the same treat at home.

However, a meal can last only so long, especially one so meager. As we both swiped a finger across our plates to swab up our crumbs, Evangeline asked, "Why are you here, Camilla?"

My finger was actually in my mouth at the time, allowing me a few seconds of grace to phrase my response. "I want to stay here for a while. With you, if that's all right."

"Why? Did Nathan send you away?"

"No," I answered, a little too quickly. The hunger in her question startled me, though it shouldn't have. Evangeline had loved Nathan longer than I'd even known him, and her affections hadn't altered after all these years.

She appeared unconvinced. "I can understand how he'd want a little time alone with his new wife."

"They've been married four months."

"So did *she* send you here?"

"Sister Amanda does not tell me what to do. If anything—"
I stopped myself, knowing that giving in to my temper would
lead me to reveal more than I wanted. "It's just . . . all of us, in
that small house. Like I said last night—we get so crowded."

"You usually stay with Rachel when you come into town."

I forced a casual laugh. "Well, Rachel's house would hardly
be the place for someone looking for solitude."

"I see." She stood abruptly, snatching my plate right out
from under me. "So you figured poor old Evangeline needs the
company, right? Never mind all the times *I* might like to have
company, or even be a guest in someone's home when it's not
time for a funeral." She dropped the dishes in the sink basin
and clapped a hand to her mouth. "Oh, Camilla. I'm so sorry.
I didn't think—"

"It's all right." I rose and placed my arm across her bony
shoulders. "Remember, you were supposed to be there for the
baby's dedication. I would have spared you the funeral had it
been in my power."

"But doesn't it give you great joy to know that your little
boy has returned to Heavenly Father?"

I carefully chose my words. "I know he's in the arms of
Jesus, and yes, that gives me comfort."

Evangeline pulled away and poured warm water from the
kettle into the washing tub. Our simple fare didn't call for soap.

"I'll never have a baby of my own, you know."

"Don't be silly," I said, bringing our cups from the table.
"You're still a young woman—we both are. And I know you'll
find a husband sometime. Soon, in fact. As soon as you like."

"You don't understand." She looked for all the world like a
woman poised on the point of confession, like she was holding
a hundred secrets at bay. I didn't pry, having secrets of my own.

Something told me that an ill-placed word might burst the dam of undesirable confession built up between us. Instead, I quietly helped her with the quick task of tidying up the kitchen, keeping my own story stopped up at the top of my throat.

"I won't make you sleep on the parlor floor tonight," Evangeline said, running a dry towel over the clean table. "You're welcome to one of the rooms upstairs, for as long as you want."

I placed the clean plates on the shelf. "I won't be a bother."

"You can take a bed warmer up with you. If you go to sleep real fast, you'll be warm enough."

"I'll be fine, Evangeline. Remember, I live in the same winter as you."

"And I won't ask you about anything, unless you want to tell me. About why you're here, I mean."

"You're a good friend. And that's all I need right now."

Seeming satisfied with both my answer and her kitchen, Evangeline led me back into her parlor. She stopped in the doorway, planting her hands on her narrow hips. "Well, it looks like we have a harder row to hoe in here, don't we?"

"I've seen worse." I picked up the tray of dishes from the small table and headed back to the kitchen, thankful we hadn't tossed out the wash water. It felt good, having something to do. I shaved soap into the water and set the dishes to soak. I pictured Evangeline eating alone by the dim light of her parlor stove, steps away from where she would bed down for the night. Her situation made her every bit as much a prisoner as I'd ever been, yet there didn't seem to be any hope for her release in sight.

By the time I returned to the parlor, she had folded up most of the bedding and placed it in a large wicker basket that she stashed behind the sofa. I opened the drapes, ushering in the morning sun, and the flooding light instantly transformed the room, giving it a cheeriness neither of us could echo.

"You can take your things upstairs," Evangeline said, nodding toward my little bundle sitting on the high-backed chair. "Any room you like."

"Don't you want to come with me?"

She shook her head. "I don't go upstairs very often anymore. I keep thinking I should take in a boarder or two. I guess I'll practice with you."

Her weak smile reassured me that her last statement was a joke, though I knew if I'd offered any sum of money, she would have snatched it from my hand.

I picked up my bag and mounted the narrow stairway, twisting around the narrow turn. The second floor had an unusual frigid mustiness, like an attic. From earlier visits I knew the far bedroom was that where Brother Moss had lain, motionless, until he took his final breath. Drawing my own shuddering one, I knew I could never stay in there. Just to my left was the boys' room—both of its narrow beds stripped clean of linens, though the walls were still littered with drawings. Curiosity drew me in, and I stepped around, observing the childish yet sincere sketches of Mormon heroes. Samuel the Lamanite facing a sea of arrows; Ammon bearing a mighty sword. These men—these figments of Joseph Smith's imagination—took precedence over the heroes of God's holy Word. Little wonder their images were left intact, while every other personal belonging was tucked away in bureau drawers.

Shuddering, I moved on to Evangeline's own room, though I didn't like to think I was keeping her from sleeping in her own bed. Still, she'd stated her preference strongly enough, and I stepped over the threshold pleased at what I saw. A cheerful log-cabin-pattern quilt was spread across what looked like a soft bed with soft pillows piled against a white iron headboard. The curtains were drawn, but I pushed them aside to reveal a view of the now-bustling street below. The braided rug on the floor was well worn, and a thin layer of dust lay across the surface of the desk and dresser, but otherwise the room was clean and tidy.

I had few enough belongings to stow away. I wore my only dress, though I had a few underthings and stockings to stash in the bottom drawer. My Bible was given a new home on the table next to the bed and finally, the three stubs of candle Colonel Brandon had given me with his rather dire instruction. At the moment, standing in a pool of sunlight, I could not imagine what terror could befall me that I would need to summon his soldiers in the night. Then again, there was a time I never would have imagined myself anywhere but in the loving arms of my husband. And before that, in the protective custody of my father. So with just a hint of ceremony, I lined the three candles—each wide enough to stand without the benefit of a holder—along the windowsill. Just seeing them there gave me an added layer of comfort, and out of curiosity, I hazarded a glance out the window to see if I could get a glimpse of one of the men sent to patrol.

But no. No mounted soldier in uniform astride a noble horse. No collection of young men gathered to stand at attention. I pressed my head closer to the glass. How would I know what to look for in a military patrol? Colonel Brandon had donned civilian garb to bring me here; it stood to reason any troops he sent out would be similarly dressed.

Then, just as I was about to step away, I noticed a man standing across the street and two houses down. On this crisp winter morning, he alone stood perfectly still. All about him, men and women bustled about their business. Men hauled handcarts full of wood; women walked in groups of two or three, lost in conversation; children wove themselves through-out, running late toward the sound of the school bell ringing in the distance.

But this man—he wore a dark-blue wool overcoat and a wide-brimmed hat pulled low over his eyes. In fact, I might not have seen his eyes at all, save for the fact that his head was tilted straight up, and he was looking right at me.

CHAPTER 9

We settled into a routine like two maiden aunts who had spent a lifetime watching life pass them by. Each meal—no matter how meager—became its own ceremony as we prepared, ate, and cleared away the same few dishes over and over. One pot of soup fueled an entire day's conversation as we sat quietly at our tasks, commenting on its delicious aroma. Indeed it was, with shreds of sausage, chunks of potato, and a generous stir-in of butter and cream just before we ate.

Still, during those first days, I experienced a hunger like I hadn't known since the final miles on the wagon trail to Zion. Evangeline lived solely on the charity of the Saints, and her allotted groceries seemed barely enough to meet her needs, let alone to share with her secretly apostate friend. We ate twice a day—a midmorning breakfast and supper one hour after sundown. Hunger became a constant companion, a cavernous voice that could not be silenced. At first, it literally sang out from within me with echoing, growling calls. But as a crying child will eventually settle into silence, so its clamor died away to be heard by my ears only.

With the hunger came fatigue, and I began to see how Evangeline, unwed and alone, spent her days. I assumed she took more trouble with her housewifery having a guest, but no single chore demanded more than an hour's labor, and then we devoted afternoons to any sort of task that required us to move nothing more than a needle. I helped with the bits of sewing and mending Evangeline did for some of the wealthier women in her ward, hoping my efforts would contribute to my keep.

"I'm usually invited to somebody's home for dinner after the Sunday meeting," Evangeline said as we wiped our dishes dry on Saturday night—a redundant act, really. We'd eaten the remnants of the sausage-and-potato soup, wiping the bowl with the shared heel of a loaf of bread. Dessert was a shared peppermint stick. "I'm sure if you're right there with me, you'd be invited along, too. Everybody always has plenty."

I focused on the task at hand, carefully choosing my reply. "I wasn't planning to go to meeting."

"Not go?" She made no attempt to hide her suspicion. "Why in the world would you not go? Now more than ever it's so important for us to remain strong in our faith. And especially you, being so far away from your family . . ."

"That's just it." I took the dishes and placed them on the shelf. "I don't want to explain why I'm here. I don't want people to think I'm discontent. Or disobedient."

"But aren't you? Discontent, I mean."

Her question came from a place of hunger no amount of food could fill.

"I know it must be hard for you to understand. It's not easy for me, either. And I'm so grateful to you for opening your home to me."

Her eyes narrowed. "I'm not sure how I feel about opening my home to someone who doesn't want to go to church."

I had the distinct feeling we were circling each other, like two cats who had just discovered each other's presence in the room. All these days, all these hours, Evangeline hadn't asked me a single word about why I wasn't in my own home. The tepid explanation I'd given that first night seemed still to satisfy her.

"It would be hard for me, too, to go to meeting without the girls. I miss them so much." Here, the catch in my voice had nothing to do with subterfuge. The next morning, Amanda would be arranging the girls' hair in their special Sunday morning curls and taking their little hands as they walked into the church house. She would sit next to Nathan on our family's bench. Lottie's soft little head would fall against her shoulder as Elder Justus's sermon ran too long. I can still feel the weight of it—an ache that brings comfort rather than pain.

"And Nathan?"

"Of course," I said, still caught up in reverie. "I miss what we had as a family."

"Well," she said, sounding short of being totally convinced, "at least you can come with me to do a little marketing."

"I don't know how I feel about that, sister. You know I have nothing—nothing at all to contribute."

She deflected my protest with a wave of her fragile hand. "It's such a treat for me to have company. I hardly ever get to be a hostess. Besides, it's what Heavenly Father calls us to do. You're giving me a chance to be something."

"Oh, darling, you are something—a wonderful friend."

"Like it says in the seventh chapter of Moroni, 'Wherefore, my beloved brethren, if ye have not charity, ye are nothing, for charity never faileth.' See? I'm nothing. Nobody. But now Heavenly Father has given me an opportunity to be something. I don't have much, but all I have is yours, for as long as you need to stay."

I barely managed to choke out a thank-you before hugging her close to me. It pained me to see her deem herself so worthless. Moreover, to see how she'd committed the words of Joseph Smith's false teachings to her heart, twisting even those that could be good. I chastised myself for every grumbling thought that came along with my grumbling stomach, and as I held her birdlike frame, I asked the Lord to forgive me, too. Yet it was her devotion to the church that compelled me to withhold the truth of my circumstances a little longer. If her conscience were ever forced to choose between following her faith or sheltering a friend, the Saints would indeed emerge victorious.

Still, I begged off accompanying her, claiming the onset of a headache—not an entire ruse, as I seemed to always have one humming just behind my eyes. I did, however, wrap her muffler around her throat with distinctly maternal affection and joked that the basket over her arm, when full, would likely cause her to topple over on the way home. Once she was ready, I watched at the door to see her safely down the steps.

And there he was. The same man I'd seen that first morning, standing just as he was that day—across the street and at the corner. I hadn't seen him since that day, but his face was so seared into my memory as to make him unmistakable. Same blue coat, same low-brimmed hat. I noticed that his beard seemed to emerge from an almost-starlike cleft in his chin. His eyes tracked straight over to Evangeline's open door. It was too late to call her back. What explanation would I give if I could? Instead, sucking back a scream, I slammed the door closed, throwing my back against it. Despite the inevitable chill in the room, beads of sweat formed on my brow, and my breath came in short, stinging spurts.

"Lord, protect me."

My prayer squeaked out from the top of my throat, and I'll admit to being hard-pressed to know just what I was asking protection *from*. After all, perhaps he was one of the soldiers Colonel Brandon had said he would send to patrol.

"A soldier . . . a soldier . . ." Simply saying so out loud gave a sense of comfort. I tried to recall his face from among all I'd seen during my stay at Fort Bridger but found no memory of his features. Certainly, though, I had not had a chance to see them all. Still, I'd found no reassurance in his gaze, and now he knew I was in this house alone. With hands shaking, I turned and slid the door's iron bolt across, taking some reassurance in its strength.

Evangeline came home some hours later, looking quite refreshed. A hearty pink infused the otherwise-pallid face beneath her freckles, and her green eyes sparkled with renewed life. I reached out to relieve her of some of the bundles she carried and was rewarded with a healthy whiff of all the scents that came from spending a winter afternoon in a big city's marketplace.

"Oh, it was lovely," she said, fairly skipping back to the kitchen. "I asked for an extra ration of salt pork, and what do you know? They gave me that and bacon *and* a ham. Can you believe it? Not just the few slices I usually get. An entire ham.

Just for the two of us. Well, really, just for me, because they don't know . . . but isn't it wonderful how well the Saints provide?"

This was the most talkative I'd seen her since my arrival, and in her I saw a shadow of the girl I became friends with back when we were both so young. Never did she pause for me to contribute anything to the conversation, and I wouldn't have dreamed of interrupting her parade of praise. Whether through a spirit of generosity or obedience, Brigham Young's followers were directly responsible for her survival. That, at least, I could not fault.

"It's God's provision," I said, lifting paper sacks of flour and cornmeal out of the shopping basket.

"Through the Saints." Her voice took on the thinness it always did if I ever said anything that even hinted at criticism of the church. "God isn't going to drop ham onto my table."

"You never know. He sent manna to the Israelites in the desert. And Jesus fed the crowd of five thousand with just five loaves of bread and two fish."

"Heavenly Father needs his people to do his work."

"That's true." I must admit to feeling grateful for Brigham's edicts to feed the poor; my mouth nearly watered as I uncovered a sack filled with two generous scoops of dried beans and, underneath, an onion. "But if you had faith in him—just him, without the Saints—he wouldn't let you starve."

"You cannot separate faith in God from faith in the prophet, Camilla. They speak in one voice. Obedience to one is obedience to the other."

I bit the inside of my lip to keep myself from contradicting her. After all, this was how God had chosen to meet my immediate needs of shelter and food. There would be other opportunities for conversation. Perhaps we'd both be of a better temperament after filling our stomachs with a hot, steaming bowl of ham-and-bean soup. To lighten the mood, I suggested as much, though we'd have to let the beans soak overnight. She did, however, have five potatoes, and we sliced one thin along with half of an onion, setting it all to sizzle with thin slices of salt pork.

It was the first smell of real cooking I'd experienced since coming to this house. Really, the first since I'd left my own home now fully a month ago, and I almost wept with the antici- pation of it. With my careful calculations, we had just enough to give each of us a generous serving—not enough to save any left over. We cleaned our plates and wiped them cleaner still with slices of fresh bread.

"And to think," Evangeline said, leaning back in her chair and rubbing her plank-flat stomach, "I'll be eating like this again tomorrow. I ran into Sister Bethany at the market, and she invited me to dinner after meeting. Said she was making a pumpkin pie. Sure you won't come with me?"

"I'm sure. Thank you for understanding." The combina- tion of good food eaten near a hot stove gave me such a feeling of weight and warmth, I could have gone to sleep right there at the table, even though it was not quite seven o'clock.

"Well then, I guess it's up to me to be the obedient one." Evangeline was in better humor too. She rose, stretching. "Leave the dishes for now. I'm going to heat water for a bath."

And so we each trekked out to the water pump just behind her house to fill her kettle and pots with water, which we set to boil. One split log after another was added to the fire, until the little kitchen glowed as warm as an August afternoon. I took it upon myself to wipe down the washbasin, just as I always did for my girls, before filling it.

I don't know why I didn't leave the room. Evangeline was a grown woman, after all—not a little girl. But something about her seemed so small and frail, I simply stayed. It was I who grazed the back of my knuckles across the water's surface to make sure the temperature was just right; I who shaved thin slices off the cake of sweet-smelling soap and dropped them into the water; I who fished around until I'd found every last pin in the crimson nest atop her head.

"I could help you wash your hair, if you like," I said as the stuff sprang to life beneath my hands.

"Oh, could you? I have such a time—it gets so snarled."

So, fully dressed, Evangeline sat on the floor and I guided her until the back of her neck rested against the edge of the basin. My own sleeves rolled to my elbows, I scooped the water up until her hair was saturated clear to her scalp. I worked the bar of soap into a lather between my hands and ran them through the wet tresses, massaging her scalp, then rinsing it with warm water. Once satisfied, I twisted it into a thick rope and wrung as much of the water out as I could, then wrapped it in a square of toweling.

Rising to my feet, I promised to comb and braid it after she'd finished her bath.

"Wait." She reached for my arm to help her stand. "Would you mind going upstairs to my room and fetching me a clean set of garments from my top bureau drawer?"

I hesitated for just a split second—almost to the point of asking for clarification—before saying, "Of course." How could I ever forget?

I took a long match from the box by the stove, touched it to the flame within, and lit a lamp.

"Are you sure you need that?" Evangeline was doubled over, unlacing her boots. "I thought you'd know your way around by now. And they're right in the top drawer."

"I won't let it burn a second longer than I have to." I'd

almost grown used to the dark in this house, but I wasn't entirely comfortable in it.

The heat from the kitchen dissipated long before hitting the second floor. I set the lamp atop the yellowed doily and opened the top drawer, my eyes immediately landing on the familiar, white cotton fabric. Though it was now folded to hide its sacred symbols, I could clearly picture the stitched images—the square and compasses across each breast, the marks at the navel and the knee. Long-sleeved, extending from its high collar to the ankle, I'd worn such a garment until the night before I left Nathan. So many burdens woven into this fabric, and yet I knew, to Evangeline, to wear it was to wear her very faith.

Garment in one hand, lamp in the other, I used my elbow to close the drawer and made my way back to the kitchen. The fire that had burned so valiantly to heat the bathwater had all but disappeared, and the chill of a near-empty house on a winter's night was slowly creeping back in.

"We should build the fire back up," I called out as I rounded the corner. "Or you'll catch your death—"

The sight stopped me midstep. Evangeline was small enough to fold herself up and bathe right in the galvanized tub, and so she had. She stood now, the water up to her ankles, wet hair heavy down her back. Her garment—identical to the one I held in my hand—clung to her, sopping wet against her skin.

"C-c-can you help me?" Her teeth chattered around the words as her fingers struggled with the tied closure.

"Oh, sister . . ." I set the lamp and garment on the table and ran to her aid. "You can take this off long enough to bathe, you know."

She kept her lips clamped shut and shook her head.

There was a tie at the top of the shirt and another midway down between the symbols stitched over each breast. This second one was knotted, and the fact that it was wet made it even more difficult to dislodge.

"Come closer to the light." I gave her my arm to help her over the tub's edge and led her to the table. The tremors that had made her hands unable to work the knot now took over the whole of her body, sending her into violent spasms. "Hold on to me," I instructed. "Try to be still."

She clutched my upper arms, further hindering my efforts, forcing me to work close—so close, I could see her very bones protruding beneath her skin.

"Do you think this might be easier if I had all ten fingers?" I said, attempting to lighten the mood.

"Maybe that's the m-m-miracle we should pray for. That they'll g-g-grow back."

Soon, though, I could see that untying the closure would not happen anytime soon. "I'm going to have to cut it."

"N-n-no!" No joking here. Her gritted teeth did nothing to lessen her insistence.

"Either that or wait until it's dry, and you'll catch a chill if you wear it too much longer."

"You c-c-can't—"

"Just here at the tie," I soothed. "And we can stitch it right back on."

"You know b-b-better."

"I know that it's silly to catch a cold." I tore myself away from her grip. "I'm going to go get a pair of scissors."

I left her with the lamplight, knowing my way well around the parlor and the exact place where her sewing basket sat next to her favorite chair. My fingers quickly closed around the cold blade, and I grabbed a wool blanket from the top of the pile of bedding Evangeline kept folded on the end of the sofa, hoping she'd see fit to wrap herself in it and allow her body to warm itself before putting on the new, dry garment.

I returned to find her just where I'd left her, only on her knees, hands folded in prayer. I, too, went to my knees, praying silently beside her.

Father, God. Thank you for freeing me from this same bondage.

Then I touched her shoulder. "I'll fix it tomorrow. While you're at church."

She nodded, and I pulled at the garment, sliding the scissors between it and her cold, pale flesh. In my mind, freedom for Evangeline would come with one quick slice. Soon enough, though, I found myself in a different scenario as I worked the blades against the wet fabric.

"When did you last sharpen these?"

"Never have." Her eyes were closed as tight as the knot.

"I don't want to dull them any more than they are. Or rust them."

"Get a knife."

"Are you sure?"

I took her silence as permission and went to the counter, where the same sharp knife we'd used to slice potatoes earlier still sat with the rest of the unwashed dishes. I exchanged the scissors for it and returned to Evangeline, who now had tears streaming down her freckled face. She looked so small, so much like a child, and I wanted nothing more than to wrap her in the blanket, take her in my arms, and rock her until she was once again warm.

"Heavenly Father," she prayed, warmed at least enough that her teeth no longer chattered, "forgive me. Forgive me for being such a fool, to not think—"

"You're not a fool." To my knowledge, I'd never interrupted somebody in prayer. Indeed, I was unsuccessful in doing so here, as she continued without stopping.

"I should have untied it first. I should have known. Forgive our violation of this sacred garment. Forgive Camilla, who sins on my behalf."

Whatever protective, loving thoughts I'd held before disappeared. This time, I did not go to my knees. Instead, I reached down, looping the two fingers of my left hand under the knotted tie. Evangeline's eyes flew open as I yanked the fabric away from her skin. In one none-too-gentle motion, I slid the knife's blade beneath the fabric. One swift slice, and Evangeline was free.

Her gasp was such that I feared I'd misjudged and nicked her as well.

I managed to ask, "Are you all right?" while waiting, breathlessly, for the sight of blood.

She fingered the jagged edge. "You can't fix this."

"Yes, I can." Though now, despite my relief that she was unharmed, I felt less inclined to do so.

"No. It's ruined."

"I'm not *that* useless with a needle. You'll see tomorrow. Good as new."

She looked up, imploring. Tiny as she was, I'd never seen my friend looking so vulnerable. Always, since the day we met, she'd had this bearing that made me think there was an iron ribbon running just beneath her skin. Perhaps it was, in fact, strength she felt coming from this that she wore under her clothes. I would not debate the garment's power just now. Or maybe ever, seeing how desperately she clung to its sacredness.

"Take this off," I said, gently tugging at the tie I still held. "Drape it on the chair to dry and get some warm clothes on. I'll put more wood on the fire and comb out your hair."

Her chin quivered. "B-but we've already used so much. . . ."

But I ignored her protest, digging through the wood box by the back door, looking for the smallest split logs I could find.

Out of respect for her privacy, I busied myself as long as I could, glancing up every now and again to see the shadow on the wall as it shed once and for all the wet clothing. Evangeline's silhouette was skeletal, lacking even the most modest of womanly curves. The moment I knew she was once again covered, I turned back.

"Don't tie it so tightly this time."

She offered a weak smile, and I knew she had given me a measure of forgiveness, though she would never accept the same forgiveness herself.

CHAPTER 10

I'd been up late in the night, having offered to press Evangeline's Sunday meeting dress. The more I labored in her honor, the less critical she was about my refusal to accompany her. This, to her, was familiar. Acceptable. Actions submitted in the name of faith.

She herself was up much earlier than our usual rising time. I could hear her singing to herself downstairs, something she would never do in my presence. I remember our singings during the journey west, when I might be sitting right next to her and hear nary a sound coming out of her mouth, despite her fervent mouthing of the words. No doubt, in just a few hours' time, she would be sitting on a hard wooden pew, surrounded by her sister Saints, miming the notes of those songs that honored her heroes.

When a final note disappeared like so much sand in a shoe, I heard her soft steps as she ascended the stairs.

"Camilla?"

She'd never ventured upstairs since my arrival. Reluctantly, I wrapped the top quilt around my shoulders and braced my feet to hit the cold floor.

"Good morning, Evangeline." I stopped at the doorway to the room, and she lingered on the top step. "Your hair looks nice." And it did, plaited into two thick braids that she'd wrapped around her head.

"Thank you. Now, you need to hurry. We'll need to leave within the hour if we're going to be on time."

She began to walk back down the stairs as if the matter had been settled. She didn't stop until I called down, "I'm not going this morning."

Turning to face me, she said, "Are you sick?" Her words held more accusation than concern, and I knew I'd never feign an illness grave enough to convince her.

I clutched the quilt tighter. "No, not really."

Then that small, tight smile, and a new, slow ascent, her hand on the rough banister, seemingly pulling her up every step. "I understand."

"Good." I wanted to retreat to my borrowed bed, but still she approached.

"We all have sin in our lives, but you cannot run away from God in heaven. He sees you. And I can only imagine what you must be harboring in your heart that would make you leave your husband and children. But maybe, if you come with me today, if you confess to your brothers and sisters, you'll find the courage to return."

By now she was not only at the top of the stairs but directly beside me, laying her light-as-a-feather hand on my arm. Her fanaticism for the false teachings we'd both once embraced was overwhelming.

"I've nothing to confess to the church."

"It's very important that we all strive to live in obedience, and here you've abandoned your family. Now it seems like you're set to abandon your church. What's next? Your faith?"

I didn't know how long I would be able to live as the serpent taking shelter beneath the rock of Evangeline's cold, bare home, but I wasn't about to announce my apostasy to Evangeline Moss this Sunday morning.

"I miss my girls," I said, relaxing my posture as if greatly comforted by her touch. "I loved Sunday mornings—getting them dressed, fixing their hair. I . . . I can't imagine going without them."

She pouted. "Poor Camilla. I understand. Well, not completely, not having children. But I can imagine. Still—"

"No." Then, softer, "Not this morning."

She sighed. "Very well, I guess. Next week."

I nodded. "Perhaps."

"No 'perhaps.'" Under any other circumstances, her tone might have come across as motherly, even mockingly so. But she was not my mother; she was my friend, and that relationship felt more tenuous with each passing moment. "I was looking forward to having someone to go to church with me this morning. Someone like a sister."

"I think what I need most is to be alone. Use this sacred time in prayer."

"To listen to your spirit?"

I held my smile. "To commune with the Lord. And watch that the beans don't scorch."

"Well, all right then. And remember I'm invited to Sister Bethany's for dinner after the meeting. I'll try to bring home an extra piece of pie. She makes the best pumpkin pie."

"That sounds wonderful." For good measure, and because I felt a genuine affection, I bent to kiss her cheek. "Now, can I do anything to help you get ready?"

"No. I'll be leaving now. If I'm early, I might get a seat closer to the stove."

I remained in the doorway until I no longer heard her steps, then returned to my bed, seeking warmth within the rumpled blankets.

Lord, forgive my lies.

That seemed to be a prayer I would be repeating for days on end. Not a complete lie, of course, because here I was already spending my morning in prayer, and I smiled at my clever excuse.

Be with my little girls this morning. Protect them from the lies spoken from the pulpit of this false church. Send your angels to distract them from the elder's voice. Let only the truth filter in—that you are God, their Father in heaven, and that you love them. Hold them close, Lord, as I cannot. . . .

It didn't take long for me to realize that I could not remain in prayer as long as I remained in bed. My head filled with too many memories—countless Sunday mornings with Melissa at my side, Lottie on my lap, their warmth fueling my heart as Elder Justus's droning voice threatened to stop it outright. Nathan's voice, raised in song, rang through the recesses of my mind, and I reached my hand across the cold sheet, missing his warmth in an entirely different way.

I lay on my side, hand on my pillow, and when I opened my eyes, the misshapen, scarred flesh loomed large in my sight. Something in me longed to see his face, nestled in feathers, looking into my eyes. And then, our last morning together, the day he took a second wife.

He'd woken up with her this morning.

If not for that marriage, Lord—that woman—I might still be with him. At home. Walking hand in hand with my little girls on our way to church. To sit as a family and listen to the message of the prophet. Knowing in my heart it was false teaching, but putting up the pretense—allowing those lies to hold me and my daughters captive.

Right then my loneliness fled, pushed to the corners of my heart by a flood of gratitude. And praise. And unbelievable peace. I had done the right thing. For my children. I might be adrift, but my daughters were safe. I was still uncertain as to how it would all work out, but my faith was now securely placed in the true God, and I knew he would prevail for all of us.

So I closed my eyes and slept. Dozed, really, as I remained aware of the sounds coming from outside the window. Conversations and greetings shouted across the street, a group of women singing an anthem of the Saints. Occasionally something would ring out loud enough to rouse me completely, and I resolved to get up, get dressed, and go downstairs, but the first little movement would bring me to a cold spot between the sheets, and I cowered back to my warm, curled-up ball.

At some point, though, the instinct for survival overtook the pleasure of sleep, and I realized that only a flight of stairs separated me from true warmth in the form of a woodstove and food to fill what was quickly becoming a hollow, nauseous pain.

It was enough to send my feet to the floor, and within minutes I was dressed, my hair loosely tied at the nape of my neck. I picked up my Bible and my journal, thinking how nice it would be to read and write in the cozy kitchen, and I thought I would spend this morning in a little church of my own making, with the words of Jesus Christ himself as my sermon. Perhaps one of Paul's letters for my Sunday school. The heels of my shoes made an echoing clatter as, newly energized, I bounded down the steps. But it was an imperfect echo, sometimes preceding each step, then continuing when I stopped. Not an echo at all, but a completely different sound.

A knock.

Two steps from the bottom I stopped. Who would visit Evangeline Moss on a Sunday morning? What Saint visits *any* Saint on a Sunday morning? Those not at meeting would die of shame before turning this sacred time into a social call. It could only be a stranger. No doubt one with a blue coat and a single, dark brow. The peace that had settled around my heart shredded, replaced by the fear I'd felt every time I'd seen that man.

Unless—and here my fear abated—it wasn't a stranger at all, but a soldier. Sent with the official duty to confirm my well-being. Either way, I had no intention of opening the door completely blind to who might be on the other side. Until I knew, I had no intention of opening the door at all. I spun around and bounded back up the stairs, once again accompanied by repeated pounding on the door. The room once occupied by Evangeline's brothers allowed an easy view to the front porch. Careful not to disturb the curtains, I placed my head against the cool glass, holding my breath in preparation for whatever sight would greet me. All, it turned out, in vain, because nothing could have prepared me for the visitor on the porch. More than that, my visitor knew exactly which window I would choose for an outlook, and she stared right back up at me.

"*Rachel?*"

Far below, she stamped her foot, and I hopped to her silent command, running down the stairs all a-clatter, practically throwing myself against the door upon arrival.

"I've been out here nearly five minutes," she said, pushing her way right past me without so much as a glance. "My hand is throbbing."

"I didn't hear you."

"Well, I'm sure it must be wonderful to adopt the life of a heathen and sleep late on a Sunday morning—"

"I wasn't sleeping. Look, all dressed."

She quirked her lips to one side and raised her eyebrows, unimpressed with my appearance.

"And by the way," I said in an attempt at my defense, "I notice you aren't at church either."

"Bother. By the time Tillman gets the wives and kids out the door, he'll never even notice I'm gone. One of the few perks of polygamy. You can just disappear for a while. But then, I guess you've already figured that out."

There was more than an imagined bit of admiration in her comment, so I allowed myself to take no offense. Instead, I invited her to the kitchen with a wide, welcoming gesture.

"Oh, Camilla. Your hand."

"Frostbite. One of the dangers of running away," I said good-naturedly.

Never one to be generous with sympathy, Rachel continued on into the kitchen. I'd noticed the basket draped over her arm from my observation upstairs, but it took on new meaning as I followed. She dropped it on the table and rubbed her hands together.

"Good glory, it's cold in here."

"Sister Evangeline is quite conservative with her fuel."

"I'll tell Tillman to send one of the boys over with a few bundles." She fed the dwindling fire in the stove and handed me the kettle. Her jeweled hands looked unaccustomed to kitchen work.

"Fill this up?"

"Of course."

I held the crock pitcher steady, pouring a stream of cold water into the kettle's narrow spout while Rachel rummaged through the basket, producing several brown paper–wrapped packages.

"Apple-carrot muffins. Maple sugar doughnuts. Cinnamon scones and a round of fresh butter. We had a few ladies over for quilting yesterday, and these were left over."

"Oh my."

"And of course—" she held up a small tin box, giving it a playful shake—"tea."

"I don't know why Tillman lets you get away with this."

"Tillman doesn't know, and neither do the sister wives, a situation I'm quite comfortable with."

"Your secret is safe with me."

"Then you'll join me?"

My mouth watered at the thought. "Of course."

"Then sit," Rachel said, taking over the role of hostess— one I was glad to relinquish. "And how is our little Evangeline?"

"Sad. And lonely, I think. She wants a family."

"She wants Nathan."

I said nothing, and Rachel let the matter drop. Instead, I took down a small dish for the butter and two cups for our tea. Evangeline had less than a cup of white sugar, but she used it so infrequently, I wagered she still wouldn't miss a few spoonfuls.

"Now," Rachel said, settling in at the table while the water boiled, "tell me everything about where you've been."

"I don't know if that's a good idea."

"You sound like you don't trust me."

"That's not it."

"Come on." Her smile, identical to her brother's, led the

way as she leaned across the table. "We'll swap. You tell me something I want to know, and I'll tell you something you need to know."

"What are you talking about?"

But by then the kettle was spitting drops of steaming water, and Rachel hopped up to fill the pretty china pot she'd brought. Her face was a calm, unreadable mask as she packed the leaves into her silver tea ball and dropped it in to steep. She returned to the table and took her place across from me, drumming her fingers expectantly. "Well?"

"What do I need to know?"

"Tell me about the soldiers."

"Why do you care? I'm back now. Safe."

"As much as I love you, Sister Camilla—and you know I do—it's not entirely your safety I'm concerned about. You know Brigham has us all up in arms about the government being on the warpath. The things he's asking us to do—did you see the temple?"

"Yes."

"So—" and here there was the slightest crack in her facade—"are we safe?"

Had Evangeline posed the same question, I would have known she questioned the safety of the Saints. But Rachel's heart was with her family—the husband she loved and shared, the passel of children that filled her home, even the sister wives she counted as family.

"They aren't seeking bloodshed," I answered.

"But they'll fight?"

"If ordered to do so. Or forced. That's why Colonel Brandon—he's commanding the troops, actually—wanted to keep my presence there a secret. So there'd be no misunderstanding and Nathan wouldn't feel led to retaliate."

"He knew."

I remembered the sound of his voice on the other side of the tent wall. "Of course he did. I'm just grateful he didn't come back."

"Brigham wouldn't let him."

"Brigham?" She might as well have picked up the teapot and cracked me over the head with it.

"Oh yes." Rachel's calm demeanor did nothing to ease my ever-increasing ire. "The minute he realized you were gone, Nathan was at Brother Brigham's office. We searched, of course, after the storm, and I don't know what possessed my brother to head for the Army's camp. But he begged for a company of our militia to go with him and bring you back. He loves you very much."

"I know." I absently fingered the ring I wore ribboned around my neck.

"But Brigham doesn't want trouble with the Army, and he doesn't care enough about Nathan Fox to brew some up." As if reminded, she lifted the teapot lid, frowned, and settled it again.

My heart began to settle, tempered by the sobering memories of Nathan's often-desperate attempts to win Brigham Young's favor. "Well, for once I'm thankful for the prophet's indifference."

"Not entirely. He said Nathan couldn't interact with the United States Army. But Brigham's personal guard? That's another story entirely."

"What are you trying to tell me?"

"That you need to be careful." She reached for a scone and set it on the plate in front of me. "Nathan knows where you are."

"Now?"

"This morning at breakfast, Tillman says, 'So did you know Nathan's wife is staying with Sister Evangeline Moss?' I just about dropped the bowl of scrambled eggs."

"I've seen a man across the street. He seemed to be watching the house. Watching me."

"What does he look like?"

I described him. Tall, broad, dark, scruffy beard growing from the cleft in his chin.

"Doesn't sound familiar, but who knows? The prophet has plenty of men to do his bidding."

Rachel picked up the teapot and filled our cups, adding, without question, a tiny bit of milk and sugar to each. Something danced in her eyes as she pushed my cup across the table. Triumph, I think, taking my surprise—my fear, in fact—as some sort of victory.

"So," she said after sending a cooling blow across the surface of her drink, "are you ready to go back home? I can arrange for Tillman to drive you."

"I'm not going back, Rachel."

"Don't be ridiculous. Brigham won't give you a divorce."

"I don't care. I'm not just leaving my marriage; I'm leaving the church, this place."

"What about your girls?"

"I'll be back for them, when I'm settled."

"Where?"

"Home. With my parents. If they'll have me, that is. I'll know this spring, as soon as the weather is safe for travel. But if I go back with Nathan now, I know I'll never leave. Not only will he never let me out of the house, he'll just . . ." I brought my cup close to my face, hoping the steam would explain the flush on my cheeks. "He lured me away once before with nothing more than his words. He'll do it again."

"Then maybe you don't really want to leave."

I took a long sip of the drink, relishing both the warmth and the rebellion of it. "If I had a choice, I'd stay. But I can't. It's like some sort of veil has been lifted, and I can just *see*. I know it's hard for you to see it too, but this religion—it's all lies. Joseph Smith was a false prophet, and now Brigham Young is abusing your faith. I know the truth now, in my heart. My life is in God's hands, my heart given fully over to Jesus Christ. And I know if it were just me, I could live here, with Nathan, and never lose that."

"So why don't you?"

"Because my girls . . ." My throat closed, tears choking the words. How could I explain? I'd read where Jesus told others to leave their families, their loved ones—to abandon their very lives to follow him. Saturated in the Latter-day teachings, Rachel didn't even know the same Jesus I followed. "I won't abandon them to these lies."

"Nathan will never let you take them."

"He'll have another family. With Amanda. Maybe even a son and other children. Maybe even another wife."

"Tell me something." She gestured with a corner of scone pinched between her fingers. "This *unveiling* of yours. Do you think you would have had your own personal revelation if Nathan hadn't taken a second wife?"

"It came long before. In my heart, I renounced the teachings of the prophet the day my son died, but I remained faithful to my marriage. I *chose* my husband over my faith. But when the time came for me to ask the same of him, I *begged* him not to bring another woman into our home, but I held no such place in his heart."

"But shouldn't a man—or woman—love God above all?"

"Yes, if it is the true God. His isn't. Brigham's isn't."

"Dangerous words, sister."

"I know." Despite her argumentative nature, I knew she spoke out of concern rather than threat.

"Brigham wants unity—in this world and the next."

"And he has a fleet of Saints at his disposal. He won't miss me."

"No, but Nathan will."

CHAPTER 11

Rachel and I cleaned up the evidence of our visit long before Evangeline was expected to be home. I insisted she take back what we didn't eat—though, in truth, that amounted to little more than a single muffin and half a scone. I'd have no way of explaining their arrival to Evangeline, and I myself would be eaten away with guilt if I kept them upstairs for a clandestine snack.

She'd hugged me close before leaving—a warmer embrace than I ever remembered between the two of us. But it did little to ease my mind. I slid the iron bar as I closed the door behind her and went immediately to my knees in prayer. Looking back, I cannot articulate exactly what my appeals to the Lord were that hour. My safety, of course, though I loathed to think of my own husband as being any kind of threat. More like the safety of my own mind, that I would remember my purpose and the promise I had of God's protection.

I went into the kitchen, where the last of the tea warmed in a small saucepan. Rachel had offered to leave me both the tea and the pot, but I would not infringe on Evangeline's hospitality so blatantly. Still, I relished the thought of savoring a final few sips while reading my Bible at the sunny table. Whatever questions plagued me, the answers would be within these pages. I curled my finger around the cup's handle and bowed my head over the precious book.

Oh, to have a prophet—a true prophet—who would walk into this kitchen and speak the words of God into my life. Give me the truth I longed to hear. I would suffer any reprimand for my choices, withstand any holy chastisement for my actions, if it meant hearing a true word.

But then, hadn't God already given his Word? It was the desire for a *new* revelation that had given Joseph Smith a foothold in the hearts of his followers.

I lifted my head and opened the Bible, turning through the pages listlessly at first, then with more purpose. If my heart sought the words of a true prophet, they were to be found here—words recorded by men who were ordained of God.

I turned to the book of Jeremiah, written to those in another time, another captivity, but meant for me in this moment as well. My eyes flew across the chapters, seeing my own sin in the sins of Israel. Hadn't I abandoned my Lord when I first ran away with Nathan? Hadn't I snubbed my nose at his blessings when I took to the wilderness?

It had been scarcely more than a month since I'd left my husband, and though I did so in order to find a new life for my daughters, I felt so lost. Misplaced, actually. Like I'd been hidden away from God's eyes, left to scramble through life's darkest corners.

And then, after nearly an hour's reading, my heart found hope, as God promised to rescue the remnant of Israel—those who clung to their faith. He promised to gather them together, and I claimed my place in that remnant.

My eyes had grown weary, but by the time I came to the twenty-third chapter, my vision became the least important of my senses, as the voice of the Lord of hosts seemed to fill the empty kitchen, shouting from the printed page. *"Am I a God at hand, saith the Lord, and not a God afar off? Can any hide himself in secret places that I shall not see him? saith the Lord. Do not I fill heaven and earth?"*

I belonged to a God who saw me, sitting in that cold kitchen sipping tea. The same God who rescued me from the snowstorm, who guided me across the plains, who would see me restored to my family. I closed my eyes and tried to see my little girls through his eyes, for surely he saw them, too. At this moment they would be walking home from church. I opened my hands, palms raised to the ceiling. In that moment I felt restored, healed, not maimed in any way.

"Oh, protect them, Father. Let the cold wind of your creation blow over them, clearing from their heads and their hearts the teachings of the Saints until I can bring them to a home built on your truth."

I wept, wondering just how many times my own mother had offered up that same prayer. Perhaps she was in such supplication right now, at her table. With her tea. Her hands outstretched, maybe grasping my father's. And had she done so every day since my leaving? True, she hadn't responded to my letters, but that didn't mean she'd abandoned me in her heart.

"Oh, God, restore us to each other, just as I've been restored to you."

The words on the pages of my open Bible blurred as I dropped my head upon it. The paper felt cool against my brow, and I breathed in the smell of—I don't know what, exactly. Ink? Leather? My own touch, as I'd pressed my palm so often against the open pages?

There had been moments before—and many since—when I truly sensed that God was at hand, but none so strong as that moment. The Mormons speak often of the "burning in the bosom," but this had no such isolated sensation. Joseph Smith had this testimony of the revealed presence of God in the forest, but I saw nothing. Heard nothing. In truth, *felt* nothing. No touch to my upturned hands, no warmth coursing through my veins, no comforting weight between my shoulders.

I simply knew.

God was here. God was within me. No power on earth could sway me from that fact. I needed no angel to come to my bedside. No vision in my path. No recitations or explanations or revelations. He filled me just as he did the heavens and the earth. I needed only my own breath with which to pray.

I sat until the tea got cold, gulping it down in one swallow the minute I heard the front door open.

The days following that Sunday morning were swathed in an almost-springlike warmth, both within the house and outside. Not that I went outside. Rachel's words bound me as much as any prison wall ever could, and I found myself startling at the least little sound. But relentless sunshine warmed the house more than any bundle of firewood ever could, even though it was the second week in February.

That Tuesday afternoon I found myself in my room, curled up on the bed with my Bible open beside me, taking advantage of the warm sunlight to leisurely write in my journal. The words I wrote required a level of privacy beyond mere solitude. This was, after all, my testimony, and would be my voice should I be prevented from speaking my own story. It had no place downstairs, where Evangeline had the windows thrown wide open, as if she couldn't truly be comfortable without some level of chill.

Upstairs, my own window was open just enough to coax the curtains into a fluttering dance set to the tune of the sounds coming from the street below. Some conversations, a crying child, the intermittent rumbling of a wagon's wheels. When I heard a knock on the front door, I brought my pencil to an abrupt halt and ran to the window. Looking down, I saw nobody on the front porch, meaning the visitor had already been welcomed in, and I exhaled a measure of relief. I crossed the room and opened my door a crack to try to listen to the conversation downstairs.

Evangeline's voice was, of course, unmistakable, but the hair rose at the back of my neck when I heard the other. Though muffled and indistinct, it was undeniably male.

For all the loneliness of her existence, Evangeline did play host to a great number of visitors, as one Saint after another always seemed to be stopping by with a small gift of food or cast-off clothing. But never—not once—had she received a man into her parlor.

Grateful for the silence of well-oiled hinges, I eased the door open and stepped into the hall, walking in stocking feet to the top of the stairs. I disobeyed every instinct that told me to stay hidden, and though my steps were noiseless, I was certain the pounding of my heart could be heard as far away as the kitchen. With each step the voices grew more clear—both hers and his. They twisted and rang inside my head, blurring the conversation while revealing the speakers. Then, as I neared the bottom step, I heard a burst of laughter as familiar as my own face in the mirror.

Only my two-fingered grip on the banister kept me from losing my balance.

There stood my husband in Evangeline's parlor.

His laughter stopped the moment I took my first step from around the stairway, and not a shred of it lingered in his eyes. Oh, the smile was frozen in place—wide as ever. Any passing stranger—perhaps Evangeline herself—might have mistaken it for an expression of joy at seeing his long-lost wife at last. For a few heartbeats, I flattered myself with the same thought. But then I noticed the clenching of his jaw, not to mention his fist—one ball of fingers nestled in an open palm. I imagine if I'd touched him, I would have felt his muscles tensed beneath his skin, making him more a man carved of marble than of flesh. Yet, given all of this, I felt no fear. Not then. This was Nathan, my husband, and while I cannot recall the steps that brought me across the room, soon I was close enough to touch him. It was this touch I feared—much as I'd feared it all those years ago when we'd stood in the shadowed woods together. I felt very much the same fifteen-year-old girl, heart pounding so hard I could barely think.

"Well, look at you," Nathan said, his eyes scanning me from head to toe.

"Perhaps I should leave the two of you alone," Evangeline said. I'd forgotten she was in the room. "Shall I go to Sister Rachel's and fetch the girls back here?"

"The girls?" I hid my wounded hand in the folds of my skirt, anticipating.

"I didn't want to bring them here and not find you." His smile never waned. "I couldn't stand for them to have another disappointment." Then he turned to Evangeline and looked at her with such a warmth I could feel her heart melting. "That would be wonderful if you could bring the girls here. They can't wait to see their mama."

Without a single glance in my direction, Evangeline grabbed a light shawl to wrap around her thin shoulders and flew out the door, promising to be back within the hour.

What can I say about the silence that followed? The parlor windows were open, letting in the occasional soft sound from the streets, but it seemed swallowed in the fluttering curtains, smothered by the unspoken mass between us.

"I went to Rachel's," he said at last, his voice thin and taut, his words measured, defiant of any identifiable emotion. "The day after you left. After the storm. Because you said you were going to Rachel's."

I choked, rather than spoke, my answer. "I know."

"Then I took my own life in my hands and went into our enemy's camp and listened to that man lie to me."

"I can imagine how much that must have hurt you."

"Can you?" He moved toward me. I didn't shrink away, but perhaps some level of fear registered on my face. At any rate, Nathan's hands—poised midgrip—stopped just short of grasping my shoulders. Then, as though he'd just lost some sort of battle, his shoulders drooped.

"You can't possibly know. You left without a word. You abandoned your children. You stole my horse."

He said all of this with such disarming humor, with his hands outstretched in some mock-pleading gesture, that I felt a welcome, familiar ripple at the base of my spine. He was offering me forgiveness, right there on the spot, without my

131

having to ask. There it was, the same boyish grin that had so long ago lured me from my father's home, and I found my lips being tugged into a smile of their own. And then, his touch. So light—just the tip of his finger beneath my chin. Slowly, I lifted my face, until my eyes met his, and there was nothing between us but a swirling mass of impetuous, dangerous decisions. I wanted to step back—not to escape his touch, but to flee this moment. Far enough to find crisp, clear air. Far enough that I wouldn't feel his breath, warm and sweet, just above my skin. Because he was drawing me closer, and just as his image blurred before me, so did any hope of reasonable thought.

Had I stepped away, I might have said something other than "Oh, Nathan, I'm so sorry," before he kissed me. But I didn't move. My next breath met his, and the weight and worry of weeks disappeared. Familiar arms drew me close, and my hands sought the promising strength of them, relishing the feel of his coarse wool shirt and the work-hardened muscles that tensed beneath my touch.

My touch.

As abruptly as our kiss began, he drew away, moving to capture my hands in his. And there, nestled in his calloused grip, my maimed little hand. The buttons of flesh where my fingers once were had taken on a sickly white hue, the jagged scars now fully sealed. An inexplicable wave of shame washed over me, and I balled the remnant into a fist—as if to hide what remained—and tried to pull away, but Nathan held me, his fingers looped around my wrist.

"What did they do to you?"

How much did he know? And how much could I say? I waited, searching his face, trying to read the mind behind the question. Protective fury? Heartfelt concern? One response might drive him to want to exact revenge, another to pour out his gratitude for saving my life.

"When they found me," I said, stalling somewhat, "my hands . . . from the cold. It—they were dying. Dead already. And the doctor said there wasn't any choice."

He brought my hand to his lips, covering my scars with his kiss, and I couldn't speak anymore. No touch had ever felt so tender, and my mind flew back to the sound of the bone nipper and Captain Buckley's odd little whistle. The memory of whiskey mixed with the lingering taste of Nathan's kiss, and all those little moments lived as one. Again, I heard myself saying, "I'm sorry," apologizing for the very weakness of my flesh.

"I just can't bear the thought of you being in such pain." He held my palm flush against his chest. I could feel the beating of his heart.

"It doesn't hurt anymore."

"But it must have."

I attempted a weak grin. "I've borne children, Nathan. This doesn't compare."

He refused to reward me with his own smile. Instead, he glanced at my other hand, then back at me.

"You aren't wearing your wedding ring."

"No. I can't, of course, on my left hand—"

"But your right?"

"I suppose I could. But it was so badly swollen at first. And now—"

"Where is it?"

I reached into my dress and withdrew the silk ribbon with the small, plain ring dangling from it.

"Hand it to me," Nathan said with a gentle control that bade my obedience. For a moment, he studied the place where the silk was knotted, but then without the slightest attempt to dislodge it, he secured the ring against his palm, wrapped the ribbon around the first fingers of both his hands, and pulled, snapping that silk as if it were little more than a dried reed. It slid out from within the ring, dropping heedlessly to the floor.

He took my left hand and touched the ring to the scarred flesh.

"The prophet says some sins are so grievous we can only seek atonement through the shedding of blood."

Then he took my right hand, slid the ring on my finger, and kissed it.

"Makes it all the more special, don't you think?" He raised his eyes to me. "Like we're getting married all over again. A new hand." He touched my face. "A new start."

Outside, the day turned to evening, like a shadow dropped through the window. Darker, cooler, and the few open inches between the window and the sill made a welcome distraction. I pulled myself from his grasp saying, "It's cold," and turned my face to the narrow, cooling breeze.

He didn't follow me. Of course he wouldn't. He didn't move at all. Not when I leaned over to take great gulps of the fresh air, not even when I pretended to struggle with the sticking frame. I could feel him behind me, though. Watching. The back of my neck burned under his gaze. He had just reaffirmed our marriage, claimed me as his wife. We'd been married by the edge of the Platte River, sealed to each other within his church's sacred teachings. A new storm could rise up between us now—here in Evangeline's parlor—and it would make no difference. He'd be there when it cleared. Or soon after. His was an inescapable power, granted to him by both his false god and his false prophet. I would have to flee their reach if I were ever to escape his.

That was the fresh start I needed. And I might have told

him that, too. My strength was almost there, but then, down the street, I saw them. Their hair like strands of corn silk, their faces sweet and pale with the bright pink patches on their cheeks that always appeared when they played outside in the cold. They were running now, leaving Auntie Evangeline, who carried a large, covered dish, a good distance behind. Even with the pane of glass between us, I could hear their laughter. My own bubbled up, like my very life returning.

I spun around and ran for the door, ready to meet them on the street, but Nathan grabbed my arm.

"Go upstairs," he said, every bit the authority he'd always been. "Wrap your hand."

"Wrap it?"

"Like a bandage. It'll frighten them as it is."

"But what—?"

"Say you burned it on the stove. Go."

By now I could almost hear their voices coming from the other side of the door, but I knew he was right. He released me and I ran upstairs, pulling out the pins that held my hair so loosely. I dragged a comb through my hair and hastily plaited it into one braid, which I twisted and pinned into the style that my Lottie always likened to a snail. Then, with a strip of gauze I found in the bottom drawer, I hastily wrapped my hand in a sloppy cocoon, tucking the edge of the fabric in at the wrist.

I took just a second to study my reflection, worried that my daughters would pick up on my gaunt appearance—especially Melissa, who never missed the slightest hint of trouble. As sharp as the planes of my face might be, my eyes were bright, my skin flush with excitement. Their excited chatter drifted up the stairs, and with a final prayer of thanks, I ran downstairs to meet them.

CHAPTER 12

Melissa saw me first. Nathan was crouched down, eye level with little Lottie, who, with her back to me, regaled him with some amazing tale of life at Aunt Rachel's. But Melissa, I could tell, had kept her eyes trained, looking for me. Initially, they popped open—big and brown like her father's—and her mouth opened in a perfect O of surprise. But then, as if remembering something quite important, she gave her head a little shake, narrowed her gaze, and appeared enraptured with Lottie's story.

My body—the same body that so ached to hold her—seized with caution. Like a doe entering a forest clearing, I took one slow, cautious step after another. Her gaze never softened. She, the six-year-old child, stared me down with an intensity that alerted her little sister that something dangerous was coming up from behind. Lottie stopped midsentence and turned—startled at first—but then her face broke into a mass of unfettered joy.

"Mama!" she cried over and over, with every little running step, repeating it still as she buried her head in the soft of my neck. Her skin was cold, but her breath was hot, as were the tears I felt wet against me.

Oh, the feel of her, tucked up against me. How perfectly she fit. I held her, pouring a silent, pleading apology through my embrace. I longed to shower her—up and down every tiny inch—with kisses. One for every day I'd missed. But that would mean pulling away, and that I could not do. Not while her cries were now deep, quaking sobs, each one rippling through her body as she clung ever closer. Her skin burned hot now. I could feel it even through her dress as I patted her back. I whispered, "Shh, shh," and looked over her head at her older sister and father, who held me in place with identical, accusing glares.

No battle line had ever been more clearly drawn.

Eventually Lottie grew calm, her breath shallow but even, and I pulled away far enough that I could look at her swollen, tearstained face.

"I tried to be a big girl while you were gone. Auntie Amanda said I shouldn't cry, so I didn't." She sucked in her lower lip and furrowed her brow. "But I wanted to."

"You're a liar," Melissa said with more venom than I thought capable of a child her age. She looked straight at me. "She cried every night when we were in bed after prayers." Something in her voice told me she hadn't shared in her sister's tears.

"Well," Nathan said, clapping his hands and rubbing them together, "there's no more need for tears now, is there? Here we are, all together again, and from what my little Lottie was telling me, we have a delicious dinner Aunt Rachel sent along."

"A whole chicken!" Lottie piped up, instantly cheerful. "She said they roasted one too many."

"How kind of her." It was the first I'd spoken since coming into the room, and the words still caught in my throat.

Lottie never left my side, and Melissa never came near me as we made our way into Evangeline's small kitchen. A three-legged stool was brought to the table, but Lottie chose to crawl into my lap to eat her supper.

Never, I imagine, had Evangeline's table ever held such bounty, neither in food nor fellowship. Melissa and Lottie each gripped a drumstick in one hand and a biscuit in the other, piles of mashed turnips left largely unattended on their plates. Nathan regaled us with stories. Not new ones, but ones drawn from memories shared by those of us around the table. He told stories from our journey to Zion, making each Indian and bobcat more ferocious than they could have ever hoped to have been. Of course, during those days I was a new bride, so newly in love with my handsome husband, and more than a little afraid of the life in front of me.

As he told his stories, I couldn't help but recall that early, fear-fueled passion. Throughout the meal our eyes would meet, and I knew we were both filling in those details not fit to be shared with our company. Those were the days when our home was nothing more than a blanket or two spread out in the shelter of a fellow Saint's wagon. His arms were my shelter, his promises my dwelling.

Evangeline had been there then, on the fringe, always watching. Now she threw herself into the midst of us. We were at her table, after all. The chicken carcass sat in the middle of the table, and abandoning any attempt at manners, we all reached across the table, picking at the remaining flesh. Sometimes I caught her looking like she was on the verge of

pinching herself. This could be her life, had she her own husband. Or had she mine. I knew—had always known—that her
desire to be Nathan's wife encompassed the core of her being.
Back then she must have felt like she'd lost a great prize, standing at the river as I was given to him in marriage. But now she
had the blessing of the prophet to stake a claim of her own in
his life, if not in his heart.

That's when it all became clear, the reason for her sunnier
disposition of late. The half-hidden smile. The generosity. The
lightness in her step. She knew he was coming; she'd invited
him here. She had told Tillman, knowing Rachel would never
betray my confidence.

Looking more catlike than usual, she ripped a wing off
the nearly meatless bird and was nibbling at the bone when
I caught her eye. Her lips, shining with fat, curled into a thin
ribbon of a grin, and I could almost feel the soft-pawed stab in
my back.

How had I not felt this before? This friendship, this hospitality—nothing more than a tortuous game, like I was bait
dangling in her grip. She'd reunited Nathan with his first love,
his first wife. Surely there would be some reward attached. A
scrap he could throw her. Just enough to release her from the
piteous charity of her sister Saints. Enough to give her a hand
into heaven.

"This is nice, isn't it?" she said as if lifting my thoughts
from my mind and setting them on the table like so many
mashed turnips.

"My sister roasts a fine bird." Nathan moved his chair
away from the table and patted his full, flat stomach.

"Oh, I'm sure it wasn't Sister Rachel," Evangeline said.
"She's never been one to do a lot in the kitchen. Marion is the
real cook in that household."

"Mama's a good cook," Lottie said. She lolled back against me, her little foot listlessly kicking against my shin.

"Oh, she was known to burn a biscuit in her day," Nathan said. "In the early days, I mean."

"That's why I was glad to have Kimana," I said. "Without her we might have starved in a house full of food."

Nathan joined me in a warm, chuckling laughter, and even Melissa managed a small smile.

"Yes," Evangeline said, seeing no humor in my statement, "but you could hardly marry Kimana, now could you? She's a savage."

I tensed, sitting up straight beneath Lottie's weight. I could see nothing but Kimana's soft brown eyes, her wide, peaceful face. I felt the pillowlike softness of her embrace and heard her halting speech in prayer. Such faith she had—such a pure understanding of God.

"Don't you speak of her that way," I said, reaching around Lottie to pound my fist on the table. "She is a part of our family. Like a mother to me."

Nathan reached his hand out and laid it on my arm. It was the first he'd touched me since our kiss, and I surprised myself at the smug pleasure I took from Evangeline's watchful gaze.

"I don't think Sister Evangeline meant any harm."

"Besides," Melissa said, her voice pointed in its purpose, "Papa's already married to Auntie Amanda."

Nothing compared to the soundlessness that followed. All our bits of laughter and conversation disappeared, like a candle snuffed out by a puff of spite.

"And to your mother," Nathan said after what seemed like far too long. He touched me still but now moved his hand to intertwine his fingers in mine, and I would not give Evangeline the satisfaction of pulling away.

Lottie twisted in my lap. "Are you going to be the new baby's mama?"

Nathan's grip tightened as I looked at him, but it was Melissa who spoke.

"Don't be stupid. Of course she isn't. Amanda will be that baby's mama, just like Mama is ours."

"That's too many mamas," Lottie said, the last word stretched out in a yawn. Maybe, under other circumstances, we might have laughed, but not that night. It was the first I'd heard of a new child, and I hadn't been gone for much more than a month. She must have known before I left, or at least suspected.

"You didn't tell me," I said, untangling myself from Nathan's grip, thus shifting Lottie.

"She wasn't sure."

"And she's sure now?"

"Yes."

"Well, isn't that nice?" Evangeline's attempt at joy did nothing to rejuvenate the mood.

"Kimana says in summer." By now both Lottie's voice and body were heavy with sleep.

Nathan stood, stretched, then bent to take her out of my arms. "Do you have a room for the girls upstairs? Because I think this one is tuckered out."

"I'm not tired," Melissa said.

"Good. Then you can help your mother and Auntie Evangeline with the dishes."

"No need," Evangeline said, and I hated that she'd taken my opportunity to win my daughter's favor. "She can go into the parlor and help make up the beds. A nice soft pallet on the floor, just like when we were on the trail." She clasped her hands. "Won't that be fun?"

I stopped stacking the plates. "In the parlor?"

"Where else?"

"I assumed they'd sleep with me. In my room."

"The parlor's warmer," Evangeline said. "Don't you want your daughters to be warm?"

"They'd be warm with me."

We might have bickered on like that all evening had Nathan not taken control. "The parlor will be fine. Like an adventure." He hoisted Lottie higher on his shoulder. "Just like the Saints on the trail."

Neither of the girls exhibited as much excitement for this manufactured adventure as did Nathan and Evangeline, but I chalked that up to their fatigue. At least on Lottie's part. Melissa seemed nothing but relieved.

Left alone in the kitchen, Evangeline and I worked together in silence. Out of the girls' sight, I finally unwrapped my bandaged hand and began scraping plates and submerging dishes in the tub filled with water that had been warming on the stove all through dinner. The chicken carcass was set in a pot to be boiled down the next day for stock. I held my tongue lest I should unleash my temper, and might have been content to do so for the remainder of the night had Evangeline not sidled up beside me with a dishcloth to say, "Isn't this nice?"

"How could you?" I seethed, returning a newly clean plate to its place on the shelf.

Her eyes popped open as wide as they could, and I wanted to use the dish in my hand to smack the innocent look from her face.

"I—I thought you would be happy to see your family again. You said you missed the girls."

"You had no right." I returned to my task. "None at all, to bring him here."

"You forget. This is *my* home. Brother Brigham says so."

"I don't forget, Evangeline. You remind me every day."

"And I was rather enjoying our time together. As friends, you know. It's nice to have another woman to talk to."

I ignored the bait, focusing on dredging up every last fork from the bottom of the basin. "I told you I needed some time away, to adjust to having another woman around."

"But how long?" Her attempt at ignorance grated. "You weren't leaving for good?"

"I don't know what I was thinking. And it's not your affair."

"But this is my—"

She stopped short, and I turned to see Nathan in the doorway. "The girls are tucked in—and tuckered out. Lottie's asleep already, but Melissa's got a little fight left in her."

"You look tired too," Evangeline said with a presumed intimacy that churned my supper. She offered to take him upstairs to show him the clean linens, but he declined.

"You ladies finish up down here. I'll be fine."

We did finish up, working in silent tandem at first, until Evangeline could no longer hold her tongue and picked right up from before our interruption.

"I'll have who I like as a guest in my house."

"Of course you will." I folded my dish towel and draped it over the back of a chair to dry. "And I am grateful to you. It was very kind of you to take me in—all of us."

I walked out of the kitchen and into the parlor, now dark, save for the bit of light glowing from the fire in the stove. Nathan had built it up, using far more wood than Evangeline would have ever allowed.

"I love your daughters." Although I hadn't heard her footsteps, I knew she'd followed me here. "If I never have the chance to have children, I wouldn't mind. I'd be happy to think of yours as my own."

Despite the warmth of the room, I shivered.

She leaned forward until I felt the heat of her breath on my neck. "Heavenly Father has a plan, I think. To bring us all together."

I turned and gripped her shoulders in an attempt to be reassuring. "God always has a plan, but it's not often the plan we would choose for ourselves. We can't always know exactly what he would have us do."

"That's why he gave us the prophet. To speak for him."

I was undecided for a moment whether to use my grip to shake her or to fold her to me in the type of embrace she'd never have from anyone else. After all, I'd loved her once—truly as a sister. Tonight, though, it became clear to me that she'd never returned that love. Not really. I was both the woman who had taken Nathan away and the woman who might somehow give him back. "Would you mind giving me just a few moments alone with them? It's been such a long time, and since I didn't get to share a story with them, I'd like to just have a few moments of prayer."

"Of course."

Melissa and Lottie were flat on their backs on a soft bed of quilts on the floor. I let go of Evangeline and dropped to my knees between them, laying one hand on each small, beating heart. That was enough at first, just to feel their life, the same as I'd felt them within me. The last child I carried would have been a year old now. While my heart took on the familiar ache it always did when I thought of my son, I marveled at that moment in God's wisdom. I had one child safely delivered to an eternity with Jesus; I had two more under my touch who would never learn the truth unless I delivered them from these lies.

"Almighty God—" I whispered his name, calling down his presence—"I give these girls to you, and I dedicate my life to making a home where they can truly know you. Take me where you will. I will be his wife as long as you bid me, but I will be their mother forever. Surely, Lord, you would have me raise them in a home that honors you. Give me that home."

Lottie remained motionless under my touch, slumbering through my prayer, but when I opened my eyes, I saw Melissa staring straight at me.

"You have a home, Mama."

It was my right hand that rested upon her, and I brought it up to stroke her face, grateful that she could not escape my touch. "I know I do, sweetie. And I miss it."

"Then come back."

"I will." I felt God himself making that promise through me.

"Tomorrow?"

I shook my head. "No. You see, I have another home, with my parents back in Iowa. I ran away from them, too."

"To marry Papa?"

"Yes. They're angry with me, just like you are. I think I need to visit them for a while."

Her little brow furrowed. "Why don't you write them a letter?"

"I've tried. You may not understand, but it's best this way. We'll only be separated for a little while; I promise. I won't let you be apart from me the way I've been apart from my mother. I promise. Now, tell me, have you been reading your Bible?"

She shook her head. "Papa doesn't let us."

I somehow managed to keep my smile. "Have you been saying your prayers?"

"Every night. And going to church meetings. And Papa reads to us from the holy book."

"He's a wonderful father." Evangeline was back, padding her way in stocking feet to the bed she'd made on the sofa.

"Yes, he is," I acknowledged, but I would not entice her into further conversation. Bending low, I kissed Lottie's soft, warm cheek before leaning over Melissa to whisper, "I love you very much."

"I know." She whispered too.

Sensing her consent, I kissed her forehead, smoothed the few strands of blonde away, and kissed it again. I didn't utter so much as a good night to Evangeline.

I left the room and went to the stairway, holding tightly to the banister in the dark, knowing Nathan was up there, somewhere. I didn't know until I rounded the corner at the top and saw faint light coming from the room across the hall that he was planning to make my bed his own.

I might have turned around right then, gone back to some small patch of parlor floor, or even ducked into the brothers' room had my door not opened to reveal him bathed in candlelight.

"I heard you on the stairs." He opened the door wider and stepped aside as if to usher me in.

I brought my steps right to him and stopped. "That's my room."

"Where else would I be?"

I pointed back down the hall. "There are others."

"None that I wanted."

He grabbed my hand and pulled me across the threshold, thus ending further discussion. The room grew unbearably small and close with him in it. Somehow he'd managed to position himself between me and the door, his shoulders seemingly broader than the frame. Light filled the space around us—more light than I ever remembered having within these walls. My shadow cast across him, and I realized the source of that light came from behind me. From the window, in fact. From the three candles burning bright against the glass.

Very clearly I recalled the moment Colonel Brandon had pressed those three stubs of candle into my hands. *"If there's ever a time when you don't feel safe, put these candles in the window."* I knew better than to think soldiers from the United States Army were stationed at the corner, but Colonel Brandon was not a man to speak lightly nor to go back on what he had spoken. How long had Nathan been up here? Twenty minutes? Half an hour? Certainly not long enough to alert the United States Army.

I went to the window and, seeing nothing, snuffed out two of the candles.

"Evangeline is so thrifty," I said. "Why burn three candles when one will do."

I regretted my decision almost the minute I turned back. In this soft, single light, Nathan looked more angel than enemy.

"Look at you," he said, his voice full of appreciation.

"You haven't looked at me in months." The bitterness in my tone surprised me.

"That's not true. You'll always be my first wife. My first love."

"But not your only."

"Amanda will never be what you are to me. She and I will never have what you and I had in our early days. You remember those early days, don't you, Mil?"

Mil. It was Nathan's special endearment, a name used only by him. More sacred than the secret name I'd been given at my endowment—the name he believed he would call to bring me from my death into eternity with him.

"But soon she'll have your child. And then maybe another.

Your early days with her are almost gone. Then what, Nathan? Another wife? More early days? You knew Evangeline before you knew me. Maybe you'd like to have a life where you can reminisce with her, too."

He did not so much as flinch at the sharpness of my words, though I felt them slicing as they left my tongue. He did, however, bridge the distance between us with one easy step and reached behind me to pinch out the remaining flame between his calloused fingers and pull the curtains closed.

The immediate memory of his face remained like a phantom in the darkness, and his body seemed to be everywhere at once. I felt him standing along the length of me, his forehead pressed to mine. His fingers were wrapped loosely around my neck, his thumbs restless against my jaw. I knew my pulse pounded against him, and I knew he had the strength to stop it cold. Fear crystallized me to utter stillness within his touch— a fear I knew well. Not any kind of pure terror, but some enticing mating of trepidation and excitement. I'd felt the same the first time he loved me. And the last. And now.

What I remember next is the struggle. Not between his body and mine. He held me in such a way that I dared not move. No, the war waged between my own mind and my flesh, my heart holding me captive as surely as his embrace. Perhaps it was the flush brought on by those memories of our early loving or the strange, unbidden jealousy knowing that he had grown so accustomed to another woman's bed. So when he chose to respond to my shrewish words with a kiss, all my accusations went unanswered as he trailed his lips, his hands, across my face, my throat. Even as he coaxed me into wrapping my arms around him, I had the distinct impression of having emerged from the battle victorious.

It is an underestimated and elusive power a woman can

hold over a man—a power seductive in its own right. My mismatched, wounded hands roamed victoriously across the expanse of his muscled back, my mouth sought refuge in the hollow of his throat. We spoke in short, gasping command, and though my defenses fell around me, I stood tall in his arms. Brave and consumed. The room must have been cold—it always was—but I felt only the invigorating heat of conflict.

Those who would judge me have never loved. I know now that I should have asked God to release me from this love, to quell the passion that I felt whenever this man was near. But our vows pardoned my sin; I was still his wife. He'd used just such persuasion to entice me to his faith. Perhaps I felt that, in some way, I could use the same to draw him to the truth. Or perhaps I was just lonely. Or cold. I'd been too close to death without him, and with him—for at least one winter's night—I lived again.

CHAPTER 13

"Do you know what they wanted me to do when we realized you'd left?"

These were the first words he spoke to me in the morning, before even the first strip of sunlight threaded its way past the curtain. I lay curled against his side, where I'd slept in the crook of his arm, just as we had every night of our married life except when my body's swelling with each of our children made such sleep impossible. He spoke as if we were in midconversation, like we'd been sitting in a comfortable silence for quite some time waiting for the next idea deemed worthy to break the silence. I was certain he'd been awake long before my first stirring, waiting for me to join him, so I cleared my head of the last vestiges of shadowy dreams and asked, "Who?"

"The bishop. And Elder Justus. They told me I should have you hunted down."

I burrowed my cheek closer to his chest, savoring the warmth of his skin. For one night, at least, his sacred garment had been cast to the floor.

"Isn't that what you did? Why you're here?"

"They didn't want me to go myself. Said your womanly wiles might keep me from following through on the work for the kingdom."

"Oh. And what would that work be?" I did not draw away, but I held my body brick-still against him.

"To bring you back into the church." He brought his hand to my chin and tilted my face to look at him. "Tell me I haven't failed."

My heart raced, and there was nothing between us to hide my fear. "I love you, Nathan. As much as I ever have. As much as any wife ever could."

"So you'll come back with me today?"

I shook my head—a small movement, for he still held me fast.

"It is your place, Camilla. As my wife—a wife who loves me. You should be there, beside me."

"You have another wife beside you now, Nathan."

Perhaps if I'd spoken with any degree of softness, made any attempt at sweet pleading, he might have been more gentle in his own right. In one swift motion the covers we'd burrowed under were swept aside and I was alone.

"I acted in obedience to God." He dressed as he spoke, reaching first for his sacred garment, though his frustration afforded it no reverence.

"You acted in obedience to the prophet."

"They speak with the same voice." He fished around

on the floor, gathering my clothing, and—without turning around—tossed it onto the bed. "Get dressed."

I sat up, and with shaking hands, I obeyed. If he'd meant to shame me, he'd succeeded. In the gray, predawn light, Evangeline's room took on the seediness of a fallen Eden, and Nathan's words swept away any hint of coming grace.

"To you, maybe. Not to me. And I love you, Nathan, but I cannot worship in a church that mistakes the will of one man for the word of God."

"You can't just choose which of God's laws you will obey and which you won't. Your salvation comes with a price of obedience. To Heavenly Father and to me."

"My salvation comes from Christ alone. If I sin, it is against him only, and his sacrifice has restored me."

"But you have sacrificed too." He dropped to his knee and took my altered left hand in his. "See? You've paid in flesh, shed blood. And why would God ask this of you if you had not sinned?"

I looked at the two little lumps of healed-over flesh, the base of my missing fingers twitching under our gaze. "There was no blood," I said at last, whispering. "I mean, I don't think there was. I slept through the . . . when he . . . But that was the problem. No blood. It was dead flesh—both of them. Useless and bloodless and black."

"Like the prophet says, for those who turn their backs on the church. That their flesh will turn black—"

"No. My flesh was black because it was rotten and dead. And that death would have spread to my heart. It would have killed me." I lifted our joined hands and held them to my cheek. "I'll die if I go back, Nathan."

"You'll die if you don't."

Not a threat, not a promise, but a plea. I looked into his

eyes and found them brimming with fear—enough to instill the same in me.

"What do you mean?"

"They'll come for you if I don't bring you back."

"Who will?"

"You know who. Brigham's men. The Danites. His 'Avenging Angels' fighting the war against apostasy. "

"Surely not," I said, attempting to shrug off such a menace. "I'm just one woman."

"Who has made her husband and the elder and a bishop each look a fool. What kind of man am I if I cannot keep control of a household as small as ours? What hope do I ever have of eternal glorification? You don't understand what's at stake, Mil. They charged me to bring you home."

"Home?"

"Our home and our faith."

"No."

He reached up and gripped my shoulders. "You will be restored, Camilla. By blood or by baptism."

"And you would give your soul over to a church that would do me this harm?"

"My soul is your soul, and I give them both over to the promise of eternity. And I choose to have my eternity with you—no matter how intent you are on throwing that away."

"I don't believe that."

"Fine." He rose to his feet and hauled me up to join him, taking me in his arms. "Don't believe. I don't care. Just come back. Act the part. Sit in church, go to the singings. Save your life now, and Heavenly Father will restore your soul later, as long as you are sealed to me."

I took a deep breath, inhaling the scent of him. Oh, how tempting his proposal. To live with him and love with him—even if only occasionally, when my flesh was weak enough to risk the pain of transgression. I could wear the mask of a Saint. After all, hadn't I done so for all of our married life? And if my life was a lie, was that not like any other sin covered by God's grace? What harm could there be in the small bit of subterfuge that would allow me to live with the man I loved, to make a home with him and our children?

Our children.

Nathan's proposition meant my daughters would be raised in a web of lies, brought up either to believe in a false god or to feel shame for the true one. And that was just our own girls. I would be spreading such deception to Amanda's child and others as the years wore on.

I reached up, cupping my hands over his ears, my fingers buried in the soft, curling hair behind them.

"I know you want nothing more than to please God. For once, forget what the spiritual leaders have said. Listen for *his* voice in your heart. What is he saying?"

He closed his eyes, and I, mine. Slowly, as if not of our own accord, we moved toward each other, our brows resting together, our breath a mingling mist between us. With all my strength I prayed for God to appear. The teachings of Joseph Smith boasted of such appearances—God himself, and Jesus, and angels from on high. Nathan had lost himself to the belief in such manifestations. But the appearance I prayed for was not so grandiose. I wanted only his still, small voice—still enough to calm my husband's fears, small enough to pierce his heart. Just a sliver of truth.

Oh, Lord Jesus, be real to him. Be truth for him.

I kept my eyes closed until I felt the feather touch of his lips on my skin.

"He brought you to me," he said.

"I know."

"You are my life."

"I know that, too."

"And I hate that you're asking me to make this choice."

Sunlight battered against the curtain, and I burned with hope. "We can go back east," I said, "in the summer. After Amanda's baby is born. She's young and beautiful—any man would be happy to have her. And I'm sure by now Papa is wanting help on the farm. We'll have a place to go. . . ."

Early on, I'd seen in his eyes that I'd misunderstood his choice, but still I kept rambling, hoping I'd say something to turn back the tide of pity that washed across his face.

"We can have so many nights—every night, if you want—like last night. And who knows—"

"Camilla."

"—maybe someday, another child. A son, like you've always wanted."

"We have a son in heaven."

"Of course, yes, I know. I think about him every day."

"A son who deserves a complete eternal family."

"Oh, Nathan . . ."

He drew me close one more time and kissed me. When he tried to pull away, I locked myself to him in a final, desperate appeal. We'd been so close—just a prayer away from building a life together. If his soul could not stand the thought of attaching itself to me, perhaps his body would. Not until he braced his hands against my shoulders and pushed would I resign, and then it was with humiliating, stumbling steps.

"I'm going downstairs," he said, "and waking the girls. I'll take them to Rachel's for breakfast, and then we're heading home. Should be a clear day for traveling." He brushed past me and went to the door, but I grabbed at his sleeve, stopping him.

"What about those who sent you to find me? To bring me back. What are you going to tell them?"

He turned and placed his hand on my cheek in a final, soft touch.

"I offered you a home. I offered you salvation and atonement. I don't intend to tell them anything unless they ask specifically." Then a wavering in his sweet, reassuring smile. "And you'd better pray they don't ask. I've seen what they can do."

It occurred to me to follow him, to overtake him on the stairs and throw myself over my sleeping daughters. Make him pry them out of my arms. But now—even more than when I felt myself nearly suffocated by snow—I felt my very life in danger. Perhaps that was Nathan's intent all along, to frighten me away from taking our children. If so, he succeeded for the time. Even more than when I left them back in our cozy home, I knew my daughters would be safer outside of my care.

I did, however, creep down the stairs, stopping just short of rounding the corner. I could hear the girls' sleepy voices, meek in their protest at the abrupt rousing. At home we always took pains to have a warm fire in the stove before bringing them out of bed to wash up and dress in its glowing light. Evangeline, of course, took no such pains for comfort, and my heart broke to hear their teeth chattering behind their questions. Where was Mama? Shouldn't she come to breakfast? Couldn't they say good-bye?

Nathan, true to his nature as a warm, loving father, answered them with gentle insistence. Mama wasn't feeling well. They would see her soon. She sent hugs and kisses.

Everything within me twisted in longing. Both Melissa and Lottie had been cajoled into giggles, lured by promises of sweet rolls and milk. Looking back, I can almost be grateful for what he spared me that morning. My daughters shed no tears, and I told no lies. But oh, the sacrifice.

Somewhere around the edge of activity, I heard Evangeline, gathering coats and scarves and hats, brushing hair and lacing boots. Her voice dripped with maternal affection, as if I were already miles away, or dead and gone, or maybe simply in the next room, accepting of the role she was playing in our life.

At some point, the door opened, then closed, and they were gone. I got up from my perch and ran up the stairs to watch them through the window. Perhaps I should have merely peeked from behind the curtain, but for the life of me I couldn't think of why I should have to hide from my own children. Nathan must not have anticipated that I would do this—unless he really was capable of such cruelty—because he lifted Lottie up to carry her through the muddied street, and as she gazed over his shoulder, she looked straight up at me. Her little hand went up in a wave, and with a throat burning with unshed tears, so did mine. She said something and Melissa, holding tightly to her father's hand, turned around, too. Our eyes met; her stare was as cold as the pane of glass between us. Only Nathan continued on without looking back. One step after another, and my little family disappeared around the corner.

God alone knew when I would see them again.

I smoothed the covers on the bed in an effort to hide the memory of my last night in Nathan's arms, then fell to my knees beside it, burying my face in the faded, worn quilt.

They are still so close, Lord. I could run right now and catch up. Hold my feet if you would keep me here.

I wished for something to drown the doubt that twisted within my mind.

Oh, God, can you not give me a vision? Can your voice not fill this room? I'm just a woman. Just one small, frightened woman. Do you really ask this of me? To make my way in this world alone? To abandon my children? To escape my enemy?

My eyes scanned the room, but I saw nothing that spoke of refuge. Nathan's warning rang in my ear. The church would have me back.

By *blood or by baptism*.

And I would not be baptized.

CHAPTER 14

Evangeline and I circled each other like cats the next day. Unfailingly polite cats, with cordial greetings and well-mannered discourse, but both of us seemed to have one eye trained on the other, except when she finally left the house for one of her endless rounds of church meetings. Wherever Mormon women gathered in a parlor for charitable work and small sandwiches, Evangeline Moss would be there to pick up the crumbs of both.

Today I knew she was telling them all. Sister this and Sister that—women whose names and faces were beyond unknown, but whose innocent gossip could seal my fate. Although she'd protected me until now, I supposed. At least no curious would-be counselors had shown up at the door, hoping to coax me back into my husband's good graces. For now, I had only Evangeline's grace to claim, and that I feared would waver in the shadow of her thwarted plan.

Down in the kitchen I built a substantial fire in the stove and set the last shreds of Rachel's chicken simmering in a broth with an onion and a few carrots. I was just mixing dough for dumplings when she came blustering in.

"Mmm . . . what smells so good?"

"It's the chicken," I called out, inviting her in with my voice. "I'm making some dumplings, too."

"I just came from the most fascinating Ladies' Aid meeting. Do you know Sister Coraline? What am I saying? Of course you don't. Living out by the quarry like you do. Or did. Well, she sang for us today, something beautiful. Brother Brigham says that he wants Salt Lake City to have theaters and opera houses just like any other big city, and we got to hear her today, and it was magical."

By the time she finished her report, she'd shed her wrap and was holding her hands out to warm by the stove.

"Sounds lovely," I said.

"Sister Coraline might sing at church meeting this week. You could hear her then."

"I don't think so."

"It won't be a secret much longer that you're here. All of Brother Tillman's household knows, and your daughters— they'll probably tell everyone in the valley. I honestly don't know what you're hiding from."

She spoke with such exaggerated innocence the hair on the back of my neck bristled.

"I was talking to some of the ladies this afternoon. And they—some of them—had the honor of *choosing* their sister wives."

"Oh, Evangeline . . ."

"He would do it, Camilla. He would marry me if you asked him to. He loves you that much. He'd do anything—"

"He didn't love me enough to keep me as his only wife, as much as I pleaded with him."

"Well, of course not. You can't expect a man to put the wishes of his wife above the will of Heavenly Father and the prophets."

"Then I suppose you will have to wait until one of them tells Nathan to marry you. At that, I promise you, I will voice no objection."

"You don't think—" and here her voice crackled with tears—"it's even a little bit possible that he might love me?"

My heart broke. Despite all of this, Evangeline was my friend, had been since the moment I met her, when she'd flashed a mischievous grin and told me to choose a favorite freckle. I wished I could offer her rescue from that hurt—the hurt she'd carried since that same day—but I could only offer the kindness of truth.

"No," I said as gently as I could. "Not in the way that you love him."

"But I wouldn't need him to love me that way. Not the way he loves you. Not like last night—" She clapped her hand to her mouth, but she might as well have used it to slap me for all the color that rushed to my cheeks.

Flustered at both her discomfort and my memories of the previous night, I busied myself getting out bowls and spoons, keeping my face well away from her.

"I wasn't sure if you'd find the extra bedding," she continued, stumbling over her words, "so I went to your room and . . . I know I should have turned around and come right back downstairs, but—"

"Stop. This isn't—You can't just *talk* about this."

But then the silence that followed was worse, because I know we were both focused on what each had heard and felt. Nathan Fox—and all he meant to both of us—was a presence in the room, consuming our senses.

"What is it like?"

"Evangeline, please—"

"I don't mean—of course it wouldn't be proper. But to have somebody love you that much. I can't even imagine."

My own embarrassment waned, replaced with something akin to pity for this woman who might never know the power of a man's touch. I should have told her that what she'd heard last night wasn't love, not exactly. My love for Nathan encompassed so much more than my body. For all of our marriage—the marriage we alone shared—he'd been my very life, sharing my every breath and thought. When I thought about last night, I still felt the glow of his touch. No sense of shame clouded my memories, but I did suffer a slight tug of regret when I considered my weakness in the face of his presence.

"That should not have happened," I said, carefully setting the wide, shallow bowls on the table. "Not here in your home. Now, don't you realize? That's what it's like, being a sister wife. It's night after night, listening in the dark, hearing your husband—the man you love—sharing another woman's bed. You have no idea how that hurts. . . ."

But I could see in her eyes that she did.

The room was quickly turning gray with evening's shadows. Desperate to get away from the topic, I amassed a load of false cheer and suggested we eat. Evangeline, even less convincing in her cheer than I'm sure I was in mine, poured us each a glass of water from the blue crock pitcher.

By the time supper was on the table, the room had grown

dark enough to warrant lighting the lamp, stretching our shadows until our heads touched along the ceiling. My appetite for the thickened stew had disappeared with the daylight, and not even the perfectly turned dumplings tempted me as Evangeline and I joined hands across the table to bless the meal.

"Your turn," she said, though I hardly thought to keep track.

I closed my eyes, feeling the warmth coming up from my steaming plate and the touch of her twiglike fingers.

"Most gracious Lord, thank you for your bountiful blessings. For the food on the table and the friendship with which we share it. May our loved ones far and near be so blessed under your caring, watchful eye. Amen."

"Amen," Evangeline echoed.

My hunger was restored with the first savory bite, then sated a bit with each one following. The only sound was the clink of our spoons and the practiced, ladylike sips as we touched our lips to the steaming broth.

"So," I said after a time, "this Sister Cora? Was that her name?"

Evangeline swallowed a sip of water. "Coraline."

"Sister Coraline. What songs did she sing?"

"Some of the songs were in German, so I couldn't understand them. But then she sang hymns."

"Sounds lovely."

"It was. When she sang about our home with Heavenly Father and all of our children yet to be born, her voice was so clear and so perfect, I could just see it. I would give anything—" she cleared her throat and lifted her glass once again—"to be able to sing like that. Or to sing like anything."

I smiled. In our younger days, especially during our westward journey, we'd all made light of Evangeline's voice, the way she'd always mouthed the words in impassioned silence.

"It's a wonderful gift," I said.

"Maybe that's how I'll sing after I die. That will be Heavenly Father's reward for my life. I could die a happy death tonight if I knew I'd wake up tomorrow able to sing like Sister Coraline."

"Well," I said, hoping to build on what was seeming like a lighter mood, "maybe you'd better put an extra log on the fire tonight to make sure you don't freeze to death. Wouldn't want to get to heaven with a sore throat."

"Easy for you to make jokes." Her voice had never sounded more tortured. "You know what's waiting for you. He's waiting for you. If anybody should wish to die tonight, it's you."

Perhaps if she'd said such a thing in the middle of a sun-filled afternoon, my body might have been spared the painful chill that scraped along my spine. As it was, the glare of the lamplight cast her face in a yellowed glow, with her freckles creating tiny pockets of darkness across her countenance—like an aged woodcut brought to life. The air outside was perfectly still—not the least bit of a breeze—but the cold was cruel, and tendrils of it crept through the kitchen like icy weeds. She'd spoken in a tone as thin and flat as the ice that floated in the washbasin.

"Don't say such things," I said, hearing nothing but the echoes of the elder's threats.

"He still loves you. You're his wife; he'll call to you."

"My life is in God's hands. It is he who will call me to heaven when my days here are over, whether it's tonight or tomorrow or fifty years from now."

"You really believe that?"

"I do, with all my heart. Jesus Christ is my Savior, and the Bible tells us that in Christ, we're all the same. No single person can lord eternity over another. Nathan doesn't hold my eternity in his hands. He is my husband, yes. And it might be that he'll be my husband for the rest of my life. But when my life ends, so does our marriage."

"But the prophet says—"

"Hang the prophet."

I got up from my seat only to find Evangeline doing the same, and we stood, facing off.

"Watch how you speak of him." There was a definite hiss behind her words.

"No, you listen to what I have to say. Don't you see what the prophet has done? How he's made you a slave to this teaching? He has you ready to feed off the scraps of some other woman's marriage for the privilege of spending an eternity with a man who didn't love you enough on earth."

"I tell you, Nathan could love me."

"Not enough! He couldn't love *me* enough to devote himself to me. He doesn't love Amanda enough to stay away from the woman who left him. And he doesn't love you enough to . . . to even *look* at you."

She raised her hand to slap my face, but I caught it, my fingers easily encircling her wrist, and I hauled her to her toes.

"Hear this," I said, my heart and words full of a strange, raging compassion. "Nathan Fox would marry you tomorrow if he thought it would bring me back to him. But I care about you too much to invite you into that kind of hell on earth. But if you wait around long enough, he just might marry you to gain Brigham Young's approval. Then you can spend your life following the whims of the prophet, and when you've worn yourself out working for the church, you can go to your grave and wait for Nathan to call you. And you can wait and wait and wait. Because I might try to save you from hell on earth, but if you put your hope in Brigham Young, there's nothing I can do to save you from the hell that waits for you after you die."

My spine curled with every word, until Evangeline was cowering beneath my arched stance. I released my grip on her wrist and stepped away, spent.

"It's late," I said. It wasn't, really, but it was dark, and the last few minutes had taken on the weight of an entire day. "Let's get this cleaned up."

"Go on upstairs. I'll take care of it."

"But—"

"I don't want your help. I don't need your help. Go to bed."

I dared not risk another word, lest she decide I wasn't deserving of a bed that very night. "Very well, then," I said. "Good night."

I took a long matchstick from the tall box on the wall by the stove and touched its tip to the lamp's flame. With my hand cupped to protect the fledgling light, I made my way upstairs, going directly to my window. One by one I touched the match to the three candlewicks on my windowsill.

"If there's ever a time when you don't feel safe . . ."

I'd no sooner touched the flame to the third candle than I heard a pounding on the door. Not my door, but the front door downstairs. Visitors to Evangeline's home weren't rare, but to have one at this time of night was unheard of. Instantly my mind went back to the last time I'd heard such insistent pounding, my last night at home with Nathan and the girls, the night Bishop Childress came to demand my renewed allegiance to the church.

And so they'd found Nathan again. Or he'd sought them out. They were at the door, and within minutes, Evangeline was at mine.

"Sister Camilla?"

She hadn't bothered to knock. Why should she? This was her house, after all, and she'd caught me with the still-smoking match in my grip. Even though the light from the candles barely reached across the room, I could clearly see triumph in the very way she held her spindly shoulders.

"Who's here?"

"Two men. They're here for you."

CHAPTER 15

I'd been up and down those stairs a thousand times, but that night it seemed one step was added for each one I took.

Evangeline followed right at my heels, hissing in my ear. "I should have told them everything you said. But I don't know if I could ever bring myself to say such things against the prophet, even if they weren't my own thoughts."

I said nothing. My heart was beating ten times with every step, and I would not waste my words defending myself to Evangeline Moss. Instead, I prayed to God, asking him to give me the strength I needed to stand firm for his truth and to soften the hearts of my interrogators.

I turned the corner into the parlor, surprised to see that

Evangeline had invited one of the gentlemen to sit on her sofa, and my stomach dropped to my feet when he stood. Blue coat, broad shoulders, heavy dark brows that knit together atop his broad nose. It was the closest I'd ever seen him, and I'd monstrously underestimated his size, perhaps because I'd only ever seen him from a distance. He was huge; the parlor sofa that served as Evangeline's bed looked like doll furniture in comparison.

"Sister Camilla Fox?"

His voice was as deep and dark as I'd imagined it would be, and not a hint of humor anywhere near it.

"Yes." Who else would I be?

"I'll leave you alone to talk with her," Evangeline said, sounding a little too eager. "Unless you want me to stay. I could be of some help, you know. I've had some experience in such things. Questioning, I mean. And helping people—women, that is—understand the true gospel. Redirecting their path for the good of the church."

The giant listened patiently, a hat crushed in his hand, and once she stopped talking, he said, "That may be, sister, but I've been asked to bring her back."

"Asked by whom?" Somehow I sounded like I deserved an answer.

"By the highest authority."

"From Brother Brigham?" Evangeline looked up at him with such adoration, one would think the prophet himself were in the room.

He ignored her. "Please, we need to be going before it gets much later."

"Will she be coming back?" I'd like to think Evangeline asked this out of concern for my well-being, but her essence of satisfaction prevented me from any such charitable thought.

"We aren't at liberty to say."

We. And that's when I noticed that, with each response, he'd been making eye contact with his companion—a figure who'd remained seated in one of the parlor chairs, keeping his back to me. The giant looked at him again, only this time he nodded, inviting the second man to stand.

At that moment, my blood ran hot up one side of my body and cold down the other. He was equally tall as the giant, but infinitely thinner. Thinner, in fact, than I remembered. It was all I could do to refrain from leaping clear off the floor, but he fixed his eyes on me with an unpracticed sternness I dared not disobey. Before that night, I'd never have guessed that Private Lambert was capable of commanding such authority.

"Yes," Private Lambert said, holding himself taller in some attempt to make his voice deeper. "We need Mrs.—Sister— Fox, Sister Camilla Fox to come with us."

"Where are you taking her?" Worry mixed with suspicion crept behind Evangeline's question.

"We aren't at liberty to reveal that, either," Private Lambert said, attempting for all the world to match the giant's tone.

"Well, of course," Evangeline said. "Heavenly Father's greatest work is often done in secret, I've always said."

"Then you are a wise sister, indeed." The giant gave her a little bow as he said this, and I did not imagine the girlish giggle that escaped Evangeline's thin, chapped lips.

"I'll help Sister Camilla gather her things," she said, "and then, don't worry; I'll have her right back down. The Lord's work shall not wait." She turned to me. "Come."

With a lightness in my heart I could not have imagined only days ago, I once again walked ahead of a whispering Evangeline.

"Now, don't be frightened. Remember, whatever happens, they are doing the work of Heavenly Father. It's for your own good and the assurance of your salvation and eternity."

"I'll try to remember."

We came back to my room.

"*Three* candles. I never noticed that before. Seems wasteful."

"They are mine; I brought them with me. I'll burn them as I see fit."

"Of course."

I found the small satchel with which I'd arrived and packed my few, meager things—stockings, petticoats, my Bible. Evangeline made no comment on what I took or didn't; she merely paced the room, wringing her hands. Poor thing seemed genuinely concerned.

"And I didn't mean what I said, about it being best for you to die tonight."

"I know." Though I was in no mood to reassure her.

"I think I'll ask again if they can't just interview you here. It's so very cold outside; I can't imagine—"

"I'm in God's hands now, Evangeline. Delivered over. You needn't worry."

I snuffed out all but one candle and picked it up to light my way back downstairs. Like some sort of faithful dog, Evangeline was at my feet, speaking what I'm sure she thought were words of comfort, but had I not known exactly where I was going, I would have had to be led from this house kicking and screaming.

"You must let them spill your blood," she said close to my ear. "Once baptized, we cannot be fully restored without suffering the same as our savior. It's the truest atonement."

I held her tight, knowing she would slash herself on any

altar for her beloved prophet. Her body shuddered against mine, and I stepped away, holding her hands. "Why are you crying?"

"I want more than anything to see you brought back to the church, Camilla. But I don't want them to hurt you."

Her face bore witness to her conflict. My confession danced on the tip of my tongue, but God held it still. I was about to walk out of this house not into a lie, but into an unspoken truth.

I gave her a soft kiss on each freckled cheek and said, "I love you, Sister Evangeline," before gathering up my satchel and returning to the parlor. There, I allowed Private Lambert to hold my bag while I put on my coat after wrapping my head and throat several times over in a thick wool scarf. Evangeline, in a final, sweet gesture, gave me a pair of mittens that stretched up to my elbows, and by the time I was ready to walk out the door, nobody—not even Nathan himself—would have recognized me. My eyes remained my only exposed feature, and I bent to Evangeline to allow her to place her own dry kiss right between them before stepping through the door held open by the giant.

In what I can only assume was part of their ruse, each man took me by the elbow and escorted me down the street. Between their strides and their heights, there were times I believe my feet were lifted completely off the ground, the way Nathan and I would walk the girls when they were little, with big, swinging steps. None of us spoke—not a single word—until we were well around the corner from Evangeline's street. There, right in front of the darkened home of some distant neighbor, both men released their grip, and I pulled the muffler away from my mouth to take my first stinging breath.

"How?" It was all I had breath to say.

Private Lambert did all he could to maintain an appropriate soldierlike facade, but his sweet face was obviously poised at the point of bursting into unabashed joy. "Good to see you doing so well, ma'am."

"Good to see you, too." I looked to the giant.

"Horace Braugen," he said with a most gentlemanly bow.

"So you're not with Brigham's militia?"

"That depends on who you ask."

I looked to Private Lambert, whose face was now an unreadable mask, then back to Braugen. "Are you a Mormon, then?"

"Was," he said, "and am when I need to be."

He bowed, took my mittened hand, kissed it, then placed it firmly in Private Lambert's, whose face I imagined turned as red as Evangeline's hair. "Private, I officially deliver to you your sainted Sister Camilla Fox."

With that, he continued walking, leaving Private Lambert and me in the middle of the dark street.

"How did you know?" I tried again.

Private Lambert tried looking me in the eye but soon straightened his spine and gazed at something over my head. "I'm not privy to the details, ma'am."

"Well, who is?"

"Colonel Brandon. He's waiting just north of town, and by my calculation we have about twenty minutes to get to him before he comes for you himself."

"Then we'd better hurry."

Normally by this time of day my body would be so worn out from battling cold and hunger that I could only long for the relative comfort of Evangeline's narrow bed and the pile of quilts that would afford enough warmth for me to eventually go to sleep. That night, however, my feet took flight, and I matched Private Lambert's loping stride with two of my steps to each one of his.

"Careful we don't seem to be running," he cautioned more than once. "We don't want to arouse suspicion."

And while the streets of Salt Lake City were largely deserted at this dark, cold hour, we did come across pockets of Saints out on purposeful strolls, returning from family visits, perhaps, or doing some last-minute church business. While, as far as I knew, the town had no officially enforced curfew, I'd never known anybody to be roaming about much after nine o'clock, and while I wagered it could not have been much past seven thirty when we left, the night was cloudless, almost oppressively dark, with a stinging cold that felt like a million shards of ice.

Once again as we approached the temple, I could hear the sounds of men working, and as the site came into view, I stopped in my tracks, shocked at the sight. It was gone—almost completely. Where the massive structure once stood as testament to the prophet's church, now something akin to a grave buried all but the heartiest corners of his people's labor.

Private Lambert tugged my sleeve, saying, "Come on, please, ma'am," and I fell in step again. Unlike Lot's wife, though, I was leaving nothing here that I loved. I turned my head, allowing the younger man's grip to guide my steps, and I stared at the crew laboring through the night to bury Brigham's dream until I could see them no more.

"How much farther?" My lungs were burning with each short breath.

"Do you need to rest?"

I swallowed. "No." But I did. My steps had now slowed to where I allowed him to get several strides ahead of me before I had to run a few to catch up, and then again.

"You can stay here if you like. I can send the colonel back with a horse."

What could draw more attention than a Mormon woman mounting a horse in the middle of town late at night?

"I'll be fine. Is he where you camped before?" I'd never make it that far.

"Yes, ma'am."

Resolute, I repeated, "I'll be fine," and I prayed that God would lift my feet in one step after another to deliver me from this place.

We passed through one fashionable neighborhood, just a few streets away from where I knew the lights of Rachel and Tillman's home would burn late into the evening. Indeed, all of these homes boasted a warm glow, and strains of music—pianofortes and singing—made their way into the crisp night air.

"Pretty," Private Lambert offered over his shoulder.

"Always," I agreed, trotting to bridge the distance between us.

Eventually houses grew fewer and fewer, and we were on nothing more than a wide dirt path that I knew to be one of the main roads into the city. Each step now was a battle, and while I hadn't even thought about what would await me once we reached the destination of Colonel Brandon, I began to crane my neck, keeping my eyes peeled for firelight, lamplight, or any sign of stopping. And then, quite silently and suddenly, he was right in front of me.

"Mrs. Fox."

Had I an ounce of strength within me, I could not excuse my actions, but at that moment my very legs gave out and I collapsed most clumsily into his arms. I clutched at his coat, though my thick mittens prevented any such purchase, so instead I wrapped my hands around the width of his arms and fell against him.

"There now," he said, and I could feel his hands giving reassuring pats to my back, "you're safe now. I'm here—we're here."

My mouth felt like it was full of winter hay, and I could not speak. Slowly, though, I tested my weight and moved away from the colonel's embrace once I knew I was able to stand.

Colonel Brandon grabbed me by my shoulders but spoke over my head to Private Lambert. "Where will they think she is?"

"Taken. Just like Braugen said."

"How long until someone comes looking for her?"

"They won't," I said, my words dry against my tongue. "Nobody would dare."

Colonel Brandon looked at me then, his eyes the only speck of warmth on this earth. "Well, then. Our job just got easier."

He turned his head, gave a long, low whistle. The bushes surrounding us rustled, and four horses—two of them saddled—emerged. Even in the darkness I could recognize her. Honey, with her blonde mane and lively prance, came straight for me, and while I should have felt some sort of joy at this reunion, I had only a nagging pang of guilt.

"This is Nathan's horse," I said, reaching out to touch her velvet nose.

"You're his wife," Colonel Brandon said. "It's as much yours as his."

"No." I turned to him. "Take her back, can't you? I don't want to be a thief on top of everything else."

"Someday." His voice rang with promise. "For now, we need her so we can give the other two a rest every few miles. Private? You ready to ride?"

"Yes, sir." Private Lambert launched into a full salute, making him look infinitely younger.

Colonel Brandon placed one foot in his stirrup and swung himself into the saddle with an ease I'd rarely seen. It wasn't until that moment that I began to wonder just how I was to ride, and then I noticed the colonel's hand reaching down for me.

"Oh no—"

My protest was cut short when Private Lambert, saying, "Pardon me, ma'am," laced his hands around my waist and, in an equally smooth motion, I was deposited—sideways—on the same horse. Colonel Brandon's arms wrapped around me as he held the reins, and—acting of its own accord—my head lolled against his shoulder. At once I was overwhelmed with the very feeling I had the first time I met this man. Safety and warmth. Through one ear I heard Colonel Brandon click to his horse; through the other I heard the creak of leather as Private Lambert mounted his own ride.

And we were off.

CHAPTER 16

Throughout the night, I attempted to doze, locked as I was in Colonel Brandon's custody. He would permit no such rest.

"Wake up," he'd say, jostling me every bit as much as did the horse we rode. "You'll freeze."

But I could not imagine such a thing. There were moments on our ride when I felt warmer than I had in weeks, warmer than any moment spent next to Evangeline's sparse fire, warmer than the hours drifting in Nathan's arms. Sweet, exquisite warmth coursing through my very blood.

And then, "Wake up!" to a sharp winter's night.

Each time we stopped to rest the horses and transfer the saddles, I stomped in my own circle, trying to work up the circulation in my feet and legs while flapping my arms—all of this at the colonel's command. Thankfully I had only the frost-covered landscape to witness my efforts.

When it was time to ride again, I protested on behalf of the poor horse that had to carry two riders.

"Nonsense," Colonel Brandon said. "You're nothing but bones and boots."

That first morning I saw the majesty of a sunrise, and I looked to the east thinking, *My home is there. My past and my future.* The air was clear and sharp as glass, and it seemed completely illogical that we couldn't just turn the horses and ride to the dawn, stopping only when we came to the river separating me from my father's farm.

We rode so long that it truly felt as if we had decided to set out for Iowa. Again and again, I lost my battle with sleep, and Colonel Brandon allowed me to surrender. I don't know how the men and the horses made that long trip with barely any rest, but somehow they did.

Finally, late in what may have been our second full day of travel, our motionlessness roused me, and I awoke to the familiar rumble of men's voices.

"Welcome back," Colonel Brandon said.

A sea of bearded faces watched from underneath stocking caps pulled low under their uniform hats. Several wore blankets wrapped around their shoulders. While I might have been an object of curiosity, none moved from their places. Just as he had several times throughout the long journey, Private Lambert jumped down from his horse and came to my side, reaching up his long arms to lift me effortlessly to the ground.

"Shall I escort Mrs. Fox, sir?"

"Yes, Private." Then, to me, "I think you will find your room much as you left it. If anything is lacking, you'll have someone stationed at your door to convey the information to me."

I had to bend my head back to look at him, positioning the setting sun right in my eyes, so he was little more than a silhouette when I said, "Thank you."

Never has a prison cell appeared more inviting. Colonel Brandon was correct in saying that little had changed. There was my bed and my table and my trunk and my stove. The narrow window still sat high in the wall, keeping the room in a darkness that now seemed to offer more comfort than gloom. The only addition was the buffalo-skin rug stretched across the floor.

Later I would learn that, during my absence, the men had cast lots to earn a night sleeping in this room—a warm, welcome change from the circular tents dotted along Fort Bridger's remaining wall. Perhaps that explained their less-than-exuberant reaction to my return. Had I known how I'd displaced them, I might not have enjoyed a single night's sleep. Or day's, for that matter. But I didn't know, and frankly when I first stepped over the threshold, I think I might have been able to summon the strength to knock over any soldier who came between me and my bed.

I remained upright and polite with Private Lambert as long as courtesy demanded, but the minute the door closed behind him, followed by the familiar sound of that sliding metal bar, I collapsed. With shaking hands I removed my mittens and scarf, tossing them to the ground. Numb fingers worked to untie my boots and loosen the buttons of my overcoat. A cozy fire lit by Private Lambert before he left certainly afforded enough warmth that I could take my coat off, and I intended to do so, but after shrugging one shoulder out, I hadn't the energy to repeat the action with the other. I still had one foot on the floor when I succumbed, at last, to sleep.

March came in like a lamb, prompting Colonel Brandon to remark that it would likely go out like a lion. It was a rare glimpse of humor, bringing a welcome softness into his face that otherwise seemed haggard with worry. Although he would never share details with me, I knew this winter was taking its toll on his men. They hadn't been prepared to spend a winter without shelter, and he'd sent many of his troops back when they first rode up to the ruins of Fort Bridger. Even so, supplies were low, rations carefully portioned.

Each time one of the soldiers came to my door with a plate of food, I bowed my head in both gratitude and shame. How could I have had such an ungrateful spirit for the meager meals shared with Evangeline, and yet feel unworthy of similar portions shared with these strangers? I had a sneaking suspicion that, were I to compare the bounty on my plate with any one of the men's, I would find I'd been given a relative feast. And with each one, a steaming mug of thick, black coffee.

It wasn't until we were weeks into April that I realized for certain I was pregnant. Until then, I attributed my fatigue and lethargy to the cold quarters and scant diet, not to mention endless days of having nothing to do. While I marked the fact that I'd missed my woman's time not once, but twice, I thought little of it, assuming I'd merely lost track of time. In fact, it crossed my mind that perhaps God was sparing me from those ministrations while living—as I did—in such close company with men.

Had I been the hale and hearty woman who was Nathan's first and only wife, I might not have recognized the small, telltale swelling in my stomach. But now, circumstances had worn away all but the most necessary flesh, and one night I lay in bed, warm under a pile of wool and pelts, and discovered the tiny, resolute mound.

"It must be," I said aloud.

I suppose any other woman in my circumstance might have been seized with panic, but my first reaction was one of gratitude. What child is not a gift? And this one had been given to me—and me alone. My arms still felt the weight of the last child I'd carried, his tiny, frail body growing heavier in each moment after his last breath. I received the new life I felt beneath my hands as a blessing and a promise.

"You, little one, will not know this church." Thin, gray moonlight illuminated my breath as I spoke. "You will be the first of my children that I will take away from this place." *And the last I will ever have*—though I could not bring myself to say as much aloud, even to the emptiness of my room. I did not have the luxury of dwelling in sorrow. I turned to my side and curled my body around the tiny being within me.

"Oh, Father God, thank you for such a gift."

I did not tell Colonel Brandon right away. Somehow I knew this announcement would bring out an even more protective spirit, and already I lived knowing that every bite of food I ate was a bite taken from those sworn to protect me.

Besides, how often does a woman have the chance to hold the secret of a child? Nathan was always so watchful, ever eager to know when our family was about to grow again. That we had several years separating our daughters and our son made us an anomaly among our neighbors. Other families filled their church bench like stair steps—one child after another, some sharing a birth year. But we had Melissa; then two years later, Lottie; then three years later, little Arlen. Two years ago, that was, when I was carrying my precious child who would fight for the few breaths God would grant him.

And now, this little one—no more than an idea in the night. An early winter baby, mid-November, I assumed. This, then, would be the first of my children my parents would hold. I continued to read my Bible daily and saw each verse as a promise made to this baby. I read aloud, hoping the vibration of my voice would wrap itself around this child, surrounding it in the rhythm of truth.

As much as the cold weather might have tempted me to a time of confinement, drifting only between my bed and my chair, I knew my body would demand more of me in six months' time. So every day, at the height of the afternoon sun, I left my cozy room to walk the length of the remaining stone wall. It was a daily gamut of tipped hats and greetings of "Afternoon, ma'am," that refreshed my spirits as much as did the cool, fresh air. Sometimes I would have an escort—Private Lambert, for example, who kept himself half a step behind me with his hands clasped behind his back. Other times Colonel Brandon walked beside me, holding his hand out at a gentlemanly angle whenever we came across a patch of deep snow or slick ice. Once or twice, I even took a turn with Captain Buckley, but his endless questions about my health—Was I eating enough? Did I feel rested?—made me wonder if he didn't have his own suspicions, especially given the knowing glint in his eyes when he asked them.

But most days, I walked alone, my face lifted to the sun, my eyes scanning the breadth of the sky, knowing that the same sun shining on the child within me shone on those I'd left to God's care, and I prayed for the day we would bask in its warmth together.

Bereft of a calendar, my outings bore witness to the passing of days and the gently turning season. Soon came an afternoon when I didn't need my scarf. Then another when I removed my hat midway through. I tucked my gloves into my coat pocket, and then I bravely stepped out without my coat at all. The ground became more mud and slush than snow. Men gathered in circles of laughter without creating clouds of steam. Everything became lighter—I felt it in my heart and in my feet.

Only the weight of the child within me grew, creating a center that seemed to anchor me to the ground. Otherwise, that afternoon when the sound of birdsong came wafting on the nearly spring breeze, I might have soared right up to meet it in the air. We had survived the winter.

"How soon can I leave?"

I could think of nothing else. There were some mornings I woke up ready to saddle Honey and ride toward the sunrise, and that afternoon my enthusiasm was met with a chuckle from Colonel Brandon that fell just short of patronizing.

"Soon, Mrs. Fox."

"Days?"

"I don't want you to feel in any way discouraged, but you must remember that my men aren't here on a holiday. I have orders to be here. No matter how noble the cause, I can't just abandon my post without permission."

"But you don't have to go, necessarily, do you? Couldn't you assign me to somebody else?"

"Are you telling me how to command my post?"

"Not at all. I wouldn't even ask if you hadn't promised—"

"I am well aware of my obligations, Mrs. Fox. Unfortunately they extend beyond you."

It was the sharpest he'd ever spoken to me, and I was thankful we'd taken our walk along the outside of the wall,

away from the curious eyes of the men. I held my tongue, waiting for his apology, but he remained equally silent, perhaps
waiting for my own.

"I had hoped to leave the first of May," I said.

"Out of the question."

"Why?"

"If any of my men were to talk to me like that, they'd
spend a month in the stockade."

"My apologies, Colonel Brandon."

We'd come to the remains of an outlying building—nothing more than a single, short wall of chinked logs that somehow
had been spared the fate of further fire. Here he stopped, and
I beside him.

"In the last post, I submitted a request for permission to
escort you home. I'm waiting to hear. Word should come with
a change in command. As soon as that happens, I'll assemble
a party, and if the weather holds, you'll be home before you
know it."

"But if you can't . . . I mean, it doesn't have to be you."

"I would like it to be."

His declaration settled between us, somewhere at our feet,
given the direction of both our gazes. He stood with his hands
clasped behind his back, while mine fidgeted, turning and
twisting one on another.

"Does it bother you still?" he asked.

"What?" Then I realized I was especially worrying the very
spot of my amputation. "Oh no. Not at all, especially now that
the weather's warmer."

He reached for my hand, and I allowed him to take it.

"It can take time for such a wound to truly heal. To the
eye, one can see that the surgical procedure has mended, but
I've known many men to report still feeling pain, even though

such pain is impossible. You think, how can something hurt that isn't there? That's the kind of healing that takes the longest."

"And I suppose, for some, it never does."

He hadn't looked at me until that moment, and when he did, whatever wall existed between us melted away. Unlike Nathan, whose eyes enticed and danced, full of glinting promises, Colonel Brandon's held a wide, open honesty. Soft and vulnerable as newly turned earth. I could offer him no less.

"I'm going to have a baby. In the fall."

Slowly, almost imperceptibly, his touch relinquished mine and he stepped away. "I suspected as much."

"Did you?" Bold as anything, I ran my hands over my somewhat-flat stomach. "I'm hardly showing."

"There's a marked difference in your face." He seemed almost as surprised as I was when he touched his finger to my cheek. Such a small gesture, but it felt like he'd reached across a canyon to bridge the new distance between us. I could sense the battle he fought to bring words to this new intimacy. "Something that wasn't there before you went back to Salt Lake City. Call it a healthy glow. It looks like hope."

"Am I really so different?" I never imagined myself as anything but pale and gaunt.

"I don't know that it would be obvious to anybody who wasn't looking for such a change. And then, too, when you walk, you hold your hands like you are now . . . protective. You might not be aware—"

"I wasn't."

"No need to be self-conscious about it now." He took on an exaggerated brusque, authoritative tone. "Like I said, most would never notice. But I remember my wife, before our son was born."

"Well, my condition actually makes me quite tired, so I think it best we head back. I'd like to lie down for a bit."

I turned, but he did not follow.

"I had wondered," he said, stopping me with his words, "if my suspicions were true, whether or not that would change your plans. If, perhaps, you would be more inclined to seek a reconciliation and return home."

"No."

"And you will be how far along if we are able to embark in May?"

I couldn't be sure if he was asking purely for my travel safety's sake, or if he wanted to confirm that some measure of reconciliation had taken place while I was away in Salt Lake City. For the briefest of moments it occurred to me to lie, make him think that I'd been pregnant when his men first found me in the snow, but if I'd stalled long enough to do the calculations, he surely would have noted my dishonesty.

"Three months."

"We'll have to ask Captain Buckley if it will be safe for you to travel."

I laughed. "Colonel, if we allowed this condition to keep us from traveling, there wouldn't be a single woman west of the Mississippi River."

"And its father?"

I met his gaze and said evenly, "This child will be part of my new life, away from here."

"And he'll never know?"

"Not until God wills that I reveal it. But don't you see? If I don't get away, if Nathan finds me, and he discovers . . . he'll never let me go."

"He won't find you."

"How can you be so sure?"

"He won't find you because he's not looking. Not anymore."

CHAPTER 17

My mother used to have a saying for those times when a mysterious chill would dart across her body.

"Like somebody's walked over my grave," she'd say, and I always found it to be the funniest thing because she wasn't even dead yet. Neither was I, of course, but Nathan must have believed I was. There could be no other reason for him to give up his search for me. So as silly as the saying was, in light of Colonel Brandon's revelation, I expected to be bombarded with such strange feelings. An eerie hollowness, a profound cavernous fear of an empty, waiting grave. Instead, I sensed only peace. In some ways, I'd been waiting for months to be taken away, tugged by force back to the church that seemed so intent on holding captive its members.

Now I was free—as free as I could be until my actual death.

As a result, I took to spending nearly as much time as I possibly could outside my little room. I walked and I walked, surging with a new energy born from the brisk breeze and sweet spring air. In fact, I might have lived my entire day among the piles of rubble and abandoned fire pits with the soldiers if I hadn't been confronted one particularly warm day by Private Lambert.

"Mrs. Fox, ma'am, if you wouldn't mind, I need to ask you . . . well, we—the company—would like to request, if you wouldn't mind . . ." He stammered and blushed, crushing his hat in his hands as he shifted from foot to foot.

"What is it, Private?"

"Some of the men, they haven't had a chance to do their washing pretty much all winter."

"And they want me to be their laundress?"

"No, ma'am. Nothing like that at all. They'll do their own washing. Thing is, they need to wash themselves, too." He grabbed the back of his neck, twisting and turning in an effort to look anywhere but directly at me. "We was going to bring the washtubs outside. . . ."

"Ah, and you'd like me to stay *inside*."

"If you wouldn't mind, ma'am."

I don't think I've ever heard anybody make such a celebration of a wash day. While my curiosity was not remotely piqued, I did lend an indulgent ear to the sounds coming from the yard outside. Laughter, mostly, and other bits of conversation I'm sure they would never have let loose had they known I could hear them, let alone had I been out among them. I hadn't seen Colonel Brandon at all that day—for that matter, I hadn't seen him in several days—which might have contributed to the general sense of revelry.

Not long after, an agreement of sorts sounded from the men outside as scattered bits of noise joined together in one collective, victorious shout. It was a familiar sound, one that I associated with my previous stay, before my time in Salt Lake City. The shouting became distinct.

"Mail call!"

This, then, another hope for spring. Never mind the tiny shoots of new grass, the songs of birds, the days warm enough to roll your sleeves. Now we had safe, open passage from east to west. More than ever, the confines of the room took on the air of a prison and I paced its length. Outside I heard a single voice take control and rise above the rest, calling out the names.

"Dufray! Minor! Pascal!"

The noise would swell and wane, and it wasn't until they fell into absolute silence that I knew Colonel Brandon had arrived. Minutes later I heard his voice in the larger room adjacent to mine. The door was closed, but that hadn't been more than a formality since my return. I came and went as I pleased, though no one entered without my express invitation and permission. Now I stood with my ear pressed up against the door, wondering if official business on the other side called for me to wait for the same indulgence.

Voices were low and muffled. Colonel Brandon's was distinct and familiar, though the words remained unintelligible. And two others. All of it sounding very official and solemn. I suppose I could have feigned ignorance and breezed right across the threshold to suffer the consequences of my disruption, but before I could fully consider such a plan, my ear rang with a sharp rapping on the other side of the wood.

"Mrs. Fox?"

I took three steps away and shouted, "One minute!" For no particular reason but to buy a bit of time, I smoothed my hair, tucking what strands I could behind my ears, and straightened my skirt.

The expression on Colonel Brandon's face proved impossible to interpret. Smiling? No, but not stern. Just serious as he said, "For you."

It bears noting, I think, that his eyes so captivated me I hadn't even glanced down to see what he held in his hand, and when I did, my own began to shake.

An envelope, long and thin, and my name written in timid, blocked letters—a hand I hadn't seen in years.

"Mama." I breathed the word as if the woman herself stood before me, because in all this time, this was the closest I'd come to such a thing.

"I'll leave you to this," Colonel Brandon said, closing the door between us.

The shaking in my hand now traveled throughout my body, and I feared my legs would not hold me long enough to take even the few steps to my chair. I dropped the letter on the table and propped my elbows up on either side of it, resting my head on my clasped hands.

"Dear Lord, thank you."

Not wanting to risk tearing the letter itself, I waited for the shaking in my hands to settle down before lifting the envelope and carefully running a finger beneath its sealed edge. In it, a single sheet of paper—so familiar. Probably torn from the very notebook I used to write my school compositions.

Years could not erase my mother's voice; I heard it in every word—soft and timid, fearful of rising above my father's.

Our dearest girl—
It is winter now. And your father is ill. Has been since midsummer. Doctors do not know. We

will wait for spring, a healing or death, they say. He can take nothing more than buttermilk-soaked bread. The doctor does not know, but I say he is too filled with bitterness to take anything else. He does not know about this letter. He thinks I don't know about the others, but I do. Every one you sent. He would not let us open or read them. But I knew. I always knew. I pray you can forgive us and I pray that you come home.

It was left unsigned, though of course I needed nothing to authenticate its sender. My eyes combed over the page again and again, frustrated with its sparseness. Her unsophisticated writing filled the page, even with so few words. Perhaps she didn't realize she could send two pages, or three, or a tome if she so chose.

Papa was sick. He was dying, even, and he hadn't forgiven me.

Spring. Healing or death.

And my mother asked me for grace.

I jumped up, folding the letter, and went into the outer office, where three men—Colonel Brandon and two others I did not recognize—stood around the heavy wooden desk, all eyes trained on a scattering of papers across its top.

"Mrs. Fox—"

He seemed on the verge of introductions when I interrupted. "It's word from my parents, Colonel Brandon. My father is ill. Quite ill, it seems. I need to go home at once."

"Mrs. Fox," he repeated, "this is Colonel Chambers. He will be assuming command in my absence."

I afforded him the briefest acknowledgment before asking, "When can we leave?"

"When will you be ready?"

"Now."

He chuckled. "Will you grant me three days?"

"Yes, sir," I said, attempting my best impersonation of Private Lambert. "At dawn?"

"At dawn."

Three days. At the time, it seemed an interminable wait, but during those three days, I witnessed the resurrection of Fort Bridger. A fleet of supply wagons arrived the morning after the mail, and barrels of flour and sugar and coffee were rolled into storehouses. Construction began on towers and barracks, and men who had spent an entire winter on bedrolls spread out over frozen ground feverishly worked to build bunks and stitch mattresses.

Through all of this, of course, they kept a vigilant eye on the events in Salt Lake City. Spring would mean some level of resurgence there, too, as everyone emerged from the dormant winter infused with renewed vigor and purpose. I took to leaving my door ajar when Colonel Brandon and Colonel Chambers met in the outer office. I suspect Colonel Brandon realized I was listening, but I surmised that he endorsed my eavesdropping, as he did nothing to prevent it.

While they talked, I worked on remaking my blue dress—one clumsy stitch at a time. Colonel Brandon briefed Colonel Chambers on my predicament shortly after introducing me, and until then I'd almost forgotten that Zion itself faced a crisis of far greater magnitude than mine. As I stitched, I learned that, by and large, farmers in the outlying towns were arming themselves, preparing for battle. Brigham had launched a campaign calling all Saints to be prepared to make the ultimate sacrifice for God and gospel.

"But we are still called to stay the course," Colonel Chambers said. "We will not fire unless fired upon."

"Correct," Colonel Brandon said. "Not even in retaliation for our men in the town. They serve in that capacity at their own risk."

"And do they report here to me?"

"No. That would be far too dangerous for them. We have our checkpoints established between here and Salt Lake City. They'll leave a sign if we need to meet to exchange information."

"That's how you knew about . . ." His voice trailed, and I knew he was talking about me.

"Yes," Colonel Brandon said. "And she's been nothing but trouble ever since."

I could sense the humor in his remark from the next room. He must have known I was listening. Had he been in the room, I might have thrown a pincushion at him. Instead, I smiled and continued with my hem. He so rarely told a joke, it seemed something to savor.

The night before we were to leave, I cornered Private Lambert and requested a washtub, hot water, and soap that I might be able to take my own spring bath. I thought the poor boy might faint on the spot, as all the blood in his body seemed to have rushed to his face, but that evening I was presented with a large tub, six kettles of steaming hot water, and just as many buckets of cool, not to mention clean linen and a dish of soft soap.

Private Lambert himself offered to stand guard outside my door, as there was no bolt on my side, and I could think of no other man I trusted more with my privacy. Safe in my room, I used a handful of soap to lather through my hair, kneeling at the side of the tub to rinse it. I wrapped it in a length of linen, then stripped to step into the warm water. For just a moment, I marveled at the shape of my body. I had no way of knowing just how many of the men were aware of my condition, but could they see me now, there would be no doubt. The winter had taken its toll on my flesh; my shoulders and knees protruded with a sharpness that threatened my skin. But the core of my body swelled with life and health.

I ran my hands along its expanse as I bathed, enjoying the warmth of the water. Once soaped and rinsed, my skin squeaked beneath my touch. I unwrapped the toweling from around my head and used it to dry my body. A modest fire glowed in the stove, and I stood next to it, every inch of myself warm and clean. My wide-toothed comb glided through my wet hair, ridding it of tangles. I slipped on a nightgown, pilfered from Evangeline's and laundered by a willing private, and brought a chair right up next to the stove, where I could sit and help my hair to dry before going to bed.

A muffled knock. "Mrs. Fox?"

I had no wrapper to cover my gown, so I draped my shawl over my shoulder and invited Private Lambert to open the door, assuming he was there to throw out the wash water.

But it was Colonel Brandon who poked his head around the door. One look at me, and his eyes shot up to the point where the ceiling met the wall; there, except for the briefest connecting glances, they would remain for most of our conversation.

"We'll leave before first light."

"I'll be ready."

"Are you certain?"

"I can be an early riser when I need to be."

"What I mean is—" and for this he looked right at me— "are you ready to leave your children?"

"I left my children more than three months ago."

"They're not much more than a hundred miles from here. Come dawn tomorrow I can take you in that direction just as easy as I can take you to meet the stage."

"My children think I'm dead."

"But you're not."

"No." I studied the ends of my hair. "But I don't have a life to offer them. Not yet. I don't have a home or a means of support."

"And you don't think you can find that here?"

"A woman alone is dependent on the charity of her community. I'll be excommunicated. Nobody will be allowed to talk to me, let alone offer charity."

"I just want to be sure you're prepared for the separation. I know what it's like to leave my family, never knowing for certain if I shall return."

"I'm escaping my war. If I stay here, I'll spend the rest of my days looking over my shoulder, fighting to keep my children away from the church."

"There are other dangers."

"Yes, I know. One of them being that I will not have the opportunity to be reconciled to my father before he dies. I must go to him, *now*. And to my mother. I need to know that they will welcome both me and my daughters into their home so I'm not left . . ."

"Wandering?"

"Dependent."

"And if they don't?"

I stood then, my shawl offering adequate modesty atop my shoulders, but aware that there was little I could do to prevent the firelight from casting an intriguing shadow as it burned behind my nightdress. "Have you changed your mind,

Colonel Brandon? Because you certainly seem intent on changing mine."

"Sometimes a strategy deserves a second thought." He
spoke, again, to the wall.

"This is not a strategy." I sat again, my back fully to him.
"I'm here by God's grace and provision. There's no reason to
think he will abandon me now."

<hr />

Honey, saddled and brushed and proud, waited for me in the
predawn light. She was one of six saddled horses, and they stood
in a formation almost as regimented as did the men standing
around them.

I'd never seen the men gathered in such official posture.
The winter had taken its toll on their uniforms, but each was
pressed the best it could be.

"Attention!"

Colonel Brandon and Colonel Chambers emerged at the
far end of the line of men and strode toward where I stood at
the front.

I don't know what I expected a changing of command to
be, but that morning's ceremony proved to be little more than
a handshake between the two colonels, followed by Colonel
Brandon's salute to the troops. At a voiced command, they
returned the salute in kind, moving in a disciplined, sharp
movement. Those men were sworn to follow Colonel Brandon
into battle, to obey whatever command he would speak, without question. They would shoot and kill other men, if need be.
They might at some time be engaged as such with my neighbors
and friends and family.

And here they all were because of me. Now, Colonel

Brandon, having relinquished all other official duties, greeted me with a very civilianlike "Good morning."

The previous evening, he had explained to me that we would ride on horseback to a way station, where we would board a stagecoach for our journey back to Iowa. Honey looked every bit as eager to go as I did, but I tugged at Colonel Brandon's sleeve to protest.

"You know how I feel about stealing Nathan's horse."

He twitched his moustache in such a way that I didn't know if he was irritated or amused, and it occurred to me that I probably should not have spoken to him outright with his men in formation behind him—an enlightenment that came from Private Lambert's puzzled, disapproving glare.

"We have an escort to ride with us; then we'll board the stage, and they will return here, bringing both my horse and your Honey with them. After which, as my final standing order, she is to be taken and set free within a mile of your husband's property, where, Lord willing, she will find her way home."

"Without me."

"Correct."

"What will he think?"

Colonel Brandon took my hand in both of his, encasing it in reassuring warmth. "He'll think, if nothing else, his horse returned."

I noted two truths in his eyes when he spoke. First, that he held my husband in the utmost contempt. Second, that he loved me. It didn't occur to me to confront him on either of these at the moment—not in front of the troops. I tucked both away, not knowing how either would serve to get me through the day's ride. I allowed Colonel Brandon to lead me to my horse, where Private Lambert was waiting with a step stool to help me mount her. Once the reins were in my hand, I busied myself arranging my skirt. Then, with Colonel Brandon by my side, two soldiers riding ahead of us, and two behind, I dug my heels into Honey's flanks.

In deference, I'm sure, to my condition, we kept the horses at an easy pace. And it was a glorious day for a ride. The air was perfumed with fresh sage, and by early afternoon we had both the warmth of the sun on our backs and a cooling breeze in our faces. Every breath felt sweet and fresh and new. Still, I held Honey's reins in my whole hand while keeping the other in a perpetual protective embrace over my stomach.

We stopped periodically to rest both ourselves and the horses, but as the day wore on, Colonel Brandon called on us to push through to our destination—as much as my ability and comfort would allow. As nobody there had more desire to reach our destination than I did, I put on my bravest face, reassuring all that I felt fine, and rode the final miles putting my faith in both Honey and God that I would see some sort of bed that night.

The way station was nothing more than a mark on the horizon when I first saw it, and by the time we arrived, it was swallowed in evening shadows. From what I could tell, it consisted of some half a dozen buildings—one large, two-story structure and several low, long ones, with a scattering of small cabins all around. Lights blazed in the largest building, and I felt God's own hand at my back, pushing me forward.

Our party was received by a motley welcoming committee, consisting of a middle-aged married couple—Mr. and Mrs. Fennel—and a rather hulking young man named Thomas, who might or might not have been their son. As we brought our horses to a stop outside the door, the three of them came out of the house, meeting us at the low, dilapidated fence that marked a modest yard in front of the large house. After greetings were exchanged that showed me Colonel Brandon was no stranger here, Mrs. Fennel led me to a tidy room with a washstand, chair, and a wide bed covered with a bright green-and-blue quilt.

"Now, I'll be servin' a supper downstairs, but you just get yourself tucked in and I'll bring up a tray. A full day on horseback is mighty hard on a woman."

"Thank you," I said with genuine relief. "You're very kind."

As she closed the door behind herself, I went immediately to the washbasin, alarmed at the vision that greeted me in the mirror. Dust had settled into every crease and corner of my face, and what wasn't tinged brown with dust was red with sun- and windburn. I filled the basin with water, rolled up my sleeves, plunged in my hands, and splashed my face. Oh, the cool refreshment. After a quick check to see that the door was locked, I stripped off my dust-soiled dress and dabbed a washcloth along my shoulders and arms, trying to ignore the quickly browning water.

The nightgown felt cool and soft against my bare skin, and it smelled of sweet cedar. It was now fully dark outside, so I didn't feel completely indulgent in crawling into the bed. The mattress was a soft straw tick, more comfortable than I'd slept on since leaving home, and for just a moment I worried that I might fall asleep before getting a chance to eat whatever smelled so delicious downstairs. My fears proved unfounded, however, when Mrs. Fennel walked in carrying a tray with a steaming dish of shepherd's pie.

"I feel like royalty."

"Well, you look half-dead. Sure you have the strength to eat?"

I nodded and sat up straighter, my mouth watering at the sight of the mixture of lamb, carrots, and potatoes in a rich gravy on the plate.

"I'd like to stay with you so's you'd have someone to talk to, but I got a room full of men downstairs that are gonna keep me hoppin'. You'll be all right?"

I nodded again, this time my mouth too full of food to speak politely. Mrs. Fennel instructed me to leave my tray outside the door after I had finished, and then she left me alone with my supper. It didn't last long. I wolfed the food in a matter of minutes, washing it down with gulps of fresh, cold milk. The last bite was a battle against fullness and fatigue, but I managed it down and fell against my pillows, exhausted. It took the last bit of my strength to get up and set the tray outside my door, where I found Colonel Brandon opening his own right across the hall.

"Mrs. Fox."

"Colonel Brandon."

It was the extent of our conversation. I set my tray on the floor, and he disappeared. I climbed back into bed and was asleep within moments.

CHAPTER 18

Never could two mirrored experiences be so different. Years ago I'd traversed this same land with Nathan. Step by step I'd crossed it, walking one plodding mile after another when I wasn't sitting on the tongue of somebody's wagon as a team of oxen took even slower steps. Five miles a day we'd covered—on a good day—and each of those miles passed one blade of grass at a time. If I closed my eyes, I could bring it all back—the relentless sun, the inescapable rain, the days upon days of seeing the same mountain peak on the horizon—no closer at the end of the day than it had been when you were washing up the breakfast dishes. Nathan and I hadn't had our own wagon, so we'd sleep under the stars, wrapped in each other's arms. Or we'd sneak off—just over a hill, maybe—to enjoy our newly married life.

And that's what it felt like. Life. Just a slow-moving home. We sang and cooked. Children played games right alongside the turning wagon wheels. Little girls spied wildflowers and made chains of them; little boys trapped lizards and snakes. Prairie dogs stood on their haunches and watched us rumble by.

But traveling by stage, I hardly knew I was making the same journey. Nothing could have prepared me for the brutality of this transport. The noise was deafening, with the constant rattle of chains, not to mention the stagecoach itself. Mrs. Fennel had indeed procured extra cushioning, which was lashed to the original seat with long leather strips. Without it, I couldn't imagine the beating my body would have taken. At our first lurching exit from the way station, I found myself tossed from my seat entirely, nearly into the lap of Private Lambert, who at the next stop volunteered to ride shotgun with our driver. This left me alone with Colonel Brandon, something that never affected me during our conversations back at Fort Bridger. But my newfound understanding of his feelings for me put me on edge, and I was actually grateful to focus my attention on remaining upright on the seat.

We stopped four times during the course of the first day— every ten miles, according to our driver. When we came to our fifth and final stop, we'd traveled approximately fifty miles, and though I felt every one of them throughout my aching body, I marveled at the distance. We'd driven the equivalent of more than a week's travel by wagon. It took me more than a season to leave home; I would be back in less than a month.

To my relief I learned that we would not ride through the night. Any sort of bed—even a straw pallet on rocky soil— would be preferable to more miles of being tossed around in that torturous seat. We'd stopped at the Big Pond station, comprised of one large structure of massive sandstone slabs and several outlying smaller buildings. Here there was no Mrs. Fennel and family bustling about to feed and serve us. In fact, I might well have been the only woman there, which renewed my appreciation for Colonel Brandon's offer of escort. Upon stopping, our driver had jumped down to go in search of someone to help with the horses, leaving Private Lambert, Colonel Brandon, and me to fend for ourselves in the main building.

The door was wide and square and heavy, if Private Lambert's obvious effort to open it was any indication, but it opened to a room that managed to be somehow simultaneously cavernous and cozy. The walls were lined with narrow bunks, stacked three high, each with a mattress covered by a neatly tucked-in blanket. Four long tables with benches created an aisle down the center of the room, stretching from the door to an enormous stone fireplace that comprised most of the far wall, where a small, inviting fire burned. Facing it was a gathering of horsehair and leather–covered chairs.

"Care to sit?" Colonel Brandon gestured with his hat.

"No thanks," I said, arching my back. "I've had quite enough sitting for one day."

"Well, it appears they've left supper for us, at least."

A large, cast-iron kettle sat on the end of one of the tables, with a stack of bowls next to it and a shallow pan covered with a white towel. At a nod from Colonel Brandon, Private Lambert went to it, lifted the lid, and reported, "Beans, sir. And corn bread, sir. They must have known they had soldiers coming." Then a small smile in my direction. "Beg your pardon, ma'am."

As it turned out, this building actually had two halls that jutted out from the far wall. To the left, according to a rough-lettered sign, was a kitchen, and to the right, a washroom. I was given leave to wash up first and was pleasantly surprised at the facility. There was a hand pump coming right up from the floor and a row of basins and pitchers set up along a shelf that ran nearly the length of the wall. To my relief, two of the pitchers were already filled, and once again I turned the water gray with a day's worth of travel dust. I knew I'd have no chance to wash anything other than my face and neck and hands, but even that little bit was refreshing. I opened the back door to dump my dirty water off the porch and paused for just a moment, gazing up into the starlight.

"Good night, sweet girls," I said, and I prayed that God would keep us all safe until we could look upon the stars together.

When I reentered the main room, two other gentlemen were seated at one of the long tables. Colonel Brandon introduced them to me as Ephraim Henness and Nicholas Farmer. Both had high brows and gray hair with neatly trimmed whiskers and were dressed in well-tailored, dark suits. They were taking the westbound stage headed for Salt Lake City. And then, in a tone that would seem natural to anybody who'd never spent countless hours in conversation with the man, Colonel Brandon introduced me as his wife.

Instantly alert, I took a step closer to Colonel Brandon and said, "Good evening, gentlemen."

I'd seen these men before. Not these particular ones, of course, but others upon others just like them, and I knew they were Latter-day Saints.

"Perhaps, then, Mrs. Brandon, you could serve up our supper?" the elder of the two said. "The station cook encouraged us to wait for your arrival. Unsavory character himself, so we're quite pleased to know we have more civilized company."

My smile remained frozen. "I'd be happy to."

Colonel Brandon and Private Lambert took turns excusing themselves to clean up in the washroom, purposefully not leaving me alone with Brothers Ephraim and Nicholas, for which I was grateful. The men exchanged small talk about the weather and travel, while I took a lamp and ventured into the kitchen. Not caring whether or not I had the resident cook's permission, I built up the fire in the cookstove and set a kettle of water on to boil, having located a tin of tea on a shelf.

Upon returning to the table, I ladled out beans, passed the corn bread, and poured glasses of cold water. When all were seated, Colonel Brandon offered to say a blessing for the meal, but Brother Ephraim raised his hand.

"May I inquire first, sir, if you are in right relationship with our Lord?"

Colonel Brandon smiled warmly, almost indulgently, and said, "Yes, sir. I am a Christian."

Now it was the Saints' turn to offer their own condescension in allowing this Gentile to lead them in prayer. At his invitation, we joined hands—Private Lambert at my right and Colonel Brandon at my left—and bowed our heads.

"Father in heaven," he prayed, and I wondered if he held Brother Ephraim's hand as tightly as he held mine, "we give you thanks for our safe journey and for the hospitality of those who will give us food and lodging this night. We ask a special blessing for them and to be held in your mercy for the rest of our travels. Please allow your healing hand to rest upon Camilla's father, that she may see him on earth before he goes on to glory. In the name of your Son, Jesus Christ, in whom alone we can find salvation, amen."

As I opened my eyes, I let my hand rest for a moment on Colonel Brandon's arm and whispered, "Thank you," as his gaze met mine.

"Your father is ill?" I detected genuine concern in Brother Ephraim's question.

"Yes," I said, welcoming the touch as Colonel Brandon's hand covered mine. "I haven't seen him since . . . well, in a very long time."

"Well then," Brother Ephraim said, "we will keep him in our prayers too. Nothing can be quite as comforting as the love of a child."

For a little while nobody spoke as we dove into the meal left for us. Whoever this unsavory cook might be, he had a way with spices, as the beans held a delicious flavoring of onion and salt and some other ingredient I could not identify but found delectable.

"Have you not yet been blessed with children?" It was the first Brother Nicholas had spoken since our introduction, other than the most minimal conversation.

Colonel Brandon and I exchanged a glance. I hesitated a breath before answering, "No." The lie taunted me. In an effort to hide my guilt, I looked to my lap, then brought my hand to my stomach, as if to protect this little one now.

Brother Ephraim pounced upon my gesture. "Perhaps I am wrong, but are you now in the midst of such a blessing?"

Just as I was wondering how I would respond, Colonel Brandon drove a knife through the pan of corn bread, saying, "I'm afraid it's rather impolite to make the lady's condition a topic of conversation, and I must ask you to apologize."

Both brothers reacted as if Colonel Brandon had slapped them in an attempt to defend my honor, and I disguised a smile behind a swipe at my mouth with the back of my hand.

"I assure you we meant no disrespect," Brother Nicholas said. "My apologies to you both."

"He's a soldier," Brother Ephraim said. He was at least ten

years older than Brother Nicholas and obviously considered himself the authority between the two. "Perhaps he sees it as his sworn duty to stir dissension."

Before he could respond, I took the knife and the pan away from Colonel Brandon and resumed his task.

"Is this your first visit to Salt Lake City, gentlemen?" I stopped myself just short of calling them brothers.

"It is to be our home," Brother Ephraim said, overstepping Brother Nicholas's attempt to respond. "We have been five years in England and Wales on mission for the Church of Jesus Christ of Latter-day Saints. Tell me, are you acquainted with our faith?"

"We are," Colonel Brandon said.

"Nope," Private Lambert said at the same time.

I said nothing.

"Well then, my young man, given these uncertain times, perhaps you would like to be acquainted with the true gospel of Jesus Christ."

"No, he wouldn't," Colonel Brandon said.

"I believe the young man can speak for himself," a newly outraged Brother Nicholas said.

"No, he cannot. He is under my command."

Private Lambert looked from one man to the other, carefully chewing his food.

"I see," Brother Ephraim said. "But my brother and I are not under your command, so you cannot stop us from sharing our faith. Oh, wait, I seem to have forgotten. That is exactly what your president is endeavoring to do, isn't it? To deny my people our constitutional rights to practice our religion? And from what I have heard in my letters from our church leadership, you are ready to wage war if we attempt to exercise our rights."

"We are here," Colonel Brandon said, the hand not holding a fork balled into a fist, "to keep peace. And—"

"And I would like to have peace at this table," I interrupted, laying my hand on his arm. "Certainly we could find a more neutral topic of conversation. Tell us, Brother Ephraim, more about England. We've never been."

The Mormon man's eyebrow shot up at my use of the word *brother*, and I realized too late the degree of familiarity I'd taken—something no Gentile would ever do. His scrutiny intensified, and I felt every bit as targeted as I had the night the bishop and Elder Justus came to demand my rebaptism.

"You, then, I sense, are acquainted with our mission?"

"I? No, nothing beyond what is common knowledge."

Brother Ephraim leaned forward in an almost-predatory posture. "And just what do you consider 'common knowledge'?"

Colonel Brandon was on his feet. "Now see here—"

And I was on mine. "I've something to attend to in the kitchen. If you all will excuse me." I grabbed Colonel Brandon's sleeve and pulled him close, speaking directly into his ear, yet loud enough for all the company. "Do not engage in battle, my darling, when I so desire a night of peace."

He sat back down and was actually apologizing for his outburst as I walked out of the room. In the kitchen, the kettle was spitting water droplets that hissed on the stove. Finding a towel to protect my hand, I poured the water from the kettle into a serviceable pot and dropped a ball of tea in to steep. Smiling to myself, I filled a tray with the teapot and five white mugs, along with a small dish of sugar.

"I'm sorry I couldn't find any milk," I said upon reentering the large room. The four men sat in sullen silence, and I wager not a word had been spoken in my absence. I set the tray on the table. "There was a little sugar, though. This should help soothe our rattled bones."

Acting quite the lady, I poured a steaming cup to serve to Private Lambert and then another for Colonel Brandon.

"I'm afraid our faith does not permit us to join you," Brother Nicholas said with more arrogance than apology. "Were you better acquainted with our teachings, you would know that."

"Oh, I'm terribly sorry." I amassed all the wide-eyed innocence I could muster.

"That's quite all right," Brother Ephraim said, and from the glint in his eye, I knew he hadn't been fooled. "Please, enjoy. It isn't easy to deny oneself such simple pleasures, even when doing so in obedience to God. I'm afraid we have so many of our Saints who have found the true path of righteousness to be more difficult to follow than they anticipated. That's why we were called back from the mission field, in part. Isn't it, Brother Nicholas?"

"It is, indeed."

Private Lambert slurped his tea, garnering a disdainful look from both brothers.

"These are very troubling times for our church, as Colonel Brandon here is quite aware."

"Not quite sure I see the connection," Colonel Brandon said.

"So many flock to our faith, searching for truth and, dare I say, finding it in the revelation of our prophet. But then, when choices have to be made—" his eyes tracked mine, holding them until I looked away to stir sugar into my tea—"they come to a crisis of faith. The rewards of Heavenly Father are great, but they come at a price. The price of obedience. Some are simply not willing to obey."

"And you have been summoned to enforce obedience?" Colonel Brandon said.

Brother Ephraim spread his hands wide in a gesture of appeasement. "You see, we have the same duties to perform. You want my people to adhere to the laws of government; I want my people to live by the laws of God. Of course our methods of persuasion are quite different."

My blood ran cold as inwardly I questioned just how different they were. After all, was I not a fugitive of this very church? I tried to nonchalantly sip my tea under Brother Ephraim's watchful eye, but even though I held it with both hands, they shook so, sending scalding droplets onto my skin.

"Are you all right?" Colonel Brandon said, taking the cup from me and offering his handkerchief to dry my spill.

"Perhaps that is why the Lord forbids that we imbibe hot drinks," Brother Ephraim said.

Too late to stop myself, I said, "It is the prophet who says so, not the Lord."

"Ah, Mrs. Brandon, I see you know more about our teachings than you let on."

"It's late," Colonel Brandon said, standing, "and we all have a long ride ahead of us in the morning. I suggest we get some sleep. Private?"

At once, Private Lambert was on his feet. "Yes, sir?"

"Perhaps you and one of the gentlemen here can scout out whoever's in charge of this place and find out where we're to bed for the night."

"I'm afraid we already have," Brother Nicholas said. "There are no suitable lodgings other than what you see in this room." He indicated the bunks lining the walls. "The surrounding cabins are not for the guests, and I, for one, am grateful.

Dens of drinking and gambling they are. No place for a lady."
He offered me a smile; his fellow Saint did not.

"So we sleep in here?" I said. "All of us?"

"I daresay your honor will be safe with us," Brother
Ephraim said. "We are married men, with wives waiting for us
in Salt Lake City. And you appear to be heavily armed."

Colonel Brandon's eyes narrowed, and I cleared my throat,
calling his attention and pleading with him not to take this
conversation further.

I cleared the table, with Private Lambert's help, and gave
the dishes a quick rinse, leaving them stacked in the empty
sink. Normally I'd hate the thought of leaving a kitchen in such
a state, but by that time I was so exhausted I could only think of
laying my head down in whatever place God had provided for
that night, even if it meant a narrow bunk in a shared room. In
fact, once I got back to the main room, Brothers Ephraim and
Nicholas had claimed their bunks—one above the other on the
left side of the room.

"Why, it's not unlike the sleeping provisions our brothers
and sisters will have on their voyage to this country." Brother
Ephraim was propped up on one elbow, speaking to Brother
Nicholas, who was in the bunk above him.

"Praise God to have this experience," Brother Nicholas
said. "I daresay to the rest of you, you will be facing some
accommodations far less comfortable than these."

Though I was loath to look, I did notice that they had
removed only their shoes and suit coats, having taken to bed
fully clothed. Both Private Lambert and Colonel Brandon wore
their uniforms—boots included—as if they had no intention of
retiring anytime soon.

"Well then," I said, hoping to keep my voice low enough to
hide my discomfort from the men across the room, "good night."

"Good night, ma'am," Private Lambert said with the slightest bow.

"Good night," Colonel Brandon said, adding, "dear," after a glance toward our companions. Then, in a gesture I'm not sure was meant only for their suspicious eyes, he came toward me and placed a soft kiss on my brow. I stood perfectly still, for if I raised my face even a fraction, I feared his kiss would trail to my lips . . . or break away entirely. At the moment, I did not know which I feared most.

Afterward, he took my hand and led me across the room, to the bunks farthest from the Mormons and closest to the fire.

"I think it best you take the top," he whispered in my ear. "And I'll be right below you."

"Very well."

My feet were about ready to swell themselves out of my boots, and after I'd settled myself on the top bunk, I began to bend forward, intending to unlace them, when I felt Colonel Brandon's hand close around my ankle. Without a word, he freed my feet, setting my shoes on the ground next to the bottom bunk.

"It's not the first time you've stolen my shoes," I said.

"I just want you to stay put," he said. "Now get some sleep."

I lay back on the surprisingly comfortable mattress, then turned on my side to press my back against the cool wall. I felt safer there, even though a short railing on the outer edge ensured that I probably would not roll out to my death in the middle of the night. I found myself eye to eye with Colonel Brandon, who disappeared for just a few steps before returning with a blanket taken from one of the unused bunks. For a moment I thought he would cover me with it, but then he seemed to reconsider and simply handed it to me, folded.

"Thank you," I said, spreading it across my body.

"Sleep tight," he said.

He instructed Private Lambert to put out all the lights in the room, and soon the only light came from the fire dwindling in the fireplace. I heard Private Lambert preparing to go to bed in the bunk next to mine, having heard Colonel Brandon instruct him to take the bottom so he would be better prepared to come to my aid if necessary.

I suppose such talk should have given me cause to be worried. What possible dangers could I be facing? True, once our conversations stopped, I could clearly hear the raucous laughter coming from the outlying cabins, where the keepers of the station and our driver were engaged in all manner of sin, but I had no sense that they had any intentions of molesting me. In fact, I don't know that they even knew a woman had arrived—certainly no pains were taken for my comfort.

That left Brothers Ephraim and Nicholas.

Already the Saints were snoring—deep, hollow sounds that threatened to keep all of us awake for half the night. In the dark confines of my upper bunk, I smiled. How could I forget those first moments of consciousness when Colonel Brandon pledged to help me? To protect me? My honor, my person, my faith—all of it had been the subject of scrutiny this night, and there he had been at every turn, throwing himself in front of any accusation that might harm me in some way.

I knew Colonel Brandon intended to sleep in the bunk below mine, and I held my body tense, waiting for that moment when I knew he, too, had settled in to sleep. But I heard nothing, felt nothing, and from my vantage point could see nothing but the dancing fire.

Then, there he was, emerging from the kitchen. He glanced in my direction and I closed my eyes, hoping the darkness in the room hid my wakefulness. I'd had them open long enough to see that he carried a tray, and on it the teapot and cup. The sound of snoring was joined by that of the tray being set down on the long, low table in front of the gathered chairs. I hazarded to open my eyes again to see Colonel Brandon, in his shirtsleeves, removing his own boots. He poured what I assumed to be tea from the pot into the cup and settled back into one of the chairs, propping his stockinged feet up on the table.

I knew with the slightest whisper, Colonel Brandon would be at my side. I wanted to thank him, to call him over and thank him for preserving both me and my unborn child, but I did not. Instead, I lay perfectly still, loath to move at all lest I attract his attention, for he could see me from where he sat.

Moments later, when he bowed his head, I knew he was not dozing, but praying. More than that, I knew the God to whom he prayed. I closed my eyes, knowing he would stay there all night. Watching me. Protecting me. Praying for me. And I wished, with all my heart, that I were free to return his love.

CHAPTER **19**

Fifteen days. Never before would I have thought to be grateful morning after morning for clear skies and dry land, but for fifteen days the Lord stretched out a road before us that seemed nothing short of a miracle. I watched through a single, small window as an entire country passed by. Mountains and rivers and endless, endless grass. We had rain that never exceeded being refreshing, sun that did nothing beyond providing warmth, and just enough of a chill at night to bring me to curl up around my growing child and drift to well-earned sleep.

Sometimes we would have the stagecoach to ourselves, but often we shared our journey with a myriad of interesting people—many of whom were businessmen hoping to profit from the burgeoning and increasingly accessible West. Never again, though, were we compelled to create the illusion that we were husband and wife. In fact, neither of us spoke of that night again for the duration of our journey. When not engaged in conversation with a travel companion, we spoke very little beyond the pleasantries of health and sleep. Private Lambert, never far from either of us, took on a role of something between a protector and a manservant, and as we neared the Nebraska border, I began to wonder just how I would get along without him.

Neither Colonel Brandon nor I ever discussed just what would occur once I was safely returned to my parents' home. Perhaps that is why he seemed to be so keen on crafting a distance between us. We continued to stop at regular intervals to rest or change out the horses, and as we came further east, each stop took on a second purpose as Colonel Brandon inquired about any kind of message he might have received. More often than not, a thin envelope with an official seal had been left with the station attendant, and he became increasingly solemn with each missive.

Because we'd taken a different route from the one that had borne me west, I traveled day after day with little knowledge of exactly where we were and how far we would travel before reaching a familiar landmark. Then came the afternoon when, at a short rest break, I learned we would spend the night at Fort Kearny. Until then I'd known only that we were in Nebraska. And Nebraska. And Nebraska. But I knew Fort Kearny. It was on the Platte River, the same river in which I'd been baptized into the church before being wedded to Nathan Fox, just days after leaving my home. Four days, if I remembered correctly. Maybe five. So far away from my husband, so near my parents, and no idea if I would ever have a home with either. When

Nathan and I first married, we needed only a blanket on the ground to have a home, and in the months since leaving him, I found I still required little more. In some of our stops along the trail, I didn't quite have that.

The lodgings at Fort Kearny, however, brought me an unprecedented level of comfort. This was no mere stagecoach station. It was barely twilight when we drove through a fortified wall; soon after, the horses came to a jangling stop outside an impressive white, two-story structure with gabled windows and a wide wraparound porch. This time, rather than the lone, grizzled attendant that so often met us at our disembarking, a man in a sharply fitted military uniform stood at attention. Colonel Brandon saluted him before offering his hand to help me down the folding steps.

Once on the ground, however, I quickly lost my position of being the center of Colonel Brandon's attention. I was handed off to a Mrs. Hilliard, who offered the same pitying lecture as had Mrs. Fennel and the handful of other women I'd encountered along the way before ushering me into the house.

Oh, and what a house.

Not since my last visit to Rachel and Tillman's had I the opportunity to see such elegance and luxury. Velvet and foil paper on the wall, a floral-patterned carpet on the floor, and mahogany wainscoting running the length of the room.

"My goodness, but you're a mess," Mrs. Hilliard said, obviously taking no pains to spare my feelings. "Here's your room—" she opened the first door on the left at the top of the stairs— "with a wrapper robe hanging on that hook right there. Take these things off. That door leads to the back stairs, and I'll have a bath waiting for you. I'll bet it's been ages since you had one."

It had, but my misgivings must have been apparent because she added, "Don't worry. None of the men stay here.

Drivers have a different lodging, and the officer will have his own quarters."

"And Private Lambert?"

"Barracks. Just us women tonight."

The tub was set up in a washroom behind the kitchen, and to my delight I learned that my dress would also receive its long-overdue laundering. It didn't occur to me until later, when I was wearing a clean, cotton gown and nestled between clean, cotton sheets, to wonder what I would wear the next day.

As it happened, I didn't need to worry. I awoke the next morning to streaming sun—the first morning since beginning our journey that I hadn't had to hang my head out of a stage-coach window to see the dawn. Panicked, I jumped out of bed, donned the wrapper, and threw open the door, only to find a surprised Mrs. Hilliard—lace bonnet perfectly in place—on the other side with a silver, dome-covered plate on a tray.

"Well, I thought you'd be hungry for breakfast, but I didn't expect this."

"Have they left me?" Although I couldn't imagine a more ridiculous question.

She offered a motherly, indulgent smile. "Of course not, dear. Your Colonel Brandon has business with the commander here—highly confidential, of course, but something to do with new orders." She spoke this last while leaning over the tray and offering me a wink. "Here's hoping he'll get a commission that'll keep him a little closer to home, eh?"

"Oh," I said, grasping her misunderstanding. "Colonel Brandon and I are not married. I have a husband. In fact—"

"Now, now—" she nudged past me with the tray—"there's them that judge and then there's me. A man gets lonely sta-tioned out in the middle of nowhere. You just be sure he does right by you. I know right well what kind of salary he draws, and it's plenty to set the two of you up someplace nice."

Clearly, by "the two of you" she meant me and the baby. At my look of surprise, she patted my arm. "Now, don't you worry. I'm sure none of those men have noticed a thing, but you can't hide your condition from a woman who has borne as many children as I have."

"Colonel Brandon is not the father of this child."

"Truly?" She looked confused but not convinced.

"Truly," I said, hoping my insistence would protect Colonel Brandon's reputation. "As much as I appreciate your hospitality, I would appreciate in turn if you would respect my privacy in this matter."

If I offended her, she gave no sign, offering instead a saucy wink as she dropped the tray on the bedside table, saying, "Indeed, m'lady," before sashaying out the door.

I knew I should chase her down and force the truth upon her, but at the time I was grateful for a hearty breakfast and a soft bed to which I was allowed to return. In fact, I slept most of that day, disturbed only by the ministrations of Mrs. Hilliard, offered with a knowing look. At supper she informed me that my presence would be required in the dining room at seven o'clock the next morning, and when I awoke, I found my dress and underthings—all clean and starched and pressed—on the foot of my bed. I'd slept through their delivery.

Colonel Brandon was waiting for me at a long oak table when I made my first appearance in the dining room. Although the table could easily accommodate a dozen diners, it was set for only two, with an empty plate to Colonel Brandon's left. He rose to his feet as I walked in, a formality never neglected in all our days of travel.

"Good morning, Mrs. Fox."

"Good morning, Colonel Brandon."

"I hope you slept well."

"I slept all day," I said, slightly embarrassed. "I was afraid you'd moved on without me."

"You are the reason I'm here," he replied, capturing none of the humor of my statement.

"And how exciting to be so close. Three more days, do you think?"

"To the Missouri, yes. I'm not sure how long after the crossing. I'll see to it that I get to a map before you leave."

"Before *I* leave?"

Mrs. Hilliard came through the swinging door with an enormous tray of cooked eggs and bacon. Neither Colonel Brandon nor I spoke until she had served us and made a slow, listening retreat.

"I'm afraid I won't be accompanying you from this point on." He made quite a show of slicing his eggs, creating a mass of yolk and white in the middle of his plate.

"Why not?"

"I'm needed here."

"Here?" It seemed to me, from my limited experience of window gazing, that Fort Kearny was a well-established entity. I could not imagine any institution needing Colonel Brandon more than I did.

"It may come as a surprise, Mrs. Fox, that there are matters in this world more pressing than your own. We are a country still at war in Utah, and quite possibly heading into another one. Brigham Young might have threatened a skirmish in the West, but relations between the North and the South are commanding our attention as well. I assure you, the stakes there are much higher."

I was thoroughly chastised by the end of his statement, unable to do more than pick at my own food.

"So I'm to take the stage alone?" I tried not to sound accusatory, but apparently I failed because Colonel Brandon could not meet my eyes.

"I've given over your charge to Private Lambert. Or if you prefer, I can see if we cannot find a woman to serve as your escort and chaperone."

"No." Perhaps in remembering Mrs. Hilliard's insinuating, I spoke too quickly, as Colonel Brandon seemed taken aback. "I am quite comfortable traveling with Private Lambert. He is quite the capable gentleman, like traveling with one's brother."

"Younger brother."

"Yes, but quite capable."

In Private Lambert, we found a common affection, and a companionable silence fell between us. Mrs. Hilliard came and went, bringing tea and milk and muffins, clueless as to how much it all tasted like dust. Had I been in any other frame of mind, it might have been delicious, and if Colonel Brandon's intake gave any indication, it was. Then again, I matched him bite for bite, tasting nothing.

After breakfast, I went to my room to wash up, and when I came downstairs, Colonel Brandon was waiting to escort me outside. I still had only my one small bag. Colonel Brandon took it from me and handed it over to a young boy in a blue cap, who offered an amateur salute and was given one in return.

"He's about your son's age, isn't he?" I took the arm Colonel Brandon held out for me.

"I'd wager," he said, and we walked out onto the front porch.

Rather than the large, rumbling stagecoach that had

driven us these past eight hundred miles, a sleek, black carriage pulled by a team of six matched horses awaited.

"It will make for a much smoother ride." He pointed out the features of the wider wheel base and the lighter cab.

"But just as fast?"

"Four mornings from today you'll ferry across the Missouri. Then—I checked the map—about half a day's ride and you should be home."

"To Kanesville?"

"To Kanesville."

"Then even sooner. My parents live about ten miles north of there."

"Then perhaps you'll be there for lunch."

"If Papa's up for it. If he'll even see me. If he's even alive."

"Now stop." With his free hand, Colonel Brandon cupped my chin and tilted my face toward him. "You haven't traveled all this way to let such doubts enter your head now. You will go home, and you will be welcomed with open arms. And I'd give anything to be a part of it."

"But duty calls here?"

"It does." From the look in his eyes, I couldn't be sure if he was fulfilling a duty or embracing escape.

I turned my face away from his touch and looked to the team of horses that stood so patiently in the cool morning.

"Then I must thank you for bringing me this far. I'll be grateful—" I turned to him—"really, forever, that God brought me to you." I meant for those to be my parting words and attempted to take my hand from his arm, but he trapped it, covering it with his.

"We have the same prayer."

"Oh, Colonel Brandon—"

"Please, can't you call me Charles?"

"No," I said, feeling my own heart break in his eyes.

There was a great deal of bustling activity at the front of the house as Private Lambert arrived with the man I assumed to be our driver—another soldier with an even younger face. Still, Colonel Brandon pulled me closer, tilting his head toward mine.

"Surely you know how I feel about you," he said, stating a fact as plainly as any I knew.

I responded with another. "I am a married woman."

"For how long?"

"In my husband's eyes, for eternity. In the eyes of the law, until I choose it to be otherwise. In the eyes of God, for now. Today, and that's all I am promised."

He stepped away. "Forgive me. I must sound like some sort of vulture."

"Not at all." I reached out, tugging at his sleeve. "I wish, sometimes, that it could be different. That we—that I—" But I stopped my speech the same way I had stopped this very thought so many times before. To wish otherwise was to deny the blessings God had given me so far—my daughters and the child I now carried. As kind and caring as Colonel Brandon was, I felt none of the stirring I'd felt the first time I saw Nathan Fox—or the last time, for that matter—and I would not allow myself to wonder if I stirred such thoughts in him.

"May I write to you, then?" he asked. "While you are with your parents?"

"Of course."

"And will you write to me? I'd like to know—" he fidgeted—"about the baby."

"I will." In fact, I was already looking forward to the first letter.

"Very well." In an instant, he was once again the military

commander, standing straight with nothing in his posture to indicate he had anything other than soldiering and strategy on his mind. Only his eyes betrayed a softness of spirit, and of all people on the earth, perhaps I alone would recognize that vulnerability. He took my hand for a final time and raised it to his lips, kissing first the back, then turning it over to kiss my palm. His moustache tickled, and the intimacy of the gesture made me want to flinch away, but I did not. Instead, rooted in place, I closed my eyes, concentrating on that place where we touched, and waiting—hoping, actually—for a racing of my pulse. But I felt nothing but safe and steady, even in the face of venturing off alone.

CHAPTER 20

The last time I crossed this river, it had been on a narrow raft of lashed-together logs piloted by a stranger while I stood wrapped in my future husband's arms. The echo of my father's voice—calling my name into the darkness—still rings in my ears. When I crossed it again, I stood on a four-hundred-square-foot barge, alongside a sleek carriage and a team of horses, accompanied—guarded—by a boy soldier from the United States Army. I cringe to think of the girl I was on that raft—reckless and thoughtless, leaving her home and family with no promise of a future other than what she wanted to believe. Years later, though, these same traits were bringing me home, and while my innocence might have been gone, my faith was stronger than it had ever been. God himself had been with me for every step in both directions.

I watched the eastern shore of the Missouri River approach at a maddeningly slow pace. More than once, Private Lambert actually clutched my arm as I was leaning forward in some sub-conscious attempt to hasten the barge.

"We were lucky to procure such an early crossing," I said to Private Lambert when he'd steadied me to my feet for the last time.

"Yes, ma'am," he replied. By then he had his hands once again clasped behind his back, and he rocked on his heels.

"Then a short drive along the coast."

"Map makes it look like about four hours."

"And I'll be home."

"Yes, ma'am. You will."

And in the end, it was just that easy. To think, after eight years of love and loss, of heartache and hope, all that remained of my journey home was little more than a Sunday drive. By the time we disembarked on the eastern shore, the sun was fully up with the promise of a warm day. The soldier appointed to be our driver had orders to stay on the other shore, so it was just Private Lambert and me riding with the black leather top of the carriage folded back.

"It's all looking familiar," I said, though I spoke more from wishful thinking. I was hardly well traveled as a child, and any landscape will change over the course of nearly a decade. How could one stand of trees seem more familiar than another after such an absence? Still, I rode leaning eagerly forward in my seat, waiting for some memory to merge with what I saw before my eyes.

And then, not long after the sun had crept to its apex, a road.

"Stop!"

Private Lambert brought the horses—we drove with just two—to a halt. "Do we turn here, ma'am?"

I stood, placing my hand on his bony shoulder to steady myself. "No. You see this road to the right? That leads into town."

"So, left, ma'am?"

I shook my head. "Straight ahead. Follow this road, and we should head straight to my father's farm."

Once I sat down, Private Lambert gave the horses a loose slap of the reins. I saw nothing of the path before us because I closed my eyes in prayer.

Oh, Father, thank you for this journey. For your guiding hand and the forgiveness for my disobedience. Whatever happens now— should my father be ready to receive me—is already in your plan. May he be gracious to me, O Lord. Give me a humble heart and the right words. Restore us to each other, just as—

"Is this it, ma'am?"

I kept my eyes closed, knowing what I wished to see upon opening them. A low rock wall extending on either side of a narrow gateway. A wide yard behind it and a loose-stone pathway leading to the front door of a small house with a sloped roof.

"Ma'am?"

And it was there. All of it. The house appeared a little more weathered, but the rock wall had been built tenfold what it was when I'd left. There were the barns and a few cattle grazing in the field beyond the yard.

Tears sprang to my eyes, and my breath came to me in short, shallow gasps.

"I don't know that I can get this rig through the gate. Is there another—?"

"I want to walk," I said, scrambling to gather myself.

"Well, hold on, then." In a flash, Private Lambert was out of the carriage and around to my side, ready to hand me down before I had even gained enough composure to stand. "Are you ready for this?"

I looked down into his sweet face—such a good and honest boy. Then I realized: he was only three years younger than I and the same age Nathan had been when I agreed to be his wife. How could I not have known there were Private Lamberts in the world?

"I'm ready."

He took my hand and, in the bumbling way we had somehow perfected, lifted me down from the carriage. I stood beside it, smoothing my dress and straightening my bonnet while he fetched my bag.

"Shall I walk you to the door, ma'am?"

"No." One less thing to explain.

"As you wish, but I'll stay here until you are safely inside."

"Very well." Before he could turn away, I reached up, placing both of my hands on his soft, shaven face and pulling it to me. His second cheek was still burning from my kiss on the first, when I said, "You're a fine man, Private Lambert."

"And you are the . . . well, the bravest woman I know."

Smiling, I picked up my bag and walked through my father's gate. Not ten steps in, the front door opened, and there she was.

My mother.

She was smaller than I remembered, and not only because of the distance between us or the few inches I'd grown since leaving. More than a matter of stature, her very presence seemed to have diminished. She held up her hand to shield her eyes, looking so very tired, like she'd been called out of the house at the dawn after a sleepless night rather than a warm spring afternoon. A shadow lurked beneath her skin; her hair had taken on the paleness of gray. She might have lived ten years for every day I'd been gone, but every minute of that time disappeared when her eyes met mine.

I don't know who started running first or who said the other's name or when the satchel I'd lugged across the country became a forgotten mass in the stone path. Her arms were around me, and while I could not recall a time when the two of us had engaged in such an embrace, neither could I imagine what power could ever rip me away from this love.

We wept and wept, our faces buried in each other's shoulder, tears soaking each other's collar, and when we pulled away to look into each other's eyes, we remained separate for only a matter of seconds before falling once again into a clutching embrace.

At some point I realized she was saying, "You're home. . . . You're home. . . . You're home. . . ."

And I said nothing, only accepting the subtle transference of power in which I became the comforter to this woman, for she had now fallen against me, and my body supported the weight of both my child and my mother. Never had I felt more complete. And yet, of course, there was one piece missing.

"Papa?" I had no idea how to frame my question.

Mama took my hand. Then, noticing my fingers, she gasped, then stepped back, seeing my pregnancy through a mother's knowing eyes. "There's so much—just so much—to tell you . . . and to ask. I don't know where to start."

"Start with Papa," I urged.

I knew she didn't want to. The shadow was back, and she looked for all the world like a creature seeking escape.

"Please, Mama. I have so much to tell you—both of you."

She wiped a tear from her cheek and tugged my hand. "Come inside."

Nothing had changed. Not a thing. Same table, same three chairs, same ladder leading up to my old attic bedroom. I might just as well have been coming home from school rather than escaping from another life. The calico curtains might have been a bit more faded and the rag rug worn a bit thinner, but the afternoon sun illuminated the same dancing dust motes of my childhood.

"Wait here," Mama said.

Instinctively I obeyed, though I did have a pang of conscience when I thought about poor Private Lambert at that gate. I took a peek out the door, however, and saw the back of the carriage as it rounded the corner. My satchel had found its way to the front porch.

"Camilla?"

I turned.

"He'd like to see you."

I'd never been summoned into my father's presence without a sense of fear. My earliest memories are of him looming over me, blocking out the sun or casting a shadow across the ceiling as I cowered at his feet. His booming chastisements still echo in my ears; my body still tenses when I recall the occasions—rare as they were—when I was punished with a switch. But it was an altogether different fear that gripped me now. An unfamiliar trepidation that turned Mama's well-swept floor into swampland with each hesitant step.

He was in their bedroom. It was, perhaps, the first I'd ever seen him in this room, as he'd been always up before the sun, and I'd often been lulled to sleep by the sound of his puttering on one project or another. This room lacked the light streaming into the rest of the house; heavy curtains—these were new—drawn across the window led me into perpetual night.

"Arlen, dear?" Mama said. "She's come home."

Had I not seen Mama kneel at the bedside, I might never have known where to find my father. The man who had once been this tower barely made a ripple under the familiar, faded quilt I'd known since childhood. His head—as bald as ever—and his shoulders were propped up against the headboard, but it seemed ages before my eyes adjusted to the light enough for me to make out the features of his face. Then I realized, my eyes were fine, as much as they could be in that shadowed room. It was his face, the very hue of his complexion, that played tricks with my eyes. When my mother told me he was sick, I'd expected to see him pale against the pillow, but I did not—could not—prepare myself for the man I saw.

It appeared as if, during my absence, some force had come upon him to drain his body of all it ever held. The coarse, sun-touched skin that had stretched across his square jaw and thick neck now hung in parchmentlike folds. And the color—dark yellow, almost to the point of orange, given the darkness.

"Pa—" The rest of the word caught in my throat. I swallowed it on my way to the other side of the bed, where I knelt, reaching for the hand that sat listless on the bed.

At my touch he turned to look at me with heavy-lidded eyes. His lips moved, emitting some semblance of my name. Had Mama not announced me, he would not have known me, as his face held no hint of recognition.

"Yes, Papa." I brought his hand to my lips, trying not to recoil at the clamminess of the waxy skin.

He said my name again, more clearly this time, and brought his other hand up to touch my face.

"I'm here. I'm home."

"Tell him," Mama said.

I looked at her, questioning, across my father.

"Tell him," she repeated.

235

Papa hadn't taken his eyes off me. All those thoughts about what I would do, what I would say if I ever found myself in my father's presence again balled up in my throat. I closed my eyes, seeing nothing but the man I used to know. The room was silent save for the sound of his labored breath, but I heard his voice, hearkening back to our past. Anger, yes—accusation, even—but beneath it all, love for me. Certainly, somewhere in his heart there had been love. Now more than ever, I needed to believe it because it seemed quite clear that I would never hear him speak the words.

"I love you, Papa. And I know you love me."

"It's not enough," Mama said, "to give him peace."

I dug in. "I'm here now, hoping that you can forgive me for my disobedience. I was young, and I was stupid and just so, so . . . blind."

Papa turned his head, looking pleadingly at his wife.

"No," Mama said to me, but she gave me no direction.

"And I've been happy, Papa. Since I left." Tears now streamed freely down my face, and my lips moved against his hand. "I married a man who—who loves me very much. And I love him. We have two daughters—you have two grand-daughters, Melissa and Lottie, and they are so, so beautiful. God has blessed me."

Here I stopped, overwhelmed with the effort of seeing only the goodness in my life. Papa was looking at me again, tears pooled in his eyes, and I felt his hand clutch at mine, and I knew.

"I forgive you, Papa."

His grip went slack and he closed his eyes. I looked across at Mama and felt her approval. I suppose I could have listed his transgressions: his anger, his judgment, his coldhearted refusal to read my letters. But how could I have known the extent to which he had tormented himself, blamed himself since that night he held his shotgun and watched his only daughter disappear?

I said it again. "I forgive you," and had I not been kneeling, I would have been thrown to the floor by the tide of grace that flowed between us. He could not speak, so I spoke for us both. "And I accept that you forgive me."

Minutes later, as I laid my head on the faded quilt next to him, I felt his hand in my hair—a gesture infused with more affection than any I'd received in all my years living under his roof. In my mind's eye I saw Nathan and our daughters, how they were constantly in his arms, on his lap, how he lavished them with such open, exquisite love. He was their world and their light. Why did I ever think I could take them away from that and bring them here?

"He wouldn't let me read your letters," Mama said, but I lifted my face and hushed her.

"It's forgiven," I whispered. "And now I can tell you everything myself."

CHAPTER 21

For the rest of that day and into the night, I relived my life from the moment I met Nathan Fox on the pathway to school until the moment I got word that Papa was ill. But for every tale I told, I spared them from another. Mama's eyes filled with tears as I told her about becoming Nathan's wife in a ceremony on the banks of the Platte River, but I mentioned nothing about my baptism in those same waters. I shared every step of the journey to Zion without mention of the graves we dug along the way. Mother cringed when I told her about the season of locusts, lifting her little feet off the floor as if she, too, felt them crunching beneath each step, and her eyes filled with wonder when I told her of the miracle of the gulls that came to eat them all.

Papa dozed in and out, though I held his hand as I brought his granddaughters to life within that room. "Melissa's birthday is this month. She'll be seven. And my little Lottie is four and a half." I struggled with my own tears as I recalled Melissa's wide, questioning eyes and Lottie's sweet, bubbling spirit. "Then we had a little boy."

Papa's eyes lit up at that, and he moved his lips to speak.

"He didn't live very long. But he was beautiful, and we named him Arlen, after you, Papa."

"But God has blessed her with another one," Mama said, her lips trembling with her smile. "And when will it be here?"

"Soon," I said, as if the word would give Papa the hope that he needed.

Mama brought in a simple supper that we ate at Papa's bedside—just bread and cheese and tea. For Papa she had a bowl of lukewarm beef broth with which she soaked cubes of bread and gently laid them on his tongue.

"Hasn't been able to take anything solid in nearly a month," she whispered, as if the man wasn't inches away.

I wondered, of course, what the doctor had told her about Papa's illness, what it was and if there was any hope for recovery, but I would not ask her within his hearing. In truth, I had only to look into his eyes to see that there was very little hope to be had.

After we'd eaten, I volunteered to take the tray into the kitchen, allowing Mama time to see to Papa's needs. Forgoing any soap and water, I simply wiped the plates and cups clean with a towel I found exactly where I knew it would be. In the next room, Mama's voice spoke so tenderly, quiet rejoicing at a daughter's return. Meanwhile, I, the daughter, felt every moment of every year lived since I was last in this kitchen. I sank into the chair that had been mine every day of my young life and ran my finger along the familiar grain of the wood.

"So where are they?" Mama's voice invaded my silence.

I didn't look up. "Who?"

"This wonderful husband and these beautiful girls."

"It's a long journey, Mama. And expensive, to take the stage."

"And you couldn't wait until this child was born?"

"It would be too late in the fall. Too dangerous to travel, and I didn't know how sick Papa was. I couldn't take the chance."

Then she was in front of me, sitting across the table, her dry, coarse hand forcing me to look at her. "You left us, Camilla, without a thought. And your father—he was so, so hurt. And bitter. I'll never forget coming home with that first letter. *Running*, if you can imagine, wanting to share it with him. Wanting us to open it together, and he took it away."

"And sent it back to me. Unopened."

"So you sent another."

"When Melissa was born."

"I tried to hide that one, but it must have been written on my face because when I got back from town, he took it. And after that, he—he forbade me to even go to our post again."

"Oh, Mama—"

"So I don't even know how many letters you wrote."

"Two a year. Every year. I have them now, if you want to read them. Or if you think he'd like to read them."

She smiled. "I think that would be nice." Then, her smile gone, "I still don't understand why you had your change of heart, even before you knew he was ill."

That was the moment she became not only my mother but the first Christian woman I'd encountered since leaving home. I don't think I realized until that moment just how much hurt I had been carrying at Nathan's betrayal, how humiliated I felt at being replaced in my husband's bed. These seemed the burdens to be borne by a woman, yet here at the table I felt once again like a little girl. But she knew what it meant to love a man, to devote herself and her life to him, even without the promise of that love in return. When had I ever seen my father speak a soft word to her? Not once had I ever seen them engaged in an embrace that was anything other than polite. Yet she loved him; I knew she did. He'd left her, in some ways, years before I did, and he was about to leave her again.

I took a deep breath. "He took a second wife."

Mama's brow furrowed. "You divorced him?"

"No."

"Then how—?"

"Another wife, Mama. A second wife, in addition to me."

I followed her thoughts as realization dawned. Confusion, disgust, and then sadness. Not pity, but the kind of sadness a mother feels when her child hurts.

"Oh, darling." She was up and around, my face buried in her soft bosom. "We heard about such things, and your father— just beside himself with worry. If he knew . . ."

"Please, Mama," I pleaded, every bit the little girl, "don't tell him."

She held me for a while—until she felt better, at least— and then sat down again, drawing her chair close to mine so she could maintain her touch, and asked, "How does that happen?"

"It's part of the teachings of the prophet." I surprised myself with the utter calmness in my voice as I went on to explain the beliefs my husband held so dear. That we would continue our marriage in heaven—ours and every marriage he entered into on earth. How he, my husband, would call me from my grave, and I would spend eternity bearing his children until he himself became a god.

"And you believed all of this?"

"Some of it, a little. For a time. But then I remembered everything you taught me, Mama. I went back to my Bible; I came back to Christ. And then I came home."

"What about your girls?"

"I want to bring them here, if I can. As soon as I can." I told her about the danger I faced as an apostate, my fear that my daughters would grow up under those teachings. "I have to bring them far away, and I had to know that I had a home to bring them to, because I have no way—no means at all—to support us."

Mama cradled my face in her hands. "Of course you may bring them here. Will your husband allow such a thing?"

I balled my fists. "I'll make him understand."

"And what about this little one?" She reached her hand to my stomach, and I felt the baby move. Our eyes met and we smiled, as if she'd felt it too.

"He doesn't know about this baby."

"Will you tell him?"

"Not unless he comes to me."

"He'd better not."

Two days later, quietly, in his sleep, Papa died.

I marvel, still, at God's timing. His grace. One more day of indecision, a day of rain, a broken wheel, or an injured horse—any or all of those things, and my father would not have died in peace. As it was, I never told him about Nathan's plural marriage, nor the danger I faced, nor the blasphemous teachings that were the milk of my daughters' faith. For all he knew, I'd come back solely to see him, and that settled well with me.

As his strength would allow, I continued to tell him funny stories—silly games Nathan played with the girls or funny things they said. I told him about Kimana, the Indian woman who shared our home, and about her deep, abiding knowledge of God as Creator. I recounted legends, making my eyes wide and round, changing my voice to match her flat native tone. I described the beauty of the Great Salt Lake—the inland ocean with the foaming shore and the violet sky. In short, I gathered every pleasant moment I could conjure and found myself overwhelmed with how many I had.

"God has been good to me, Papa." They were the last words I ever said to him.

Since Papa's illness, Mama'd kept on a crew of six hired men to run the farm, and that morning she sent one of them into town to fetch the doctor.

"I know it won't do no good," she said, "but I just figure he should know."

People who do not know my family—specifically who do not know my mother—might think it odd to see the woman who had just lost her husband of over thirty years so detached at his departing. She shed few tears, and those she did were wiped away quickly, not soon to be replaced. If anything, her manner became more brusque, her lips set in a permanent, thin frown, like all of this was just a bother. But ours had never been a house filled with joy, and if tears are the counterpart to laughter, it is little wonder that both were scarce within our walls.

That very afternoon, Dr. Davis walked across the street to tell Elias Dobbins, who served as our town's coroner, mortician, and sometimes barber, and the two of them came out together in Dobbins's wagon, bringing a casket and other necessities to prepare Papa for his viewing. I'd known Dr. Davis since I was a child, of course, but Dobbins had moved to town just a few years ago. Still, a flicker of recognition crossed his face when Mama introduced me, and he greeted me with "Oh, *you're* the daughter."

The smattering of friends and neighbors who heard the news and came out to offer condolences met me with some measure of the same. Of course they knew my story—most of them knew me—and each new visit seemed to be as much about seeing the wayward daughter as an outpouring of sympathy. Thank goodness my pregnancy could still be concealed by a full skirt. That would be another test of the community's goodwill, one that I would happily save for another day. One by one the women came, bearing loaves of bread or pies or platters of sliced meat. They set their offerings on the table and went straight to my mother, taking her in an awkward embrace dictated by Christian duty, and then they came to me.

"How awful you had to come home to such tragedy."

"Thank God you made it back in time to see him before he passed."

I could see in their eyes they would much prefer a story about how I'd come to be here for my father's funeral rather than some dull tale about his last hours on earth. But I only smiled as warmly as I could manage and thanked them for their loving concern.

Between visits, the day charged on with custom and efficiency. The furniture in our parlor was pushed back against the walls, making an open area in the middle of the room where people could gather in sight of the casket, which was set up on Dobbins's tall, narrow table in front of the cold fireplace. Meanwhile, the bed Papa died in was stripped—one of the women took the bedding home to wash—and the very mattress and pillows removed. By evening I would hardly have known this was the same room. The curtains were open, as were the windows, and the sour smell of disease was already drifting away.

Just as people had trickled in throughout the day, so they left with the onset of darkness. Many had offered to stay the night, sitting up with Mama in the parlor, but the obvious relief in their eyes when Mama turned them down belied the sincerity of their offers.

We stood in the yard watching the last of our company leave. Mama's hand took mine, and I think we both loathed the idea of going back inside, but there was not much else we could do. Silently, we turned and walked through the front door, finding ourselves in a kitchen full of more food than had ever been in this house.

"Are you hungry?" Mama asked.

"Starving, actually."

She assembled a plate of food for me, a smaller one for herself, and we took our places at the table. I dove in, shaking with fatigue as I took those first bites, but Mama simply sat, her hands in her lap, staring at the center of the table.

"I did love him, you know."

"I know you did, Mama."

"It wasn't easy, always. He made it almost impossible sometimes . . . but you know that."

We ate in silence after that. I cleaned my plate down to the crumbs while Mama barely picked at her food.

"I'm going in to sit with him," she said at last, when she could no longer keep up the pretense of eating. Leaving her full plate on the table, something I'd never imagined her capable of doing, she stood, squared her shoulders, and stared at the door leading into the parlor.

I stood too and said, "I'll go in with you."

We left the lamp on the table, as the parlor had its own

glow coming from a dozen or more candles throughout the room. Mama went straight to the casket and I followed. We stood side by side looking at the masklike face of my father.

"He hated being sick," Mama said. "He wouldn't admit it at first, that anything was wrong. Just kept workin' and workin'. Then one day he couldn't even get himself out the door."

"He's not sick now. Just think about it. He's with the Lord, full of such peace and joy."

"If he is, it's because God's put him to work doin' somethin'. Can't see him happy any other way."

We spent the night in that parlor, sitting together on the sofa, leaning against each other, dozing on and off until the dawn. Mama was adamant that Papa be buried that next day, but not on our property. We were due to arrive at our small church cemetery by nine o'clock in the morning for a short ceremony, followed by a gathering at our home.

Sometime in the middle of the night, I realized I had nothing suitable to wear to a funeral of any kind—not even a small gathering of people who were virtually strangers to me. To my humble relief, Mrs. Dobbins arrived early the next morning with a simple black dress for me.

"Elias mentioned your . . . circumstances," she said.

I thanked her and went into my parents' stripped room to change. Mother was already dressed in a simple, sturdy black frock that she had begun sewing the first day Papa couldn't get out of bed.

In the meantime, Elias Dobbins and the hired hands transferred Papa's casket to Dobbins's wagon and headed for the cemetery. Mama and I were driven in our neighbor's carryall. We arrived to find some dozen mourners, though it was their presence more than their demeanor that would classify them as such. Nobody wept, though it did warm my heart to see how sweetly my mother was received. At some point it occurred to me that I might have better served my father by staying home today, as I could not escape the curious sidelong glances of those gathered under the pretense of paying respect to the man being lowered into the ground.

It wasn't until Reverend Harris stood at the head of the grave and cleared his throat that the eyes and attention of those gathered turned to the circumstances at hand. The minute he began to speak, I was transported back to my childhood, when I'd spent every Sunday morning of my life in a wooden pew listening to men who sounded just like this. This morning, like all of those, the pastor's voice held so little life, such a lack of passion, that I found my mind wandering even at my own father's funeral. I know he quoted Scripture after Scripture: the vanity of life spoken of in Ecclesiastes and the reminder that we had come from dust and to dust would return.

I wanted to scream. All around me heads nodded in solemn agreement. Meaninglessness and dust. But my father's life had not been meaningless. He loved his work, loved his farm, loved his family, and though his stern nature masked his passion, loved his Lord. He was not dust. His body, yes, was now an empty shell—it had nearly become such the moment he fell ill. But he himself was beautifully restored. Healed. Why couldn't Reverend Harris speak of that?

I had fled this church, run from these teachings, chasing the light in Nathan Fox's eyes—a light I didn't see in a single person gathered here. I thought about the promises given to the Mormons. No good Saint ever considered himself as meaningless dust. His work on earth bought him glory hereafter. He would be glorified, blessed with wives and children, himself a god. None of it true, but all of it enticing. Why, then, at the funeral of a good Christian man must we dwell on the emptiness of life? Who would trade deity for dust?

My hands clenched into fists at my side, and God himself held my mouth shut. Somehow, above the arguments whirling in my head, I heard Reverend Harris speak my name. Torn from my silent tirade, I looked to him, questioning.

"I have one more Scripture I would share on your behalf."

It was, as far as I can recall, the first time he had ever spoken to me directly.

"I should like to read the words of our Lord from the fourteenth chapter of the Gospel of John." The pages of his Bible rustled in the spring breeze as he read the familiar words: "'Let not your heart be troubled: ye believe in God, believe also in me. In my Father's house are many mansions: if it were not so, I would have told you. I go to prepare a place for you. And if I go and prepare a place for you, I will come again, and receive you unto myself; that where I am, there ye may be also. And whither I go ye know, and the way ye know.'"

He closed his Bible, holding the place with one finger, making the book an extension of himself. "Camilla, Ruth, let not your hearts be troubled." Then, to those gathered, "Our friend and neighbor Arlen Deardon has been received unto Christ. Even now, he resides in the house of our Lord, in a place prepared for him. Such a place is prepared for all of us. Jesus Christ has said it is so."

This time when the heads nodded, I joined them, privately humbled at my criticism of Reverend Harris's message.

"There are those," he continued, looking at me again, "who would have you believe that the hereafter is a mystery, and they would seek to solve that mystery by creating their own vision. But we must be ever vigilant to seek only the truth in Scripture. Jesus promises to give us what we long for every day.

A home. After life's long journey, we are given a home. What more could man want?"

The question hung between us, but I felt no accusation. Only questioning, as if he needed confirmation. Silently I held out my hand, requesting his Bible, which, after a brief raising of his eyebrows in surprise, he handed to me.

Carefully, I took the book, keeping the same passage marked with my own finger. "May I continue?" I asked, startled at the strength of my own voice.

"Of course," Reverend Harris said, his eyes full of knowing.

"'Thomas saith unto him, Lord, we know not whither thou goest; and how can we know the way? Jesus saith unto him, I am the way, the truth, and the life: no man cometh unto the Father, but by me.'"

I was given no chorus of agreement, which I attribute to the crowd's shock at having a woman—a recently heretical woman—read Scripture at the funeral of a good Christian man. It was my mother who responded first, saying, "Amen."

Gently, Reverend Harris retrieved his Bible from me. "I would hope that thus is the testimony of all gathered here."

At that, a subdued amen tumbled through the crowd, my own affirmation a choked whisper.

"Then it would seem," he continued, "that we gather today to acknowledge another homecoming as well. Just as Arlen Deardon is welcomed to his mansion in heaven, so is his daughter welcomed into our lives. Let us gather together in rejoicing."

CHAPTER 22

The rest of the day following Papa's service was an endless round of curiosity veiled as sympathy, much like the previous day, though the presence of Reverend Harris proved to be a comfort in the end.

"I should like to have a long talk with you sometime, young lady," he said when given the opportunity to corner me in the parlor. "I feel you have much to teach me."

I smiled at the compliment. "I don't claim to know very much. Only what I have read in the Scriptures."

"I mean about *them*, their teachings. Is it, after all, so very different from what we as Christians believe?"

For a fleeting moment I felt such pity for this man, a man

of God, to have even the slightest hint of doubt. "One wouldn't think so, at first," I said by way of sparing his pride.

"And so it is a movement birthed in deception."

"I can think of no better description."

"May I ask, then, what it was that brought you back to the truth?"

"The Holy Spirit," I answered without hesitation. "God never left me."

Thankfully, our friends had mercy on us and our house was empty just after noon. Mama and I were both walking dead on our feet, and it was Reverend Harris's wife who finally shooed the last of our guests out the front door.

While we were at the graveside service, helpful neighbors had come into our home, sweeping it from top to bottom and organizing the gifts of food that had been brought. This, of course, proved a great help during the time of reception, but it wasn't until Mama and I found ourselves once again alone that we realized the greatest favor of all. The room that had served as a place of sickness for so long had itself been renewed— scrubbed clean, with fresh, light curtains hanging in the place of those meant to block out the sun. A new, plump tick sat on the bed, covered with a thick, luxurious-looking quilt. Nothing in the world had ever looked so inviting. The countless sad hours piled on top of each other, and in one motion, Mama and I dropped down on top of it.

Side by side we rested, holding hands, cooled by the afternoon breeze coming through the open window.

"When you was very little," she said, speaking to the ceiling, "I would put you down for an afternoon nap in here. And I would tell your father, 'Oops! I just heard the baby cry,' and then I'd sneak in here and lie down beside you. You was always fast asleep, but I'd pretend you needed me, just to get some rest for myself."

"I do the same with my girls." My mind filled with visions of those long, snowbound days when we might cuddle and rest for an entire afternoon.

Mama squeezed my hand. "I can't wait for you to bring them home."

"They'll love it here. Lottie especially. She loves cows. She might prove to be a better hand than I ever was."

I paused, giving Mama time to respond with something—maybe a reassurance that I'd always done the best I could or even a joke about just how inept I was at dairy farming—but all I heard was a low, whistling snore. Her grip went lax, and I turned on my side to look at her. Lying down, her face smoothed back to the one I knew as a child. Never beautiful, but familiar. I curled up beside her, drawing my knees as close as I could to my body, and after a few minutes wondering if I wasn't actually too tired to sleep, found myself slipping into sweet, safe darkness.

We slept until morning—late morning, actually. I awoke with such a pressing need, I worried I would not make it out across the yard in time. I threw myself off the bed, leaving Mama in a fit of childish giggles, and flung open our front door. The sight of the man on the other side nearly made me lose my battle with the morning's necessities. Not that he was frighten-ing, just unexpected, and this sight of him with his hand raised midknock made me think that perhaps it was he who woke us.

"Good morning." He actually tipped his hat, revealing a head full of thick, ash-gray, close-cropped hair. "Is Mrs. Deardon at home?"

"Yes, yes," I said, ushering him in. I yelled, "Mama!" over my shoulder before excusing myself and, as dignified as I could, blustering past him. I made sure the door was firmly closed behind me before tearing out for the privy.

Later, relieved, I walked back into the house to see Mama and our guest sitting at the table, an open portfolio in front of them and the kettle hissing on the stove.

"So that *is* you, Miss Camilla. I thought I'd heard that you were back, but one can never take too much stock in rumors; at least I've always thought so."

I looked at him harder.

"You don't remember me, do you?" He held out his hand. "Michael Bostwick. My son, Michael Junior, was your schoolmate."

"Ah yes," I said, barely able to recollect a soft, round-faced boy who even as a child wasn't nearly as handsome as the distinguished gentleman now in our kitchen.

"Mr. Bostwick's son is at Harvard," Mama said, offering an oddly unnecessary bit of news.

"Law school." He puffed with pride. "Like his father."

"Well, that's wonderful," I said, unconvinced.

"I'm here to go over the details of your father's will. Oh, pardon me—so sorry for your loss."

"Thank you."

The hissing kettle begged for my attention, and I busied myself making tea while Mr. Bostwick settled into his place at the table.

"You need to join us, Camilla," Mama said. "This concerns you as much as it does me."

"Very well," I said, stalling. Something about Mama's cool, calm demeanor unnerved me. It was as if every minute of the past few days—the past few months, maybe, with Papa's illness and death—had led up to this moment. I poured each of us a steaming mug of tea and found a bowl full of assorted muffins left over from yesterday's meal. Mr. Bostwick looked over the selection with a critical eye, finally choosing a perfectly rounded specimen. He brought his tea to his lips, sniffed, blew, and slurped before setting the mug down in front of him.

"Now," he said, "you'll be happy to know that I have a buyer for the farm."

"You're selling the farm?" Nothing—not one word—had been said about this as even a possibility, let alone a plan, but from the look of relief on Mama's face, it was clear this came as no surprise.

"It's what your papa wanted," she said. "And me, too. I can't run it on my own. Don't want to even if I could."

"Who's buying it?" I tried to picture strangers sitting at our table, cooking at Mama's stove. But then, I'd abandoned this home long ago. Perhaps I had no right to question.

"Nobody you know." Mr. Bostwick shuffled through papers as he talked. "A family moving into the community. Cousins of the Lindgrens, I believe."

"It doesn't matter," Mama said, recapturing his attention. "How soon can they be here?"

"Mama, where are we going to live?"

The *we* seemed to have caught her attention, and I instantly regretted my selfishness. Of course she'd had no way to know of my arrival or my plans. Still, I was here now, and pregnant, and if nothing else, she needed a roof over her head. Like her, I turned to Mr. Bostwick.

"You have options." He found more papers to shuffle. "Mr. Deardon—God rest his soul—owned a building in town that he currently rents to, well, me. My office is downstairs, and since my wife's passing, I live in the apartment above. You would be perfectly within your legal rights to evict me from the living quarters, if you would like to occupy those for yourselves. But I would appreciate some notice—"

"I have no plans to evict you from your home, Mr. Bostwick," Mama said.

"Which I appreciate," he said, lifting his mug of tea in tribute. "Not to mention that my continued tenancy will provide a modest income. Now, your husband—your father, Miss Camilla—also owned the adjoining lot, which is currently vacant, and a smaller piece of land right on the edge of town, just behind the school."

My head swam with all of this. "How long has he owned these properties?"

More paper shuffling, but it was Mama who provided the answer. "He was always a good businessman. I knew about the lots in town, but not about the other."

"It was purchased about six years ago." He looked up at me. "Maybe soon after you left?"

"So you'd have a place to come home to," Mama said softly. "Do you think, Mr. Bostwick, with the sale of the farm and the lot next to your building we'd be able to build a house on that land?"

"Mama, I don't want to be a financial burden to you."

"Now wait," Mr. Bostwick said, "you have an inheritance of your own coming to you."

"I do?" I wrung my hands as I always did when I was nervous, especially worrying the place where my fingers had been amputated. I caught Mr. Bostwick's eyes staring, a hint of discomfort in them, and I stopped, bringing them to rest in my lap.

"The will was last updated six months ago. Just after Mr. Deardon's health took a turn for the worse." He now gave a look across the table to Mama that almost endeared him. "From the sale of the farm, if the final price allows, he wants five hundred dollars to go to you directly, Camilla, and one hundred dollars to any grandchildren known or unknown."

"Oh my." Once again my hands twisted upon themselves. I looked at Mama. "Did he know?"

She shook her head. "We always hoped, from the day you left nearly, that you'd come back."

"But with children?"

"Left that up to God, of course," Mama said. "We just wanted our own child home."

Mr. Bostwick took a pinch of muffin and pointed at my stomach. "Looks like you've got a hundred-dollar bun in that oven."

In other circumstances, his familiarity might have been taken for impropriety at best and lasciviousness at worst. But I merely gave myself a pat. "So it would seem."

Mr. Bostwick scrutinized the document in front of him. "It appears Mr. Deardon was quite clear that this money is to go to you, Camilla. And your children, should you have any. Set up in a trust in your name so your husband would be excluded." He looked at me over the rim of his glasses. "Is there a husband?"

"I am married, yes. And I have two daughters. Papa didn't know, exactly, about the children. And my husband . . . well, he doesn't know about any of this."

This brought a new posture to Mr. Bostwick. He sat up straighter and addressed me with almost-protective attention. "Do you mean he has abandoned you?"

"I have left my husband."

"Divorced?"

"No."

"Intend to divorce?"

"As the Lord leads, Mr. Bostwick. I cannot make any decisions outside of his guidance."

"Of course, of course. Couldn't have it any other way. Now—" he looked about the room, even under the table—"these children?"

"They are in Utah. With their father."

"And are we waiting to see what the Lord has to say about that?"

"No." I reached across the table and took Mama's hand. "Of that I have no question. I need to bring them here."

"Well, then." He brightened, then dug into his leather satchel and produced a pad of paper and a small box containing an inkwell and pen. "I think it's a good thing you met a lawyer today."

"There's one other thing. The circumstances under which I left were . . . unusual. It's likely that my husband believes me to be dead, and it's certain he knows nothing of the child I'm carrying now."

"So the first order of business will be to convince the man that you're alive? Not to worry, my girl. I wouldn't be much of a lawyer if I couldn't do that."

"But not just yet," I said, willing his pen to stop in midair. "I don't want him to come and fetch me home."

CHAPTER 23

Strange how, with just a few words on a page, a few strokes of a pen, my life took on a shape I never would have envisioned. Mama and I spent the rest of that summer giving life to those words.

We sold the dairy farm, though the new owners allowed us to continue to live there while we hired men to build a new house for us on the land at the edge of town. Twice a day, in the cool of the morning and evening, Mama and I walked to what would be our new home—not only to measure the progress but for our own general health. Mama had spent months taking care of Papa, and the freedom to simply walk out of the house for an undetermined errand was one she hadn't enjoyed when he was healthy and alive. We would walk and talk, my body growing stronger with each step, while the words we exchanged bonded together and grew to fill a longing I'd never before recognized. I'd grown up without her. True, my mother was in our home all my childhood years, but moments like those we now shared had been nonexistent.

I didn't intend to enter a summerlong correspondence, but when I wrote to tell Colonel Brandon of my father's passing, he responded with such sympathy I felt compelled to write again, reassuring him of our restored state. With each letter he expressed more and more interest in the progress of our new home and the sale of our old one. Soon those details became too mundane even for me. Abandoning my journal, I wrote to him of some of the smallest things, like finding a beautiful pair of silk shoes in the back of Mama's armoire, though, as I wrote, *"when either of us will ever have the opportunity to wear them remains a mystery."*

In every letter, Colonel Brandon inquired of my health, to which I answered, *"I am very tired much of the time, doing little more than cook and eat and nap between walks with Mama. I both hate and love to sleep because my dreams are filled with Lottie and Melissa. I see them and hear them, and for those hours they are as close to me as the child I carry."*

I awoke from such a dream one afternoon and walked into the kitchen to find Mr. Bostwick at our table with his usual folio of papers scattered about. His presence was not unusual, as he always seemed to have one trivial legal matter or another that warranted an invitation for Sunday dinner or Tuesday supper or Friday evening pie. I met this visit with an unusual pang, however, as it was the first time I hadn't greeted him at the door to usher him in like any other guest. He was simply *here*, at our table, with Mama bustling about offering fresh cream for his cobbler. Only the smattering of documents made this anything other than a family gathering, as it seemed clear I was the only one not at ease.

"Darling," Mama said, "I was just about to wake you. Mr. Bostwick has some good news."

The man's eyes were closed in an expression of pure enjoyment as blueberry cobbler and cream trickled from the corner of his mouth to be caught expertly by his handkerchief lest it stain his expensive suit.

I smiled despite myself, wondering what his esteemed colleagues would think of the sight. "Does he?"

He opened his eyes and looked at me. "Indeed." With obvious regret he laid his fork to rest on the plate. "I've been in contact with a judge in Salt Lake City, and there should be no impediment to your success in suing for divorce and gaining custody of your children." He offered a wink to my ever-expanding stomach. "*All* of them."

"Well . . . ," I said. It was, of course, the freedom I had longed for, but to hear it condensed into such simple, legal terms belied the hidden complexities. "You make it sound so easy."

"With Brigham Young no longer in political power, it is. The new governor is quite sympathetic to the cases of the polygamous wives, calling the legitimacy of their unions into question."

"But I'm a first wife. Legal in every respect."

Mr. Bostwick waved me off, giving in to the lure of the cobbler and forking another bite into his mouth. He spoke and chewed at the same time. "Giving you the claim of adultery and alienation. A few days in court, a few weeks to process, and you and your daughters could be back here before the first snow."

"Back?" Mama set a small plate of bread and butter and cheese in front of me—my customary afternoon snack. "What do you mean *back*? She's not going anywhere."

"Mama, if it means getting my girls—"

"What it means is having that baby out in the middle of nowhere."

"The baby's not due until November. We could be back by then. Isn't that what you said, Mr. Bostwick?"

"With a private stage and ideal proceedings, yes." Though, in light of my mother's scrutiny, he seemed far less convinced.

"Just what do you mean by *ideal*?" Mama might not have been an educated woman, but this question was not asked in ignorance. She joined us at the table but kept her eyes trained on me as Mr. Bostwick gave his answer.

"Given that Mr. Fox does not protest the divorce."

"You said I had legal grounds."

"You do. But the wonderful thing about the law, my girl, is that there are two sides to every story. Still, I'm certain we'll prevail."

"Even if she's standing right there? Belly full of his child?"

Mama's bluntness took me aback, but I was even more struck by her intuition. My mother had never met Nathan Fox, yet she seemed to possess an understanding of him that, in this instance, far exceeded my own.

"She's right," I whispered, barely loud enough to break through Mr. Bostwick's legal rebuttal. "This child might be a son. He'd never give that up without a fight."

Mr. Bostwick's volume took our kitchen for a courtroom. "Does he not have that other woman to give him sons?"

"He doesn't love that other woman," Mama said with a gentleness that seemed to deflate the man's bluster.

"Well, then—" Mr. Bostwick began to listlessly shuffle his papers—"I suppose I shall go on my own and file the case on your behalf. Truly, your presence is only a formality. I daresay I shall be no temptation for the lovelorn Mr. Fox. And I've no legal obligation to disclose the details of your delicate condition."

Mama looked triumphant, but I could not share in her victory. "What about my daughters?"

"I will establish proof that you have a home and means of support. Your absence will not alter the fact that you have every right to gain custody."

"But how—?"

His square, heavy hand patted mine in a gesture I'm sure was meant to be reassuring. "I'll bring them to you safe and sound; rest easy."

I looked at Mr. Bostwick through the eyes of my daughters. To me, yes, he was growing to be a familiar fixture in my home, his loud voice and long speeches resting on the shore of endearing. I could see the protective nature behind his bravado, and the barrel-like body beneath his ornate vest denoted strength as much as a healthy appetite. But to Lottie and Melissa, he'd be nothing more than a stranger—a large, imposing, unknown man taking them away from their beloved father to the vague promise of a mother they'd probably been told was dead. All very legal, all very proper, but nonetheless terrifying.

"We'll wait," I said, hating the very words in my mouth.

Mr. Bostwick seemed ready to take the stand when Mama, with nothing more than a gentle nudge of his cobbler plate, kept him silent.

"This is my daughter's decision. And I know how much it pains her."

"In the spring." I nearly choked on the familiar-sounding promise. "One more winter, and we'll leave in the spring."

"And just what," Mr. Bostwick said, heedless of his condescension, "would you like me to do until then?"

"Nothing." I tore off a corner of my bread, then set it back on my plate. "Nothing at all."

By the first of August, our new home was ready, and having allowed the women of the church to sweep all the floors and clean the windows, Mama and I drove our farm wagon, laden with all our earthly possessions, for the last time. Over the course of a morning, the heart of our old home became that of the new. The furniture arranged in a sunny front parlor, the table in the kitchen at the back.

"It'll be so nice to receive visitors at the front of the house," Mama said.

I can recall throughout my childhood half a dozen times we ever had ladies come to call in the morning. What farmer's wife had time for such socializing? Since my arrival our visitors were numerous and frequent, bringing a new interest in friendship thinly veiled in curiosity. After all, my condition could no longer be concealed, and the veiled looks I garnered whenever I went into town had grown into full stares. Then, through the guise of inquiring as to my health, the questions began.

I told only enough to sate them. That I had married, that indeed my husband had sought to take a second wife, and that I hoped to bring my daughters here to live. I shared, too, the story of being lost in the storm and my rescue, for that gave me an opportunity to be a witness for God's miraculous care. But I told nothing of my fears, the assumption of my death, the threat of atoning for my sins with the shedding of my own blood. Our town was far enough north of Kanesville to be free of the Mormons' constant encampment, but close enough to come into contact with them frequently. My father's fear and mistrust had driven me away; I would do nothing to fuel more of the same.

Our house was a spacious, two-storied structure, but as the

baby grew, climbing the stairs became an uncomfortable chore, and I knew it would soon become prohibitively cumbersome. We had a bedroom downstairs that was to be Mama's, hoping the children and I would occupy the three upstairs, but she insisted that until the baby was born, I should take the first-floor bedroom.

That first night in our new home, the minute I hit the ticking, the baby sprang to life, rolling and twisting within me with such exuberance I feared I'd never get to sleep. I put my hand on my stomach and sensed the movement beneath my palm.

Tears sprang to my eyes as I remembered sharing our unborn babies' movements with Nathan. We'd lie in bed, his hands covering the width of me, and I'd see his eyes light up in perfect synchronization with the baby's kicking.

"She's dancing like she did in heaven," he'd said of our Melissa. I remember marveling at both his prediction that she'd be a girl and the idea that she'd already lived an entire life before being born. Nathan was unshakingly convinced of both, and he'd captured me in his predictions.

But not with this child.

I knew beyond knowing that this child had no life before Nathan and I created it. And more than with any other of my children, I had no sense of its gender. I hadn't even allowed myself to picture its birth, its life. As much as I might miss those sweet, warm moments sharing the growth of a child within me with its father, I relished this selfishness. For the next few months, this baby was mine alone. New life, yes, but life dependent on me, unlike my daughters, who thrived under another woman's care; unlike my son, who hadn't thrived at all.

In essence, that night it was my child who rocked me to sleep as my prayers of gratitude drifted into dreams.

CHAPTER 24

Mama spent one night in a bare room upstairs, sleeping beneath the moonlit breeze, and the next night she was downstairs with me, lying side by side, whispering about all that we'd missed in each other's lives. Exactly why we whispered, I don't know. There was certainly nobody to disturb, even though we did have the comfort of a neighbor in view. Most nights, at least once, something would set us to laughter.

For every letter I sent to Colonel Brandon detailing the joys and frustrations of this time, he responded in kind, though he offered few details of his duties at Fort Kearny. Instead he wrote of his son—bits and pieces of news he'd learned from the boy's own letters. When I thought to inquire after Private

Lambert, Colonel Brandon provided news that he was well, too. On several occasions he recalled something amusing from our journey east together, and I would smile as I read. How strange it seemed to have formed memories with this man, and I always shared these with Mama, who had an insatiable hunger to know of every possible moment of my life during the time we were separated.

"*How odd to think,*" he wrote sometime near the end of August, "*that so much time must pass between our correspondences, when we are not so very far away from each other.*"

I did not imagine the request between those lines, nor did I acknowledge it. Instead, I posted a chatty inventory of the curtains to be hung in the new house and a few thoughts about the benefits of keeping chickens.

"*Might I come to visit you?*" his next letter inquired plainly. "*I would like to see where you live so that I can better picture you in my mind when I read your letters.*"

"*Perhaps,*" I wrote in my response, "*I have failed in my duties of description.*" After which I gave a detailed list of my intentions for the girls' bedroom—the delicate furniture I'd commissioned from a carpenter in town and the yards and yards of pastel gingham Mama and I were fashioning into coverlets for their beds. At the time I did not realize my underlying thoughts—that there was no room for him in this household. I described our table as so small that we would need a new chair if we were to have a family dinner. Two chairs, should Mr. Bostwick choose to join us.

Gentleman that he was, Colonel Brandon neither acknowledged my evasiveness, nor did he solicit another invitation. Not in the next letter, nor the next, nor the next.

About a month after our move, Reverend Harris and his wife came to call. The four of us sat in Mama's sun-filled parlor drinking fresh ginger water and sharing a platter of cheese sandwiches.

"Now, Miss Camilla," Reverend Harris said, gesturing with a sandwich corner, "when can we expect to see you in church? To my recollection you haven't attended since your arrival back home."

I felt myself blush, even though his voice held nothing but kindness. "I'm sorry. It's difficult to go, knowing . . ."

Mrs. Harris leaned forward, her face all gentleness. "Knowing what, dear?"

My hands covered my stomach, now obviously pregnant. "Knowing what they all must think of me, a woman without a husband. And given the circumstances, how I left . . ."

"Do you give us so little credit for grace?"

"Of course not," I rushed. "It's just so difficult, not to feel scrutinized."

"Do you assume you are the first of our congregation to be lured away to this church? Or the last?"

"I don't know of any."

"They don't all find their way out to Brigham Young's new Zion. You know as well as I do that there are settlements up and down the river. Some we lose forever, but others, like you, dabble for a while. And we always rejoice at having a lamb return to the fold."

"I did far more than 'dabble,' Reverend Harris. My husband is a Mormon, and my daughters are with him. So not only am I a woman expecting a child alone, I'm doing so because I abandoned my family."

"You aren't expecting the child alone," Mama said. We were sitting next to each other on our narrow sofa, and she placed a comforting arm around me.

"Of course not, Mama." Now, as it happened nearly every

269

day, my throat and eyes burned with tears. "Everybody at that church, though, will judge me on one of two counts. Either I was an unfaithful Christian or an unfaithful wife."

Mrs. Harris reached to pat my knee. "We do not judge—"

"You cannot speak for your congregation." The words came out much more harshly than I intended. "Forgive me. Everybody has been kind and wonderful. I'm just afraid of what people might be thinking."

"Are you worried, too, of God's opinion?" Reverend Harris asked.

"No," I said, adamant. "I know I am fully restored to him and that my salvation is secure. And don't think I don't worship. I do, in my own way. I read the Scriptures—I've read the entire Bible, in fact. And I pray. I spent so many long days—you can't imagine how many days—like a prisoner, almost. Even before I left my husband, my home, I felt so alone with God. And then last winter, when I *was* alone with God. There's a strength he gave me, and I think I'm afraid of losing that strength."

Reverend Harris looked at me with a quizzical expression, something I imagined he was not known for. I'm sure the times were rare indeed when this man encountered a statement he was not prepared to process, but clearly I'd stumped him. Soon enough, though, he drew himself up, prepared for conversational battle. "How could attending church possibly *diminish* your spiritual strength?"

"When I was a child, I was in church every Sunday." I patted Mama's leg. "She made sure of that. And I listened; I did. But sometimes what the preachers said would be so far beyond my understanding. I listened, but I didn't hear."

"I know just what you mean," Mrs. Harris interjected. "Even my dear husband's preaching can be a bit dry at times."

Reverend Harris looked sheepish, and I felt compelled to come to his rescue.

"You're a fine man of God, a good Christian, and—" I looked at Mrs. Harris—"an excellent preacher, but all the time I was in church as a child, I never felt connected to God. I think that's why it was so easy for me to be deceived. I didn't know or care enough not to be. Then, while I was away, when I went to their services—"

"You felt excited by the new teachings." Reverend Harris attempted to complete my thought.

"At first, yes, but it was as much Nathan—my husband— as anything else. But once again, I found myself in a pew, listening. And this time, hearing, and knowing deep down it was wrong but doing nothing."

I began to weep again, and Mama gave me a handkerchief. We all sat in silence, presumably to allow me to regain my composure and my thoughts, but I had no desire to do either. In fact, I wished heartily that the topic hadn't come up at all. I tried desperately to think of some way to avoid giving an explanation I felt I owed no one.

"Now, stop," Mama said, rubbing small, soft circles on my back. "And tell us what it is you're afraid of."

I took a deep breath and wrapped the handkerchief around the two fingers on my left hand.

"I've grown so close to God." I looked straight into Reverend Harris's eyes. "Closer than I ever thought possible. Closer than I was ever *taught* could be possible. I *hear* him. And I know he hears me. I don't want anything to come between us. I don't want to hand over the control of what I know and hear and believe to somebody else. I don't want to be *told* what God's Word says because that's what *they* do. They tell you where the

Bible's right and where it's wrong and what it means. I have a mind and heart of my own."

"But Reverend Harris knows the Bible is never wrong." Mama nearly leaped out of her seat in his defense.

"And he knows what it all means," Mrs. Harris added.

"Ladies, please." Reverend Harris held up his hand, chuckling. "I understand exactly what our Camilla is saying."

"You do?" My question meant no disrespect, but Mama jabbed me anyway.

"I do, and I cannot but respect a woman so dedicated to her knowledge of her Savior. So I will only encourage you, out of a sense of community and familial love, to consider joining us in worship. And please don't feel ashamed of the precious child you carry. He is the very picture of new life found in Jesus Christ." Suddenly, his heavy brows rose and he gulped down the rest of his water. "I may just have my text for next Sunday's sermon. Come along, Alice." He stood and placed a motivating hand on his wife's shoulder. "I must get back to my study."

***

I could not ignore such a warm invitation to fellowship, so the first Sunday morning I felt good and strong enough for the walk, I got up and dressed myself in the new sage-green dress Mama had been sewing for me since I'd arrived home. The bodice featured two rows of buttons, which, when the time came, would make feeding the baby an easier task, and the skirt featured an inner fastening to expand and, later, form to what I hoped would be my shrinking waist. It was one of the few new dresses I'd had since marrying Nathan, as I was an impatient seamstress who had relied heavily on clothes donated by her sister Saints.

I breathed in the sweet scent of freshly cut lumber as I finished my preparations at the mirror, fashioning a complicated
series of ringlets. My fingers fumbled with the pins, and I was
about to abandon the style altogether and resort to my usual
brush, braid, and coil, when I heard a soft knock on my door.

"Camilla?"

I turned—well, twirled, actually, quite pleased with my
appearance despite my fullness, even with the unfinished coif-
fure. "How do I look, Mama?"

An odd smile came across her lips. "More beautiful than
I ever remember."

I held out a palm full of pins. "Can you help me?"

"I'd love to."

I sat on the corner of my bed, as Mama was a bit shorter
than I, and gave myself over to her.

"I feel like I'm preparing you for your wedding." Mama's
lips were clenched over the pins, so I wasn't sure I heard her
correctly at first.

"I'm already married."

"Seems Mr. Bostwick can undo that."

"Mama, please."

"A woman shouldn't miss her daughter's wedding. Not all
of them, anyway."

I turned my head, causing the pin she was inserting to
jab my scalp, but I didn't care. "I don't know that I'm going to
divorce Nathan, let alone ever marry again."

"Well, we don't always know what's down our road, do we?"

She pushed in the last pin and declared we would be late
if we didn't leave soon. In her absence, I stood to admire myself
as fully as possible in the mirror hanging over the four-drawer
bureau. Although I knew the curls would be lank and lifeless
by the end of the day, they did look pretty now as they framed

my face in soft spirals. The hard edges along my jaw and cheek-bones were softer now, owing as much to a summer feasting on fresh cream and beef as anything. I looked at myself in profile, smoothing my hands along the soft, freshly pressed dress, enjoying every bit of my figure, determined not to let anyone bring me to shame.

Mama's voice called from the kitchen, so I picked up my Bible and went to find her. There was Mama, still wearing that unreadable smile, only now she stood next to a large box.

"One last thing," she said, "to celebrate."

The box was tied with a string fashioned in a simple knot, and within moments I had it open, eager to see the contents.

"Oh, Mama. It's beautiful."

And it was—the perfect hat to wear with my dress. The wide straw brim created a nice frame for my face yet was generous enough not to smash my complicated curls. A small bouquet of spring flowers graced its crown, and a wide silk ribbon, exactly matched to the green of my dress, was woven through. I ran to the mirror, put it on, and tied the ribbon in a jaunty bow just under my left ear.

"Lovely," Mama said, and I agreed.

Our walk to the church house was short, with the school just over the first swelling hill midway.

"My girls will go there someday," I said, enjoying the sight of it nestled in its valley.

At the thought of my daughters, my heart lost some of its buoyancy. While I loved the child in my womb with every fiber of my being, it was hard not to resent, at times, the delay it created. Once again I was left with no choice but to commit my daughters, and my plans, to the Lord. As if reading my thoughts, Mama said quietly, "If the Lord wills it."

"Of course." I thought I had no doubt God would restore

my family, but just that little phrase knocked the tiniest chip in my faith. I could not leave it as such. "I mean, of course he will."

The church sat at the head of our town's main street, with rows of shops and business buildings stretched out on either side of it. The doors were thrown open; the towering steeple stood out against the blue, late-summer sky, and on top of that, the cross. My heart raced at the thought of finally worshiping God beneath a cross, and I quickened my step.

People had gathered in small family groups in the yard in front of the church; children played beneath the large shade tree at its side. As I suspected, eyes locked on Mama and me the moment we came into view, but I soon enough found myself enfolded. The men largely ignored me, giving nothing more than a polite nod and wide berth, which suited me fine.

Slowly I made my way to the steps. The last time I had walked through those doors, I was a child in every possible way. My mind raced with the excitement of being in a true house of worship and the haunting anxiety of feeling helpless in just such a place. Mama hadn't missed a Sunday during all of Papa's illness, nor one since his death. This morning she was my strength, close at my side. We, then, were a family, just like any other group gathered here.

Just before I crossed the threshold, I heard what was by now a familiar voice call my name and turned to see Mr. Bostwick making his way up the steps, his round hat in his hand.

"You look quite well this morning, Mrs. Fox." He winked at the formality.

"Why, thank you, Mr. Bostwick," I replied. By now I knew that a recognition of health was as close to flattery as Mr. Bostwick was ever prone to offer.

He craned his neck to look beyond me and asked about

my mother in such a way as to make me think she was just as much a reason for his presence as the Lord himself.

"She's here somewhere," I assured him. "Perhaps talking with Mrs. Harris?"

"Ah." He rocked back and forth on his heels.

Our family had always occupied a pew close to the back of the church, and I found myself being pulled right to it, with Mama just behind me. She slid in first, and I was about to follow when Mr. Bostwick cleared his throat and imposed himself between us. I appreciated our position. Having only two rows of pews behind us greatly reduced the number of eyes I could feel on the back of my neck.

When all were seated, Reverend Harris took his place behind the small wooden pulpit at the front of the church and, with a simple clearing of his throat, brought us all to silence.

"Brothers and sisters, I shall open with the words of Paul, as he wrote in his letter to the Ephesians—" he opened his swollen Bible to its predetermined page— "'That we henceforth be no more children, tossed to and fro, and carried about with every wind of doctrine, by the sleight of men, and cunning craftiness, whereby they lie in wait to deceive; but speaking the truth in love, may grow up into him in all things, which is the head, even Christ.'"

He closed his Bible and set it on the pulpit. "Fellow Christians, we all know there are men who teach false doctrine, who speak Scripture laced with lies, who proclaim an unsound gospel."

By the end of this short litany, Reverend Harris had everyone's attention and approval. I felt my face burning within my bonnet. Had he so warmly invited me to church simply so that he could humiliate me?

"And sometimes we wish to condemn those who follow

such doctrine. We call them heathens, blasphemers, and other names not fit to be spoken in this place."

Still, nods of agreement and approval, with a bit of tittering at the last.

I wanted to die. I'd heard all of those words spewed by my own father when the Mormons were encamped near our home. I heard him shouting them on the banks of the river when I ran away. In fact, it could very well be that some of the men in this room had sat there on horseback, torches in hand, watching me go. I would give anything to go away now. Just when I thought Reverend Harris's words could not be more hurtful, he said my name, and he asked me to stand.

Surely, I thought, he couldn't be this cruel. But when I gazed down the tunnel of my bonnet, I saw his watery blue eyes focused right on me, and as if by his will, I stood.

"Many of you know this woman," he said. "And if you know her, you know that she has been gone these past years as a follower of that doctrine."

A sound went through the congregation. Something like a pitiful hiss.

"I want you to see her not as the woman she is today, but as a child. A helpless child. A child caught in the rushing waters of deception. And I urge you all—just as many of you already have—to welcome her with Christian love. To speak of her only in words of Christian love. Not only because I, the leader in this church, request; but because it is what Jesus Christ, the head of our church, demands. Are we in agreement?"

Then came a soft, though not reluctant, amen from the congregation, and I was instructed to once again sit down.

I didn't hear another word.

CHAPTER 25

October 14, 1858

Dear Colonel Brandon,

    The changing leaves are putting on a glorious show for us. Another hard frost this morning, but no snow yet. After last winter, who would ever have thought that I would long to see the stuff again, but how dreary to be simply cold with nothing but bare trees and hard-packed earth to show for it. I believe I shall, for the rest of my life, have my own predictor of snow, as I get a particular, sharp ache deep in the bones at

*that spot where Dr. Buckley performed his effi-
cient surgery. The pain is enough to immobilize
my hand, and though I lived with it for only
one winter, it proved itself as accurate as any
almanac.*

"Another letter?" Mama brushed past the writing desk on her way to open the curtains wider, letting in the brilliant autumn sunshine that did little to heat the room.

"Colonel Brandon is a faithful correspondent," I said, taking advantage of the time of conversation to let the ink dry on the page.

"Faithful suitor is what he is."

"Faithful friend."

My correction, however, was lost as she tossed one dry log after another onto the fire, sending spitting sparks out onto the hearth. I got up from my little desk and went to help stamp out those few sparks that made their way to the carpet and, once there, held my aching hand to the heat.

"The cold bothers you, does it?"

"It's awful," I said. "To have pain in something that's not even there. I feel haunted by my own flesh."

"Might feel better in the kitchen. It's warmer in there and I could use some help with the cobbler."

"For tonight?" The two of us usually had very simple suppers.

"Mr. Bostwick has asked to come over. Official business," she added quickly with the slightest blush to her cheeks.

"Of course." I knew this to be nothing more than the business we always discussed during Mr. Bostwick's visits. A new tenant, perhaps, in our storefront building or the tax note due on the land. Still, there would also be an opportunity to talk of my business—perhaps news of the changing government in Utah Territory, more testimony of Brigham Young's diminishing power—all of which bolstered my hope in the promise waiting at the end of winter.

I slipped my unfinished letter inside my desk and capped the ink bottle. "Perhaps afterward I'll have more to write."

Mr. Bostwick arrived promptly at five o'clock, just as Mama was taking the boiled potatoes out of the pot. Rather than leaving our guest to the parlor, Mama invited him into the kitchen.

At first our conversation was little more than idle chitchat about the dampness of the cold and the latest price of cornmeal. Such easy, genial talk, as if this were any man coming home at the end of a day. It had been half a year now since Papa's passing, and I wondered if both Mr. Bostwick and Mama were using the question of my marriage to Nathan as an excuse to spend time together. Somehow I, the daughter, had become a chaperone, lest anyone in town think either of the two were acting with impropriety.

After we'd eaten, Mama took on the job of clearing the dishes while Mr. Bostwick emptied his portfolio of papers across the table.

"I believe," he said, "we have all we need to proceed. With your mother's permission, I have transferred all of your holdings into your name. With this, your assets far outweigh your husband's. You are a property owner here, to which our Mr. Fox can have no claim."

"Even though he is my husband?"

"He is not mentioned by name, nor is any husband acknowledged in your father's will. Mr. Fox could, of course, make such a claim for it, but as you did not come into the marriage with any such property, and you are not asking to take

281

anything from the divorce settlement, we will initially take the chance that he will follow suit."

"Would I have any right to ask anything of him?"

"Given that we are charging him with adultery, of course."

I thought about the modest home and Nathan's workshop in the barn, full of unfinished projects and his desire for Brigham Young to recognize him as a craftsman. There was nothing of any value. "I only want our children."

He presented another sheet of paper filled with his tiny, precise writing. "Of whom we are asking full custody. And what with his unwholesome behavior—"

"I've told you, it's the way of the church."

"A year ago, with Brigham Young holding both religious and legislative power, that might not have worked in our favor. But it's a new era in Utah."

"I know, the Gentile governor. But that doesn't make Brigham any less powerful."

"What Brigham Young wants is statehood, an institution incompatible with polygamy."

"But it's the practice of the church."

"Then its leader will be forced to make a choice. In the meantime—" he redirected my attention to the page—"we will insist that the three children will better thrive in the home of their mother."

"Do you mention the new baby in that document?"

"Of course, although we are not yet able to specify the child's gender or name," Mr. Bostwick said, indulgently.

"You said you had no reason to mention my 'delicate condition.'"

"By the time we go to court, we will have something far more tangible than a delicate condition. God willing, we will have a healthy, living child."

"So we have to mention the new baby in the papers?"

"If I am to represent you in court, yes. I will not be anything less than truthful. Mr. Fox is, indeed, the child's father?"

Mama and I gasped in unison, and she appeared ready to rear back and slap him.

Mr. Bostwick held up his hands to fend off the attack. "I'm only posing the questions that the court will ask if the child is ever discovered. By including him in the divorce proceedings, you are validating his legitimacy. He was conceived within the confines of your marriage, and were circumstances different, you would expect Mr. Fox to claim him. We are dealing here with the same legal principle."

"He'll fight it," I said through the lump in my throat. "And he'll have the entire church on his side."

"Rest assured, he will not. If Brigham Young has showed anything, it's that he doesn't want conflict in his holy land."

"But he raised an army. They were at war."

"A war without a battle, ended with his surrender. The Mormons are a quiet, insidious people. Their leader will not welcome a spotlight on their flawed faith."

Mama reached across the table to squeeze my hand. "I worry what will happen when he sees the baby."

"He need not see the child," Mr. Bostwick said. "Nor you, Camilla, as a point of fact. Remember, I need only have your signature, and I am perfectly capable of representing your interests alone. If you hadn't rejected my idea to leave two months ago, your darling daughters might be at the table with us this very minute."

"I told you, it didn't seem prudent—"

"At least," Mr. Bostwick said, unable to leave us to our peace, "allow me to send word that you are, indeed, alive and well and intending to sue for divorce."

He had made this very request countless times, and my answer never wavered.

"No. I know my fears may be unfounded, but right now my existence is the only advantage I have."

⁂

As fall deepened into mid-November, I came to expect the arrival of my baby any day. The days grew cold and bleak, and my joy at the anticipation of welcoming this new child warred with my despair over the many months that must pass before I might again lay eyes on my first two. Despite the dreary weather, I tried to get out and stretch my legs each day lest cabin fever drive me to distraction. And so it was on my walk home from our post office in town that I felt the first pains of labor. In the wee hours of the next morning, with Mama holding my hand, my son was born.

We'd enlisted no one to help us—no midwife, no doctor. I'd be lying if I didn't say that, as welcoming as our community tried to be, there was always a shade of disapproval in their eyes whenever their gazes dropped to my waist.

Before the birth of my girls and my first son, I'd spent countless hours knitting—alone or with a circle of women—creating tiny garments and such to welcome the new child into the world. This boy came into the world, vibrant red and squalling, with little more than a few cotton shirts and diapers to call his own. Those and the unmistakable glint of his father's eyes.

"Oh, he's beautiful," Mama said, even as he took his first breaths in this world.

"He is," I agreed, holding his wet, squirming body close to mine. More than beautiful, he was instantly, vibrantly alive. His arms and legs thrashed; his cries filled the room. Mama took him and washed him and returned him to me a clean, healthy pink with a soft cap of blond hair.

"Have you thought about a name?" Mama asked.

I hadn't.

His cries quieted as we looked at each other; his waving fists grew still. There was only one name I could give this boy.

"Charles." I looked to Mama not for confirmation but for understanding. "Charles Deardon Fox."

He took to the name immediately, wrapping his hand around my finger and turning his perfect head toward the sound of my voice.

"Does he look like your girls?" Mama asked. "Like they did when they were born?"

I pulled him closer. "He's bigger. The girls felt like they didn't weigh anything at all. His face is rounder, like his father's. And his eyes are darker. And his smile . . ."

"Nonsense." She brought a basin of warm water and began to wash me. "Babies don't smile when they're just born."

I didn't argue, but she was wrong. Already, within these few minutes, my baby's mouth stretched itself into a tiny version of his father's enticing, sometimes wicked, grin.

"Oh, baby boy," I whispered, "I'm so happy to have you to myself."

The arrival of baby Charles brought a new flood of visitors and food and gifts. I suppose something about new life initiates forgiveness. Reverend Harris and his wife came with the cradle last used by his youngest son—now ten years old—and several small, soft blankets. When we gathered in the parlor to pray, Reverend Harris held Charlie in one arm and lifted the other high.

"Most sovereign Lord—" his deep, rich voice filled the room—"we rejoice in the safe delivery of this child and the health of his mother. May he be raised in your truth and dedicated to a life of Christian righteousness."

Such a burden I felt under those words. With Charlie safe in Reverend Harris's grasp, my own arms felt so empty. How clearly I recalled handing my girls over to Elder Justus as he spoke similar words over them, and I had stood by, silently, ignorantly, pledging to raise my daughters to believe the lies of a false gospel. What I wouldn't give to have had them at my side that day, gathered to me as we prayed for their brother. I hazarded to open one eye to look upon my son, nestled in the arm of a godly man, and emptied my own prayer into the room.

Father, hold my girls. Keep them safe, even as you kept this little one safe within me through so many trials.

I knew our reunion would be in his time and his way, and I knew the choices I'd made to this point weren't perfect ones. I could have refused to let Nathan into my bed, but then I would not have this precious life. I could have refused to leave without my children, but then I might have fallen victim to the discipline of the church. Still, never had I felt farther away from my daughters than I did at this moment. More than the separation of a thousand miles, it was an unfathomable spiritual expanse. I would not rest easy until I'd brought them to the other side.

CHAPTER 26

December 9, 1858

Dear Colonel Brandon,

How wonderful to hear that you will be able to spend Christmas with your son. And to travel by train—how I long to do so someday. Why, there were moments when riding the stage felt like absolute flight! It is hard for me to even imagine what it would feel like to ride on a train. Please give my regards to Robert. Though I have not met him, I've heard you speak of him so often, I feel almost as if we are long-lost friends.

To this, I add what must be much-anticipated news for you. I, too, will be spending Christmas with my own son, as he was born to me just a few nights ago. He and I are both feeling well, though we match each other for hours slept throughout the day. I confess that when I look into his face, I see his father's features, but I have you to thank for his safe birth here in this place. I have learned that the passion of youth can fade, but I do hope that our friendship will transcend such erosion, and it is in that light that I gave my son the name of Charles. It is a strong name, shared by a man whose strength may well have saved my life. I hope I have not imposed too much.

Now, to your journey. Mama, I fear, will be disappointed. I was under strict orders to invite you to join us for Christmas supper in my next letter. . . .

It would be my first Christmas away from my daughters, and throughout the season of Advent, I prayed it would be the last. This year, however, I devoted myself to creating gifts to lavish them with when we were reunited. For Melissa I made her own apron, as she was always busy about the kitchen helping me or Kimana. I'd become quite adept at all sorts of needlework despite my handicap, and I embroidered a scene of frolicking kittens on each of the apron pockets. For Lottie I painted a simple bouquet of flowers on a piece of canvas to be stretched over a ring and serve as her first attempt at stitching. She'd need only follow the painted lines with the different colored silk thread, and in the end she'd have something far more beautiful than a simple alphabet. Of course, I also knit each of them a new pair of mittens and a matching scarf, though I'd not yet decided on what fashion of hat each would like.

"You're planning to spoil those girls," Mama said. It was two days past Christmas, and she was newly returned from town. Snow created lace on the other side of the window and blew in with a halfhearted flurry before she could close the door behind her.

"It keeps me busy."

"That little one doesn't keep you busy enough?"

"He's napping," I said, even though she was already on her way to the kitchen. Minutes later she returned with a box wrapped in brown paper. "What's that?"

She studied the package. "It's from your Colonel Brandon."

"He is not *my* Colonel Brandon."

"It's addressed to you."

I set my knitting aside and, with the eagerness of a school-girl, welcomed the package to my lap. Mama handed me our letter opener, which I deftly used to break the string and the sealed edges of the paper. Inside the box were three smaller ones, each wrapped in white paper: one for Mrs. Fox, one for Mrs. Deardon, and one for Baby Charles, according to Colonel Brandon's fine, bold script.

"Shall we wait for the baby to wake up?" Mama's eyes shone with her own childlike excitement.

"Don't be silly. You first."

Carefully, Mama peeled the paper away from the square, flat box. "Oh, my lands." She lifted a pale blue square, and I could see it was silk. There were five handkerchiefs in all, each in a different pale pastel, and Mama touched each to her cheek.

"I never known such luxury," Mama said. "You'll have to thank him in your next letter."

"I'll let you thank him yourself," I said. "I'm sure he'll be pleased to hear from someone other than me."

"I wouldn't bet on that," Mama said. "Will you open yours? Or would you rather be alone?"

I ignored her comment and unceremoniously ripped at the wrapping. Inside was a long, flat box with the words *Carson Bros. New York City* stenciled on the top. I lifted the lid and gave my own little sound of pleased surprise when I saw what was nestled inside.

It was a beautiful pair of green kid-leather gloves, long enough to reach well past my wrists.

"Lovely," Mama said as I held one up for her approval. "Try them on."

I dropped the box to my forgotten knitting, pulled on the right-hand glove, and thrilled at the warmth.

"They're lined," I said, almost squealing. How any craftsman had been able to work in such soft wool and still have a glove that fit the hand so beautifully, I'll never know. Eagerly, I pulled on the left as well, and what had been pleasant surprise turned into another kind entirely.

"Mama, look."

I held up my hands. Both of them, whole. Something, perhaps batting from the same wool that lined the fingers, had been rolled and inserted into the fourth and fifth fingers of the left hand. The circumference was identical to my own fingers, and each was tapered and bent at a slight-enough angle to appear completely natural.

"Well, look at that," Mama said. "Custom-made."

"He remembered the shape of my hands," I mused aloud, all the while testing myself to see if I remembered his. I didn't.

"It's a very thoughtful gift," Mama was saying. "Why, with those on, you can't tell at all."

"So I'm to wear gloves every day for the rest of my life?" An unwelcome resentment bubbled within me, and I yanked the offending glove off my hand. "Is this something to hide? Something to be ashamed of?"

"Of course not." Mama settled the lid back on her box of handkerchiefs and loosely wrapped the paper around it. "The man loves you."

"I know." I slowly tugged off the other glove. "But I don't love him, Mama. I wish I did, but I don't."

"Pshaw. You loved that Mormon, and look where that got you."

"Did you love Papa?" An odd question, given their marriage of more than thirty years, but I hadn't a single memory of any true affection between them, and she seemed detached from any semblance of mourning.

"Of course I did." Suddenly she appeared far too practical for silk handkerchiefs.

"Were you happy?"

"Oh, my girl." Mama got up from her seat and came to my side, drawing my head into her bosom and planting a kiss in my hair. "Your papa and me might not have had some great romance, but we prayed together every morning and every night. He took care of me, even makin' sure I'd be taken care of after he'd gone on."

"And that was enough?" I pulled away and twisted in my chair to look at her. Every year of her marriage seemed etched across her face, leaving behind tracks of sadness.

She smiled gently at me. "I had a home and I had you. Later, I had hope that you'd come home."

"So do you think I'm doing the right thing? Divorcing Nathan?" I asked, suddenly craving her advice.

"I'm not the one to be tellin' you that."

"Do you think, then, that I should continue to write to Colonel Brandon? He is such a dear friend."

"Have you promised him anything more?"

"No." Surely, I hadn't.

"Then keep writing. You'll be glad, someday, to have such a friend."

February 1, 1859

Dear Colonel Brandon,

It is a bitter, black-cold day. Mama and I have not stepped a foot outside the house since returning from Church on Sunday. (And how thankful we were to have made it safely home.) The house is so cozy, though. We've a fire burning in the kitchen, and I have moved myself and Charlie into the downstairs bedroom for the time being. Right now a venison stew is simmering on the stove, and Charlie is cooing in his basket. One would think my heart would be overflowing with joy, but instead it is one of those days choked with trepidation. I fear you and Mama and even Mr. Bostwick assign me more strength and courage than I possess. You were right when you said that I tend to be impetuous. Perhaps I take advantage of the mercy of our Lord. What if I've relied once too often on his goodness? What if—?

I stopped, tore the paper to bits, and tossed those bits in the kitchen stove. It was too cold to write at my parlor desk, as we'd adopted the frugal Evangeline's practice of heating only one room at a time.

"Change of heart?" Mama was at the table too, hemming new diapers for Charlie.

"I can't find the right words."

Colonel Brandon's letters had grown bolder in his affections since Christmas, and I'd been so careful to respond with friendly, cool detachment. I feared that pouring out the emptiness of my heart would be extending to him an invitation to fill it. What I'd been about to write was pain better suited to prayer.

In the bleakness of this winter, sometimes an hour—even an entire afternoon—might go by, and my daughters wouldn't cross my mind. This morning, I woke up, and they had not been my first awareness. If I experienced these lapses, what must be happening in their young, ever-changing minds? I used to worry about whether they would forgive me; now I found myself plagued with the chance that they might forget me.

But I'd share none of this with Colonel Brandon, nor would I share it with my mother. Where he would reply with a letter full of praise for my strength as well as a reminder of why it was so important to have a partner with whom to share such fears, Mama would just look up from her sewing and tell me that my fears were silly.

I dipped the ladle into the stew and brought it to my lips. "This is ready," I said over my shoulder.

"It's not suppertime." Mama didn't even look up.

"I think I'll eat early, though, and go to the prayer meeting at church."

That got her attention.

"Tonight? It's too cold for you to go out there."

"It's cold, but it's clear." I reached down a bowl from the cupboard, as if the question were already resolved. "I'm feeling a bit cooped up. I need the walk as much as anything, and if I leave early enough, I'll get to the church before dark."

"It's too cold to take the baby."

"I don't intend to take him, Mama. Nor do I want you to go with me. I need . . ." How could I explain? My spirit felt like an extension of the winter sky. Clear, yes, but gray. No new prayer fell from my lips, and everything I'd lifted to the Lord seemed to have fallen back to my feet like the old, packed snow on which I would walk. I needed to be surrounded by fresh voices. I needed the prayers of others to reinforce my own.

"You need to be careful," Mama said, finishing my thought. "Fill up with that hot stew, and wear your wool petticoat. And mittens over your nice lined gloves."

By the time I reached the main road into town, I was almost to the point of regretting my decision. My breath crystallized on the scarf wrapped up to my nose, and the very air stung my eyes. Each breath was fresh, though it might have pained my lungs to take it, and my legs grew stronger with each stride. Still, the sight of smoke billowing from the church's chimney was the sweetest I'd seen in days, and I hastened my pace toward it.

Though the clock on the wall showed I was early, I was far from the first to arrive. I walked in to a sea of hushed conversations, none of which my presence would interrupt, even as I made my way back to the stove. In the glow of its warmth, I unwound my scarf and peeled off my gloves. Now recognizable, I garnered a little more attention. Reverend Harris's wife asked about the baby, and Mrs. Pearson sent her regards to Mama. Their welcome did as much to warm me as did the stove. Soon I could take off my coat, and as more people came in, I relinquished my spot. Mrs. Harris patted the seat beside her, but I chose a seat on the aisle just three rows up and bowed my head.

"Good evening, my brothers and sisters in Christ." The voice of Reverend Harris came through my darkness and I opened my eyes to find him smiling right at me. "How sweet to come together in this hour of prayer. And a special thank-you to Mr. O'Ryan for getting here early to lay the fire."

The room echoed with appreciation.

When we were quiet once again, Reverend Harris led us in a prayer dedicating the next hour to the petitions to be brought to the Father, and upon our collective amen, he invited those gathered to share their hearts. There was, of course, the usual array of those to lift up the sick and the weary. I learned that one of our oldest members—Miss Goldie—would surely meet her Savior before the end of the week. We also collectively praised God for the Stinsons' new baby and the fact that their oldest seemed to have weathered the measles. I listened to their stories and joined my heart with theirs in prayer, though not out loud. While I felt I had found my place in this church, I'd not yet found my voice.

When the hour was nearly up, Reverend Harris surveyed the small gathering. "I feel there is one more among us in need."

Had he said as much when I first walked in, I might have melted in my seat. Instead, whether it was the brisk walk in the cold or the hour spent surrounded by true brothers and sisters too humble to call themselves saints, I felt a new layer of strength just under my skin. The church was quiet—mine the only head not bowed in prayer. Slowly, subtle whispers filled the room like steam, and I found myself rising from my seat. My hands ceased to cling to each other, and I held them—palms up—in front of me, warmed from above.

"Yes, Camilla?" Reverend Harris said. Neither he nor any of the townspeople ever addressed me as Mrs. Fox. "How may we pray for you?"

In a thousand hours I could never have spoken all my needs, nor was this the place to make them plain. I could not tell this room full of husbands and wives that I prayed God's blessing on a divorce. As kind and Christlike as these people appeared, I knew there were those who viewed me as a woman who had forsaken her husband and abandoned her children. And given all that, how could I share my dilemma about Colonel Brandon? That I longed to love one man while I was still married to another?

All of this I lifted to the Lord with renewed faith that he would answer, but I spoke aloud only one pressing need.

"I ask only that the Lord bring a swift end to this winter."

April 23, 1859

Dear Colonel Brandon,

This will be a short letter, and quite possibly my last for a while. If you question the erratic penmanship, let me explain that my excitement is such I can hardly hold the pen. Mr. Bostwick joined us for dinner this afternoon—an official visit as my attorney. Not long after Mama cleared the dishes, he presented me with the written receipt for our paid passage to Utah via the Overland Stage. We are due to leave within the next two weeks. I am breathless with anticipation. I do not know how I am to sleep or eat or

*perform the most mundane of household chores.
My heart and mind are filled with the voices of
my children. Charlie cries, and I hear Melissa; he
chortles, and there's my Lottie. My arms ache to
hold them. Mama and I have spent a good amount
of time this winter making pretty new quilts for
their beds. How I long for the night we will kneel
together and pray. I look out the window and I
see them playing with tiny teacups beneath our
tree. I pray each and every night that they will
find it a joyous thing to come live in this home.*

I paused to allow the ink to dry on the page and took in the scene around me. How could my girls feel anything but love and comfort here? Mama was at the stove boiling milk, to which she would add a bit of sugar and a drop or two of cod-liver oil—a concoction Charlie would take from a rubber-topped bottle when it cooled. The question of weaning the baby so early had been my greatest concern for my journey west. But he'd taken to the bottle as easily as I could hope, given that I still nursed him in the morning and late at night. He'd also taken a few bites of mashed yam and had gummed a small bite of milk-soaked bread.

"I'll keep that boy fit as a fiddle while you're away," Mama said as she stirred. "You tell that to your Colonel Brandon."

I smiled. "Perhaps you can take over my letter writing while I'm away."

"Oh, I don't think the man wants to hear from the likes of me."

"Colonel Brandon is my friend, Mama. Nothing more." Though I was certain he wished more of me. He had not openly professed his love, but his letters consistently conveyed an affection I fought to keep out of mine. And while I wrote endlessly about the current happenings in our home, he often alluded to the future. He'd yet to specifically include me in that future, but he never failed to reference a time when we would see each other again. I'd felt a certain safety in writing—our correspondence had been a way to pass the long, hot summer days of my growing pregnancy and the long, bleak winter days as I waited to embark on this journey. But now, on the brink of such change, I knew there would be a shift in his pursuit. Soon, God willing, I would no longer be married, opening the door for a courtship, even if only through letters. Still, I was no more prepared to enter such a relationship than I had been the day I first awoke to Colonel Brandon's searching eyes.

Mama gave a knowing *hmmm* and continued stirring as I turned the page over and continued.

I shall not write to you again until my family is here restored. It's not that I wish to keep you uninformed; I simply do not know what opportunities I will have.

I took this journey once before with you, and I will bring my never-ending gratitude with me once again. I shall miss the strength of your presence, but I hope I can rely on the strength of your prayers. In the meantime, I know Mr. Bostwick will take good care of me. He is an exceedingly kind man, and traveling with him will be akin to what it must be like to travel with an attentive father.

As for what my new distinction in life will mean to our standing with each other, I beg of you to be patient with me. I travel tomorrow with a mission to bring my daughters to a home where they can grow to know Jesus Christ. What that entails for my marriage I cannot say. The matter is not entirely in my hands. Moreover, I cannot claim my heart as my own. It is now given to my Savior, and only he can direct my path. Rest assured, my dear, dear friend, I have nothing but the greatest appreciation for your regard.

Your letters hint often of a future we might share together. To that I have only this to say: I cannot give you an answer of any kind. You've no right to expect more. I am not angry; I simply implore you to remember my state. Do not cause me to sin by introducing thoughts no married woman should entertain.

You have made your case. Allow me to make my peace.

Seeking courage,

I remain your dearest friend,

Camilla Fox

CHAPTER 27

I saw the unfolding of the city through a narrow slit of window, holding the blind to the side as the stagecoach made its way through the streets. It was well past dark—nearly nine o'clock according to Mr. Bostwick's timepiece. We were delivered right to the Salt Lake post office, which seemed fitting, as we shared the coach with a dozen sacks of mail. Mr. Bostwick commented that such an amount spoke to the growth of the city, or perhaps the lingering enthusiasm for the restored postal contract. I only knew that they caused me to twist and turn uncomfortably in my seat, and my face still bore the burlap-sack pattern where I'd taken advantage of the rough, uneven pillow.

The way the two of us comported ourselves, one would

be at a loss to determine who was visiting this city for the first time. Mr. Bostwick solicitously handed me down from the stage, and I folded myself against the cool adobe wall. Despite Mr. Bostwick's normally persuasive powers, nothing would convince our driver to take us to the Hotel Deseret on West Third Street.

"I ain't a cab," he'd said through a haze of cigar smoke.

"We could walk," I said when Mr. Bostwick poked his head back inside to deliver the news. "It isn't far, and I would love a chance to stretch my legs."

"And what of our bags? You're coming back with much more than you had when you left."

"Of course."

Hard to believe I was the same woman who'd fled first through the snow, then in the night with little more than a bundle of belongings. Now we would need to hire a porter at the station to load and unload my two trunks, and Mr. Bostwick's luggage besides. Where once I'd worn a sadly adapted dress from a charity barrel, I now wore one of two stylish traveling suits. True, I'd been wearing it for over a week with just the barest of dust brushing and a daily changing of shirtwaist, but the cut was impeccable and the wool somehow perfectly weighted to ward off the chilly mornings and evenings without being swelteringly hot in the afternoons. Besides these, I had two calicoes that, except for the fact that they were crisp and new, would dress me identically to any Mormon woman. On this I insisted, though Mr. Bostwick would rather I represent myself as a woman of considerable means.

"I am thankful enough to have a home and the comfortable living God has provided," I'd said. "I'll not boast of having more."

The second, smaller trunk was full of things for the girls.

Two new dresses apiece and thin, dark canvas riding coats to protect them from the inescapable dust. I also had two small, soft down pillows and one of Mama's older quilts to help keep them comfortable both during the ride and in whatever overnight stopping places we would encounter. At Mama's suggestion, I'd refrained from bringing them any new dolls or toys.

"They might want to bring something more familiar from home," she'd said, and I marveled that there was ever a time in my life when I'd disregarded her counsel.

Within fifteen minutes Mr. Bostwick had procured a young man—maybe fifteen years old—with a shock of yellow-blond hair feathering out from beneath a black knit cap. He had a team of slow-moving horses pulling a flatbed wagon and agreed to take us and our luggage to the hotel for whatever amount Mr. Bostwick had folded into his palm. Mr. Bostwick rode in the back of the wagon after I had been handed up to the springy seat next to the boy.

"First time in the city?"

"No." Fortunately, the chilliness in my voice discouraged further conversation.

We rolled through the streets at such an excruciatingly slow pace, the horses might have been hauling a temple stone rather than our modest party. The boy himself slumped and sloped at the reins, his head bobbing in rhythm to the horses' rumps.

Though I'd been gone for just over a year, the change that had been wrought on the city was obvious, even at this late hour. Maybe it was a matter of season. We were, after all, quick on the heels of winter, without having given spring much of a chance to take hold. Everything looked damp, unkempt. Not exactly lifeless, but lacking the vibrancy I'd known this city to have.

I held my breath as we turned onto Temple because I knew

we would soon be taking a slow pass in front of Rachel and Tillman's home. At this hour, the children would all surely be in bed, but I fully expected to see the downstairs windows full of blazing light as she and her sister wives gathered in the parlor to read or sew. I craned my neck but saw only utter darkness lining the street.

Turning in my seat, I asked Mr. Bostwick the time, as it must have been later than I imagined.

"Not quite ten."

"And everybody packed up in bed?"

"Everybody packed up and gone," the boy said.

Fear collided with the cool evening air, turning my blood into winter ice. "Gone? Where?"

He shrugged. "South, mostly. Order of the prophet. Pretty soon this place is going to be running over with Gentiles." He glanced my way. "No offense, ma'am, if you are one."

"What has that to do with anything?"

"Don't want to let them all profit on what Heavenly Father gave to us. Wouldn't do—"

"Stop," I said. We were right in front of Rachel's home, and there wasn't a spark of light to be seen. Without waiting for any assistance, I climbed down from the wagon seat and walked through the front gate, straight up to the front door. Somewhere behind me, Mr. Bostwick was calling my name in a strained whisper, but I paid him no mind. Acting against logic, I knocked on the front door, then pounded, calling, "Rachel! Tillman?"

Soon I felt a comforting hand on my shoulder and heard Mr. Bostwick gently, quietly leading me away.

"Camilla, my dear. The windows—they're boarded up. There's nobody here. We don't want to call undue attention to ourselves."

Looking up and down the street, I wondered just whose attention we would attract, as there didn't seem to be anybody in any of the houses. Still, I allowed him to lead me down the front steps and back toward the wagon.

"It doesn't make sense." I spoke in a hushed tone straight into the sleeve of his jacket.

"Oh, but it does. Brigham Young feels he's lost a war. This is his way of leaving a scorched earth to the enemy."

"But how could he make them abandon their home?"

"You are much more acquainted with the power of his influence than I."

The thought I'd been too terrified to speak until now came to the surface. "What if Nathan is gone?" I clutched his sleeve, panic rising. "I'll have no idea where my girls are."

"How long is the drive to your home?"

"Half a day."

"We'll leave at first light."

By now we were back at the wagon, where our driver looked on in unconcealed curiosity. "You know the folks who lived here?"

"Yes." I refused to say more.

"What's your name, son?" Mr. Bostwick asked as he helped me back into my seat.

"Seth Linden, sir."

"Tell me, Seth, where can I hire a rig to drive us to Cottonwood Canyon tomorrow?"

He scrunched his face. "My pa's got a brand-new runabout, but tomorrow's the Sabbath, sir. He won't do business with you. Won't nobody."

Mr. Bostwick got back in the wagon with what I thought was admirable flexibility for a man his age. This time, though, he didn't dangle his legs over the back edge. Instead, he scooted one of the trunks clear up to the driver's seat and sat on it. Seth clicked to the horses, and as they began their task anew, Mr. Bostwick leaned forward and said, "Trust me, young man. I'll find somebody to do business with tomorrow."

"Nope. Not in this town."

"What is your father's rate?"

Seth gave a quick glance backward. "Two dollars a day."

All of a sudden, Mr. Bostwick's arm appeared between us, palm up, a small pile of coins stacked in the center. "Perhaps we can do the transaction tonight, then. And you can deliver the buggy first thing in the morning, long before you're due in church."

The boy eyed the money. "That's too much, sir."

"I might need it for two days."

"Pa will have my hide promisin' business on a Sunday."

"Or he'll think you an enterprising young man indeed for knowing enough to conduct the business tonight."

A few more seconds' thought, and the coins were dropped in a small pocket on the front of Seth's vest. "You want a one-horse or a two-horse team?"

"Two horses," Mr. Bostwick said. "And I'll need them delivered before dawn."

<hr />

The Hotel Deseret was a plain, square, three-story structure that occupied a corner lot. The sign above the door read, "For Businessmen Who Need a Home in Our Great City." Mr. Bostwick gave Seth another nickel to lift our trunks down from the wagon and carry them into the front room of the establishment.

We walked in to find a large room with several tables

scattered about, each occupied by one or more gentlemen reading newspapers or engaging in conversation. To the far left was a long oak counter, and behind it a tall, dignified-looking gentleman with coal-black hair and spectacles pinched to the top of his nose. He was writing in an enormous ledger as we approached and continued to do so for several seconds until Mr. Bostwick quietly cleared his throat.

"May I help you?" He looked at me and one eyebrow rose above the rim of his glasses. "Sir?"

"I am Michael Bostwick, an attorney-at-law. I would like to rent two rooms, please."

"I'm sorry, sir. But we do not allow women to stay at the hotel."

His implication was clear, and even if it wasn't, the stares I felt on the back of my neck gave further clarification. My lips twitched with amusement even though my embarrassment felt close to the edge of shame.

"She is my client," Mr. Bostwick said, then, softly, "and my daughter."

"I'm sorry, sir. This is an establishment for businessmen, and we insist on not having the distraction of a woman on the premises."

"It is only for one night."

The clerk remained unflappable. "I'm sorry. There's nothing I can do."

"It's the middle of the night," Mr. Bostwick said, growing in agitation. "Can you recommend someplace else?"

I listened to this exchange feeling numbing fatigue threatening to take over my body. *Home*. That's all I wanted. No, tonight, even less than that. Shelter. Bed. Someplace to collect my thoughts and pray before tomorrow. This close to my daughters—within a day of holding them again—and I could think of nothing but Rachel and Tillman's boarded-up home. Mine—or the one I left—could be the same. If it even existed. I had to know.

Even if the Hotel Deseret would rent me a room, I knew I'd get no sleep, being tortured with such a possibility. I could not ride in a rented buggy down into the little valley of our home, only to find it deserted. I had to know, and there was only one way to find out tonight.

"It's all right," I said, a quieting hand on Mr. Bostwick's arm. "You stay here with our bags. I have someplace else I can go. A friend."

"Don't be ridiculous." Mr. Bostwick knew exactly who was on my mind. I'd entertained him and Mama with enough stories after Sunday suppers. "I'm not letting you go out alone at this time of night."

"I'll be fine. Look, that young man is just bringing in the last of our things. He'll take me."

"Let me go with you."

"No. It's bad enough I'm showing up at her door at this hour. I can't have a strange man with me as well."

"Pardon me," the clerk on the other side of the counter interjected. "Sir, will you be taking the room or not?"

"Please," I said, beseeching, "I'm exhausted. I need a place to sleep. And it's not far, just a few blocks. Just a few minutes away."

"You don't even know if she—"

"Oh, she'll be there."

Mr. Bostwick looked past me and got Seth's attention, pressing yet another coin into his hand, directing him not only to take me to my destination but also to remain until I was safely inside.

"I'll wait up for one hour," he said, keeping a firm grip on my arms. "Come straight back here if anything goes awry. If you don't come back, I'll assume all is well."

"That sounds very wise," the hotel clerk said, and it was then that I realized we'd attracted the attention of every man in the room, with the exception of Seth, who looked like he was beginning to wish he'd never taken our fare.

"I'll be fine," I said again, hoping to reassure us both. Then, on an impulse, I fell against him, wrapping my arms as far as I could around his boxlike torso. He hugged me close, and I was reminded of the words he'd said to the hotel clerk just moments before, calling me his client, his daughter. In that moment, I truly believed the lie.

"Give me the address," he said finally, "and I'll be there to get you early in the morning."

I told him, making sure that Seth heard and understood before the two of us walked out of the Hotel Deseret to the waiting wagon outside.

"I'm sorry to be such a bother," I said once I was seated beside him.

"Likely Pa won't mind. Business has been slow of late."

It wasn't long before we were on very familiar streets indeed, with row upon row of identical clapboard houses, more dire in their need of paint than ever before.

"So you got a friend waiting for you?" Seth asked.

"Something like that."

We drove past the Square, and though I didn't want to look, I hazarded a glance to where the temple was being rescued from its grave. Nothing miraculous here; the moonlight shone upon evidence of hard labor—carts of earth sat with shovels still propped beside them, as if the workers had been pulled away with the slap of sunset.

"It's going to be glorious," Seth said, following my gaze. "I can't hardly wait to see it."

"And I never shall."

He shrugged and clicked to the horses, and to my surprise they actually picked up their pace. Perhaps they sensed my impatience—or my fear. Either way, the new bounce to their tails was encouraging, and the jostling in the seat made conversation uncomfortable, so the rest of our ride was both brief and silent. In what seemed too soon, we turned onto Evangeline's street, and to my surprise—and Seth's—I called out a "Whoa" to the horses.

Seth complied, pulling the reins to bring the team to a halt just down the street from the house I'd taken as a home for a few weeks last winter.

"Is this it?"

"Yes." I wouldn't wait for him to help me down from my seat; indeed, he showed little inclination to do so. I thanked him as my feet hit the ground.

"The gentleman told me to wait for you." He was sitting up straighter, affecting a charming protectiveness beyond his years.

"You've done quite enough already." If I was going to be thrown out on my ear, I didn't want to burden the poor boy with another destination, especially when I had no idea what that destination would be. It took little more to convince young Seth to agree, and I found myself alone in the dark, in front of the very door through which I'd once escaped.

Looking back, I might have been more reluctant to be left in such a vulnerable spot if it weren't for the light I saw in the second-story window, from the very room I briefly called my own. Of course, it had been Evangeline's room long before I could lay any claim to it, and from the soft glow within, it seemed she'd reclaimed it. The thought gave me an odd sense of comfort, perhaps because my memories of her as the miserly spinster curled up on her parlor sofa every night spoke of such hopelessness. Certainly this spoke of a healing to her spirit—a healing that might translate to forgiveness. Or mercy, though I hadn't resolved whether I was to be on the giving or receiving end of such grace. True, she had given me shelter when I needed it, but she had also openly coveted my husband and covertly wished me harm. But I was here now, in need of not only a bed but also information, for I knew she would never have allowed Nathan to step one foot away from her reach without her knowledge. I raised my hand to knock on the door.

No response.

Patiently, I waited. It was too late in the evening to raise a ruckus by pounding on the door, and while the light in the window indicated that she had not yet retired for the night, it could be that she'd dozed off with the candle burning, or she was looking for a wrap to throw over her nightgown before opening the door. So, after what I estimated to be five minutes, I knocked again more forcefully.

A familiar sound seemed to be coming from inside the house, and I leaned my ear against the door to listen. Soft it was, and muffled, but unmistakable. A child's cry—more specifically, a baby's.

Blood rushed to my face and I panicked, stepping away to double-check the number written above the door. There was just enough light to confirm this was indeed Evangeline's house.

A child? It certainly wasn't out of the realm of possibility. After all, I'd had a child since last living here. She was a young, healthy woman. Perhaps she'd found the love she so desperately sought. Or at least the marriage she fervently desired. Either way,

I felt ever more the intruder than merely an uninvited guest, and I was turning to leave when I heard the door open behind me.

"Who are—?" he said, and I might have made my escape if something in his voice hadn't forced me to turn around. But I did, and there he was, looking just as he did the first time I saw him and, to be truthful, the way I pictured him in every memory—bathed in light. Sometimes from the sun, other times the moon. Tonight it was a single candle held aloft, casting his shadow on the open door.

"Camilla?"

"Hello, Nathan."

It was all I could say, as a million words—both unspoken and yet to be—nested in my throat. He apparently suffered a similar malady, as he stood, mouth agape, something between shock and a smile. We might have stood there all night, silent as that moment between darkness and dawn, if it weren't for the intrusion of two other voices. A squalling baby's cries were every bit as dry and tortured as the shout that came from the darkness. "Who is it at this hour?"

"See for yourself." And with that wicked grin I knew so well, Nathan swung the door wider and stepped aside, inviting Evangeline Moss into his circle of light. But then, as I saw her small, pointed features unfurl from pinched curiosity to a triumphant sneer, I knew she wasn't the spinster sister anymore. She sidled up to Nathan's side, fearless of the candle. Both of them wore an expression of smug victory, nothing like the reception I'd been expecting.

"You don't seem surprised to see me." I wavered somewhere between suspicious and sad, but I kept my voice cool as steel.

"We should never be surprised at the work of Heavenly Father," Nathan said before directing Evangeline to step aside and let me in.

CHAPTER 28

The baby cried and cried—long, scratchy wails that sounded like tree branches brushing against the wall. At Evangeline's jostling, part of the blanket fell away, and I could see it was a tiny thing, red and scrunched up like a bean with wrinkled, skinny arms shooting out. The newborn demanded my attention, serving as the center point around which the rest of the picture formed. Slowly, like ripples coming to rest behind a skipping stone, I gained a clear picture of my surroundings. Evangeline's parlor, yet not hers alone. A neatly folded pile of the Deseret News—a luxury she would never have afforded herself. The unmistakable scent of freshly carved wood, assuring me that somewhere—probably at the kitchen table—a project had been abandoned to the night. A few embers still glowed in the little parlor stove, meaning the room had spent the evening in a state of luxurious warmth.

Then, of course, there was Nathan himself, comfortable and authoritative as he touched the candle to the table lamp, filling the room with soft light. My eyes tracked that little light, and my breath caught in my throat as it touched the wick. There it was, a frosted blue globe etched with the image of young women dancing, a length of twisting ribbon linking them. I knew that lamp as well as I knew the man; it had been painted for me by his sister, Rachel, and had been a special gift to me after one of his trips to Salt Lake City.

The light seemed to irritate the baby, or at least magnify its cries.

"Take her upstairs," Nathan said, and for a moment there was confusion as Evangeline and I looked at each other, wondering exactly which one of us he addressed and just who was to be taken upstairs.

It wasn't until he snapped, "Go!" that I realized Evangeline's immobility wasn't due to confusion, but stubbornness. She jutted her chin and said, "This is *my* house," heedless of the squalling infant in her arms.

That's when Nathan softened, reaching out to touch first the baby's tear-streaked face, then Evangeline's hollow, freckled one. "Just see if you can get her to settle down."

"She won't. I've been trying everything."

"Sounds like colic," I said, though what possessed me to join in the conversation I'll never know. I suppose standing there with so many unanswered questions, I felt some need to interject what I did know. "Try rubbing warm oil on her stomach."

Evangeline's gaze narrowed and she held the child closer.

"Don't tell me what to do. I'm every bit as good a mother as you ever were. Better, even. I would never—"

"That's enough."

Nathan's voice held the same ability to command obedience and attention it always had. Evangeline and I both cast our eyes to the floor, and there mine stayed until the relative silence assured me she had left the room. When I faced Nathan again, he was gesturing toward the sofa, inviting me to sit, as if this were a social call. Numb, I complied, part of me relieved to have something familiar to do. I smoothed my skirts as I sat, he took one of the high-backed chairs opposite, and when we were quite settled, I cleared my throat and asked the question that had been burning on my tongue since the moment he opened the door. "What has happened here?"

"I've taken Evangeline as a wife."

"Obviously." Then, curtailing my sarcasm, I gathered my thoughts, my strength, for after all this time, it would take all of my will and wits to maintain the humility Nathan seemed to have grown accustomed to. "I know it's late, but can I please see the girls? I promise not to wake them."

"See the girls?"

I couldn't quite read his expression. Every muscle in his face was perfectly relaxed, not a hint of the tension that so often ridged his jaw, nor the humor that twitched the corners of his lips. His eyes were hooded, devoid of light, and my mind raced with the possibilities in his lack of response.

"I know they must be sleeping, but I could just—"

"They're not here."

"Not here in the house?" I fought for calm.

"Not here in the city." There was the smile I knew—broad and victorious.

My hands clawed at the fabric of my expensive traveling

suit, and I willed myself not to rip it to shreds. Every breath strained against the corset that, at the moment, was the only thing holding me upright.

"Then where?"

"They're at home, Camilla. Where they belong."

I noticed he didn't say that I belonged there too. That, coupled with the relief of knowing they were safe, helped me breathe a little easier. I couldn't imagine Melissa tolerating Evangeline's narrow permissions, and Lottie would wither away without sunlight and wide, green fields in which to run. I said none of this, however, having learned long ago how changeable Nathan's humor could be.

One particularly long squawk came from upstairs, and we both winced at the shrillness of it.

"What's the baby's name?" I was still in shock at her existence.

"Sophie. I haven't had a decent night's sleep since she was born," Nathan said.

I removed the pins from my hat and settled it on my knees, hoping he would see me—for now—as an ally. At least until I'd learned all I needed to know. "It gets easier, remember?"

"None of ours ever cried like that."

"Of course they did. Lottie, especially."

His smile was dangerously warm now. "I don't remember."

"You must have been in your workshop or here in town. She had a terrible time. Kimana used to make me an herbal tea. Fennel, I think. And something else. That seemed to help. Perhaps Evangeline—"

"She's nowhere near the rebel you are, my dear. She knows better than to trust a Lamanite concoction."

The harshness of his words startled me from my fond reverie of the wise woman who'd taught me so much about how to be a wife and mother, but this did not seem the proper time to defend her. "I've never considered myself a rebel."

"Really? Not when you left your father? When you left me? When you left the church?"

"I wasn't rebelling, Nathan. I was . . . escaping. I ran away with you to escape my father. I ran away from you to escape the church."

"And now?"

I didn't know how to answer. I pictured my cozy little home, my son—*our* son—sleeping in my arms. An entire life he knew nothing about. And by the same token, here I'd walked into a tableau I never knew existed. Here was a new sister wife and a child. Somewhere was another. And my own children scattered to the wind—by my hand and his—like so much chaff. But I would not blame him, not now, not yet. Nor would I beg his forgiveness. Instead, I settled in and forced my own face into what I hoped was an impassive mask. "I could ask you the same thing. Is Evangeline your escape?"

He seemed truly amused for a moment, as if this cramped, dull house and the dour woman who came with it could be anyone's haven. But then his expression turned serious, and he focused his attention on his work-worn hands—the only part of him that failed to exude youthfulness after all these years.

"After you left—"

"Do you mean after you left me? Without even letting me say good-bye to my daughters?"

He remained unfazed. "After I heard that you'd been . . . taken away—"

"To shed blood for my supposed sin."

"Will you stop!" He'd raised his voice and then lifted his eyes to the ceiling. I think we both noticed for the first time the new quiet coming from upstairs. He collected himself and continued in a hushed tone that I'd always found far more disturbing than any volume. "I came back for you, and you were gone. I waited and waited. . . ."

"What did you think had happened?"

"I didn't know. So I went to Brigham himself. Because we hear stories and rumors, but I don't think I ever believed—" He stopped, as if catching himself on the brink of doubt, and set his jaw to continue. "Brigham claimed to know nothing. Only that we were living in precarious times and we had to do all we could to defend the unity of our faith."

"So you thought they'd carried out their threats?"

He wouldn't meet my eyes.

"You knew I wouldn't be rebaptized. Did it give you pleasure to think I'd been restored by my own blood?"

"Don't." Everything in his voice and demeanor made the word a threat. "You can't imagine the pain we've—*I've*—been through. I went to Brigham hoping he'd give me an answer—a different one. One that didn't include apostates being disciplined so . . ."

"Harshly?"

"When Brigham didn't have an answer for me, and I knew he was hiding the truth, I wept. Like a baby, right there in his office."

"Over my supposed death or your supposed faith? Nathan, what more could it take for you to see that this—*man*—" I spat the word—"is not the infallible prophet you set him up to be?"

I'd rarely seen him exhibit any weakness, but he seemed close to tears at that very moment. So I watched, waiting to see if any would be shed in my presence. Was there any hope at all that I might still reach him with the truth?

I took his hand. "This is hardly the dream we imagined when we set off together."

He looked at me, and I saw a bit of the youthful spark in his eyes, the dashing young man who spirited me away all those years ago.

"It's not too late, Nathan. I know you still love me, and together we can make a home for our children. A home where we can teach them to know the true God, to love and serve Jesus Christ. He has sustained me through these months, and he can give our family a new start."

His eyes brightened, and for a brief moment, I allowed myself to imagine it was a real possibility.

Finally he blinked under my gaze. "So Brigham was right. You were—and are—a heretic of the worst sort. You would have been better off if you'd been restored by blood, rather than dying outside the faith. He said you were waiting for me. And that we would have more children throughout eternity."

"And that was enough to comfort you? That you'd call me from my grave? Can you not see what an empty promise that is?"

But he couldn't. His eyes were darkened, and he refused to open them to the truth. I, however, was beginning to understand more truth than I had bargained for.

As if to confirm the direction my thoughts had taken, Nathan continued to explain. "Brigham asked me about my trade, and when I told him I was a carpenter, he offered me work in the temple."

As he spoke the word *temple*, the light in his face outshone the softness coming from the lamp. How well I remembered all those years, his sincere, frustrated attempts to capture the prophet's eye with his handiwork, only to be rebuffed time and time again. He'd hewn stone from the quarry and given the same tithe of labor as any other Saint, but his longing to be an artisan . . .

"That must have felt like a dream coming true." *And your so-called prophet knew just the right time to dangle it before you,* I thought but did not say.

"In a sense, yes. He—"

"And was Evangeline a part of Brigham's compensation for my life?"

He gave me a wary look, as if he, too, realized he'd lost his foothold. "One day, about a year ago, Evangeline came out to the house. She was riding my horse. The one you'd taken."

"Honey." The horse that had saved my very life.

"She said the horse had shown up here one morning, the reins tied to her porch. Said she thought it was a word from Heavenly Father himself, bringing us your blessing from the grave."

He went on, but it was Evangeline's voice I heard in all its familiar religious rambling. Hers, at least, was a faith fervent enough to match his own.

"And," I said, interrupting, "you get the added benefit of a house in town, close to your work at the temple, when so many others have fled the city."

"Heavenly Father has blessed me in many ways."

Suddenly I felt like I'd invaded a private little joke. Only rather than being amused, I was feeling increasingly empty. Everything I'd ever loved about this man had fallen to ruin, and I now despaired of keeping even the smallest affection in my memories. His boyishness, immaturity. His impulsivity, thoughtlessness. And the last—that I'd trusted him to be a devoted parent to my daughters, that they would, indeed, be better for a time in his care—tore at me. When opportunity called, he'd abandoned them without a second thought.

"Why don't you have the girls here with you, Nathan?"

He squirmed, the way all men do when faced with the

peculiarities of women. "There were, shall we say, difficulties between Amanda and Evangeline."

"Ah yes. Amanda. My *other* sister wife. I take it she wasn't as complacent at being replaced as I was?"

"You were never replaced, Camilla. Never meant to be, at least. Heavenly Father's plan—"

"It is God's plan that a man loves his wife—"

"I loved you, Camilla."

"—and cares for his children. You abandoned my heart, Nathan, giving yourself to another. And now you've abandoned her. And our children. And—" a memory, one I hadn't considered until now— "*her* child. What did she have?"

His face lit up. "A boy. We have a son."

The sentence hung heavy between us, while I carried more than my share of its burden. Did he know? Could he possibly? My mind raced behind the eyes I fought so hard to hold steady. Master that he was, not even Nathan Fox would be able to control his anger at what he would see as an ultimate betrayal. Truth be told, in my darkest moments, I cloak that night—our final night together—in shame, even as I rejoice in the child that came from it.

I fought to swallow this last, great lie. "What did you name him?"

"Nathan, of course."

"Of course. You must be so pleased."

"He's an answer to prayer."

"I'm surprised you were able to leave him behind."

"Apparently we both have a knack for abandoning our children."

"Don't say that." But the truth of his words burned like a slap across my face.

In that moment, all my noble intentions crumbled, as

did any pretense of strength. Evangeline's parlor and all its shabby shadows warped behind a wash of tears, each one holding the days and hours since that first moment of recklessness when I closed the door on the little family Nathan and I had created. He said nothing in reply, only now both of my hands were in his, and I glanced down to see them nestled in his grip. I could not fully recognize the intent behind his touch. His thumb—coarse with labor—moved purposefully across my skin, which was pleasantly smooth due to a newfound luxury of hand cream and leather gloves. Still, we could not ignore the awful spot of amputation. Nathan turned my hands palm up and touched his finger along that ghostly spot in a curious, almost-investigative caress.

"Last summer," he said, speaking like a man gathering a half-forgotten memory, "we had the privilege of attending a lecture given by two of our finest missionaries, newly back from England."

I stared at the top of his head, swallowing my first taste of fear.

"They were concerned—" he looked up and offered one of those sideways, winking smiles—"we all were, about the strength of the church, the dedication of the faithful, and the threat of war. They told about one strange encounter with an Army general."

Colonel. Colonel Charles Brandon. I didn't blink.

"He was with a woman—a Mormon woman, from what they could tell. And they were quite distraught to see one of our own married to the enemy." Nathan broke off his gaze and looked down again. "Even more disturbing was the fact that this woman seemed not to care about the risk such a journey could pose to a woman in her condition."

Stone still, I fought the instinct to snatch my hands away

and hold them as a shield over my long-empty womb. Rather, a stronger, more protective intuition rose up, and like the doe in the brush whose slightest movement would call the attention of the hunter, I willed my very breath to match Nathan's own.

"You see," he said, looking up again, "she was with child."

I nearly gasped at what I saw. There, before me, in the brightness of his eyes and the very angle of his head, I saw my son—our son—and the man he would grow to be, handsome and strong. I could feel the confession on the tip of my tongue. The words repeated over and over inside my head. *She was carrying your son.*

But a force stronger than my guilt kept them silent. I thought of the words written on the pages in Mr. Bostwick's portfolio. He would find out soon enough, but not from me. Not until I had my daughters safely in my arms. I remembered the promises I made to create a home for my children that would protect them from the lies of my husband's faith. If God could forgive all I'd done, he could forgive a lie—even one I fought not to tell.

"If being pregnant forbade women from such a journey," I said, hoping the lightness in my tone didn't sound too forced, "there would be far fewer children in Zion."

I could tell by the set of his jaw that he was straining not to speak. Whatever battle raged in his mind remained hidden from me. He awarded victory to silence. The few inches between us were bridged by the touch of our hands, our eyes fixed on my particular disfigurement—the one that would surely set me apart from any other woman in Zion. Certainly that detail had made its way into the elders' report, though its relevance would be lost on all but Nathan. And Evangeline. That's when I realized I would not have to lie, nor would I have to confess.

"You've known all along that I'm alive."

CHAPTER 29

Nathan changed his grip, pressing his fingers against my wrist, at my pulse, but remained silent.

"You knew I was fearful for my life, carrying your child, and you did nothing."

"What was I supposed to do?"

"You knew—you had to have known that I'd gone back home."

"Of course I knew," he said, his words tinged with contempt. "But my home is here. I wasn't about to abandon it to chase you across the country."

"Comforting words, indeed." They pierced like a knife in my back. I needed little effort to extricate myself from his grip.

Indeed I began to feel, for the first time, that I was on the way to becoming truly free from him.

It would be years before I realized that with this final, twisting pain came a release for which I should have been praying all along. It was not enough that I longed to love a godly man; I needed to be liberated from desire for this one. But now, any bit of love I'd hidden in the darkest crevices of my heart skittered out into the light of this final betrayal. My heart became a lifeless mass within me. Not stone, for that would subject me to a permanent, cold death. No, more like the stump of a hollow tree that for so long holds all the appearance and grandeur of health and life and possibility, masking its fragility. One touch, and it crumbles. My destruction, however, brought peaceful, detached freedom.

I was no longer his wife in any sense that mattered. And soon enough, I would no longer be his wife even in name. "I've traveled with my attorney, Mr. Michael Bostwick. He'll be here first thing in the morning with all the paperwork necessary to proceed with our divorce."

He stood and found me, gripping my arms and pulling me close. "You can't—"

"I can," I said, feeling an odd sense of pride in the fact that it was my own feet holding me up. "I have legal grounds. Adultery. You've taken two wives while married to me, and your prophet is no longer the law of the land. Polygamy is illegal, whether he wants to admit it or not. You know as well as I do that I'm a complication he would rather not face. In fact, why don't you discuss it with him? I dare you. Tell him the wife he wanted you to believe was dead is alive and well and ready to fight for her children. All of them—including the secret son she stole away."

His face changed at this as anger dissolved with his grip. "A son?"

I instantly regretted letting this bit of truth slip, but I gave my foot a little stamp, determined not to lose the ground I'd gained. "Yes. A little boy. And he'll be forever your son just as Lottie and Melissa will be your daughters. But I won't be your wife. Your home won't be with us." My eyes took a long, final look at the dark corners of Evangeline's shabby parlor. "You've already made your choice."

And then, he changed. There was a moment, years ago, as I held our first son through his short hours of life, when Nathan had sat by my side, his entire body straining against itself as if he could take on the power of the Lord and snatch the inevitable fate from God's holy hands. Then, after our tiny baby took his last breath, Nathan seemed to take his first—his body soft and fluid like an empty shirt on a line. He'd been defeated by death, but he walked away from the battle somewhat relieved.

Now, in this moment, I saw him set down the same shield. If I could have peeked under his skin, I wouldn't have been surprised to see a mass of broken bones, with only the miracle of pride holding him upright. He seemed to shrink before me, the fight leaving his eyes as they became more level with mine. A power beyond my own brought my forever-wounded hand up to touch his cheek as my heart refused to let me fully enjoy the victory of the moment.

"All I ever wanted," he said, his voice as hollow as the body from which it came, "was a family."

"I know," I said, allowing pity to summon tears but calling on the Lord to hold them at bay. "I tried to give that to you, but it wasn't enough."

"Tell me, Camilla, did you ever believe? When you were baptized the day before our wedding—all of our teachings . . . were you ever a true believer?"

My hand still touched his face, and I felt the slightest

quiver from under his skin. I moved my thumb to graze his lip before taking it away, knowing this would have to suffice as our final kiss.

"I believed in you, Nathan. I believed in you before I loved you."

"And now?"

What could I tell him? That the strong, vibrant, passionate man who lured me away from my home with a smile and a few vague promises now presented himself as nothing more than a pathetic, empty shell? "Now I understand the danger of believing in a man. I don't want our children to make the same mistake."

He crossed his arms, and the outline of his muscles showed through the fabric of his shirt. Only I would know to look for the twitch at the corner of his jaw signaling a renewed strength. Slowly, his stance grew as that disassembled skeleton within him found its form, and there was no hint of defeat in his voice when he said, "I won't fight you."

"Thank you," I said, relieved just the same.

"I'm not going to drag my faith and our family through that kind of humiliation."

"I understand."

"Now I think she should go."

I whirled around to see Evangeline standing in the dark shadows at the foot of the stairs. I had no idea how long she'd been there or how much she'd heard. If Nathan knew, he certainly gave no indication; neither did he seem surprised now.

"We can't send her out into the night." Nathan spoke without acknowledging Evangeline's presence with even the slightest glance.

"No." I'd slipped my gloves on and was in the midst of securing my hat, eager for escape. "The hotel isn't far."

"See?" Evangeline said, slowly making her way into the light. "She can take care of herself." By now she was at my shoulder and I could feel her breath on the back of my ear as she offered to show me out.

Unwilling to ignite an argument, I allowed Evangeline to take my elbow and lead me to the front door.

"Wait," Nathan called out. "Tomorrow's the Sabbath."

"A lot she cares about that," Evangeline muttered.

I said nothing, only turned back to Nathan. "What do you mean?"

"I won't meet with your attorney friend tomorrow."

"Of course," I said, feeling the first flutters of distrust. "Monday morning then?"

His smile, to anyone who didn't know him, was genuine. "Monday, first thing."

At that, my little redheaded warden renewed her grip on my arm and sped our steps to the door. She opened it with a flourish, ushering in the night air that seemed much colder than before I entered this house.

I was bracing myself lest she attempt to literally kick me out into the street when she stood to her tiptoes and pulled my ear close.

"Sorry we don't have a barn to offer you, but we do rent a stable in the livery on the corner. You can sleep there if you like."

Odd how, after feeling so victorious only moments ago, one word from this little woman could bring about such shame. Did she know? She must have—how I'd slept in our own barn back home those first nights after Nathan returned with a new wife. How triumphant she must have felt, displacing me from my husband's bed. I heard the click of the front door and turned to see the parlor window go dark. In fact, every house was dark, and I took just a moment to get my bearings. Bad enough to be wandering the streets of Salt Lake City at night without wandering in the wrong direction.

The wind blew against my face, bringing with it a bit of misting rain, and suddenly the few blocks between me and the Hotel Deseret seemed an insurmountable journey. Still, in all these years I'd learned there was no such thing, so I braced myself for the first step, stopping after a hundred or so when I found myself outside the livery. I knew it well. The place stood on four lots, with a wide yard surrounding all sides. At the back, those wealthy enough to own them paid a small fee to store their wagons or buggies or other such conveyances in an enormous building. Two longer buildings ran along either side of the property. Before embarking on their missionary career, Evangeline's own brothers worked here, mucking the evenly spaced stalls and caring for the horses lodged within.

Though I was certain Evangeline had no charitable motive in whispering this place into my mind, the warmth and the shelter it offered beckoned me now in an irresistible way.

Mindless of any sort of consequence, I contorted my body to fit between the wide-spaced railings of the fence surrounding the property, stepped into the yard, and made my way directly across it to the nearest barn. Thankful for the saintly love that invited such trust, I opened the unlocked door, instinctively patting the wall along its frame until my fingers found the shape of a square tin lamp and a box of matches.

Though the horses hadn't acknowledged my entrance, stamps and snorts rippled down the line at the sudden, sulfurous spark that filled the barn until I could get the flame safely subdued within the punched walls of the tin lamp. I blew out the match and, when it was cool to the touch, let it drop to the hard-packed dirt floor.

The room was long and narrow. My steps were muted as I made my way past the stalls that lined the right side of the room. The sweet smell of fresh hay spoke well of the horses' care, and I saw no fear in their large brown eyes as, one by one, I held up the lamp to shine its speckled light. Finally, six stalls down, I saw her. Even in the low light I recognized the burnished blonde of her well-curried coat. Wishing I had an apple or carrot or any such treat, I reached my hand and allowed Honey to nuzzle against it.

"Hello, old friend."

I suppose the idea began the minute Evangeline joked about my bedding down here for the night, but it took full form when I turned to see the saddle and tack hanging opposite the stall. Later I would have time to regret my impulsive decision, as I had regretted so many of them in my lifetime. But at that moment, my choice seemed inevitable.

"*Monday, first thing,*" he'd said, with a smile that wasn't all there. All of a sudden, everything he'd said—his gracious admission of defeat, his show of compassion for my soul, his promise of Monday morning—all of it was so clearly tainted by the man I knew him to be. Nathan's intentions weren't clear, but if Rachel's household of four wives and countless children could disappear, who was to say that Nathan couldn't spirit away his own family while Mr. Bostwick and I bided our time at the Hotel Deseret. My own experience taught me that lives could be ripped away in the span of a night. I dared not wait until Monday morning. I dared not wait until dawn.

CHAPTER 30

I reined Honey to a stop at the edge of the thicket. Beyond the trees, the church house of Cottonwood Canyon sat in the clearing, bathed in the sunlight of this damp spring morning. We'd ridden all night after a brief stop at the Hotel Deseret, where I left a note for Mr. Bostwick. The clerk, more irritated at my return than at having been roused from sleep, had flatly refused either to allow me to go upstairs or to fetch Mr. Bostwick down to me. He did, however, produce a sheet of stationery and a pencil before turning his head to allow me a bit of privacy as I wrote.

The message was short. Only that I'd taken it upon myself to ride out to Cottonwood Canyon and that he would find Nathan at the address I'd given him.

The clerk had provided no envelope, and I've no doubt his eyes glanced over my words long before Mr. Bostwick's did. But I didn't care, as long as the message was delivered at dawn.

Then, the ride. Sometimes at a breakneck pace with my body bent to Honey's neck, trusting her thundering hooves to navigate the hard-packed road, other times at a slow, easy gait while I sat tall and slack in the saddle, rocked by her steps. All night I'd heard only the sound of her hooves accompanying the prayers in my head. Now, as I held her still at the edge of the church house clearing, I could hear the voices of the people I'd once called my neighbors—my brothers and sisters—strong and unified, raised in song.

Come, all ye saints of Zion, and let us praise the Lord;
His ransomed are returning, according to his word.

I smiled, wondering if they would sing so lustily, knowing just who among them was returning—a fallen Saint on a stolen horse, here to snatch her children. Almost as quickly as the smile twitched across my lips, though, doubt swelled within me. I was coming home now as one resurrected. My daughters and I had spent more than a year mourning each other, but I'd done so with the luxury of hope.

The saddle leather creaked as I swung myself to the ground, rearranging my skirts upon landing. I led Honey to the edge of the trees before loosely looping the reins around a branch. I stepped into the clearing just as the Saints in the church house launched into the second verse of the hymn, calling the dispersed people of Judah to gather in the latter days. I remembered singing that song and the flushed, fervent faces of those singing around me. Nathan always sang with an impassioned marching motion, and my own foot never failed to tap. Even now the tune strained to be hummed into the morning air.

I took my first steps into the clearing, looking back over my shoulder as I'd done since the first miles Honey and I took together. If Mr. Bostwick remained true to our plan, he and Nathan had already encountered each other, and no doubt both were unhappy with my rash behavior. Sabbath or not, I trusted Mr. Bostwick to plead my case. Moreover, I knew he would buy me time. I could only pray it would be enough.

I wasn't alone in the clearing; scattered families were making their way to the church house. Inside, the congregation implored Israel to rejoice, as God would encounter them wherever they were found. Somehow, God kept them from finding me, as I moved along the building in full view, yet attracting no attention. While I wouldn't go inside, having left once before with a vow never to return, I would hazard a peek through a window once the Saints were settled, just to see my girls.

But I would need no such opportunity, for as I came to the front of the building, just at the corner, there they were, just cresting the swell of land at the edge of the churchyard.

"Come on, girls. We're late." It was the first time I'd seen my husband's second wife, Amanda, since the day before I left this place, but she looked like she'd lived a decade within the year. Her hair was still black as a raven's wing, but the sheen that brought it close to blue was gone. Gone, too, was the elaborate styling of braids and loops. Instead, she looked like any other of her pioneer sisters, with long locks unceremoniously secured at the back of her head, framing a face that had gone from porcelain perfection to being simply pale. Shadows lurked below her eyes, and the figure I'd once envied in its fashionable dress had settled within serviceable calico.

With her head turned to look behind, I had the smallest

fraction of a second to duck around the corner, yet I remained frozen. My daughters were behind those skirts, but before I could see them, I'd have to get through my scowling sister wife.

And she'd seen me.

Never had I considered Amanda a person to be feared, and I think it was the expression of sickened terror on her face that made me feel like I'd seen a phantom reflected in a looking glass. Immediately I stepped back, pulling the hood more closely around my face. Still I could see them, if only through my narrowed, secret view. Melissa first—oh, Melissa. Her hair was darker than I remembered, or perhaps she was simply destined to leave her blonde locks to her childhood.

She'd always been my serious girl, and that hadn't changed. When Amanda moved aside, Melissa stepped forward, her eyes lifted up to the church house door as if waiting for a miracle to emerge.

"Go on in," Sister Amanda said, tinged with impatience. She opened the door and gave an imaginary little swat to hurry Melissa along, but my daughter needed no encouragement. The congregation was singing the fourth verse of the hymn, and the clear, sweet voice of my child joined them.

Tho wicked men and devils exert their pow'r, 'tis vain,
Since he who is eternal has said you shall obtain.

Already, before I'd even had a chance to touch her, I stung from her rejection, but I could not dwell on that defeat, as I looked over to see my Lottie coming up behind. Never—not since her first step—had this child ever moved without seeming to spring up from within. Now she walked as if temple stones were strapped to her boots.

"Come on, come on," Amanda urged, snapping her fingers.

Lottie, however, would not hurry. Her blonde hair was plaited and pinned to make two rings fastened with bows, and her dress was clean and starched, but her downcast face belied such prettiness. Once she reached the bottom step, Amanda took hold of her sleeve and, heedless of Lottie's little yelp, yanked her across the threshold. The gesture lit a fire in me and I lunged for Sister Amanda myself, but she deflected my grasp and held me at bay saying, "Go sit with your sister. I'll be in directly," as if she had little more to do than dispose of a fly on the wall.

The moment the girls were safely inside, however, she spun around, her face a chalky white save for two strawberry-red spots on her cheeks. "So you're alive, are you?"

Such an odd question. Light-headed from the shock of seeing my little girls after a long, sleepless night, I found myself without any clever response and said simply, "I am."

She stomped around to the back of the church house and I followed, compelled by the grip she had on my sleeve.

"I knew it," she said, her chapped hands clenched into fists. "Nothing that man ever told me turned out to be true. Told me you'd been dragged away in the middle of the night. 'Atonement by blood,' he said, lest I ever take it in my head to follow your steps. Oh, he was broken up and sad about it for a while. Talked you up like a saint. A real one, like the Catholics. Every night filling your girls' heads with stories, telling how they look like you. 'Image of your mother,' he'd say."

When she quoted Nathan, her face transformed to the very image of him, and I almost laughed at her talent.

"But then he stopped. He changed. Married himself that horrible woman in town and left me out here with that Indian woman and three children—"

Her voice was shrill, and the accent of her homeland, England, became more pronounced.

Now it was I who touched her sleeve, calming her as best I could. "I'm so sorry," I said, not sure if I was apologizing for leaving, for coming back, or for the months in between.

Suddenly she was crying, and she wiped both her eyes and nose on the sleeve of her dress—something the woman I'd known before would never do. "Not your fault. You got away. I just can't understand why in heaven's name you'd ever come back."

Her words carried the weight of confession. Both of us knew the danger of discontentment, but we stood in that instant free from its burden—she for the moment, at least. It was like a yoke lifted from both our necks. Never in our months together as sister wives had we shared such a moment of kinship, and we silently granted each other permission to give in to cautious laughter.

"Now tell me," she said as the last giggle faded, "what are you doing here?"

"I've come for my girls." For the first time, my mission held a ring of joy.

"What you saw—I know I seemed a bit short with them, but it was the shock of seeing you—"

"I understand," I said, though I doubted it was the first they'd seen of her temper. "Do you—will they be happy to see me?"

"Oh, sister—" tears sprang to her eyes again—"little Lottie prays every night for Jesus to keep you safe. Then Melissa chastises her, saying you're in the grave waiting for Papa to call you to heaven, and Lottie just cries and cries. I never know what to say, but Kimana tells them that Jesus can keep you safe wherever you are, and that gives them some comfort, but still—"

"What did Nathan tell them?"

"At first, nothing. Just that you were at Evangeline's. Then later, that you'd simply vanished. Left us all to go back to where he found you and would never be back. He said he didn't want to scare them." She gave a furtive look around and behind us. "I don't want to frighten them now. And if those people in there . . . Well, I can't imagine the scene. Go back to the house. Kimana's there with the baby."

"Your little boy?"

Her face brightened, and I saw the first hint of the vibrant woman I'd known. "Little Nate. He's my life, my very life."

"So you understand why I have to take my girls with me. I have a home ready for us with my mother back in Iowa."

"Away from all this?" She inclined her head toward the wall on the other side of which a new song burst forth, singing of Adam-ondi-Ahman. I remembered Nathan teaching our girls that song before bedtime, telling them of Adam and Eve, sent from the Garden of Eden to live after their fall.

"Just think," he'd said, "the mother and father of all mankind living in the land we call Missouri. And to think, one day, it will once again be the holiest of places with a gathering of all the prophets."

How my ears had burned listening to such lies. I blamed the firelight for the flush on my face, unable to voice the shame I felt at my silence. And now, there they were inside, singing the lies I'd allowed them to learn.

"I don't expect you to understand."

"Oh, but I do," she said. "Not about the church so much. Seems one's as good as another. But I don't much like sharing my husband, and I don't know that I'd want my daughters growing up to do the same."

"I'm divorcing Nathan. Legally," I added when her eyes narrowed in suspicion. "I don't know what that will mean for you. There's still Evangeline, but the girls and I will be gone. I guess that will make you first wife."

She offered a weak smile. "I do love our husband, you know."

"He's your husband," I said, "not mine. But I know what it means to love him."

Silence again inside the church house.

"I'd better get inside," Amanda said. "The girls'll be worried. You can wait for us at the house. If you like, I can talk to them on the way home, tell them it was an awful mistake and you've just been traveling. . . ." Her voice trailed as she grappled with what would be an impossible conversation.

"No. Don't say anything. Just come home as quickly as possible. And don't invite Elder Justus for dinner."

"Well, that's not likely to happen anyway." In a spontaneous burst of camaraderie, she took me in a surprisingly strong embrace before disappearing around the corner.

I made my way back to the grove to find Honey waiting patiently. A hooded woman astride a horse would surely attract attention in our small town, and truth be told, my legs relished the idea of a long, stretching walk. So, assured that all Saints were safely tucked inside the church house, I led her along the edge of the clearing. Dew still sparkled on the ground despite the efforts of the sun. I dropped the reins and allowed Honey to follow of her own accord. I peeled off my gloves and untied the cape's thick ribbon, instantly refreshed as I lifted the heavy wrap from my shoulders. The tiniest breeze touched my skin and cooled my scalp.

From inside came another round of singing, this time one of the rare hymns shared by Mormons and Gentiles alike. I recalled the warm familiarity I felt lifting it with my voice within those very walls, and now, with them well behind me, I hazarded a soft utterance to the morning.

A mighty fortress is our God, a tower of strength ne'er failing.

For just a moment the volume of the congregation increased, calling back my attention, and just as they and I proclaimed our God a mighty helper, there they were—my little girls framed in the church house doorway. I saw their lips mouth, *Mama!* and my world was reduced to four little running feet as the expanse of dewy grass between us grew smaller and smaller. I fell to my knees within seconds of their touch and held them to me—one in each arm. Still I remember the sweet smell of their hair, the hot, wet tears on my neck, our sniffling, soft words saying nothing of any great meaning. Honey gently stepped aside as our reunion became one great, silly, rolling mass with bits of blue sky appearing and disappearing behind the close, beautiful faces of my children.

Once we'd righted ourselves, I looked past them in time to see Amanda step back inside and close the doors.

"Lottie looked out the window and thought you were a ghost," Melissa said, sounding as mature and authoritative as ever. "And she pestered Auntie Amanda to let us go outside and see."

"But Auntie said I mustn't disturb."

Hearing Lottie speak brought new tears to my eyes. Gone were the soft, round sounds of the little girl she'd been. Her voice had thinned along with her face, and traces of Amanda's accent were unmistakable.

"So we waited for the first prayer," Melissa began.

"—and I prayed and prayed that you weren't a spirit—"

"—and when we started singing, Auntie Amanda told us to go see for ourselves."

"Well, what a wonderful thing for Sister Amanda to do."

"Do we have to go back inside?" Lottie's pout harked back to the child of my memories.

"Of course we do," Melissa said, already attempting to stand.

"No." I grasped her hand and held her close. "Think of the ruckus we'd cause. Let's go home. We can surprise Kimana. And besides, I'd love to meet your little brother."

At this Lottie erupted in new glee and leaped to her feet. She reached for my hand to help me up and, with unbridled childish horror, recoiled at what she saw. "Mama, your fingers!"

This captured Melissa's attention, but she appeared more intrigued than frightened. "Frostbite?"

"Yes." I stood, feeling more than a little self-conscious as I brushed my skirt. "Do you see why I always tell you to bundle up?"

"Will they grow back?" Lottie's nose hovered inches above my scarred flesh.

"Of course not, silly," Melissa said. "They're flesh and bone."

Lottie looked up, her eyes wide as dollars. "Did it hurt?"

"Not as much as being away from you."

I could tell it took all of my little girl's strength to reach out and touch that unfamiliar hand, but when she did, I felt the years slip away. I held my other out to Melissa, but she preferred to take Honey's reins, recounting how angry her papa had been when I'd taken the horse the first time.

"But you're both back now," she said, setting the pace with slow, resolute steps.

"Yes." I tried to guard my reply from falsehood.

We walked along the narrow stream leading to our house, the chatter of the girls running as fast as its water. They told me of Amanda's son, Nate, but I said nothing of the brother awaiting them elsewhere. Lottie had started school, and she loved it, though arithmetic gave her fits. Melissa had memorized Mark Antony's speech from Shakespeare's *Julius Caesar* and was quoting the last familiar line when the little home we'd shared came into view.

Even from this distance, I could see that the property had taken on what my papa used to call a "widow's look." The small fence around the house had fallen into disrepair with its gate hanging at an unlatched angle. The woodpile was down to just a few split logs, and nary a tool was to be seen. Still, a thin ribbon of smoke came up from the chimney like a beckoning promise, and I answered with my quickening step.

Some would be puzzled as to how I could feel this to be a homecoming, knowing that my true home was a bright-yellow house hundreds of miles east. They might not understand how, having so recently reunited with my mother, I could ever hold my arms out to the small, brown woman who had walked so slowly from the front door, only to stand perfectly still at the gate. But those people, I think, have never been held in arms as soft as Kimana's.

I fell into her that morning the way I imagine one would land in a cloud. She smelled, as always, of flour. Speechless, we held each other until I stepped away. Her round, unlined face was just as I remembered, though she'd grown more streaks of silver in her hair. Small, button-brown eyes brimmed with tears, and her chin quivered in an effort to maintain a calm demeanor.

"So," she said, her voice the same iron-flat, "the mother fox has come back."

I nodded, too enthralled with this woman to speak. It was she, I knew, who had fed my children, tucked them in at night, brushed their hair, and bandaged their wounds. Most of all, I knew her prayers blanketed them head to toe, night and day. Stronger and closer than even my own.

Kimana took my face in her broad, soft hands. "I knew it. Even when Mr. Fox said you passed over, our Creator told me you were still alive. I have prayed for this day, Mrs. Fox. I have spoken your name in the night and the morning."

"I know you have." Unlike Kimana, I allowed my emotions to flow unchecked. Tears, however, weren't enough, and I felt my knees give out beneath me, sending me once again into her embrace. My body, it seemed, had used its final bit of strength to get me here, but I could not take another step on my own.

"Poor child," Kimana said, half-leading, half-carrying me to the house.

I felt Lottie's hand in mine. "Is Mama sick?"

"No, little one," Kimana soothed. Whatever other words of comfort she shared, however, were lost to the darkness that overcame me before I even saw the door.

CHAPTER 31

In my dreams, a child cried, and I reached for him. Rather than finding a familiar, soft bundle, I found myself tangled in thin arms, my fingers entwined in silk.

"Mama, can you hear me?"

The voice at the edge of the darkness was both familiar and not, as was the face I saw when my eyes fluttered open.

"Mama, are you awake now?"

Lottie, of course. Nose to nose beside me on the goose-down pillow. She'd taken her braids down and her hair made a golden cloud in the afternoon sun pouring through the window.

"Are you ready to get up?"

That made three questions before I could peel my lips

apart to work up a response. I closed my eyes and nodded, humming an affirmative answer, and drew her closer to me. She remained still for a few minutes but soon became a mass of wiggling elbows and knees.

"Auntie Amanda's been home from church for hours, and Kimana has biscuits and gravy waiting for you."

At the mention of food my stomach turned itself inside out as my brain scrambled to remember the last time I'd had anything to eat. More than a day, by my fuddled calculations.

"Tell her I'm coming." The last word was stretched around an enormous yawn that sent Lottie into her own. Playfully, I nudged her out of the bed, and she scampered out of the room announcing my imminent arrival.

I don't know if I should blame the night's ride or the morning's nap while wearing a corset, but every muscle, bone, and sinew in my body ached with movement, and once Lottie was out of the room, I indulged myself in all manner of wincing and groaning like I'd suddenly been transformed into a woman twice my age. I swung my legs over the side of the bed and sat, taking in the familiar surroundings.

My room. Never shared with my husband. I remembered well how Nathan had expected it to compensate, somehow, for ousting me from our marriage bed upon Amanda's arrival. It had its own cozy fireplace and expansive window—everything that, under different circumstances, might have felt luxurious. But I'd taken it as a place to hide away during the long winter nights when the girls were asleep and Nathan and his new bride chatted away beside the front room stove. By the time they were ready to take themselves off to bed, I'd be gazing into my embers or huddled down under my quilts.

Now I could see that nothing had changed since my departure, save for the missing lamp that now adorned Evangeline's parlor. Everything, including an abandoned knitting project, gave the impression that I'd only gone to the market for the afternoon, rather than across the country and back again, having lost a father and gained a son along the way.

Somebody had thought to remove my boots, and my stockinged feet padded across the thick braided rug as I made my way to the mirror hanging above the bureau. I don't know what I expected to find, having had no opportunity for close personal scrutiny in several days, but I found myself pleasantly surprised. My hair was, understandably, falling out of its pins, resulting in soft waves framing my face.

"You're here," I said to the woman in the glass, though I refrained from a gloat of total victory. My cheeks might have been flushed from new sleep, but there was a lingering fatigue in my eyes.

I plunged my hands into the water in the washbasin below the mirror and brought it up to splash my face. A square washcloth was draped over its edge, and I soaked this too, wrung it out, and patted it along the back of my neck, under my collar. I longed for a bath, remembering evenings with the large, galvanized tub right here next to my fireplace, stepping quickly in and out of my sacred garments long after I'd given any credence to their power. Opening the top drawer of my bureau, I found my bone-backed brush, strands of my hair still wound around its bristles. Despite my hunger—which was by now to the point of nausea—I considered taking out my hairpins, giving myself a good brush, and pinning it all up again. Not so much for vanity's sake, but as a diversion from what awaited on the other side of the door. Sometime within the next few hours I would be telling my daughters that we were leaving this place—their home—forever.

Still bootless, I walked into our front room in time to see

the familiar sight of Kimana pulling a tray of piping-hot biscuits from the oven. A pot of sausage gravy bubbled on the stove, and in less than a minute, a mass of both mingled on a plate in front of me. I restrained myself long enough to thank the Lord for my safe journey and ask for a blessing on this meal, digging in even as I opened my eyes at amen. Lottie and Melissa sat across from me, each with their own biscuit and a dish of jam between them. So much time melted away in that moment, as though God had set back the calendar of my days and it was any other Sabbath, with Nathan just out in his workshop or walking a dinner guest halfway home.

"May we join you?"

Amanda emerged from the front bedroom, having taken the time to rebrush and braid her hair since I'd last seen her. On her hip sat little Nate, happily occupied with a wooden block.

"Of course," I said through a mouthful. How odd it must be for her to feel she needed to be invited into her own home.

"Look, Natey," she said, "your auntie Camilla has come to visit."

She used the boy's body itself to point in my direction, and the child fixed his eyes on me with the curiosity and expectation of one who hadn't reached his first year.

"Hello, Nate," I said as she plopped the child on the table in front of me. My eyes welled with tears for my own little boy, but I whisked them away before anyone could question. Not that they would, as it was immediately obvious that Nathan's son commanded the full attention of everyone in the room. Kimana's voice jumped to an octave I'd never heard before as she bustled about the room finding the perfect biscuit for his little hand and pouring milk into what must have been his special tin cup. Lottie and Melissa were about the business of tweaking his toes and offering him new blocks to play with while Amanda looked upon all of this with well-coiffed maternal pride.

A new twist of guilt wedged itself in my gut, and I worked my fork around in the newly unappetizing dish.

"Isn't he the sweetest thing?" Lottie proclaimed, willingly giving up her place as the baby in the family.

"Auntie Evangeline's baby is ugly," Melissa said, causing all of us to gasp in protest, through which my older daughter remained unfazed. "Have you seen her?" she pointedly asked me.

"Just a glimpse," I said, uncomfortable under her suspicion.

"So you went there first before you came here?"

"I came in a stagecoach." I tried to lay a groundwork of enthusiasm. "It arrived in Salt Lake City, so I stopped by to visit."

"You saw Papa?" Lottie's whole face shone with love for the father she adored. "Was he so very happy to see you?"

"I'll bet Auntie Evangeline wasn't," Melissa said with a womanly cynicism I chose to ignore.

"I did see your papa, and we had a long talk." I set my fork down entirely, regretting every bite I'd taken as each seemed determined to climb up my throat and choke my words. "Your papa is married to your auntie Amanda, and now your auntie Evangeline, too. And . . . well, when I was gone for such a long time, I decided that maybe I shouldn't be his wife anymore."

I don't know what I expected their reaction to be, but certainly I'd expected something other than the vague, puzzled look on Lottie's face and the outright contempt in Melissa's.

"You can't do that," Melissa said. "When a man marries a woman, she is his forever, here and in heaven."

Amanda chose that moment to lift her son from the table and cuddle him in her lap. Lottie, too, sensing something was amiss, climbed up into Kimana's softness, leaving Melissa and me to face each other over food that might just as well have been little piles of dust.

"In a sense," I said, venturing into an explanation with all the care of walking on a frozen pond, "but marriage is also a promise, and your papa and I have both broken promises to each other."

"You're not supposed to break a promise," Lottie said, breaking my heart with her disappointment. Kimana looked away.

"You're the only one who broke a promise when you ran away from all of us." Melissa's voice held nothing but cool condescension. "What promise did he break?"

Before I could stop myself, I glanced at Amanda, who hid her face in her child's thick, black hair.

"Oh," Melissa said. "You don't want him to be married to Auntie Amanda."

My mind went back to the cheeky, brazen woman who'd invaded our home—nothing like the woman sharing this table with me. Now, in contrast to the coldness I'd initially greeted her with, I felt a tug of affection. And while, yes, her arrival had delivered a deadly blow to my marriage, it was hardly the first, and I would not lay blame at her feet.

"Not while he was still married to me."

"So why did you come back?"

That's when I knew that, while I'd been sleeping in the next room, Melissa had been building up the story behind my return, and I was about to begin tearing it down bit by bit.

"Because even if I'm not Papa's wife, I'm still your mother. And I miss you girls so very much."

"Can you live here if you're not married to Papa?"

"No," I said.

"Are you going to live in Kimana's cabin with her?" Lottie asked. "She's not married to Papa either."

At any other time, we might have greeted such an inno- cent question with the same abandoned laughter that Amanda and I had shared in the shadow of the church house, but all of our hearts were too heavy to go far beyond a flickering, indul- gent smile.

"We're going to live back home. My old home, with my mama. Your grandma. You've never had a grandma before, and she can't wait to meet you."

I watched as understanding dawned upon Melissa. Whatever truth she'd envisioned disappeared, buried by the weight of new revelation. Her eyes narrowed, her brow fur- rowed, and her lips twisted into a sneer stolen straight from her father. "*All* of us?"

"Both of you."

Little Nate squirmed in his mother's embrace and was set on a rug near the hearth, where a whole box full of blocks awaited him. Both the girls looked at him with such longing, I took a deep breath and announced, "You have another little brother. He's waiting for us back home."

Amanda looked shocked, and Kimana, pleased.

Melissa seemed not to have heard me. "This is our home."

"Your home is with your mother," Amanda said, reaching for Melissa's hand in a gesture of distant affection. "You need yours and she needs hers. Mine died when I was little, like you, and I miss her every day."

"I don't want to miss you anymore," Lottie said, and she crawled from Kimana's lap and ran around the table to me.

"A wife has to obey her husband," Melissa said. "Papa won't let you take us away. He'd never see us."

"He hardly ever sees us now." Lottie spoke such quiet,

unemotional fact, we all sat in silence, giving her words space to settle.

I prayed silently, begging my Lord to give me the words to say. Bad enough that I had naively thought I'd just slip them away, but never had I anticipated this divide between my daughters. Something told me that if I spoke the whole truth about wanting to shield them from the Mormon teachings, Melissa would dig her little heels in all the more. So long ago, in those first moments of waking after the storm, when Colonel Brandon declared we would have a battle on our hands, I had no idea the hardest fight of all would come between me and my eldest child. I had to give her a grudging respect for having such strength of conviction. Even at her young age, she was prepared for theological debate. Her father had taught her well. Too well, and thus I strengthened my stance.

"The law gives me permission," I said, then, softer, "and your father must obey."

"Even if he doesn't want to?" Her eyes begged for reassurance.

"Even if he doesn't want to."

To that, Melissa had nothing to say, and for a while the only sound in the room was the happy banging of wood on wood as Nate played with his blocks. I craned to look at him over Lottie's head. Perhaps he had his father's carpentry skill in his blood.

"When will you be leaving?" Amanda's question sounded almost wistful.

"I don't know," I answered truthfully. This final leg of the journey would be in Mr. Bostwick's hands. I would not budge from this place without his legal approval and paternal blessing.

"Are we going to walk the whole way?" Lottie asked.

This time her innocence did get a chuckle out of me. No

doubt she was thinking of those poor emigrants who came pushing handcarts, having walked the entire journey across the plains.

"Goodness, no. We're going to take a stagecoach." I jostled her on my knee, bouncing her until she giggled. "There'll be a grand team of eight horses, all with great chains jangling, and the ground is just a blur before your eyes."

She twisted in my lap. "Can Kimana come?"

All eyes turned to the silent woman at the table, each of us with our own personal longing.

"No," she said before any of us could make our plea. "My family is here, buried in this ground. And little Nate—" she nodded toward the child—"and more little ones someday."

Sister Amanda blushed and whispered, "Maybe, if Heavenly Father brings my husband home."

CHAPTER 32

From that afternoon on, I felt like one of the ten virgins in the parable who waited for the bridegroom to come in the night, only I had no idea exactly what I was waiting for. It is with a begrudging spirit that I admit to seeing a glimpse of Joseph Smith's vision for his polygamous doctrine. I found my heart opening to Sister Amanda and saw how we might have been friends—just as Evangeline and I once were—had we not been forced to share a husband.

When we had quiet corners of time, I shared the stories of my journey since I was last here. If the girls were listening, I talked about Charlie, imitating his funny little laugh, or about my mother and what a gentle, kind spirit she had. In the evenings after they were asleep, I sat with Sister Amanda and Kimana, reliving my journey—the horror of the amputation, my dreadful sojourn with Evangeline, and the bittersweet reunion with my parents.

"My father's gone too, you know," Amanda said, mopping her eyes with the corner of a pristine apron. "These people ran him out when he wouldn't join their church."

I didn't comment on her gaffe—that this was her church too—but I did click my tongue in sympathy. "Where is he now?"

"California, far as I know. That's where the money is, isn't it?"

"Just wait." I leaned close, as if conspiring. "This church has built a great city, and its leader has lost his power. My Mr. Bostwick says this will be the next great city of the West."

But I shared my deepest fears with Kimana alone.

One morning, when I'd been there more than a week, as Kimana and I worked to hang wash on the line, I told her of the sweet regard I harbored for Colonel Brandon. Sometimes talking with Kimana felt like dropping my thoughts into a deep, soft pool. She said little, merely rearranging my words and offering them back to me as questions to be pondered in a new light.

"He is a good man?" she asked after I'd gone on at length about his faith, his courage, his commitment to bring me home.

"One of the best I've ever known. And I think—I know he would marry me."

"And that is enough for your heart? To marry a good man?"

"You don't understand, Kimana. I'm going to be a divorced woman. No other man is going to want me."

"Here." She handed me one of Sister Amanda's nightgowns, soft white cotton trimmed in silk and lace. This was a change in our working pace, as I'd been handing the garments to Kimana to pin. Still, I took hold of the garment, shook it out, and draped it over the line. I waited for her to hand me the pins to secure it, as I would have, but she simply stood, arms crossed against her ample bosom, until I reached into the bag hanging from the line and retrieved them myself.

Hanging wash had never been my favorite chore, but I'd disliked it all the more since suffering the handiwork of Captain Buckley. With the loss of my fingers, I'd lost the ability to deftly pass the pin from one hand to another while clutching the cloth to the line. These days I held both pins in my right hand, folding my left wrist over the garment to hold it in place until it was secured. Frustrating work, even on mild, windless days like this one. Kimana witnessed my struggle in silence, simply taking a step away from the basket of wash on the ground, and waited for me to bend, lift out a petticoat, and start the process again. At this pace, my hands would be red and chapped, and the particularly sharp, chilling pain was already taking form at the place of my amputation. As I bent to the basket again, however, Kimana stopped me and said, "Hold up your hands."

I did, my fingers splayed against the clean white fabric.

"Tell me, Mrs. Fox, what do you see?"

"My hands." A simple answer, yes, but all I could think to say.

"How do they appear?"

Kimana never asked idle questions, so I studied the image in front of me, searching for the understanding she wanted me to find. "They look . . . incomplete."

"But is there anything you cannot do now that you could do before?"

"Wear a wedding ring." A small joke, more for my benefit than hers. Still, she granted me a rare, small smile and took my left hand in her coarse, but gentle, work-worn grip.

"You have learned to work through the emptiness. Here—" she traced her finger across the scarred flesh—"is mark of healing. Sealed up. When a woman loses her man, it is like the flesh being torn away. You need time to heal, to let that wound seal itself."

"But what if I never have another chance?"

Again she looked to my hand. "Do you hate the fingers that remain?"

"Of course not."

"A woman's hands are never idle. This hand is your womanhood. Your childhood is gone. Your husband, now, is gone. But your children remain. Do you call this hand worthless next to the other one?"

Slowly the picture took shape in my mind. God had given me these children. He kept my son safe in my womb through a perilous time and brought me safely back to my daughters. The home I would bring them to had its beginnings in my own childhood. All of this grace in the light of my own willful disobedience and ill-conceived actions. Why, then, should I fret over another man's affections? Why should I doubt that everything God had given me would forever be enough? This was the woman to whom I'd entrusted the lives of my children. I knew I could trust her words of wisdom for my own.

Just then I heard the girls' voices raised in a fresh, gleeful shout. Indecipherable at first, but then the words "Papa! Papa!" rang clear as morning. I moved the petticoat to the side and saw a wagon coming over the crest.

It was a moment I'd lived so many times before—Nathan coming home. For a moment, the past two years disappeared, and joy gathered in my knees and soared through my heart, taking my breath with it. My first instinct was to run and wait at the place where the hill meets the meadow, and I might have if Kimana had not held me.

"Do you see?" she said. "New skin can fool us into thinking a wound is healed when it is not."

I swallowed and dug my heels into the earth, watching my girls run to meet their father. But Nathan was not alone in the wagon. The reins were in the hands of my Mr. Bostwick, and between them, looking more diminutive than ever, sat Evangeline, clutching her swaddled Sophie.

At the bottom of the hill, Nathan hopped down. Melissa and Lottie ran into his arms. He swung Lottie up on his shoulders and held Melissa's hand for the rest of the way, arriving at our little fence just behind the wagon. I stayed at the clothesline as Amanda, with her son balanced on her hip, waited at the gate. There, depositing Lottie on the ground, Nathan greeted both with a kiss. If he even saw me, he gave no indication.

I looked to Mr. Bostwick, who pulled the horses to a stop outside our yard, greeting me with a tip of his hat and a reassuring nod.

Leaving the toddler in his older sisters' care, Nathan and Amanda made their way to the wagon, where Amanda took the baby as Nathan helped Evangeline from her seat. The child might have been Amanda's own, given how her face lit up. Anxious at the separation, little Nate ran through the open gate and straight for his mother's skirts. Soon after, I felt little hands clutching at my own, and I looked down to see my Lottie, her arms wrapped tight around me.

Still at the gate, Melissa. She looked on the gathering at the wagon with a longing I felt in my own heart. When she turned her eyes to me, I knew that my daughters and I would forever share the same wound of my divorce from their father, and hers would run especially deep. At some point, Kimana had melted away, and I held my hand out to my elder daughter. Finally, with slow, purposeful steps, her head cast to the ground, she came to me. She stiffened under my touch, but I would not take it away. I knew we would need to heal together.

Mr. Bostwick climbed down from the wagon and walked through the front gate with all the confidence he showed in everything he did. Nathan barely afforded him a glance as he walked by.

"These are your lovely daughters, I presume?" Mr. Bostwick said as he approached.

"They are." I introduced each one, but Lottie only clung tighter, and Melissa stared at his spit-shined shoes.

"Well, well. What a lovely family."

I thanked him, then shooed the girls off so we could talk alone.

Mr. Bostwick changed his stance, forcing me to turn my back to Nathan and the others, and said, "There's a stage leaving first thing tomorrow morning. I think it's best you and the girls be on it."

"Already?"

"What did you expect?"

I had no answer, only that the familiar peace of these few days made everything else seem almost dreamlike.

"The divorce?"

He puffed out his big barrel chest, hooking his thumbs in his vest pockets. "You can imagine my surprise when I was given only a few scribbled words to explain such a perilous decision."

"I'm sorry. I didn't know what else—"

"You should have waited for me, Camilla. It was bad form to come out here."

"I had to."

"And stealing the man's horse?"

"Legally, she is still my horse too."

Mr. Bostwick rocked back on his heels, looking like he almost admired me on that point. "Well, not any longer. Mr. Fox has agreed not to contest the divorce. He has signed, and I need only file the papers in court. You are, for all intents and purposes, a free woman." I don't know what I expected to feel at that moment. When I was first declared Nathan's wife, I had such spinning joy I feared I would fall over if it ever stopped. Later, when we were sealed together according to the Mormon teachings, I'd given way to a more solemn content-ment. Perhaps, at our dissolution, I should have experienced direct opposites of both. Swallowing despair, giddy fear. In truth, both would visit me frequently, but at that moment, I felt only a peculiar void of emotion.

"And our girls?"

Mr. Bostwick leaned closer. "You have full legal custody of all three children."

Suddenly the boarding of the early-morning stage couldn't come soon enough. Throwing all propriety aside, I flung my arms around Mr. Bostwick, an embrace he endured with good humor before gingerly disengaging himself. "You and your daughters need to gather your things. I told young Seth I'd have the rig back this evening."

"How long?"

Mr. Bostwick checked both the sun and his timepiece. "Within the hour."

Within the hour.

There have been moments in my life I would trade all those remaining to live again, and others which there is no grave deep enough to bury. The moments that followed live in both camps. Somehow, one of Sister Amanda's pretty carpetbags was filled with nightgowns and favorite blankets, stockings and knit caps and Sunday best dresses. Never mind that trunks of new clothes and things were waiting for them. How could I have thought that such things could ever replace what they'd known all their lives?

All of us moved as if through molasses, except for Kimana, who maintained her reliable, steady pace as she sliced two loaves of bread to make butter-and-cheese sandwiches and wrapped a jar of pickles in a clean, white cloth. The house was crowded with wives and babies, though Amanda and Evangeline largely stayed at the table taking turns trying to soothe the increasingly inconsolable Sophie. The girls inspected every corner of the house, looking for any treasure they might want to take, and I was at their heels, reminding them that there would still be children growing up in this home. Mr. Bostwick remained in the wagon seat, his lap littered with papers, and Nathan had secluded himself in the workshop in the barn, presumably to gather materials to take to the temple upon his return.

That was where I found him when all had been loaded into the wagon bed. Never again would I smell fresh lumber and not think of this place, this moment. It was nearly two o'clock in the afternoon, and dust motes danced in the beams of light pouring through the narrow windows. Nathan sat upon his workbench, his broad back to me, head bowed low over hands clasped between his knees. He did not hear me come in, and I took a last look at him. Undoubtedly he was in prayer, and I joined him.

Father God, here is a man who so desperately wants to please you. He is a good man—as good a man as he's been taught to be.

When I opened my eyes, he was looking at me, and I dared not take one step, lest I be turned to salt on that very spot.

"It's time for us to go," I said, my voice barely above a whisper.

"Then go."

"Won't you come out and say good-bye?"

"Good-bye."

"To the girls?"

"And just how am I supposed to do that? Tell me how I can look my little girls in the eye and say I'm never going to see them again."

"Just tell them that you love them. And that you'll miss them. Who are we to say that God won't cause our paths to cross again?"

He took one step toward me, then had the grace to stop. "Are you sorry they crossed in the first place?"

"No. Otherwise we wouldn't have our children."

He looked like he wanted to speak but again showed grace with silence.

"Do you remember where you first met me?"

"Like it was yesterday," he said, and I believed him.

"At my house, where we're going to live now, if you go to the edge of my property, there's a large rock, and if you stand on top of it, you can see that very spot."

He smiled. "Shall we make a monument?"

"I want you to know I'll share that story with Lottie and Melissa. They'll know every moment of our courtship, every story of our lives. And if you write, I promise not to hide the letters."

"I'll write."

"To them," I emphasized.

"To them."

"They'll like that."

I heard Mr. Bostwick call my name, and I hesitated just long enough for Nathan to come to my side, and we walked together into the sunshine. Kimana was at the gate, on her knees, wrapped within the combined embrace of Lottie and Melissa. At their father's voice, however, they let go and ran to him.

Whatever they said to each other in those final, private moments remains unknown to me. I went to Kimana, my sister and sometimes mother, and simply stood.

"Close your eyes," she said.

I obeyed, still seeing the lingering shadow of the sun in my darkness. Then I felt her wide, warm palm on my forehead, and she spoke in the short, nasal syllables of her native tongue. It was, I knew, a blessing, and I moved my lips in silent agreement. Though our languages were different, our faith was the same, and somehow we came to say amen in unison.

I opened my eyes.

"I will not see you again, Mrs. Fox. Not in this lifetime."

"I know," I said, though it ached to say it.

"But one day I will go to sleep, and I will wake up in the presence of the Creator, where your little one is waiting. I will hold him and sing him the songs of my people, and we will watch for you."

"Thank you for loving my children, Kimana."

"And now I have others that I will love." She winked. "That I will teach."

I wrapped my arms around her and for the last time took in her nurturing scent. When I turned around, Lottie and Melissa were already in the wagon, peeking over the side, and the team was beginning to prance impatiently. I paused long enough to give Sister Amanda a kiss on her powdery-white cheek, as well as one atop little Nate's jet-black hair. Faced with Evangeline, however, I found no such compulsion. Baby Sophie, forever squalling and red, squirmed against her bunting, and Evangeline held her like a shield between us.

"Good-bye, Sister Evangeline," I said with a simple touch to her sleeve.

"You're no sister of mine," she said. "Not in any way."

I grinned as widely as the Lord would allow. "I hope that changes someday."

I walked to the wagon, where Nathan waited to help me up to my seat, and I'm not ashamed to say I still remember that final touch. I turned back to the girls to see that they were ready.

"Yes, Mama," Lottie said, but Melissa merely stared at the tailgate.

Apparently satisfied, Mr. Bostwick gave the horses a gentle slap with the reins and was turning them around when I called out, "Wait!"

"Camilla, my dear," he said, his patience wearing thin, "we really must—"

"Just wait."

Without giving much thought to the spectacle I must be creating, I swung my leg over the wagon seat and our luggage, finding a clear spot on the floor of the bed. Immediately, Lottie scooted into my lap, and the first lurching movement of the wagon knocked Melissa off her knees.

"Come here, Missy," I said, beckoning, and she crawled over to my side. Each girl clutched her favorite doll, treasures their papa had brought home to them years ago, and I included their names as I said a prayer for our safe journey. By the time I finished my prayer, we were at the crest of the hill, and I looked out over the tailgate to see one man, his wives, and their children gathered in front of what was once my home. We'd spent one hour together living as a family built of false prophecy, and now my daughters and I served as anchors for each other, leaving them behind. Silently, as I held my girls, I begged God for two things:

that he would change Nathan's heart, and that he would keep mine strong. One prayer would be repeated and answered in that moment, and in every moment, in every mile that followed.

The other, I would not repeat again.

⚬⚬⚬⚬⚬

We arrived in Salt Lake City well after dark. By then the girls were sound asleep against me. Mr. Bostwick drove capably on, but when we did come to a stop, I noticed he was at least as tired as either of the children he peeled away from me.

"Where are we staying?" The effort of getting down from the wagon bed without waking Lottie gave me little chance to take in our surroundings.

"This is Aunt Rachel's house." Melissa spoke through a yawn, and she stood sleepily, unsteady on her feet.

"Rachel's?" I was on the ground now too, Lottie heavy against my shoulder as I turned to verify. Sure enough, the dark, rambling house beckoned, looking as welcoming as a cave.

"Our Mr. Fox had a key," Mr. Bostwick said, producing said object from his vest pocket. He inserted it into the lock and opened the door to the cold, damp room.

Melissa was able to walk in under her own power, and my aching back sang in relief as I laid Lottie on the sofa barely discernible under a white sheet. Of the three sofas that once furnished this room, only this one remained.

Mr. Bostwick followed us into the house. "It will be my residence for the time being, until I can find something more suitable."

This was a revelation I had not expected, and I sent Melissa—obviously in dire need—out to the privy so he and I could discuss it in private.

"You're not coming with us tomorrow?"

"I must stay until your case is settled, and I have a feeling there might be other women in this city who will need my help. It's a strange phenomenon indeed when a lawyer is a welcome resident. I feel I must take advantage of the situation."

Propriety aside, I planted a kiss on his square cheek. "We'll miss you, Mr. Bostwick. We all—Mama especially—have grown quite fond of you."

"And I as well," he said, stepping away from my embrace and making a show of taking an envelope from his breast pocket. "Will you give this letter to your mother? And tell her you both may look for me at summer's end, when I will no longer need your legal matters to lend an excuse for me to call."

I noted the strong, bold hand on the front of the envelope: *Mrs. Arlen Deardon (Ruth)*. The sight of it called to mind an unfulfilled promise.

"Will you post a letter for me as well? After we leave?"

"I'd be honored. For our young colonel?" He held out his hand as if expecting me to hand it over on the spot.

"Yes," I said, though not indulging his assumption. "I'll write it tonight and leave it on the foyer table." Another of the few furnishings that had been spared uprooting.

"Well then—" he rocked back on his heels—"it has been a long day, and I shall leave you to settle yourselves to sleep."

Only two of the rooms upstairs still had serviceable beds. Mr. Bostwick chose one, and I tucked Lottie and Melissa together in the other one, planning to squeeze myself between them later.

One would think that, given the day, I would have taken myself fast asleep. Instead, I took a candle and stole downstairs to Rachel's pretty writing desk—much more ornate than my own back home—and secured the light in a sconce on the wall.

Not sure if she would have left such supplies behind, I was relieved to find the desk well stocked with stationery and envelopes, pen and ink. Upon bringing it to the light, I noticed the stationery bore Rachel's monogram—an ornate *R* nestled within a beehive, surrounded by green vines. I thought at first to make a small note to identify myself, explaining the circumstances under which I came to write this letter on such a page, but abandoned the idea. After so many letters, Colonel Brandon was sure to recognize my handwriting, and the story itself could wait for another time, should such a time ever come.

The ink had settled within its small jar, and it took a vigorous shaking to bring it to any useful form. Even so, my first few attempts created nothing more than blotches upon the page, and I knew I would have to choose my words carefully.

I ran my hand over the page, praying that God would take my hand and guide it. Then, as he has surely answered every prayer I've uttered since the first, he proved himself mighty and true again.

All my convictions and all my misgivings remained in the recesses of my mind, just as many of my words remained lost in the shadow of the hand that wrote them. I could only trust my years of practice with a pen to know that each was borne upon the page in its intended form. Minutes later, I took my hand away, and my message stood firm on the ivory page.

My daughters have been restored to me.
Our family will be reunited soon.
All is well.

By the grace of God, I remain,

Camilla

ABOUT THE AUTHOR

Award-winning author Allison Pittman left a seventeen-year teaching career in 2005 to follow the Lord's calling into the world of Christian fiction, and God continues to bless her step of faith. The first book in her Sister Wife series, *For Time and Eternity*, was a finalist for the 2011 Christy Award, and her novel *Stealing Home* received the American Christian Fiction Writers' Carol Award. She heads up a successful, thriving writers group in San Antonio, Texas, where she lives with her husband, Mike, their three sons, and the canine star of the family—Stella.

READING GROUP GUIDE

A CONVERSATION WITH THE AUTHOR

How did the idea for the Sister Wife series come to you?

I knew I wanted to write a love story, but not a romance. The character of Nathan came to me fully formed—this deeply passionate, wounded, charismatic, charming man. Then, having grown up in Utah, I knew that Christianity played almost no role in the early history of the state, so I needed Camilla to be a woman seduced away from not only her family but also her Lord. In fact, I saw the understanding and worship of God as being almost a third element in a love triangle. I wanted Nathan and Camilla to love each other as much as they loved God.

You seem to know a lot about the Mormon faith and community. How did you research this story?

I lived in Utah as a child, and my husband is an excommunicated Mormon who came to know Jesus as his Savior when he was in high school, so I had a lot of anecdotal experiences to pull from. But to get a real feel for the history, I spent some time in Salt Lake City. The pioneer women's museum there is a treasure trove of artifacts, all the little household trinkets that made up a woman's life. The blue lamp is just one of the artifacts I fell in love with.

I think what really struck me—and this is something I've shared and confirmed with other Christians—is the spirit of Temple Square in Salt Lake City. The city is beautiful and meticulously maintained, but there is an oppressive air. It's quiet, but not serene. Something about that huge, white temple topped with a golden angel is unsettling.

I also spent a lot of time browsing websites and discussion boards reading posts by ex-Mormons. They gave me a clearer understanding not so much about why people join the church, but why they stay and why they leave. It's heartbreaking, the stories of bitterness and betrayal, even more so seeing how so many leave the Mormon faith with a mistrust of God and religion in general. I wanted to capture that sense of a desperate need for love and acceptance in Nathan's character. There are many anonymous people out there who were so helpful in my efforts to capture both Nathan's fervor and Rachel's just-beneath-the-surface disdain.

The first book in the series, For Time and Eternity, **had an interesting ending. What made you decide to end the story that way? How have readers responded?**

It wasn't an easy decision. Wait, I take that back. In my mind, even before I wrote the first word, I knew I would end the story with Camilla in a snowstorm. Trade sunshine for snow, and it was, in many ways, a total rip-off of Dickens's conclusion to A *Tale of Two Cities*. Read it closely, and there are hints and visions that all will be well for Camilla and her children. This ending leaves us with the fundamental conflict in Camilla's life resolved: She has restored her faith in Jesus Christ. She is completely given over to his direction, will, and protection. Given that, what could possibly go wrong?

How have readers responded? With, um, enthusiasm. Total strangers have pleaded for advance copies of the second book, and friends have been a little threatening, to tell you the truth. Not a week went by that I didn't get an e-mail from a reader wondering what was going to happen to Camilla—and I loved it! I felt such a huge responsibility not to let anybody down.

Why did you decide to make the story into a two-book series?
I knew Camilla's story would fill more than one book. It would cover both her journey back to the Lord and her journey to save her family—and I didn't want to shortchange either of those. I think sometimes in Christian fiction we oversimplify the process of faith. Too often, it's the matter of a realization and a prayer, and that's it. (I've been guilty of the same in other books.) But given the alternate theology of the Mormon faith, I knew I needed to be more careful. I felt a responsibility to try to *show* the truth of the gospel of Jesus Christ. Then, once I'd given Camilla a firm foundation of faith, she was free to go on a more rip-roarin' adventure. I think readers will appreciate having gone through this journey with her, rather than simply taking her Christianity for granted.

Camilla and Nathan are reunited for a short time in this book. Why did you decide to bring them back together?
Frankly, I missed Nathan. Now, normally, I hate it when authors speak of their characters as if they're real people, but Nathan Fox totally got under my skin. That's one reason. Also, I wanted the stakes to be a little higher for Camilla in terms of the menace he could be. Finally, the first time she left, she did it with little forethought. I wanted to pose the question of whether she would leave again, having suffered serious consequences for her earlier actions.

The leaders of the Mormon church decide that Camilla must make a "blood atonement." What does that mean? Was this a common practice in the early Mormon church?

"Blood atonement" simply echoes the fact that, without the shedding of blood, there can be no atonement for sin. Thus, under the law, the Israelites brought animals to sacrifice at the Temple. As Christians, we know that the shed blood of Jesus is the eternal, and final, atonement for our sin. There were those in the early Mormon church who felt that some sins were so egregious that only the shedding of the sinner's blood could make atonement. Please note that this is *not* the official teaching or practice of the LDS church. It was, as we see in many religions, a practice espoused by extremists. The extent to which it was actually practiced in the early Mormon church is impossible to know.

In the previous book, Rachel tells Camilla that she has to let Nathan take another wife. "You have to. You're his salvation. Joseph Smith was his savior in life, giving him direction. Your job is to save him in the next one." What does it mean that she's his salvation?

This touches on the Mormon concept of celestial rewards. According to their teaching, if Nathan is ever to achieve the highest, godlike, eternal status, he needs to have at least one eternal wife to bear his spiritual children. She is not so much his "salvation" in terms of his eternity, but in terms of the quality of that eternity. I think it's important to note here that the Mormons believe that women must be "called" into eternity by their husbands, which explains Evangeline's plight.

Today Mormons are intentionally aligning themselves with evangelical Christians. What similarities in their beliefs enable them to do this? In what crucial ways are their beliefs different from biblical Christianity?

Mormons believe Jesus Christ is the Son of God and that he died on the cross for our sins and rose again after three days.

They love and admire Jesus. They pray in his name. They identify Jesus as a redeemer and savior. But they do not acknowledge that Jesus' death and resurrection constitute the full completion of our reconciliation and salvation. To the Mormons, this act is incomplete, and true salvation depends not only upon one's belief in the death and resurrection of Jesus Christ as depicted in the Gospels, but also an acceptance and belief in the prophetic writings of Joseph Smith and the practices of the Mormon church.

What was the biggest challenge you faced in researching or writing this series? The greatest reward?
More so than any other project I've done, I had to give this one over to God. I knew I had to go beyond the average spiritual content found in most Christian fiction. I tried very hard to represent the truth of the gospel of Jesus Christ in contrast with the lies of the Mormon faith without making the books sound like 350-page tracts. It was quite challenging to craft theology into dialogue, to make the deepest questions about salvation relevant to the characters' relationships. So I hope I pulled it off!

The greatest reward? Honestly, I came away with such a deeper understanding and appreciation for my own salvation. As I wrote about Nathan's struggle to be "good enough" for God, I felt so loved by my Savior. I realized how wonderful it is to worship a God I cannot fully understand with my finite little mind.

What do you hope readers will take away from these novels?
First, I'd love readers to recognize that, despite any outward appearances, many Mormons are empty, wounded people. As I tried to get inside the head of a Mormon, I spent a lot of time online reading through forums devoted to those who had left

the church, and there was so much sadness and bitterness there. I think most Christians approach Mormons in one of two ways: we either avoid any opportunity to witness because doing so is usually fruitless, or we relish the idea of arguing with them. We need to simply love them.

Second, we need to be so rooted in Truth that we can recognize any aberration of the gospel, no matter how subtle. Mormonism and Christianity use largely the same vocabulary; the differences in theological text can seem little more than spin and semantics. We must be wary of works and messages that openly claim to be a "new" way of understanding Scripture.

DISCUSSION QUESTIONS

1. How does Camilla come to terms with leaving her children behind? Have you ever faced a decision where you felt like neither option was completely "right"? How can a Christian approach such situations?

2. Colonel Brandon is a true friend to Camilla in her time of need. Why do you think he is so attracted to her? Is she right to keep him at arm's length? Even when she is legally free to love him, she gives him no commitment, despite his obvious feelings for her. Why do you think she makes that decision?

3. Camilla is blessed with the opportunity to see her father again before he dies and to both extend and receive forgiveness. Have you lost someone close to you before you could be reconciled? How have you handled that? Is there someone in your life now that you wish you could be reconciled with? Is there anything you can do to take the first step?

4. Camilla is filled with gratitude for the blessing of a new child, even though her circumstances at the time are precarious. Have you ever been given a blessing—either a child or some other tangible expression of God's love—that was something of an inconvenience? Why is it sometimes hard for us to accept God's timing and plans for our lives?

5. The pastor in Camilla's hometown extends an unexpectedly warm welcome to her. Why is she so surprised? Has there been a time in your life when you were unsure of the reception you would receive by family, friends, or church? Have you ever had the opportunity to assure someone else of God's love and acceptance when they felt unworthy? What are some practical ways we can do that?

6. As a lawyer, Mr. Bostwick is able to address Camilla's situation with a certain amount of objectivity. When faced with a crisis, do you tend to react with an emotional response, or do you tackle problems with an air of calm observation? What are the benefits and drawbacks of each approach? Is there someone in your life who helps to balance your natural tendencies in this area?

7. Why does Nathan agree to let Camilla leave and take his children? What is he afraid of? How did this scene affect your feelings toward Nathan?

8. Melissa, it seems, will have a hard time letting go of the teachings she's been raised with. What advice would you give Camilla in regard to bringing up a child who is resistant to the Word of God?

9. The circumstances of the time period call for Camilla to take some drastic actions. How might her story be different today? What aspects of it would be the same?

THE SISTER WIFE SERIES

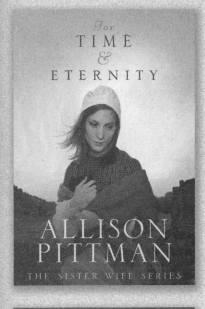

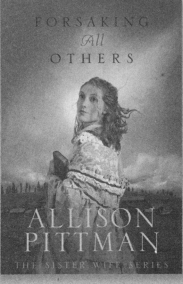

I never stop to ask myself if I should have done anything different. I have lived now nearly forty years with my choices, and sometime hence I will die in His grace. That is the hope no man can steal from me.

Not again.